PRIZE STORIES 1983 : THE
O. HENRY AWARDS
C1983.
37565005908099      CENT

PRIZE STORIES 1983

*The O. Henry Awards*

# PRIZE STORIES 1983
## *The O. Henry Awards*

EDITED AND WITH
AN INTRODUCTION
BY WILLIAM ABRAHAMS

DOUBLEDAY & COMPANY, INC.
GARDEN CITY, NEW YORK
1983

The Library of Congress Cataloged This Serial as
PZ1 Follows:
.O11
    Prize stories. The O. Henry awards. 1919–
      Garden City, N.Y., Doubleday [etc.]
          v. 21 cm.
Title varies: 1919–46, O. Henry memorial award prize stories.
Stories for 1919–27 were "chosen by the Society of Arts and Sciences."
Editors: 1919–32, B. C. Williams.—1933–40, Harry Hansen.—1941–
    Herschel Brickell (with Muriel Fuller, 19  –46)

  1. Short stories.  I. Williams, Blanche Colton, 1879–1944, ed.  II.
Hansen, Harry, 1884–    ed.  III. Brickell, Herschel, 1889–    ed.
      IV. Society of Arts and Sciences, New York.
        PZ1.O11     813.5082
    Library of Congress   [r5oq⁸3o]  Official
      ISBN 0-385-18115-9
Library of Congress Catalog Card Number 21–9372 rev 3*

Copyright © 1983 by Doubleday & Company, Inc.
ALL RIGHTS RESERVED
PRINTED IN THE UNITED STATES OF AMERICA

# CONTENTS

# PUBLISHER'S NOTE

This volume is the sixty-third in the O. Henry Memorial Award series.

In 1918, the Society of Arts and Sciences met to vote upon a monument to the master of the short story, O. Henry. They decided that this memorial should be in the form of two prizes for the best short stories published by American authors in American magazines during the year 1919. From this beginning, the memorial developed into an annual anthology of outstanding short stories by American authors, published, with the exception of the years 1952 and 1953, by Doubleday & Company, Inc.

Blanche Colton Williams, one of the founders of the awards, was editor from 1919 to 1932; Harry Hansen from 1933 to 1940; Herschel Brickell from 1941 to 1951. The annual collection did not appear in 1952 and 1953, when the continuity of the series was interrupted by the death of Herschel Brickell. Paul Engle was editor from 1954 to 1959 with Hanson Martin coeditor in the years 1954 to 1960; Mary Stegner in 1960; Richard Poirier from 1961 to 1966, with assistance from and coeditorship with William Abrahams from 1964 to 1966. William Abrahams became editor of the series in 1967.

In 1970 Doubleday published under Mr. Abrahams' editorship *Fifty Years of the American Short Story,* and in January 1981, *Prize Stories of the Seventies.* Both are collections of stories selected from this series.

The stories chosen for this volume were published in the period from the summer of 1981 to the summer of 1982. A list of the magazines consulted appears at the back of the book. The choice of stories and the selection of prize winners are exclusively the responsibility of the editor. Biographical material is based on information provided by the contributors and obtained from standard works of reference.

# INTRODUCTION

This is the seventeenth successive O. Henry Prize Stories collection that I have had the privilege, pleasure, and responsibility of assembling. After so prolonged an "immersion" in the contemporary American short story, one might feel justified in falling back on the sort of generalizations that allow an editor at least a temporary glow of omniscience—his topic, so to speak, at an imaginary Writers' Conference: The state of the story past and present, and what of its future?

Paradoxically, however, I feel less confident and more reluctant to generalize now than when I embarked on this enterprise in 1967, a case of opinion inhibited by knowledge. Having chosen 314 stories from among several thousand for the seventeen volumes I have assembled, I am increasingly aware that what is most immediately noticeable about these contemporary stories is their quite astonishing variety in theme, subject, style, character, narrative method, and how deftly they elude classification. To be sure, the rubric for the O. Henry Awards is so elastic, so open to the most generous constructions—stories of outstanding excellence by American authors that have appeared in American magazines during the preceding calendar year—that it encourages variety, even as it discourages emphasis upon a particular genre at the expense of quality.

I should add that variety makes for the unpredictable. One starts the search for the stories of a given year with no certainty as to what one will discover among the magazines that have published them. It is this anticipation of surprise—only rarely disappointed—that is the reward for the partisan or addict of the story. I use the latter word recalling a remark of Doris Lessing's I quoted in the introduction to *Prize Stories 1967:* "Some writers I know have stopped writing short stories because as they say 'There is no market for them.' Others like myself, the addicts, go on, and I suspect would go on even if there really wasn't any home for them but a private drawer."

In 1967, a comparative innocent in such matters, I detected in "the current state of short story publication cause for alarm." If I no longer believe this, it is not because the market has improved —if anything, it has worsened—but because I understand the deep logic of Mrs. Lessing's position. Addicted writers will go on writing, market or not, and will find somewhere to publish their stories, more often than not in the little magazines. There, in due course, they will be discovered by addicted readers.

In the past seventeen years, the meeting place for such writers and readers has been dramatically altered. Little magazines, once, were where one started from. Now, established writers, in the full mastery of their art—Joyce Carol Oates in *The Kenyon Review*, Raymond Carver in *Ploughshares*—seem as well-served by them and as appropriate to their pages as in the magazines of large circulation where they appear with equal frequency. But these latter magazines, at the most generous estimate, can be counted on the fingers of both hands—in this year's collection are stories from *The New Yorker*, *The Atlantic Monthly*, *Yankee*, *Redbook*, and *Mademoiselle*—whereas the little magazines, precariously financed and too often mortal, are in a conspicuous majority. Granted, it is not an ideal situation, but I think it is one we must become accustomed to, at least for the foreseeable future.

If the novel continues to please, in some instances, a vast public, the short story addresses itself to a smaller audience, who welcome it for what it offers, a distillation of experience very different—another order of being—from those slick entertainments and quasi-literary diversions aimed at the largest number of paying customers.

The notion that public events and personalities ought to be incorporated in their public reality into fiction—a phenomenon already underscored in a whole new breed of "non-fiction" magazines, the gossipy gospels of our transient culture—not surprisingly has had little acceptance among writers of the serious story. Which is not to say that what they write exists in a vacuum, apart from the real world. However little attention they overtly pay to the public life of our time, these stories reflect in a more truthful way, at however indirect an angle of vision, the realities of contemporary life as most of us know it. There is sadness, bleakness, emptiness; also love, passion, and even, as rarely as in life, moments of high-spirited comedy.

I should like to reserve some final comments for Raymond Carver's deeply affecting story, "A Small, Good Thing." An earlier version—little more than a stripped-down synopsis of what it would ultimately become—appeared in Carver's collection of stories *What We Talk About When We Talk About Love*. And there it might simply have languished, one of its author's lesser achievements. It has always seemed puzzling to me that, whereas painters, sculptors, composers, and poets have been quick to recognize the advantages of revision, of fresh starts with familiar material, of variations on a beloved theme, writers of stories have not chosen to take advantage of the same privilege. Now Raymond Carver has done so—the first publicly acknowledged example of the process I can recall. He has lengthened, deepened, enriched, enlivened; and in so doing, he has produced a story of extraordinary power. What was latent in the original version, here finds ever deepening expression. Out of the simple sketch (and the analogy to painting seems peculiarly justified), a full-scale portrait, in all its lights and shadows, has been brought to the page.

—William Abrahams

PRIZE STORIES 1983
*The O. Henry Awards*

# A SMALL, GOOD THING

## RAYMOND CARVER

Raymond Carver was born in Clatskanie, Oregon, and grew up in Yakima, Washington. He is professor of English and teaches in the creative writing program at Syracuse University. His work appears in *The New Yorker, Esquire, Antaeus, The Atlantic Monthly,* and in other magazines here and abroad. Several of his short stories have been included in the annual collections, *Prize Stories: The O. Henry Awards* and *The Best American Short Stories.* He has been the recipient of a Guggenheim Memorial Fellowship, a National Endowment for the Arts award in Fiction and in Poetry; and a Wallace Stegner Literary Fellowship. He has published three books of poems. His collection of short stories, *Will You Please Be Quiet, Please?* was nominated for a National Book Award in 1977. His *What We Talk About When We Talk About Love* was published by Alfred A. Knopf in 1981. Capra Press has recently published a collection of selected poems, stories and essays; and Knopf will issue another collection of short stories in the fall of 1983.

Saturday afternoon she drove to the bakery in the shopping center. After looking through a loose-leaf binder with photographs of cakes taped onto the pages, she ordered chocolate, the child's favorite. The cake she chose was decorated with a space ship and launching pad under a sprinkling of white stars at one end of the cake, and a planet made of red frosting at the other end. His name, SCOTTY, would be in raised green letters beneath the planet. The baker, who was an older man with a thick neck, listened without saying anything when she told him the child would be eight years old next Monday. The baker wore a white

Copyright © 1982 by Raymond Carver. First appeared in *Ploughshares,* Volume 8, Nos. 2 and 3. Reprinted by permission.

apron that looked like a smock. Straps cut under his arms, went around in back and then to the front again where they were secured under his heavy waist. He wiped his hands on his apron as he listened to her. He kept his eyes down on the photographs and let her talk. He let her take her time. He'd just come to work and he'd be there all night, baking, and he was in no real hurry.

She gave the baker her name, Ann Weiss, and her telephone number. The cake would be ready on Monday morning, just out of the oven, in plenty of time for the child's party that afternoon. The baker was not jolly. There were no pleasantries between them, just the minimum exchange of words, the necessary information. He made her feel uncomfortable, and she didn't like that. While he was bent over the counter with the pencil in his hand, she studied his coarse features and wondered if he'd ever done anything else with his life besides be a baker. She was a mother and thirty-three years old, and it seemed to her that everyone, especially someone the baker's age—a man old enough to be her father—must have children who'd gone through this special time of cakes and birthday parties. There must be that between them, she thought. But he was abrupt with her—not rude, just abrupt. She gave up trying to make friends with him. She looked into the back of the bakery and could see a long, heavy wooden table with aluminum pie pans stacked at one end, and beside the table a metal container filled with empty racks. There was an enormous oven. A radio was playing country-western music.

The baker finished printing the information on the special-order card and closed up the binder. He looked at her and said, "Monday morning." She thanked him and drove home.

On Monday morning, the birthday boy was walking to school with another boy. They were passing a bag of potato chips back and forth and the birthday boy was trying to find out what his friend intended to give him for his birthday that afternoon. Without looking, he stepped off the curb at an intersection and was immediately knocked down by a car. He fell on his side with his head in the gutter and his legs out in the road. His eyes were closed, but his legs began to move back and forth as if he were trying to climb over something. His friend dropped the potato chips and started to cry. The car had gone a hundred feet or so and stopped in the middle of the road. A man in the driver's seat looked back over his shoulder. He waited until the boy got unsteadily to his feet. The boy wobbled a little. He looked dazed, but okay. The driver put the car into gear and drove away.

The birthday boy didn't cry, but he didn't have anything to say about anything either. He wouldn't answer when his friend asked him what it felt like to be hit by a car. He walked home, and his friend went on to school. But after the birthday boy was inside his house and was telling his mother about it, she sitting beside him on the sofa, holding his hands in her lap, saying, "Scotty, honey, are you sure you feel all right, baby?" thinking she would call the doctor anyway, he suddenly lay back on the sofa, closed his eyes, and went limp. When she couldn't wake him up, she hurried to the telephone and called her husband at work. Howard told her to remain calm, remain calm, and then he called an ambulance for the child and left for the hospital himself.

Of course, the birthday party was canceled. The child was in the hospital with a mild concussion and suffering from shock. There'd been vomiting, and his lungs had taken in fluid which needed pumping out that afternoon. Now he simply seemed to be in a very deep sleep—but no coma, Dr. Francis had emphasized; no coma, when he saw the alarm in the parents' eyes. At eleven o'clock that Monday night when the boy seemed to be resting comfortably enough after the many X rays and the lab work, and it was just a matter of his waking up and coming around, Howard left the hospital. He and Ann had been at the hospital with the child since that afternoon, and he was going home for a short while to bathe and to change clothes. "I'll be back in an hour," he said. She nodded. "It's fine," she said. "I'll be right here." He kissed her on the forehead, and they touched hands. She sat in a chair beside the bed and looked at the child. She was waiting for him to wake up and be all right. Then she could begin to relax.

Howard drove home from the hospital. He took the wet, dark streets very fast, then caught himself and slowed down. Until now, his life had gone smoothly and to his satisfaction—college, marriage, another year of college for the advanced degree in business, a junior partnership in an investment firm. Fatherhood. He was happy and, so far, lucky—he knew that. His parents were still living, his brothers and his sister were established, his friends from college had gone out to take their places in the world. So far he had kept away from any real harm, from those forces he knew existed and that could cripple or bring down a man, if the luck went bad, if things suddenly turned. He pulled into the driveway and parked. His left leg began to tremble. He sat in the car for a minute and tried to deal with the present situation in a rational manner. Scotty had been hit by a car and was in the hospital, but he was going to be all right. He closed his eyes and ran his hand over his face. In a minute, he got out of the car and went up to the front door. The dog was barking inside the house. The telephone rang and rang while he unlocked the door and fumbled for the light switch. He shouldn't have left the hospital, he shouldn't have. "God dammit!" he said. He picked up the receiver and said, "I just walked in the door!"

"There's a cake here that wasn't picked up," the voice on the other end of the line said.

"What are you saying?" Howard asked.

"A cake," the voice said. "A sixteen-dollar cake."

Howard held the receiver against his ear, trying to understand. "I don't know anything about a cake," he said. "Jesus, what are you talking about?"

"Don't hand me that," the voice said.

Howard hung up the telephone. He went into the kitchen and poured himself some whiskey. He called the hospital. But the child's condition remained the same; he was still sleeping and nothing had changed there. While water poured into the tub, Howard lathered his face and shaved. He'd just stretched out in the tub and closed his eyes when the telephone began to ring. He hauled himself out, grabbed a towel, and hurried through the house, saying, "Stupid, stupid," for having left the hospital. But when he picked up the receiver and shouted, "Hello!" there was no sound at the other end of the line. Then the caller hung up.

He arrived back at the hospital a little after midnight. Ann still sat in the chair beside the bed. She looked up at Howard, and then she looked back at the child. The child's eyes stayed closed, the head was still wrapped in bandages. His breathing was quiet and regular. From an apparatus over the bed hung a bottle of glucose with a tube running from the bottle to the boy's arm.

"How is he?" Howard said. "What's all this?" waving at the glucose and the tube.

"Dr. Francis's orders," she said. "He needs nourishment. He needs to keep up his strength. Why doesn't he wake up, Howard? I don't understand, if he's all right."

Howard put his hand against the back of her head. He ran his fingers through her hair. "He's going to be all right. He'll wake up in a little while. Dr. Francis knows what's what."

After a time he said, "Maybe you should go home and get some rest. I'll stay here. Just don't put up with this creep who keeps calling. Hang up right away."

"Who's calling?" she asked.

"I don't know who, just somebody with nothing better to do than call up people. You go on now."

She shook her head. "No," she said, "I'm fine."

"Really," he said. "Go home for a while, and then come back and spell me in the morning. It'll be all right. What did Dr. Francis say? He said Scotty's going to be all right. We don't have to worry. He's just sleeping now, that's all."

A nurse pushed the door open. She nodded at them as she went to the bedside. She took the left arm out from under the covers and put her fingers on the wrist, found the pulse, then consulted her watch. In a little while she put the arm back under the covers and moved to the foot of the bed where she wrote something on a clipboard attached to the bed.

"How is he?" Ann said. Howard's hand was a weight on her shoulder. She was aware of the pressure from his fingers.

"He's stable," the nurse said. Then she said, "Doctor will be in

again shortly. Doctor's back in the hospital. He's making rounds
right now."

"I was saying maybe she'd want to go home and get a little
rest," Howard said. "After the doctor comes," he said.

"She could do that," the nurse said. "I think you should both
feel free to do that, if you wish." The nurse was a big Scandinavian woman with blond hair. There was the trace of an accent in her speech.

"We'll see what the doctor says," Ann said. "I want to talk to
the doctor. I don't think he should keep sleeping like this. I don't
think that's a good sign." She brought her hand up to her eyes
and let her head come forward a little. Howard's grip tightened
on her shoulder, and then his hand moved to her neck where his
fingers began to knead the muscles there.

"Dr. Francis will be here in a few minutes," the nurse said.
Then she left the room.

Howard gazed at his son for a time, the small chest quietly
rising and falling under the covers. For the first time since the
terrible minutes after Ann's telephone call to him at his office, he
felt a genuine fear starting in his limbs. He began shaking his
head. Scotty was fine, but instead of sleeping at home in his own
bed he was in a hospital bed with bandages around his head
and a tube in his arm. But this help was what he needed right
now.

Dr. Francis came in and shook hands with Howard, though
they'd just seen each other a few hours before. Ann got up from
the chair. "Doctor?"

"Ann," he said and nodded. "Let's just first see how he's
doing," the doctor said. He moved to the side of the bed and
took the boy's pulse. He peeled back one eyelid and then the
other. Howard and Ann stood beside the doctor and watched.
Then the doctor turned back the covers and listened to the boy's
heart and lungs with his stethoscope. He pressed his fingers here
and there on the abdomen. When he was finished he went to the
end of the bed and studied the chart. He noted the time, scribbled something on the chart, and then looked at Howard and
Ann.

"Doctor, how is he?" Howard said. "What's the matter with
him exactly?"

"Why doesn't he wake up?" Ann said.

The doctor was a handsome, big-shouldered man with a tanned face. He wore a three-piece blue suit, a striped tie, and ivory cuff links. His gray hair was combed along the sides of his head, and he looked as if he had just come from a concert. "He's all right," the doctor said. "Nothing to shout about, he could be better, I think. But he's all right. Still, I wish he'd wake up. He should wake up pretty soon." The doctor looked at the boy again. "We'll know some more in a couple of hours, after the results of a few more tests are in. But he's all right, believe me, except for that hairline fracture of the skull. He does have that."

"Oh, no," Ann said.

"And a bit of a concussion, as I said before. Of course, you know he's in shock," the doctor said. "Sometimes you see this in shock cases. This sleeping."

"But he's out of any real danger?" Howard said. "You said before he's not in a coma. You wouldn't call this a coma then, would you, Doctor?" Howard waited. He looked at the doctor.

"No, I don't want to call it a coma," the doctor said and glanced over at the boy once more. "He's just in a very deep sleep. It's a restorative measure the body is taking on its own. He's out of any real danger, I'd say that for certain, yes. But we'll know more when he wakes up and the other tests are in," the doctor said.

"It's a coma," Ann said. "Of sorts."

"It's not a coma yet, not exactly," the doctor said. "I wouldn't want to call it coma. Not yet anyway. He's suffered shock. In shock cases this kind of reaction is common enough; it's a temporary reaction to bodily trauma. Coma. Well, coma is a deep, prolonged unconsciousness that could go on for days, or weeks even. Scotty's not in that area, not as far as we can tell anyway. I'm certain his condition will show improvement by morning. I'm betting that it will anyway. We'll know more when he wakes up, which shouldn't be long now. Of course, you may do as you like, stay here or go home for a time. But by all means feel free to leave the hospital for a while if you want. This is not easy, I know." The doctor gazed at the boy again, watching him, and then he turned to Ann and said, "You try not to worry, little mother. Believe me, we're doing all that can be done. It's just a

question of a little more time now." He nodded at her, shook
hands with Howard again, and then he left the room.

Ann put her hand over the child's forehead. "At least he
doesn't have a fever," she said. Then she said, "My God, he feels
so cold though. Howard? Is he supposed to feel like this? Feel
his head."

Howard touched the child's temples. His own breathing had
slowed. "I think he's supposed to feel this way right now," he
said. "He's in shock, remember? That's what the doctor said. The
doctor was just in here. He would have said something if Scotty
wasn't okay."

Ann stood there a while longer, working her lip with her
teeth. Then she moved over to her chair and sat down.

Howard sat in the chair next to her chair. They looked at each
other. He wanted to say something else and reassure her, but he
was afraid too. He took her hand and put it in his lap, and this
made him feel better, her hand being there. He picked up her
hand and squeezed it. Then he just held her hand. They sat like
that for a while, watching the boy and not talking. From time to
time he squeezed her hand. Finally, she took her hand away.

"I've been praying," she said.

He nodded.

She said, "I almost thought I'd forgotten how, but it came
back to me. All I had to do was close my eyes and say, 'Please
God, help us—help Scotty,' and then the rest was easy. The
words were right there. Maybe if you prayed too," she said to
him.

"I've already prayed," he said. "I prayed this afternoon, yesterday afternoon, I mean, after you called, while I was driving to
the hospital. I've been praying," he said.

"That's good," she said. For the first time now, she felt they
were together in it, this trouble. She realized with a start that
until then it had only been happening to her and to Scotty. She
hadn't let Howard into it, though he was there and needed all
along. She felt glad to be his wife.

The same nurse came in and took the boy's pulse again and
checked the flow from the bottle hanging above the bed.

In an hour another doctor came in. He said his name was Parsons, from Radiology. He had a bushy mustache. He was wearing loafers, a western shirt, and a pair of jeans.

"We're going to take him downstairs for more pictures," he told them. "We need to do some more pictures, and we want to do a scan."

"What's that?" Ann said. "A scan?" She stood between this new doctor and the bed. "I thought you'd already taken all your X rays."

"I'm afraid we need some more," he said. "Nothing to be alarmed about. We just need some more pictures, and we want to do a brain scan on him."

"My God," Ann said.

"It's perfectly normal procedure in cases like this," this new doctor said. "We just need to find out for sure why he isn't back awake yet. It's normal medical procedure, and nothing to be alarmed about. We'll be taking him down in a few minutes," this doctor said.

In a little while two orderlies came into the room with a gurney. They were black-haired, dark-complexioned men in white uniforms, and they said a few words to each other in a foreign tongue as they unhooked the boy from the tube and moved him from his bed to the gurney. Then they wheeled him from the room. Howard and Ann got on the same elevator. Ann stood beside the gurney and gazed at the child. She closed her eyes as the elevator began its descent. The orderlies stood at either end of the gurney without saying anything, though once one of the men made a comment to the other in their own language, and the other man nodded slowly in response.

Later that morning, just as the sun was beginning to lighten the windows in the waiting room outside the X-ray department, they brought the boy out and moved him back up to his room. Howard and Ann rode up on the elevator with him once more, and once more they took up their places beside the bed.

They waited all day, but still the boy did not wake up. Occasionally one of them would leave the room to go downstairs to the cafeteria to drink coffee and then, as if suddenly remembering and feeling guilty, get up from the table and hurry back to

the room. Dr. Francis came again that afternoon and examined
the boy once more and then left after telling them he was coming along and could wake up at any minute now. Nurses,
different nurses from the night before, came in from time to
time. Then a young woman from the lab knocked and entered
the room. She wore white slacks and a white blouse and carried
a little tray of things which she put on the stand beside the bed.
Without a word to them, she took blood from the boy's arm.
Howard closed his eyes as the woman found the right place on
the boy's arm and pushed the needle in.

"I don't understand this," Ann said to the woman.

"Doctor's orders," the young woman said. "I do what I'm told.
They say draw that one, I draw. What's wrong with him, anyway?" she said. "He's a sweetie."

"He was hit by a car," Howard said. "A hit-and-run."

The young woman shook her head and looked again at the
boy. Then she took her tray and left the room.

"Why won't he wake up?" Ann said. "Howard? I want some
answers from these people."

Howard didn't say anything. He sat down again in the chair
and crossed one leg over the other. He rubbed his face. He
looked at his son and then he settled back in the chair, closed his
eyes, and went to sleep.

Ann walked to the window and looked out at the parking lot.
It was night and cars were driving into and out of the parking
lot with their lights on. She stood at the window with her hands
gripping the sill and knew in her heart that they were into something now, something hard. She was afraid, and her teeth began
to chatter until she tightened her jaws. She saw a big car stop in
front of the hospital and someone, a woman in a long coat, got
into the car. For a minute she wished she were that woman and
somebody, anybody, was driving her away from here to somewhere else, a place where she would find Scotty waiting for her
when she stepped out of the car, ready to say "Mom" and let her
gather him in her arms.

In a little while Howard woke up. He looked at the boy again.
Then he got up from the chair, stretched, and went over to
stand beside her at the window. They both stared out at the
parking lot. They didn't say anything. But they seemed to feel

each other's insides now, as though the worry had made them transparent in a perfectly natural way.

The door opened and Dr. Francis came in. He was wearing a different suit and tie this time. His gray hair was combed along the sides of his head, and he looked as if he had just shaved. He went straight to the bed and examined the boy. "He ought to have come around by now. There's just no good reason for this," he said. "But I can tell you we're all convinced he's out of any danger. We'll just feel better when he wakes up. There's no reason, absolutely none, why he shouldn't come around. Very soon. Oh, he'll have himself a dilly of a headache when he does, you can count on that. But all of his signs are fine. They're as normal as can be."

"Is it a coma then?" Ann asked.

The doctor rubbed his smooth cheek. "We'll call it that for the time being, until he wakes up. But you must be worn out. This is hard. I know this is hard. Feel free to go out for a bite," he said. "It would do you good. I'll put a nurse in here while you're gone, if you'll feel better about going. Go and have yourselves something to eat."

"I couldn't eat anything," Ann said.

"Do what you need to do, of course," the doctor said. "Anyway, I wanted to tell you that all the signs are good, the tests are positive, nothing at all negative, and just as soon as he wakes up he'll be over the hill."

"Thank you, Doctor," Howard said. He shook hands with the doctor again. The doctor patted Howard's shoulder and went out.

"I suppose one of us should go home and check on things," Howard said. "Slug needs to be fed, for one thing."

"Call one of the neighbors," Ann said. "Call the Morgans. Anyone will feed a dog if you ask them to."

"All right," Howard said. After a while he said, "Honey, why don't you do it? Why don't you go home and check on things, and then come back? It'll do you good. I'll be right here with him. Seriously," he said. "We need to keep up our strength on this. We'll want to be here for a while even after he wakes up."

"Why don't you go?" she said. "Feed Slug. Feed yourself."

"I already went," he said. "I was gone for exactly an hour and fifteen minutes. You go home for an hour and freshen up. Then come back."

She tried to think about it, but she was too tired. She closed her eyes and tried to think about it again. After a time she said, "Maybe I will go home for a few minutes. Maybe if I'm not just sitting right here watching him every second he'll wake up and be all right. You know? Maybe he'll wake up if I'm not here. I'll go home and take a bath and put on clean clothes. I'll feed Slug. Then I'll come back."

"I'll be right here," he said. "You go on home, honey. I'll keep an eye on things here." His eyes were bloodshot and small, as if he'd been drinking for a long time. His clothes were rumpled. His beard had come out again. She touched his face, and then she took her hand back. She understood he wanted to be by himself for a while, not have to talk or share his worry for a time. She picked her purse up from the nightstand, and he helped her into her coat.

"I won't be gone long," she said.

"Just sit and rest for a little while when you get home," he said. "Eat something. Take a bath. After you get out of the bath, just sit for a while and rest. It'll do you a world of good, you'll see. Then come back," he said. "Let's try not to worry. You heard what Dr. Francis said."

She stood in her coat for a minute trying to recall the doctor's exact words, looking for any nuances, any hint of something behind his words other than what he had said. She tried to remember if his expression had changed any when he bent over to examine the child. She remembered the way his features had composed themselves as he rolled back the child's eyelids and then listened to his breathing.

She went to the door where she turned and looked back. She looked at the child, and then she looked at the father. Howard nodded. She stepped out of the room and pulled the door closed behind her.

She went past the nurses' station and down to the end of the corridor, looking for the elevator. At the end of the corridor she turned to her right and entered a little waiting room where a Negro family sat in wicker chairs. There was a middle-aged man in a khaki shirt and pants, a baseball cap pushed back on his head. A large woman wearing a housedress and slippers was slumped in one of the chairs. A teenaged girl in jeans, hair done in dozens of little braids, lay stretched out in one of the chairs smoking a cigarette, her legs crossed at the ankles. The family swung their eyes to her as she entered the room. The little table was littered with hamburger wrappers and Styrofoam cups.

"Franklin," the large woman said as she roused herself. "Is it about Franklin?" Her eyes widened. "Tell me now, lady," the woman said. "Is it about Franklin?" She was trying to rise from her chair, but the man had closed his hand over her arm.

"Here, here," he said. "Evelyn."

"I'm sorry," Ann said. "I'm looking for the elevator. My son is in the hospital, and now I can't find the elevator."

"Elevator is down that way, turn left," the man said as he aimed a finger.

The girl drew on her cigarette and stared at Ann. Her eyes were narrowed to slits, and her broad lips parted slowly as she let the smoke escape. The Negro woman let her head fall on her shoulder and looked away from Ann, no longer interested.

"My son was hit by a car," Ann said to the man. She seemed to need to explain herself. "He has a concussion and a little skull fracture, but he's going to be all right. He's in shock now, but it might be some kind of coma too. That's what really worries us, the coma part. I'm going out for a little while, but my husband is with him. Maybe he'll wake up while I'm gone."

"That's too bad," the man said and shifted in the chair. He shook his head. He looked down at the table, and then he looked back at Ann. She was still standing there. He said, "Our Franklin, he's on the operating table. Somebody cut him. Tried to kill him. There was a fight where he was at. At this party. They say he was just standing and watching. Not bothering nobody. But that don't mean nothing these days. Now he's on the operating table. We're just hoping and praying, that's all we can do now." He gazed at her steadily.

Ann looked at the girl again, who was still watching her, and at the older woman who kept her head down, but whose eyes were now closed. Ann saw the lips moving silently, making words. She had an urge to ask what those words were. She wanted to talk more with these people who were in the same kind of waiting she was in. She was afraid, and they were afraid. They had that in common. She would have liked to say something else about the accident, told them more about Scotty, that it had happened on the day of his birthday, Monday, and that he was still unconscious. Yet she didn't know how to begin. She stood looking at them without saying anything more.

She went down the corridor the man had indicated and found the elevator. She waited a minute in front of the closed doors, still wondering if she was doing the right thing. Then she put out her finger and touched the button.

She pulled into the driveway and cut the engine. She closed her eyes and leaned her head against the wheel for a minute. She listened to the ticking sounds the engine made as it began to cool. Then she got out of the car. She could hear the dog barking inside the house. She went to the front door, which was unlocked. She went inside and turned on lights and put on a kettle of water for tea. She opened some dog food and fed Slug on the back porch. The dog ate in hungry little smacks. It kept running into the kitchen to see that she was going to stay. As she sat down on the sofa with her tea, the telephone rang.

"Yes!" she said as she answered. "Hello!"

"Mrs. Weiss," a man's voice said. It was five o'clock in the morning, and she thought she could hear machinery or equipment of some kind in the background.

"Yes, yes! What is it?" she said. "This is Mrs. Weiss. This is she. What is it, please?" She listened to whatever it was in the background. "Is it Scotty, for Christ's sake?"

"Scotty," the man's voice said. "It's about Scotty, yes. It has to do with Scotty, that problem. Have you forgotten about Scotty?" the man said. Then he hung up.

She dialed the hospital's number and asked for the third floor. She demanded information about her son from the nurse who answered the telephone. Then she asked to speak to her husband. It was, she said, an emergency.

She waited, turning the telephone cord in her fingers. She closed her eyes and felt sick at her stomach. She would have to make herself eat. Slug came in from the back porch and lay down near her feet. He wagged his tail. She pulled at his ear while he licked her fingers. Howard was on the line.

"Somebody just called here," she said. She twisted the telephone cord. "He said, he said it was about Scotty," she cried.

"Scotty's fine," Howard told her. "I mean he's still sleeping. There's been no change. The nurse has been in twice since you've been gone. They're in here every thirty minutes or so. A nurse or else a doctor. He's all right."

"This man called. He said it was about Scotty," she told him.

"Honey, you rest for a little while, you need the rest. It must be that same caller I had. Just forget it. Come back down here after you've rested. Then we'll have breakfast or something."

"Breakfast," she said. "I don't want any breakfast."

"You know what I mean," he said. "Juice, something. I don't know. I don't know anything, Ann. Jesus, I'm not hungry either. Ann, it's hard to talk now. I'm standing here at the desk. Dr. Francis is coming again at eight o'clock this morning. He's going to have something to tell us then, something more definite. That's what one of the nurses said. She didn't know any more than that. Ann? Honey, maybe we'll know something more then. At eight o'clock. Come back here before eight. Meanwhile, I'm right here and Scotty's all right. He's still the same," he added.

"I was drinking a cup of tea," she said, "when the telephone rang. They said it was about Scotty. There was a noise in the background. Was there a noise in the background on that call you had, Howard?"

"I don't remember," he said. "Maybe the driver of the car, maybe he's a psychopath and found out about Scotty somehow. But I'm here with him. Just rest like you were going to do. Take a bath and come back by seven or so, and we'll talk to the doctor together when he gets here. It's going to be all right, honey. I'm here, and there are doctors and nurses around. They say his condition is stable."

"I'm scared to death," she said.

She ran water, undressed, and got into the tub. She washed and dried quickly, not taking the time to wash her hair. She put on clean underwear, wool slacks, and a sweater. She went into the living room where the dog looked up at her and let its tail thump once against the floor. It was just starting to get light outside when she went out to the car.

She drove into the parking lot of the hospital and found a space close to the front door. She felt she was in some obscure way responsible for what had happened to the child. She let her thoughts move to the Negro family. She remembered the name "Franklin," and the table that was covered with hamburger papers, and the teenaged girl staring at her as she drew on her cigarette. "Don't have children," she told the girl's image as she entered the front door of the hospital. "For God's sake, don't."

She took the elevator up to the third floor with two nurses who were just going on duty. It was Wednesday morning, a few minutes before seven. There was a page for a Dr. Madison as the elevator doors slid open on the third floor. She got off behind the nurses, who turned in the other direction and continued the conversation she had interrupted when she'd gotten into the elevator. She walked down the corridor to the little alcove where the Negro family had been waiting. They were gone now, but the chairs were scattered in such a way that it looked as if people had just jumped from them the minute before. The tabletop was cluttered with the same cups and papers, the ashtray was filled with cigarette butts.

She stopped at the nurses' station just down the corridor from the waiting room. A nurse was standing behind the counter, brushing her hair and yawning.

"There was a Negro man in surgery last night," Ann said. "Franklin was his name. His family was in the waiting room. I'd like to inquire about his condition."

A nurse who was sitting at a desk behind the counter looked up from a chart in front of her. The telephone buzzed and she picked up the receiver, but she kept her eyes on Ann.

"He passed away," said the nurse at the counter. The nurse held the hairbrush and kept looking at her. "Are you a friend of the family or what?"

"I met the family last night," Ann said. "My own son is in the hospital. I guess he's in shock. We don't know for sure what's wrong. I just wondered about Mr. Franklin, that's all. Thank you." She moved down the corridor. Elevator doors the same

color as the walls slid open and a gaunt, bald man in white
pants and white canvas shoes pulled a heavy cart off the elevator. She hadn't noticed these doors last night. The man wheeled
the cart out into the corridor and stopped in front of the room
nearest the elevator and consulted a clipboard. Then he reached
down and slid a tray out of the cart. He rapped lightly on the
door and entered the room. She could smell the unpleasant
odors of warm food as she passed the cart. She hurried past the
other station without looking at any of the nurses and pushed
open the door to the child's room.

Howard was standing at the window with his hands behind
his back. He turned around as she came in.

"How is he?" she said. She went over to the bed. She dropped
her purse on the floor beside the nightstand. It seemed to her
she had been gone a long time. She touched the child's face.
"Howard?"

"Dr. Francis was here a little while ago," Howard said. She
looked at him closely and thought his shoulders were bunched a
little.

"I thought he wasn't coming until eight o'clock this morning,"
she said quickly.

"There was another doctor with him. A neurologist."

"A neurologist," she said.

Howard nodded. His shoulders were bunching, she could see
that. "What'd they say, Howard? For Christ's sake, what'd they
say? What is it?"

"They said they're going to take him down and run more tests
on him, Ann. They think they're going to operate, honey. Honey,
they are going to operate. They can't figure out why he won't
wake up. It's more than just shock or concussion, they know that
much now. It's in his skull, the fracture; it has something, something to do with that, they think. So they're going to operate. I
tried to call you, but I guess you'd already left the house."

"Oh, God," she said. "Oh, please, Howard, please," she said,
taking his arms.

"Look!" Howard said then. "Scotty! Look, Ann!" He turned
her toward the bed.

The boy had opened his eyes, then closed them. He opened
them again now. The eyes stared straight ahead for a minute,

then moved slowly in his head until they rested on Howard and Ann, then traveled away again.

"Scotty," his mother said, moving to the bed.

"Hey, Scott," his father said. "Hey, son."

They leaned over the bed. Howard took the child's hand in his hands and began to pat and squeeze the hand. Ann bent over the boy and kissed his forehead again and again. She put her hands on either side of his face. "Scotty, honey, it's Mommy and Daddy," she said. "Scotty?"

The boy looked at them, but without any sign of recognition. Then his mouth opened, his eyes scrunched closed, and he howled until he had no more air in his lungs. His face seemed to relax and soften then. His lips parted as his last breath was puffed through his throat and exhaled gently through the clenched teeth.

The doctors called it a hidden occlusion and said it was a one-in-a-million circumstance. Maybe if it could have been detected somehow and surgery undertaken immediately, they could have saved him. But more than likely not. In any case, what would they have been looking for? Nothing had shown up in the tests or in the X rays.

Dr. Francis was shaken. "I can't tell you how badly I feel. I'm so very sorry, I can't tell you," he said as he led them into the doctors' lounge. There was a doctor sitting in a chair with his legs hooked over the back of another chair, watching an early morning TV show. He was wearing a green delivery-room outfit, loose green pants and green blouse, and a green cap that covered his hair. He looked at Howard and Ann and then looked at Dr. Francis. He got to his feet and turned off the set and went out of the room. Dr. Francis guided Ann to the sofa, sat down beside her and began to talk in a low, consoling voice. At one point he leaned over and embraced her. She could feel his chest rising and falling evenly against her shoulder. She kept her eyes open and let him hold her. Howard went into the bathroom, but he left the door open. After a violent fit of weeping, he ran water and washed his face. Then he came out and sat down at

the little table that held a telephone. He looked at the telephone
as though deciding what to do first. He made some calls. After a
time, Dr. Francis used the telephone.

"Is there anything else I can do for the moment?" he asked
them.

Howard shook his head. Ann stared at Dr. Francis as if unable
to comprehend his words.

The doctor walked them to the hospital's front door. People
were entering and leaving the hospital. It was eleven o'clock in
the morning. Ann was aware of how slowly, almost reluctantly
she moved her feet. It seemed to her that Dr. Francis was making them leave when she felt they should stay, when it would be
more the right thing to do, to stay. She gazed out into the parking lot and then turned around and looked back at the front of
the hospital. She began shaking her head. "No, no," she said. "I
can't leave him here, no." She heard herself say that and thought
how unfair it was that the only words that came out were the
sort of words used on TV shows where people were stunned by
violent or sudden deaths. She wanted her words to be her own.
"No," she said, and for some reason the memory of the Negro
woman's head lolling on the woman's shoulder came to her.
"No," she said again.

"I'll be talking to you later in the day," the doctor was saying
to Howard. "There are still some things that have to be done,
things that have to be cleared up to our satisfaction. Some things
that need explaining."

"An autopsy," Howard said.

Dr. Francis nodded.

"I understand," Howard said. Then he said, "Oh, Jesus. No, I
don't understand, Doctor. I can't, I can't. I just can't."

Dr. Francis put his arm around Howard's shoulders. "I'm
sorry. God, how I'm sorry." He let go of Howard's shoulders and
held out his hand. Howard looked at the hand, and then he took
it. Dr. Francis put his arms around Ann once more. He seemed
full of some goodness she didn't understand. She let her head
rest on his shoulder, but her eyes stayed open. She kept looking
at the hospital. As they drove out of the parking lot, she looked
back at the hospital once more.

At home, she sat on the sofa with her hands in her coat pockets. Howard closed the door to the child's room. He got the coffee maker going and then he found an empty box. He had thought to pick up some of the child's things that were scattered around the living room. But instead he sat down beside her on the sofa, pushed the box to one side, and leaned forward, arms between his knees. He began to weep. She pulled his head over into her lap and patted his shoulder. "He's gone," she said. She kept patting his shoulder. Over his sobs she could hear the coffee maker hissing in the kitchen. "There, there," she said tenderly. "Howard, he's gone. He's gone and now we'll have to get used to that. To being alone."

In a little while Howard got up and began moving aimlessly around the room with the box, not putting anything into it, but collecting some things together on the floor at one end of the sofa. She continued to sit with her hands in her coat pockets. Howard put the box down and brought coffee into the living room. Later, Ann made calls to relatives. After each call had been placed and the party had answered, Ann would blurt out a few words and cry for a minute. Then she would quietly explain, in a measured voice, what had happened and tell them about arrangements. Howard took the box out to the garage where he saw the child's bicycle. He dropped the box and sat down on the pavement beside the bicycle. He took hold of the bicycle awkwardly so that it leaned against his chest. He held it, the rubber pedal sticking into his chest. He gave the wheel a turn.

Ann hung up the telephone after talking to her sister. She was looking up another number when the telephone rang. She picked it up on the first ring.

"Hello," she said, and she heard something in the background, a humming noise. "Hello!" she said. "For God's sake," she said. "Who is this? What is it you want?"

"Your Scotty, I got him ready for you," the man's voice said. "Did you forget him?"

"You evil bastard!" she shouted into the receiver. "How can you do this, you evil son of a bitch?"

"Scotty," the man said. "Have you forgotten about Scotty?" Then the man hung up on her.

Howard heard the shouting and came in to find her with her head on her arms over the table, weeping. He picked up the receiver and listened to the dial tone.

Much later, just before midnight, after they had dealt with many things, the telephone rang again.

"You answer it," she said. "Howard, it's him, I know." They were sitting at the kitchen table with coffee in front of them. Howard had a small glass of whiskey beside his cup. He answered on the third ring.

"Hello," he said. "Who is this? Hello! Hello!" The line went dead. "He hung up," Howard said. "Whoever it was."

"It was him," she said. "That bastard. I'd like to kill him," she said. "I'd like to shoot him and watch him kick," she said.

"Ann, my God," he said.

"Could you hear anything?" she said. "In the background? A noise, machinery, something humming?"

"Nothing, really. Nothing like that," he said. "There wasn't much time. I think there was some radio music. Yes, there was a radio going, that's all I could tell. I don't know what in God's name is going on," he said.

She shook her head. "If I could, could get, my hands, on him." It came to her then. She knew who it was. Scotty, the cake, the telephone number. She pushed the chair away from the table and got up. "Drive me down to the shopping center," she said. "Howard."

"What are you saying?"

"The shopping center. I know who it is who's calling. I know who it is. It's the baker, the son-of-a-bitching baker, Howard. I had him bake a cake for Scotty's birthday. That's who's calling. That's who has the number and keeps calling us. To harrass us about that cake. The baker, that bastard."

They drove out to the shopping center. The sky was clear and stars were out. It was cold, and they ran the heater in the car. They parked in front of the bakery. All of the shops and stores were closed, but there were cars at the far end of the lot in front of the cinema. The bakery windows were dark, but when they looked through the glass they could see a light in the back room

and, now and then, a big man in an apron moving in and out of
the white, even light. Through the glass she could see the display cases and some little tables with chairs. She tried the door.
She rapped on the glass. But if the baker heard them he gave no
sign. He didn't look in their direction.

They drove around behind the bakery and parked. They got
out of the car. There was a lighted window too high up for them
to see inside. A sign near the back door said, "The Pantry Bakery,
Special Orders." She could hear faintly a radio playing inside
and something—an oven door?—creak as it was pulled down.
She knocked on the door and waited. Then she knocked again,
louder. The radio was turned down and there was a scraping
sound now, the distinct sound of something, a drawer, being
pulled open and then closed.

Someone unlocked the door and opened it. The baker stood in
the light and peered out at them. "I'm closed for business," he
said. "What do you want at this hour? It's midnight. Are you
drunk or something?"

She stepped into the light that fell through the open door. He
blinked his heavy eyelids as he recognized her. "It's you," he
said.

"It's me," she said. "Scotty's mother. This is Scotty's father.
We'd like to come in."

The baker said, "I'm busy now. I have work to do."

She had stepped inside the doorway anyway. Howard came
in behind her. The baker moved back. "It smells like a bakery
in here. Doesn't it smell like a bakery in here, Howard?"

"What do you want?" the baker said. "Maybe you want your
cake? That's it, you decided you want your cake. You ordered a
cake, didn't you?"

"You're pretty smart for a baker," she said. "Howard, this is
the man who's been calling us." She clenched her fists. She
stared at him fiercely. There was a deep burning inside her, an
anger that made her feel larger than herself, larger than either of
these men.

"Just a minute here," the baker said. "You want to pick up
your three-day-old cake? That it? I don't want to argue with
you, lady. There it sits over there, getting stale. I'll give it to you

for half of what I quoted you. No. You want it? You can have it.
It's no good to me, no good to anyone now. It cost me time and
money to make that cake. If you want it, okay, if you don't,
that's okay too. I have to get back to work." He looked at them
and rolled his tongue behind his teeth.

"More cakes," she said. She knew she was in control of it, of
what was increasing her. She was calm.

"Lady, I work sixteen hours a day in this place to earn a living," the baker said. He wiped his hands on his apron. "I work
night and day in here, trying to make ends meet." A look crossed
Ann's face that made the baker move back and say, "No trouble
now." He reached to the counter and picked up a rolling pin
with his right hand and began to tap it against the palm of his
other hand. "You want the cake or not? I have to get back to
work. Bakers work at night," he said again. His eyes were small,
mean-looking, she thought, nearly lost in the bristly flesh around
his cheeks. His neck was thick with fat.

"I know bakers work at night," Ann said. "They make phone
calls at night too. You bastard," she said.

The baker continued to tap the rolling pin against his hand.
He glanced at Howard. "Careful, careful," he said to Howard.

"My son's dead," she said with a cold, even finality. "He was
hit by a car Monday morning. We've been waiting with him
until he died. But of course, you couldn't be expected to know
that, could you? Bakers can't know everything. Can they, Mr.
Baker? But he's dead. He's dead, you bastard!" Just as suddenly
as it had welled in her the anger dwindled, gave way to something else, a dizzy feeling of nausea. She leaned against the
wooden table that was sprinkled with flour, put her hands over
her face and began to cry, her shoulders rocking back and forth.
"It isn't fair," she said. "It isn't, isn't fair."

Howard put his hand at the small of her back and looked at
the baker. "Shame on you," Howard said to him. "Shame."

The baker put the rolling pin back on the counter. He undid
his apron and threw it on the counter. He looked at them, and
then he shook his head slowly. He pulled a chair out from under
a card table that held papers and receipts, an adding machine
and a telephone directory. "Please sit down," he said. "Let me

get you a chair," he said to Howard. "Sit down now, please."
The baker went into the front of the shop and returned with two
little wrought-iron chairs. "Please sit down, you people."

Ann wiped her eyes and looked at the baker. "I wanted to kill
you," she said. "I wanted you dead."

The baker had cleared a space for them at the table. He
shoved the adding machine to one side, along with the stacks of
notepaper and receipts. He pushed the telephone directory onto
the floor, where it landed with a thud. Howard and Ann sat
down and pulled their chairs up to the table. The baker sat
down too.

"Let me say how sorry I am," the baker said, putting his
elbows on the table. "God alone knows how sorry. Listen to me.
I'm just a baker. I don't claim to be anything else. Maybe once,
maybe years ago I was a different kind of human being. I've forgotten, I don't know for sure. But I'm not any longer, if I ever
was. Now I'm just a baker. That don't excuse my doing what I
did, I know. But I'm deeply sorry. I'm sorry for your son, and
sorry for my part in this," the baker said. He spread his hands
out on the table and turned them over to reveal his palms. "I
don't have any children myself, so I can only imagine what you
must be feeling. All I can say to you now is that I'm sorry. Forgive me, if you can," the baker said. "I'm not an evil man, I don't
think. Not evil, like you said on the phone. You got to understand that what it comes down to is I don't know how to act
anymore, it would seem. Please," the man said, "let me ask you
if you can find it in your hearts to forgive me?"

It was warm inside the bakery. In a minute, Howard stood up
from the table and took off his coat. He helped Ann from her
coat. The baker looked at them for a minute and then nodded
and got up from the table. He went to the oven and turned off
some switches. He found cups and poured coffee from an electric coffee maker. He put a carton of cream on the table, and a
bowl of sugar.

"You probably need to eat something," the baker said. "I hope
you'll eat some of my hot rolls. You have to eat and keep going.
Eating is a small, good thing in a time like this," he said.

He served them warm cinnamon rolls just out of the oven, the
icing still runny. He put butter on the table and knives to spread

the butter. Then the baker sat down at the table with them. He waited. He waited until they each took a roll from the platter and began to eat. "It's good to eat something," he said, watching them. "There's more. Eat up. Eat all you want. There's all the rolls in the world in here."

They ate rolls and drank coffee. Ann was suddenly hungry, and the rolls were warm and sweet. She ate three of them, which pleased the baker. Then he began to talk. They listened carefully. Although they were tired and in anguish, they listened to what the baker had to say. They nodded when the baker began to speak of loneliness, and the sense of doubt and limitation that had come to him in his middle years. He told them what it was like to be childless all these years. To repeat the days with the ovens endlessly full and endlessly empty. The party food, the celebrations he'd worked over. Icing knuckle-deep. The tiny wedding couples stuck into cakes. Hundreds of them—no, thousands by now. Birthdays. Just imagine all those candles burning. He had a necessary trade. He was a baker. He was glad he wasn't a florist. It was better to be feeding people. This was a better smell anytime than flowers.

"Smell this," the baker said, breaking open a dark loaf. "It's a heavy bread, but rich." They smelled it, then he had them taste it. It had the taste of molasses and coarse grains. They listened to him. They ate what they could. They swallowed the dark bread. It was like daylight under the fluorescent trays of light. They talked on into the early morning, the high pale cast of light in the windows, and they did not think of leaving.

# MY WARSZAWA

## JOYCE CAROL OATES

Joyce Carol Oates's most recent novel is *A Bloodsmoor Ro-
mance*. She is currently on the faculty at Princeton.

Agent provocateur. In room 371 of the Hotel Europejski in Warsaw a bellboy in a tight-fitting uniform is asking Carl Walser a
question. In English. But it is not an English Carl or Judith can
understand—like Polish it slips and hisses on the tongue, and
flows past their heads too rapidly. Does he want a larger tip,
Judith thinks, shocked and angered (for she has brought to
Poland hazy but stubborn ideals about the "people"), is he offer-
ing them a service of some kind—? Her mind hits upon, and immediately discards, one or two possibilities.

The bellboy is not a boy, he is perhaps thirty years old. His
lips stretch in a quick unconvincing smile, as if he is in the presence of fools or deaf-mutes; his short blunt nicotine-stained
fingers make an appeal that is both prayerlike and impatient. As
he repeats his question to Carl—only to Carl, he ignores Judith
—Judith cannot stop herself from observing that his skin is unpleasantly oily, his teeth are crooked, his eyes are slightly
crossed. (She has been noticing teeth in this part of Europe.
East Europe. She suspects that her penchant for noticing details,
for being struck in the face by details, will soon become a curse,
and is in any case a symptom of her Western frame of mind—
her morbidly sensitive consciousness. A hyperesthesia exaggerated by travel.)

Yes? What? Carl is saying. His robust good humor at simply
being here, in this country, in this city, in this hotel, and in this

Copyright © 1981 by Joyce Carol Oates. First appeared in *The Kenyon
Review*, Volume III, No. 4 (Fall 1981). Reprinted by permission.

room, has become strained; Judith notices the twitch at the corner of his mouth. —I'm afraid I don't understand.

Dollar, says the bellboy, grinning nervously, now glancing from Carl to Judith as if seeking her help. He has given the word a peculiar accent but Judith recognizes it. Dollar—zloty—change —money change? In his outgrown costume—a short green jacket with red collar and cuffs and small brass buttons—he has an almost charming theatrical air, both comic and sinister.

Ah, says Carl, grunting, I see: please get out of this room.

Judith is surprised at his words but the bellboy, sweating and smiling, does not understand.

Dollar, zloty?—he says. Money change?

No, Carl says, no thank you, *no*. Will you leave—?

The bellboy retreats, grinning in Judith's direction, his gaze hopelessly out of focus. Judith does not know which eye to engage, she would make a sign to the poor man of courteous regret, or even of reluctant disapproval, but the exchange has taken place quickly and she is most struck by her lover's sudden anger.

The incident leads into their first serious quarrel since leaving New York. Though Judith has vowed not to quarrel with Carl— not to succumb to the childish instinct in herself for contradiction, for opposition and spite. Though she has vowed to force her behavior in this man's presence to accurately represent her feeling for him. —Why were you so rude, she hears herself saying, so upset she cannot unpack her suitcase, why did you treat him like dirt?—the poor man!—you know how poor they are. Carl is hanging things in the closet methodically. Without glancing at her he says, You know what we've been told. She says incredulously, You *don't* think that poor man was an agent provocateur, do you!—that's ridiculous. Carl does not reply. That's ridiculous, Judith repeats. (The official rate of exchange is 33 cents American currency to one zloty; on the black market, $1.50. Though the Deutsche mark is even stronger.) The term *agent provocateur* pleases Judith secretly, it is so chic, so grand; but she resists saying it again. —Do you really think he was working for the police? she asks. Carl says mildly, as he sets his small portable typewriter on the bureau, For all I know they all are.

Judith wears: a black suede jump suit with innumerable zippers. Slantwise across each breast; at her thighs; at each knee—
one horizontal, the other vertical. Kidskin boots (for even in
May it is quite cold here), gloves. She is striking to the eye,
even dandyish; the Poles will simply not know how to take her.
A woman?—a *womanly* woman? But no. But perhaps: after all
she is wearing an inordinate amount of jewelry (three rings on
her right hand, two rings on her left; and several necklaces—
beautiful sullen-heavy silver that looks, and is, very expensive).
Her gray eyes are wide-set in her strong (slightly Slavic?) face,
her mouth in repose appears tremulous: but that is surely a mis-
conception since Judith Horne thrives on combat, intellectual or
otherwise. Her fingers are long and slender, the nails badly
chewed as if she were a nervous schoolgirl; her mannerisms are
abrupt and curiously appealing. Olive-dark skin, unlined, innocent of makeup—except for a *very* minimal eye makeup which
she justifies to herself because, without it, her lustrous intelligent
eyes simply don't seem to exist and cannot engage others'; strong
cheekbones, a strong squarish jaw; dark brown slightly coarse
hair worn, for the season, for the European tour, in a braid that
falls between her thin shoulder blades—a fashion that is most
stylish in the West but might strike East European eyes (Judith
is aware of the tantalizing possibility) as mysteriously *peasant*.
Her voice clear and dauntless as a bell, in public. Her bright
brittle intelligence never in question. (Though only a few of her
essays on American culture have been translated into Polish, and
not one of her books has been published, the intellectual Poles
—and there are many—seem to be quite agreeably familiar with
her work.) She is enviable, she is formidable. She is a successful
American—which is to say, an American. With her American
passport she can travel anywhere, or virtually anywhere. Her restless curiosity, her blunt questions, will never get her into trouble of any official nature: it's a miracle to observe, to realize,
that Judith Horne and Carl Walser and the other Americans
who have come to Warsaw for the First International Conference on American Culture can *never* get themselves arrested or
imprisoned or even interrogated for anything they might say or
write. Anything. So they are formidable in their brazenness,

which they try to wear without ostentation; they are enviable. Perhaps they will even be helpful.

About Judith Horne there are two mysteries, not related. The first is spurious—*Is* she a womanly woman, a female in the classic sense of the word? The black jump suit armored with its almost too prominent zippers; the expensive but unpolished leather boots; the squarish combative jaw and the mouth that curves up into a characteristically droll smile. . . . But, after all, there is Carl Walser with whom she is traveling. There is Carl Walser about whose masculinity there can be no public doubt. They are not married, those two—though perhaps, secretly, they are?—and the Horne woman simply chooses to retain her maiden, which is to say her professional, name? A trivial mystery, but one which engages some speculation. For even in East Europe the private life is hardly over.

The second mystery: her background.

Horne is an English name, a nullity of a name. But Judith. What of Judith? *Judith.*

Everyone knows what "Judith" is—biblical.

And her dark somewhat kinky hair, and her dark uneasy eyes: the restlessness of her imagination. Her American fame too. Her prominence. (Which her Polish hosts have generously exaggerated.) All of which is to suggest—the biblical Judith, the Hebrew Judith.

(Judith will keep her background to herself, which seems to her nothing more than discretion in this part of the world. She sees no reason to burden her hosts with the dreary and possibly too-familiar recitation of facts—another American with Jewish ancestors, Jewish relatives, come to visit Poland. And Judith is only obliquely Jewish anyway: she has some Jewish "blood," that is all. Remote aunts and uncles, cousins, who lived in a farming village northeast of Warsaw, and who were shipped away—all were shipped away—to Oświęcim; that is, Auschwitz. But Judith will not bring up the subject, she considers it pointless, in any case a possible embarrassment to her hosts.)

Thirty-three thousand feet above the earth, traveling eastward in defiance of the sun, Judith was mesmerized by the cloud tundra above which the plane moved with so little apparent

effort. In transit, in motion. Motion is inertia—perhaps the ultimate inertia. America behind, Poland ahead. An unfair balance—
but no "balance" at all. In size America is a continent, a complete
world. In size Poland is New Mexico.

Beside her Carl Walser sits with his lightweight typewriter in
his lap, typing notes, ideas, suggestions to himself. He will write
a story on the "atmosphere" of Poland; after Poland he will
spend two weeks in West Germany, interviewing German civil-
ians. What are their feelings about the United States—the presence of American GIs throughout their country—how do they
feel about the recent arrests of drug dealers, the recent scandal
involving so many GIs: heroin, hashish, cocaine, marijuana
being sold to Germans, many of them teenagers. Carl works
steadily, typing on an oversized sheet of yellow paper; he has no
mind for, no interest in, the familiar cloud landscape beyond the
plane's wing. Nor will Judith distract him by calling his attention to it. They are not newlyweds, after all. They are not
obliged to share every sensation.

*The Awkward Age* lies unread in Judith's lap. A paperback
edition acquired in a bookstore at the airport precisely because
it struck Judith as totally inappropriate to her circumstances; ex-
traterrestrial in its claims. A tragedy with the tone and pace of
comedy, or was it a comedy with the pretensions of tragedy. . . . She cannot focus her attention on it, she is forced to
think of other things.

Do you think you should risk it, Judith, Carl asked. Meaning
the trip—the visit to Warsaw.

You don't know me very well, do you, Judith said.

She is not thinking about her Jewish "blood"—whatever that
means. (She is after all more directly, more significantly, English; the Hornes originally came from Manchester.) She is not
thinking about Carl Walser whom she loves, she supposes, with
an emotion that is humiliating and demeaning and futile and
necessary. In a sense she is always thinking about him, or about
the aura of emotion that surrounds him; there is no need to
focus upon it. She is really not thinking at all, her mind drifts
idle and alarmed, fascinated by the cloud landscape which is in
one version *extraordinarily beautiful* and in another version *a*

*nullity, a blank, nonhuman.* She sits rigid in her seat as if her seatbelt still strapped her in place.

Sleepless in the hours after takeoff she was a witness (as Carl, sleeping, was not) to the 2 A.M. sunrise which, though expected, though inevitable, was nevertheless astonishing. One moment there was only dark—Melville's blackness ten times black—and then, abruptly, wonderfully, the light appeared. It was incorrect to say that the sun rose, or even appeared; instead, *there was light*. A bronze glow deepening in the plane's massive wing . . . the sea of cloud gradually becoming visible. The darkness fled, they were being hurtled east, plunging through time. An extraordinary experience no matter how often it occurs. . . . Judith stared at the lunar landscape, the rivulets and gullies, the ravines, the abysses, and felt both elation (for it *was* sunrise, her body responded with eagerness) and a curious impersonal dread: what did human claims mean, after all, at such a height? —what did "time" and "history" mean? The *minuteness* of personality, wisps of vapor contained tremulously in human skulls, inside human bone, like the feeble souls of extinct creatures— magnificent void of light that, below, would be casually called the "sky" and did not draw a deep breath out of a terror of either bursting into tears, or laughing hysterically. Her love for Carl Walser was now nearly a decade old; it had substance, down below; it had a history; a future; it was *hers*. Slender as a thread, delicate as a vapor . . . but hers. Thirty-three thousand feet in the air it was possible that neither "Judith Horne" nor "Carl Walser" existed in any meaningful sense of the word, but still the emotion, the obsession, existed—for why should she feel such dread at its loss? She stared, she stared. Frozen. Her wide reading in philosophy and Eastern religion instructed her that the very inhumanity of the universe is a consolation; but she felt no consolation; only a bone-chilling loneliness. While her lover slept beside her, his breath arrhythmic and moist, his strong hands docile on his lap like tools temporarily set aside. And other passengers, stirring, annoyed by the dawn, pulled down their opaque shades.

Smoke. In every Pole's fingers a burning cigarette. Meeting
rooms, restaurants. Smoke. A smoke-haze that stings Judith's
eyes, permeates her clothing, makes her hair and (so she imagines) her very skin stink. Even Carl, who smokes, is annoyed.
No ventilation, that's the problem, he says, they can't afford air
conditioning here. . . . Layers of smoke-cloud in the shabby
coffee shop of the Europejski Hotel, drifting layers of smoke-
cloud at the luncheon hosted by the Polish Writers' Union and
*Literatura na Swiecie*. Even at the ambassador's residence, at
the jammed cocktail reception. Ten o'clock in the morning, cigarettes and coils of smoke, vodka served in cylindrical glasses, the
polished wood of meeting tables, tea served Russian style: a
glass set in a silver holder, wedges of lemon; and always, in the
background, tiptoeing, old Polish women carrying trays, carrying
trays, serving, unobtrusively interrupting the flow of remarks, always serving, tea and cream and sugar, vodka, cognac, warm
mineral water: taking ashtrays away to empty them, bringing
clean ashtrays back. In every Pole's fingers a burning cigarette.

What do you make of it, Judith asks Robert Sargent, an American poet here for the conference, a slight but old acquaintance,
sweet and mandarin and not very political (the only other international conference Robert has been invited to was a "Festival
of the Arts" organized by the sister of the Shah of Iran some
years ago—Robert accepted the invitation without question, attended the festival without precisely absorbing the "climate of
opinion" surrounding Iran at that time, and came away admira-
bly innocent); what do you make of it—the compulsive smoking, the drinking? Judith asks.

Robert appears to be considering her question. His eyes are a
pale frank childlike blue behind the round schoolboyish lenses
of his glasses. But then he says apologetically that since the
flight from Kennedy he has been in a peculiar state of mind and
isn't altogether certain *what* he thinks about anything, or if he is
capable of thinking. Flying so terrifies him, he naturally takes
several Valium; and on the plane he has one or two or several
drinks; and after that—a rocky but uninterrupted oblivion. The
change of time has certainly affected him too, he feels both
wretched and inappropriately elated; he has not been particu-

larly aware of smoke in Warsaw—either smoke from cigarettes or exhaust from traffic—since fresh air, being drafty, upsets him. In a curious way I feel I am in my own element, Robert says. The run-down hotel, the secret cocktail bar in the basement— did you know there's a cocktail bar there?—it isn't advertised— the Stalinist architecture, the sad-eyed people, the long queues— the sense of time having stopped in the early Fifties—and, in a way, in 1944: something in it appeals to me.

You don't think the smoke is a political gesture, Judith says.

A political gesture? says Robert, leaning politely forward. (He gives off an agreeable odor of alcohol and talcum powder. The tiny white lines radiating from his eyes suggest his age—forty-eight, fifty—but do not detract from his boyish air.)—A *political* gesture?

Judith is always conscious, nearly always conscious, of the possibility she risks of seeming ridiculous: her blunt dogmatic stirring judgments are sometimes (her detractors claim) frankly absurd. But she pursues them, she is merciless toward what might be called her social self, her vulnerable "womanly" self. Political, she says. Smoking and drinking compulsively. In the Soviet Union—which I haven't visited, though Carl has—it's said to be worse. Smoking and drinking and religion. Here in Poland especially: haven't you noticed that they're all Catholic?

All Catholic? says Robert, blinking.

Catholic.

Ah—*Catholic,* says Robert. The religion. Ah yes—very nice— Roman Catholicism—I've been attracted to it myself intermittently.

Judith waves away a cloud of smoke. Her throat constricts in protest, in anger. She says in an undertone so that their Polish hosts do not hear: The smoke-haze of Warsaw is no less political than the smoke-haze of their religion. This is a *tragic* nation.

It is? says Robert, startled.

Pogrom. Weeks ago Carl said to Judith in her apartment on 11th Street as they sat drinking tepid coffee with their lives— their life together—in snarls and knots about them, as usual: Do you really think you should risk it, Judith?

Risk what? she said irritably. —Don't speak in riddles.

(Though he was not speaking in riddles. And rarely did.)

The Polish tour, ten days in Warsaw. You know.

His voice was uncharacteristically light, his manner uncharac-teristically gallant. Judith perceived that her lover's famous ironic tone was now in suspension: which meant that he was being consciously and systematically *nice*. Which enraged her.

Yes? What about it? You'd prefer to go alone?

That isn't what I mean.

Then what do you mean?

Carl's quizzical thick eyebrows, dark and straight and mean. His intelligent (and slightly embarrassed) frown. A former for-eign service officer—he had quit both because of the Vietnam War and because the State Department was going to ship him to Reykjavík, Iceland—he knew a great deal and had a way, some-times charming, of hinting that he knew even more. So that his pretense of being baffled and nonplussed was always distressing. What do I mean . . . ? he repeated blankly.

Rain was drumming on Judith's window. *Her* window, *her* apartment—they had experimented with living together on three occasions, but none had been a success; Judith appeared capable of making the effort—the surrender—of having no real privacy or sanctuary in her life, but Carl, who had lived alone for too long and who cherished his loneliness, evidently could not. Though he protested that he loved her: he really *did* love her. And wanted to try again.

Rain, past one o'clock, coffee in ceramic mugs (his the blue one, hers the red-orange one with the hair-thin cracks), motorcy-cles racing by on Seventh Avenue. Do you think you should risk it, Judith's lover casually inquires, as if he does not know her at all.

A tape is being made which will be played at a later date. Television, radio. Their conversation has that capricious air of unreality. A tape is being made; time is consequently denied. Judith thinks: If the tape is being made *now* then *now* isn't ur-gent. Can't hurt. Because *now* won't be played—won't take place—until later. And then we'll be somewhere else. *Later* will become *now* but we'll be gone. We'll be other people.

She was not drunk. Not on tepid coffee. Blackly bitter.

She had done many tapes, in her profession. As had Carl.

Sometimes they asked the questions and sometimes they were asked the questions. Neither quite knew at which point in their lives they had been promoted from the rank of interviewer to interviewee. Journalists of the highest rank now interviewed themselves.

Tapes are being made constantly, Judith thinks. And then forgotten. And then replayed, much later.

The caprices of memory.

Did the blood too possess memory?—but what precisely was "the blood"?

You've sometimes been upset by circumstances, Carl is saying evenly. And this Warsaw conference—Poland—your family background—

You're provoking me, Judith says.

Preparing you. Us. Both.

She does not look at him. At such moments the anxiety of her love for him—for his queer remorseless authority—is so keen, she believes that the slightest touch of his hand would cause her to burst into angry tears. Rigid she sits apart, rigid she holds her head, high. A swan's graceful neck. Does she compel his awe with her beauty? Or was Judith Horne's "beauty" fictitious? (Lovers, Judith knows very well, flatter each other innocently. And shamelessly. But if love is withdrawn the lies too are withdrawn. You aren't *really* so exceptional. So beautiful, so graceful, so wise. You aren't *really* going to live forever.)

Poland has a tragic history, I think we can agree on that, Carl is saying reasonably. I've been in Warsaw several times, though not for a while—it's very somber. The Uprising might have been only a few years ago, the wounds are that fresh. They won't forget—they don't want to forget—they loathe and are terrified of Germans. It's all very real. You might think, there, that anti-Semitism is an invention of the Germans and the Russians . . . if you didn't know Polish history.

Perhaps you exaggerate my weakness, Judith says.

You are hardly a weak woman, Carl says.

My sensitivity, then.

East Europe is a strain on anyone. The more sensitive, the more strain. Judith cannot resist: Do you know, there was a pogrom in a village outside Warsaw. In 1946.

Carl sips at his coffee. Frowns into a corner of the room.

1946, Judith says.

1946! says Carl, whistling. But as if it were expected of him.
—Why? Why a pogrom, for Christ's sake, in *1946*?

Judith smiles and shakes her head. "Tragic" Poland. . . .

In 1946, says Carl. My God. Why?

Not why—we know why, Judith says. She is fairly quivering
with dignity, control. We always know why, we Jews. The question in this case isn't *why* but *how*.


Glass. Judith strides toward a glass door, a double door. She is
late for a meeting with the Polish Writers' Union; the other
Americans are already there. In her stylish jump suit, chains
about her neck, she is hurrying, staring at the pavement, her
mind is jammed with mere shards of thought. And Polish words.
The marvelous dizzying cascade of Polish words—like a mountain stream breaking and crashing about her head, and immediately flowing past—sibilant, melodious, utterly unintelligible.
(Though one of her guides has been trying to teach her a few
elementary expressions.) For one who lives so profoundly in language, with such customary control, it is unnerving—in a way
frightening—to journey into a country whose language is so very
foreign. Not a word, not a phrase is familiar; even the hand gestures confuse her; she tastes panic and wonders if her mind is
slipping away. If she were in France, or in Italy, or Spain—or
Germany!—then, *then* she would have a chance.

She strides along the dirty pavement, her leather shoulder bag
swinging at her side. The morning is cold for May; damply cold;
not very pleasant. She is acquiring a reputation—not very fairly,
she thinks—for always being late for meetings and luncheons
and dinners. But there are so many meetings and luncheons and
dinners. . . . She is always hurrying, she is always late, toweling
her long thick hair dry in the hotel room, in the dismal bathroom, dressing hurriedly while Carl waits for her, impatiently
rattling the oversized key to the room. They will misunderstand,
he says mildly, they will think you're indifferent to them, or even
disrespectful, why can't you get ready on time?—and Judith, her
face burning, cannot tell her lover that she is not quite herself
here in this country, so far from home, so far from her own lan-

guage, her own identity. She cannot tell him that the architecture depresses her, the smoky air is making her sick, the odor
of fried onions, the sight of Pepsi-Cola bottles everywhere, displayed on banquet tables like bottles of French wine, the half-
fearful half-brazen references to Soviet Russia ("The light
doesn't always shine from the East!"–the boldest statement she
has heard a Pole say), the shabby dirty hotel room in the hotel
their Polish hosts are obviously proud of because it is "European." . . . She cannot tell him that she feels unreal, a fiction:
shaking so many hands, smiling and being smiled at in return:
that she does after all feel weak. And queerly Jewish. And
womanly–in the old, rather sick sense of the word. A Jew, a
woman, a victim. Can it be?

Robert is even later than I am, most of the time, she says
sullenly. And that Marianne from the State Department–

Is it the State Department? Carl asks. Some foundation for the
arts, I thought.

I can't help it, Judith shouts. I hurry but I'm late. I don't know
why. I can't sleep until three or four in the morning–I wake up
at six–I try to sleep again–I fall into a light sleep and have
murderous dreams–then you wake me up and it's almost nine
o'clock and we're late, we're late again, I'm late, I can't move
any faster, I feel like a zombie, my stomach is upset, it's been
upset since we left Kennedy, I can't help it, go on without me,
make apologies for me, for Christ's sake don't stand there *gazing*
at me with that look of pitying reproach!–for Christ's sake! *Go
on without me!*

Her mind is jammed with shards, mere shards, of thought.
Nothing is really whole. Nothing is logical, let alone "profound."
Since the age of fifteen Judith Horne has had an exaggerated
terror of being banal, of uttering commonplace thoughts; now, in
Warsaw, she has developed a terror of saying, *even in English,*
thoughts that are simply stupid. (Which–she has noted, with
unease–one or two of her fellow conferees have not resisted.
Perhaps it is the late-night drinking, the smoke-haze, the intensity of conversations not public and official–?)

She strides toward the glass door. Which is an automatic door.
Which will open when she breaks a certain invisible force-field.
She is late, she means no disrespect, something is happening to

her in Poland, she is not to blame. Then again this is all nonsense: she is fully in control. Her amiable Polish guides Tadeusz
and Miroslav are parking the car up the street. They have just
brought her from the modest office of her Polish publishers
where she received, with some ceremony, her Polish royalties,
held in trust for her in Warsaw these many years. (Several essays of Judith's have been translated for anthologies of American
writing in the sixties and seventies.) Six thousand four hundred
and twenty-three zlotys! Which must be spent in the country.
Which cannot be taken out of the country.

Abashed, self-conscious, Judith believed at first that the
money was worth far more than it actually was. The "senior editor" of the publishing house, an elderly female clerk, Tadeusz
and Miroslav, and one or two others—all stood watching her as
she signed papers in triplicate, as if this were a significant moment. Six thousand four hundred and twenty-three zlotys: how
will she spend it all!—what will she do! She must give gifts to
them all, she must treat people to dinner, gaily she will get rid
of the zlotys, but how much, precisely, are they worth?—and she
detests people who throw money around, she detests public generosity, the inescapable taint of patronizing, condescension. So
very typically American. . . .

She glances up, sees her hurrying reflection in the door. And
at that moment Tadeusz calls out: Miss Horne!

She had been about to walk head-on into the door.

She had been about to walk into it, thinking (but why?) that
it was a seeing-eye door, that it would open automatically with
her approach.

Thank you, Tadeusz, she murmurs, her face burning, I was
distracted, I—I wasn't thinking.

She pushes the door open. As if nothing were unusual. As if
she had not almost crashed into the plate glass and seriously injured herself.

An incident to tell Carl, she thinks. Though of course she will
not.

Madonna. The Old Town District, restored since the devasta-
tion of 1944; Castle Square; Market Square; the Adam Mickie-

wicz Museum (where Judith and the other Americans are presented with a bilingual edition of Mickiewicz's *Complete Poems*). Monuments, churches, cathedrals. Rococo statues of the Virgin, a stone effigy of the head of St. John the Baptist. Medieval alleyways, a Gothic guardhouse, nineteenth-century street lamps, plaster facades, vaulted gates, forged iron doorcases and knockers, barrel-organs. It's very beautiful, Judith says, staring, deeply moved, not knowing in which direction her emotions might rush next. Her guides are young and enthusiastic and somewhat shy; she suspects they feel extremely vulnerable (for what if the American visitors don't praise this rebuilt district, what if the Americans simply look about and murmur a few courteous pleasantries?). She reads a plaque: Market Square of the Old Town Monument of National Culture and Revolutionary Struggle of the People of Warsaw Turned to Ruins by Fascist Occupants in 1944 Raised from Ruins and Returned to the Nation by the Government of People's Poland in the Years 1951–1953.

They pass the Jesuit Church, which is so jammed with worshipers at this hour of the evening—8 P.M.—that people are standing out on the cobblestone street. In a light cold drizzle. Judith and Carl get as close as possible to listen to the priest, who is giving an impassioned sermon—in Polish of course—through a loudspeaker. He sounds young, his voice is melodious and intelligent and reasonable. Judith listens, her head bowed. When she hears a foreign language she always feels a queer fierce sensation, as if she were *about to understand;* as if, concentrating with all her strength, she could will herself to understand. At such moments her mind seems to come to a stop, her brain is entirely empty. . . . I want to understand, she thinks helplessly. I want to know.

But she despises their religion, of course. The Roman Catholic Church. It alarms her, it puzzles her, that all their guides—these wonderful young literary people—declare themselves Catholic. Genuinely Catholic. Tadeusz and Miroslav and Andrzej and Jerzy and Maria and Elzbieta.

Aren't there any Communists in Poland? Carl joked at a small dinner at the ZZPK Club honoring the Americans.

But none of the guides laughed. After a moment Jerzy said with a droll half-smile: No, Mr. Walser. But there are plenty of police.

Tadeusz is working on a doctoral degree at the university in linguistics; Miroslav, the recent father of a baby girl, does night-school teaching—Polish, English—and "free-lance" translations. Andrzej and his wife are both high school teachers who live with Andrzej's parents in one of the crowded high-rise apartment buildings in the suburbs; they have been waiting for an apartment of their own for eleven years. Jerzy is a junior editor in a publishing house specializing in textbooks; Maria is an American studies scholar, a graduate student who has visited the States (she spent a year at the University of Iowa). Elzbieta is married, has a four-year-old son, teaches when she can get a course and does "free-lance" translations too: she is very enthusiastic about a project she will begin as soon as the conference is over —the translation of Jane Austen's *Emma* into Polish. Would you like to travel, the Americans ask, would you like to study abroad, and the answer is always a slightly startled *Of course— everyone wants to go abroad.*

The United States, England, Sweden, Italy.

To be awarded a fellowship for study abroad, to be invited to the West for a semester or a year—the young people agree quietly that this would be a great thing for them.

But the competition is so strong, Miroslav says. Those awards go to professors, important editors. Older men.

Tadeusz says, No, there isn't much chance for most of us—we have to be realistic. My brother, for instance—he's in Stockholm —he isn't coming back—so it would be very difficult for me to get a visa now. Maybe I will never be given a visa again.

Discreetly, the Americans query the Poles about the Communist party—that is, the Polish United Workers Party—and about the Soviet Union. Censorship, repression, arrests. But the Poles are reluctant to speak. And Judith wonders if the conversation isn't perhaps dangerous: Carl has told her that there are certainly police agents involved in the conference, and that their guides, however friendly they appear to be, and are, will surely be interrogated afterward. I suppose one might inform on the others, Judith said. She considered them—she had grown so fond of them, so quickly—Tadeusz and Miroslav and Andrzej and Jerzy and Maria and Elzbieta—and it frightened her to think that one might inform upon the others, or that all might, in some way, be forced to "inform" to some degree.

But it depresses her even more that they are Catholic. Though of course she can understand—she can certainly understand—why.

*Aren't* there any Communists in Poland, Robert Sargent asks, disappointed, slightly drunk, I was expecting to be attacked, to be challenged—to be denounced as degenerate. But everyone I met likes me. When I said that the United States is an imperialist nation, one of the Poles shrugged his shoulders and said, Who is better? And they're all Catholic which is so wonderfully *bizarre*.

Judith tells him: Their religion is all they have, Robert. When one can't move horizontally, one must move vertically.

Church bells are ringing across the city, young priests stride along the streets, masses are always crowded. Judith shuts her eyes and thinks: Censorship, repression, exploitation of women, anti-Semitism, pogroms.

The Church.

The Church of Rot.

The young Poles are eager to know—What do Americans think of the Pope? Pretty blond Marianne from the arts foundation in Washington, more diplomatic than her face and her clothes and her charming finishing-school manners suggest, elects to speak for the American contingent—answers quickly before anyone else can reply. The Pope, very popular of course, intelligent, remarkable, world leader, international stature, extraordinary. A force for morality and justice and freedom in the world. A force for good.

Of course—there are millions of Poles in the United States, one of the guides says with a shy smile. Which might account for his popularity there. And Marianne says, Oh no—no—America in general admires him immensely—he *is* an extraordinary man.

Judith considers saying a few words. She has been uncharacteristically silent. Moody, disoriented, not "quite right"—a consequence perhaps of the trans-Atlantic flight, loss of sleep. But if she begins she might not be able to stop. The Church, Polish history, Jews, discrimination, pogroms, death.

Their religion, after all, Carl says, means Poland and not Russia—their own history and their own language.

Hatred of Jews, says Judith, pogroms, discriminatory laws, the repression of women, censorship, ignorance, rot. A church of rot.

Yes, says Carl. But their own.

Still, the young priests in their ankle-length black skirts, fresh-shaven, handsome, swinging along the streets—isn't there something engaging about them, something really quite remarkable? Judith stares, stares. At one point, in a group including Robert Sargent, she realizes that she is looking upon these young men with the startled appreciation of a male homosexual.

Madonnas in niches, enshrined in courtyards. The Soviet-built Palace of Culture in the center of the city—a rainstreaked monstrosity with Byzantine spires and domes—Stalinist chic—a dingy wedding cake. Ah, can't you see why people fall in love with East Europe, says Carl expansively, everything is so sad here, even the smiles and jokes are sad, one's heart lifts in East Europe, we mean so much here, Westerners on the streets, milling about in the lobbies of hotels, eager to change hard currency into zlotys. . . . They like us Americans nearly as much as they like Germans.

That's an absurd thing to say, Judith says.

I thought it was a vicious thing to say, Carl laughs.

The smoke-haze, cigarettes burning in fingers, lifted to mouths, everywhere. The odor of fried onions. The tolling church bells, the worshipers hurrying to Mass, in a shabby courtyard off a side street near the university, "protecting" a tenement building so old, so derelict, it must have been spared in the Nazi attack, an extraordinary sight: a sooty-skinned madonna and child in a niche about eight feet above the pavement, both plastic flowers and real tulips—red tulips—arranged before it. What is that, Judith asks, and Elzbieta, who is accompanying her and Carl for the afternoon, says with a shy smile, The Virgin —protecting the people who live here—you know—protecting? —I mean they believe in her, they believe in her power. To protect them.

I see, says Judith.

They are—perhaps—they are slightly superstitious, the young woman says, looking from Judith to Carl. I mean in this district. . . . It is something they believe in, they like. The statue.

Yes, says Carl, but why is the Virgin black?—that *is* black skin, isn't it?

Elzbieta considers the question. The Madonna is dusky-skinned but not otherwise Negroid; the infant, secure in the crook of her arm, is clearly a northern European baby. Judith is moved by the ugly plastic flowers, the red tulips several days past their prime, the shadowy dirt of the niche, the impoverishment of the tenement building. If she draws her breath in deeply—which she will not—she will smell the odors of grease, potatoes, onions, damp. She is moved by the young translator's shy embarrassed smile in which there is a margin, however small, of pride. And tries not to notice the crooked teeth.

Well I think probably, Elzbieta says after a long moment, I think probably they found this one somewhere—a store with old things—maybe in rubble—you mean because she is black?—yes—probably this is the only statue of the Virgin and Child they could get. The people who live here, I mean. They are very, you know, devoted to her.

Are they, Judith says.

Dissidents. In the elegant drawing room of the residence of the U.S. Deputy Chief of Mission the American conferees are being introduced to a number of Polish dissident writers—eight, in fact. Judith notes that all are men.

She finds herself in a spirited conversation with a tall sad-eyed man of early middle age who publishes translations under a pseudonym. He will not tell her, but she has learned beforehand that he was fired from his teaching position at the university, and cannot publish under his own name, as a consequence of his open criticism of the government. Nor will he tell her that he lives in a single room—a hovel, really—in a crowded tenement building.

She is introduced to Wladislaw, Witold, Andrzej. The high-ceilinged room fills up with smoke. There is vodka, there is cognac, there is tea. A servant appears and disappears discreetly; a man. Judith drinks tea and feels some concern that her saucer and teacup rattle—are her hands trembling? She rarely looks at Carl, at such times. Crowded social occasions. He is eloquent, wise, warm, funny, he can be argumentative, he can be bullying. She loves him and is humiliated by her love for him and will not watch him, at such times. —Tell me about Werblan, he says, referring to a high-ranking Communist of whom Judith has heard, though she knows nothing about him. Tell me about Khoyetzki. Konwicki.

Robert Sargent and a young American filmmaker named Brock and Judith become involved in a large general conversation with three Poles and a member of the U.S. Embassy—the cultural attaché, in fact. Unfortunately the Poles know only rudimentary English; everything must be translated. Judith, whose natural speaking voice is rather fast, has to force herself to speak slowly . . . slowly. Is the situation worse or does it remain the same, she asks, frowning, squinting, are there periods when the censorship lets up? Is there any logic to it? Is it true that you're forbidden to own duplicating machines?—that you can't even print up wedding or funeral announcements without the censor's seal of approval?

Talk of Brodsky, Günter Grass, Bienkowski. Judith nods and squints and tries to absorb it all, every name, every nuance of expression. Some handshakes are vigorous, almost painful; others are disturbingly weak. Any meaning? Any significance to the fact that, in this group, the Poles direct most of their comments to Robert Sargent and the young filmmaker . . . ?

A fired editor, a fired professor, a white-haired gentleman who has been arrested eleven times in the past five years, but only kept overnight at the police station: the U.S. Embassy is very much aware of him. Judith feels a queer despondency. She is angry, she is baffled, the sibilant words crash and flow about her head, do they speculate about her blood, her Polish blood, her Jewish blood?—or have they no awareness of her at all? She is led forward to meet a "prominent" culture critic, the editor of the country's leading Catholic journal. She shakes hands, she is vigorous and animated, she hears herself asking about Miroslav Khoyetzki—are they acquainted?

Khoyetzki became famous for having been arrested for the

twenty-first time a few weeks previously. By applying different articles of the criminal code the police were able to "legally" take from his apartment cans of meat, a jar of curry sauce, a pair of scissors, blank paper, a typewriter, jazz recordings, scientific journals. (Khoyetzki is a chemist.) He is guilty of publishing illegally—bringing out books banned by the censor. Is he in jail now? What has happened to him?

Judith excuses herself, the smoke is so thick. In the bathroom —which is modern, elegant, "American"—she helps herself to a two-inch wad of pink Kleenex, since there are no tissues in her room at the Europejski. She studies her face in the mirror without affection and decides that her sallow skin and the shadows beneath her eyes emphasize her Semitic blood. The pores of her nose are greasy, one of her heavy silver chains has worked its way around so that the clasp shows.

I know your position on censorship by the Communists, she will ask, but what is your position on censorship by the Church?

Carl is talking animatedly with a frizzy-haired youngish Pole, close beside him stands Marianne Beecher, of whom it was whispered (perhaps not seriously) that she is a spy—she travels about East Europe spying on foreign service people for their mutual employer, the State Department. But her official identity has to do with a science foundation—or is it an arts foundation —and Judith cannot underestimate the young woman's intelligence simply because she is so very beautiful. A linen suit, deep pink; a pale gray blouse; gold earrings; fingernail polish; extraordinarily high heels; lovely slender legs. And the face is too striking to be studied, to be granted Judith Horne's conspicuous attention.

You get the impression, don't you, an American murmurs in Judith's ear, that Poland is an occupied country. It isn't a Communist country.

Yes, says Judith. She fusses with her necklaces, she bites at a fingernail. Not watching Carl. And they have never heard of anti-Semitism, have they? Here. No, it's the Germans—it's the Russians. Poland is absolutely innocent.

He glances at her, startled.

Yes, she says, relenting, it's an occupied country. I can feel the poison in the air.

It *is* a poison, her companion agrees. Even when people talk openly—as they are tonight—you can sense the contamination, the fear. They can't really trust anyone, they can't even trust one another.

Judith sees the sad pouched eyes, the bracketed mouths. Stubborn men. But they too can be broken down. "Tragic Póland." The Uprising of 1944, Hitler's command that Warsaw must be completely destroyed: razed to the ground. Can one forget? Even the younger people—born as late as the fifties—refer to 1944 as if it were only a year or two ago.

And in our country, Judith says with an ironic smile, history is something that happened a few weeks ago—or didn't happen.

Marianne is laughing, her head tilted prettily to one side. She has a Ph.D. from Boston University in art history, she has traveled virtually everywhere, has worked in Washington for the past eight years. In her early thirties. But very young, very much a girl. In this room of dour hangdog men in ill-fitting suits the vision of Marianne is almost disconcerting. (That morning in the Europejski coffee shop she entertained a table of fellow Americans by telling of how she is always being mistaken for a Polish prostitute. Especially when she sits in the hotel lobby by herself, or has a cup of tea in the restaurant. Or tries to hail a cab. It's my blond hair, she says, grimacing, it's my jewelry or shoes, and the fact that I'm usually unaccompanied. The other day a Japanese businessman sat beside me and pushed a bill toward me on the table. American money—a fifty-dollar bill. I tried to ignore him but he was very persistent, he pushed the bill toward me and tried to knock it into my lap. I felt like bursting into tears or screaming at him, the little Jap bastard, finally I got to my feet and walked away . . . my heart was pounding so hard I thought I might faint. All I was doing was sitting in the lobby having a cigarette! . . . Afterward I thought, why didn't I take his money, take it and walk away, it would have served him right. The arrogant little bastard!)

Layers of smoke, vodka and cognac, cherry cheesecake, a convoluted tale—a complaint—about the Polish P.E.N. organization, which discriminates against young people. The translators never cooperate—they are suspicious of one another—they never tell anyone what their projects are. A sad country, someone murmurs. Too much history.

The party leadership is becoming more reactionary. Stalinist, in fact. Though Poland isn't nearly so tight as Czechoslovakia. Or East Germany. Still, it's an unhappy era. . . .

Is there anything we could do to help, Judith says impulsively. Witold and Andrzej stare at her. I mean—we Americans—could we form a committee, could we write about your situation and publicize it—could we help finance visits to the States?—or England?—or Sweden?

The cultural attaché draws near. He is obviously very pleased with Judith's response. Tall and handsome and dressed like a stage diplomat in a three-piece charcoal gray suit. Anything you can do for these good people, he says softly, would be greatly appreciated. But I don't think that visits to the West are feasible —they can't get visas.

Yes, says Judith, embarrassed, of course not, I realize that.

But anything you might do back home to publicize their difficulties, perhaps a committee of some kind, you might work through P.E.N. in New York, you might donate some money to the Index on Censorship effort in London—you're familiar with it?—yes?—anything at all, the cultural attaché says, smiling. In fact I can deliver mail to certain individuals, just send it to me in care of the embassy, our post office box is in New York City— I'll give you my card.

Yes, says Judith. I will. Yes. Whatever I can do.

The Poles stare hungrily at her as her words are translated. Judith smiles, smiles. She is overwhelmed with guilt—fairly sickened with guilt—for her freedom, her American spirit. After this strained meeting she and her friends can simply walk away! —simply walk away. And no one will follow them.

I'll give you my card, the attaché says in Judith's burning ear.

The awkward age. Propped up in bed, reading the James novel, unable to sleep. Alone. Twice the telephone has rung— that is, it has almost rung. The bell jingles, twitters. But does not ring. Carl is away at a meeting of Polish filmmakers which Judith, feeling unsteady on her feet, has declined. Now she is alone, and lonely. Now she has time in which to contemplate her thwarted jammed-up life.

The "awkward age" is an entire era, an entire swath of idle English society; it also refers specifically to the age of a young woman—no longer a girl—as she steps out into the adult world. No vocation, no fate, no life but marriage. Nanda *must* marry.

And so, Judith thinks, must I.

Except: I have outlived my girlhood. The period of my availability.

She is in love and suspects that her love is not returned. Not pound for pound, ounce for ounce. Her passion is greater than Carl's, her ferocity and despair and capacity for hurt. Consequently she hates him and hates herself for her humiliating weakness.

In mourning for her youth, her nearly forgotten Jewish blood, the sick sad futile sentiment of maudlin thought. She has wanted only to be a woman of independent means—a woman with a career, a public reputation—a woman whose name is comfortably *known:* and all this she has, and more. Her books and articles bring her a steady income, she tours the United States giving lectures (and her fee is not modest), she has only to pick up a telephone or write a letter and an academic appointment would be offered her at once. The East Coast, the West Coast, Iowa, Michigan, St. Louis, Seattle. . . . She is a thoroughly successful woman in a bitterly competitive field yet her thoughts turn helplessly inward toward love, marriage, Carl, a life with him, a life shared with him in every *conventional* sense of the word.

Fortunately, Judith thinks, I'm too old—or almost too old—to have children. *That* temptation is nearly past.

The telephone's bell makes an almost inaudible tinkling sound. Judith picks up the receiver. Yes? Yes—?

It is nearly midnight, and then it is nearly twelve-thirty. She takes off her reading glasses and rubs her eyes.

Carl is very late returning from the meeting.

Carl is very late.

Earlier today Judith Horne gave a quite successful lecture at the university. Crowded into a tiered auditorium were nearly three hundred students. And a scattering of professors. There was a small contingent from the U.S. Embassy, there were a number of newspaper and magazine reporters. Judith Horne the distinguished American writer. Judith Horne the distinguished American cultural critic. She was late for her own performance and entered the crowded overwarm room flanked by her Polish guides, who had been clearly worried, and who chattered at each other across her, while Judith in a gray corduroy jacket and dark, not recently pressed slacks, and a white turtleneck sweater (for May in Warsaw continued to be cold), hid her nervousness and walked briskly to the podium at the front of the enormous room. She felt inordinately elated—a symptom of her habitual panic before large groups—and her cheeks were flushed, her eyes bright. No longer a beautiful woman, precisely; but certainly a handsome woman. The distinguished American woman of letters.

Carl had been away, in another part of the city. Interviewing two men who were involved in the "Flying University"—an informal and indeed illegal organization that offered courses late at night on subjects forbidden by the official universities.

These days, Carl was being patient with her. And watchful. And the "Jewish" business was never raised.

Judith spoke with her customary passionate authority. The topic assigned to her was wide and generous enough: Contemporary American Culture. It was a subject she could talk about for hours, tirelessly, but in Warsaw she found herself discoursing on censorship in America. It did not escape her patrician notice that her audience was *very* interested.

Censorship in America?

By the state?—by religious groups?

But no: the censorship she meant was less formal, less direct. It was the censorship applied to serious writers and poets, "literary" people, those who write difficult, uncommercial books. The demand that a writer be *popular*—be a financial success for his publishing house—is different only superficially, Judith charged, from the demand that he write books that placate or flatter the state.

Her voice took strength, a flush rose from her throat. The talk was extremely well received, even by Judith's fellow Americans, who might have been concerned about her topic—for Judith Horne had the reputation of being quirky, provocative, provok-

ing. It was not until hours later that Judith realized she had forgotten to speak of censorship by the Church.

I hear it went beautifully, Carl said, rummaging in his suitcase for something, I hear everyone was impressed. Why did
you worry?

I didn't worry, Judith said.

She shrugged her shoulders and ran both hands roughly
through her hair, which needed shampooing—but she loathed
the shabby unclean bathroom, and dreaded spending much time
in there.

You're not disappointed that I couldn't make it—?

Certainly not.

She took the bouquet of flowers from the bureau—six red
roses, baby's breath, daisies, carnations—and dropped it into the
wastebasket.

What the hell—! Carl said, staring.

I don't like flowers, Judith said. I don't deserve them.

Why did you do that?

I don't deserve them.

They were very nice—it was a thoughtful gesture—who gave
them to you?—why are you throwing them away? Carl said,
staring at her as if he had never seen her before. There was a
tiny red nick on the underside of his chin; he had just shaved for
the second time that day.

I don't like flowers, I don't like the assumption behind them,
Judith said, not quite coherently, I mean a bouquet—a woman
presented with a bouquet—especially in public. I resent having
to pretend to be grateful in public. It's such a— She made a dis-
mayed wriggling gesture with her fingers. It's such a masquer-
ade.

Carl stared at her for a long moment. Then turned back to his
suitcase. He rarely troubled to unpack his suitcase of small
things—underwear, socks—even when he was staying in one place
for a week or more.

I don't deserve them, Judith said.

That's absurd, Carl said.

I don't *want* them, Judith said.

You deserve them as much as anyone does, Carl said.

Shit, said Judith.

The telephone rings, now full-throated. Judith lays *The Awkward Age* aside—James's highly embellished dialogue has made her both sleepy and dimly apprehensive—and picks up the receiver and says, unforgivably, Carl?—hello? But of course it is not Carl: it is a man speaking a language she cannot comprehend, even to refute its assumptions. No, no, I'm sorry, no, this is room 371, you must have the wrong number, I don't speak Polish, no, I'm sorry. But the man persists. He sounds bewildered. No, I'm sorry, try the operator at the switchboard, Judith says, and though her voice is steady enough her pulses race alarmingly.

My Warszawa. Long queues in Centrum. Futile to try to shop there, simply to spend her zlotys, and anyway the goods—the women's clothes—look second-rate. Long queues at fruit stands: withered lemons, small shriveled apples. The ugly Palace of Culture—a grit-darkened wedding cake which dominates the skyline. SMAK bars, SPOOTEM restaurants, signs for Pepsi-Cola and Coke and Hot Dogs. Kiosks. Church steeples with graceful Moorish lines. (Which is the church in which Chopin's heart is buried?—Judith must visit it.) Red trolley cars hurtling along the larger streets. Red buses, jammed, emitting poisonous exhaust arguably more virulent than that of New York City buses. Crowds, noise, rain in the morning and sunshine at noon, a pervasive chill. Cobblestone streets. Monuments. The elegant Park Łazienkowski. The Palace Marszatkowska. —How many Jews live in Warsaw at the present time? Judith asks, and her guide replies, There are no statistics.

Driven from place to place, from meeting to meeting, in a handy Boy Scout sort of van owned by the U.S. Embassy, or in Soviet-built Fiats—perky little vehicles possessing the size and grace of tin bathtubs. (Judith's teeth rattle, the cobblestone streets are not easy to navigate.) Where was the Jewish ghetto, Judith asks, and one day, finally, she and Robert Sargent are driven to it—nothing to see but pavement, high-rise apartment buildings, a monument. When you say that Warsaw was completely rebuilt, Judith murmurs, you don't of course mean *completely*—the ghetto wasn't rebuilt.

Robert Sargent takes a picture with his Olympus camera. Or

tries to—in fact he can't make the camera work. I've lugged this
disappointing thing around with me for miles, he says, for days,
and I can't get the film to move—I mean it just doesn't turn the
way it's supposed to. Judith tries to help him but of course it's
futile: what does Judith Horne know about cameras! Her long
fingers, her bitten nails. Trembling.

The monument is rectangular, made of a lightless tearstained
stone. Five prominent figures, all male; heroic; "noble"; with
muscular chests and arms; all male. (A female in the background, emerging feebly from the stone. Judith can tell the
figure is female because it is equipped with breasts and carries a
frightened baby.) It hardly needs to be pointed out that the heroic stone figures boast a craggy Aryan look—nothing remotely
"Jewish" about them.

Judith thrusts Robert Sargent's silly camera away. She begins
to laugh. What the hell has this to do with *anything*—! she says.

How many Jews live in Warsaw at the present time? Judith
asks someone else. This time the answer is more helpful: Maybe
seven hundred. . . . Seven hundred and fifty. . . . But very few
children. Perhaps no children.

Her teeth rattling in the Soviet-built Fiat, her senses stung by
something acrid in the air. Is there a poison here?—but what is
it?—where? She does not want to be morbid or sentimental; she
really *isn't* the kind of person who feeds personal hungers with
grandiose "historical" notions. Warsaw is a city that was destroyed by the Nazis but rebuilt itself—almost completely. Look
at Old Town, they are right to be proud of Old Town, Judith
and Carl stroll through it in the early evening, grateful to be
alone after a day of meetings and receptions, speeches, handshakes, smoke-filled rooms, cognac, tea with lemon, smiles
disclosing sad stained teeth, grateful for the open cobblestone
square, the freedom from traffic and exhaust. . . . The facades
of the buildings on the market square are almost *too* perfect.
Less absurdly ostentatious than the Grand Place of Brussels, but
touristy nonetheless—almost quaint—handsome olive greens and
pale russets and gray and brown and subdued red brick: all very

clean, very neat. Too bad the Soviets are bleeding them white,
Carl observes. They could fix up the rest of Warsaw.

Hills, cobblestone streets. Rozbrat, Krakowskie Przedmieścic,
Wybrzeze Gdanskie, Bolésce, Rybaki, Kozia. The same damp
chill. Polish spring. "Moneychangers" approaching them on the
street, quite openly, even insolently: Change—? Change money—?
Dollar—? Zloty—? Following after them, hands extended. Like
beggars. No thank you! Judith says angrily. She is ashamed for
her Polish friends.

Warsaw, Judith thinks, occupied city, occupied zone. She
stares coldly at herself in the dim bathroom mirror. What is happening to her here? *Is* there a poison in the air? —While her
lover dresses in the other room, groggy with morning. For he
was out very late last night. She has thousands of zlotys to
spend, must buy gifts, must take everyone out to dinner, perhaps
on the last day of the conference. Or will this strike the young
Poles who are their guides as simply an "American" gesture—
charity, condescension?

She forgives her lover his most recent infidelity. Infidelities.
She hasn't even any curiosity about the woman though she
might wonder—she might wonder, had she time—if it was an
American, or a Pole.

No time to think, to brood. Not here. Driven about in the embassy van, in someone's Fiat, Robert Sargent jostled against her,
smelling of shaving lotion. She hasn't time because she must
think, she must think very carefully, fighting her recurrent panic,
her almost physical distress at the sound of Polish—the melodic
tumble of words, the structure of the compound sentence with
its many variations: the subordinate clauses, the coordinate
clauses: which Judith imagines she can "hear" without being
able, of course, to understand.

My Warszawa, Judith thinks idly. The place of my undoing.

(Because—incredibly—she has failed to learn any words at
all. She has tried, and failed. The guides have been patient with
her, perhaps even flattered by her interest, her touching zeal, she
has parroted their words after them, anxiously watching their
lips—but a minute later and she has forgotten. The words, the

delicate pronunciations, are simply erased from her mind.
—Someone comes along, I can almost see his bulk, she says, and
with a damp sponge, an enormous damp sponge, erases the
blackboard. And the words are gone. And I am blank.)

But no time to think, no time to brood. She gnaws at a fingernail. Carl was unfaithful to her but the significant thing is that
he lied to her and expected her to believe it; *that* she cannot forgive.

No time to herself, shaking hands, squinting against the
smoke, accepting a glass of tea Russian style, declining sugar,
cream, and lemon: Thank you, no. No. Thank you. No time, she
cannot brood about the monument to the martyrs of the ghetto,
the Jewish resistance; it seems curiously beside the point to be
bitter or even "interested" at this point in history—for 1944 *was*
a long time ago. And should she take the troupe out to dinner,
perhaps at the famous Crocodile on the square. Or will they
sneer behind her back. Or do they genuinely like her, admire
her. (Why else the flowers?—dropped into the wastebasket in
the hotel room.) She has not forgiven, or has tacitly forgiven,
her lover; which comes to approximately the same thing.

There isn't time, they are being herded into the embassy van,
Judith is listening with enormous interest to an anecdote told by
the American cultural attaché whose last post, evidently a perversely cherished post, was in Saudi Arabia: 130-degree heat,
damp heat, public stonings, yes, but worse, even worse, and
women, of course, *there,* don't exist. Judith is concerned with her
digestion, capricious at all times but malevolent on this tour.
Judith dreads the very look, the odor, of the bathroom in her
hotel room. The enormous crazy roaring splash when the toilet is
flushed. (I thought my toilet was attacking me! Robert Sargent
says with a shudder.) The oilcloth shower curtain with its faded
floral design. The stained sink, the stained tile floor. Judith and
Carl divide the wad of Kleenex between them. Judith's eyes
water, her head reels: she must concentrate on a not quite co-
herent but possibly hostile charge being made by a red-bearded
young playwright: they are both on a five-member panel organized by P.E.N. to discuss the problem of translating. The young
man's English has a distinct Scots accent, unless Judith is imagining it. (She will inquire afterward and learn that he did, in-

deed, live in Scotland for some time.) Other accents are British, Midwestern. Judith assiduously inquires after names and addresses, printed cards. Perhaps she can help to get books translated into English, perhaps she can interest American publishers. She would certainly like to be of aid. She knows of exchange-student programs, she can inquire about grants for study in the States, there is Iowa, there is Columbia, there is Stanford, she will write letters of recommendation, she will be tireless. She hopes to form a committee to help the Polish dissidents who have lost their jobs and are "nonpersons"—she will make contact with Polish dissidents in exile in the States. Exhaustion rings her eyes, her hands tremble, she is aware of not being energetic enough, dedicated enough, she is aware of being "American" and therefore immune to harm. Does anything we say or write or publish *matter*, she thinks, when we risk nothing? —but there isn't time to puzzle over the situation, the embassy van is about to leave, Tadeusz is waiting, today Marianne Beecher is wearing trousers and a casual suede jacket as if in imitation of Judith's style, there will be a television interview at 2 P.M., it continues to dismay her that she seems incapable of pronouncing the simplest Polish words. Tadeusz smiles his shy, exquisitely courteous smile, and corrects—but very softly—her pronunciation of Mickiewicz.

Occupied zone. She turns abruptly from him, would hide in the bedclothes, leaden-boweled. Judith?—he murmurs.

Down on the street, morning traffic. In the corridor workmen moving furniture, maids with vacuum cleaners. The same chill pale light. Warszawa. She has awakened—again—to her city.

Judith, says Carl, I think we should hurry, there's a meeting at ten. You have an interview at nine-thirty.

Her "Warsaw" self—she sees that it is a victim. Meek, docile, even grateful for lies.

Are you all right, Carl asks cautiously. For of course she isn't.

But perhaps he isn't lying to her, she thinks, her eyes shut, perhaps he always tells the truth, it is she who distorts everything, quick to see meanings, significance, even in the wallpaper, heraldic designs too faint to catch a more robust eye.

That woman journalist who wants to interview you, Marta

something, she's probably downstairs in the coffee shop waiting, Carl says, peering at his stooped reflection in the bureau mirror, I think you'll like her: she's very intelligent.

Marta who? Judith says groggily. I don't remember any Marta.

I met her the other evening, she has read most of your essays, in English, she's very eager to meet you, you won't have any difficulty with her English either. . . . Are you all right, Judith? Is something wrong?

Nothing.

Why didn't you telephone the other night, why didn't you make a gesture, however false and strained, toward "treating me with respect" in the old American style, were you too drunk, was your companion too marvelous. . . . Though of course she doesn't say a word. She lies very still. Listening to the thuds and thumps in the corridor. You bastard, Judith thinks. Fucker.

I don't remember any Marta, I don't remember any appointment for an interview, Judith says aloud.

I have the woman's card here, Carl says. Judith does not look over at him. —She's a journalist but she has also written some fiction. I think. Kazimierz was telling me that she's quite good. Marta something.

Fuck Marta, Judith murmurs.

Yes? What?

Carl is in the other room, the bathroom. Running water. The plumbing hums, shudders, sings.

Today Judith will be taken to the Jewish cemetery in Warsaw. She has not told Carl—who is busy with other engagements, in any case—because she knows that he will frown and purse his lips and *say nothing at all.*

The other night, last night, Carl begins, and fumbles, as if not remembering: *was* it last night? or the night before? (Time is passing so very queerly in Warsaw. Even Robert Sargent has remarked upon it.)

Night before last, Judith says curtly.

She is up, brushing her hair, one impatient stroke after another. Curly kinky dark hairs in the hairbrush.

Yes, says Carl. When I came in so late. I'm sorry that I didn't telephone but I lost all track of. . . .

Yes, says Judith. I was grateful to be alone.

I thought you might be, Carl says.

I was reading *The Awkward Age.*

Which is—?

Not a Polish sort of story.

I mean, how do you find it?

Very slow, very rich, very dull, very profound. In fact heartbreaking.

But then James always is, Carl says, if you read him correctly.

I make an effort, Judith says slowly, to read most books "correctly."

Of course you do, Carl says, rummaging again through his suitcase. You're the star of the conference, the queen, the A+ student, you put the rest of us to shame, the Poles adore you, you're the only one of us they want to interview. . . . What are we arguing about? Are we arguing?

I don't know, Judith says evenly, are we arguing?

Carl says nothing. Judith continues her brushing, unhurried.

They were asking me yesterday about the NATO thing, Carl says. Now his tone has shifted. It is light, ironic, more public. He is *trying.*

NATO "thing"—? Judith asks.

In Norway. You must have read about it. They've decided to install 572 new missiles, I think it's a five-year plan.

Missiles, says Judith, where?—you mean because of the Soviets.

Carl says impatiently, letting the lid of the suitcase fall, The joke of it is that NATO is begging the Soviets to negotiate on an arms control agreement, but the Soviets won't negotiate unless NATO abandons its plan. Does that make sense?

What has Norway to do with it?

The meeting was there. I don't know. Norway has nothing to do with it—no more than any other country.

Judith drops the hairbrush on the bureau top. Yes I know about that, she says, or something exactly like it. I read it on the plane coming in.

Well—this is newer news.

It's all the same shitty news.

They were asking me about it yesterday. Not exactly—you

know—with an unfriendly intent. Because of course they don't really know what is going on here. They don't *really* know anything. The government controls the news, of course, but can they trust Western reports?—they don't really know.

They don't even know their own history, Judith says.

Does anyone? Carl says brightly.

Don't be paradoxical: *yes.* Yes, some of us do know.

We know what we've been told, what we read.

We make it our business to be told and to read a great deal.

Carl says conversationally: West Germany is quite willing to go along with the NATO plan, for obvious reasons. England and Italy as well.

But the Soviets have missiles too, Judith says, frowning. Why are we arguing?

We're *not* arguing, Carl says, I agree with you, the Soviets have thousands of missiles—they manufacture one a week. Most are aimed at West Europe but some are aimed at China.

Yes, says Judith, we know. And North America.

It *isn't* new news, you're right. It's shitty old news. You're right.

Judith is now hunting through her suitcase, through her purse. Passport, notebook, wallet, crumpled pink Kleenex, a loose ballpoint pen rattling about. A street map of Warszawa. Why am I here, she thinks, staring at something in her hand, why am I in this room, in this city, with this stranger— She stares at the item in her hand for a long time; eventually it becomes a plastic toiletries grip.

Carl says abruptly: Judith, I feel that I am confronting an adversary in you. It's gotten much worse this past week. The tension, the continual strain—

An adversary in *me,* or an adversary *in* me? Judith asks absently, not turning to look at him. After a moment, when he does not reply, she says lightly: Maybe you just feel guilty.

Why should I feel guilty? Carl laughs. I'll meet you downstairs.

Epiphanies. The mystical interpretation of the universe, Judith thinks, is probably the correct one. Each day is precisely *the* day, each hour and each moment, an eternal present, immutable.

The world is awash in visions yes I know. But to explain to melancholy Robert Sargent on the way to Gezia Cemetery . . . as the poor man recites his litany of bad luck (his camera was "lost," he seems to have set it down on a counter somewhere, or perhaps it was on the floor, by his feet, in that charming noisy restaurant in the Old Town; and this morning he awoke at ten-thirty already late for the first session of the day, lying in a pool of harsh sunlight on the carpet of his room, fully clothed, for a long time he couldn't move at all he was paralyzed stricken unable to remember where the hell he was New York or Paris or where? Warsaw?—how very long he has been here!—his soulmate back home has surely abandoned him by now and broken into the forbidden liquor cabinet as well, being a creature incapable of delaying gratification, let alone fidelity in the usual sense of the word: so he awoke, did Robert, a vile taste in his mouth, sand stinging his eyes, saliva drooling in a thread down his chest, Robert Sargent the unassuming though much-acclaimed post-modernist poet who will quietly admit in interviews that yes he is related, in fact directly related, to John Singer Sargent that extraordinary genius, but what good does that do him!—what good!—he awoke to the terrifying odor of vomit not his own and the conviction that his traveler's checks were gone and all his zlotys and hard currency as well, and personal papers, notes scribbled over with first drafts of poems, and after ten minutes of paralysis he managed to crawl to a chair and hoist himself on his feet and yes everything *was* gone—stolen—everything except the zlotys and the notes for poems!—has Judith ever heard anything so pathetic?) . . . sitting beside Judith in a Fiat driven most dextrously by the young Polish editor Bruno whose last name Judith cannot pronounce though she has heard it countless times and whispered it to herself . . . sitting shivering in a tweedy sport jacket baggy at the shoulders and worn at the elbows, a true poet's costume, appealing to Judith for aid or advice or sympathy or simply shared amusement at his predicament. The cultural attaché has been very kind, very helpful, Robert says doubtfully, of course the embassy has to take care of us, they couldn't . . . abandon us here. I mean he didn't scold. He didn't express disgust, though he may have felt it. I *thought* I saw a slight twitch in his lip. . . . But

no matter! He's going to cable home for money for me, he knows
exactly what to do, I had a horror of being forced to go to the
police, you know I'd never do such a thing, the young man was
very, very naughty to run off with my things but can I exactly
blame him . . . I mean after all . . . an American out for adven-
ture in Warsaw . . . an American of my type so clearly a victim
. . . good-natured victim . . . who's to blame . . . anyway I
couldn't describe him, my glasses had fallen off . . . my vision is
quite deteriorated in my left eye, in fact it's gotten worse here in
Poland . . . on Judith we've been here so long! . . . dear Judith!
. . . you won't laugh at me back home, will you, and spread
tales. . . .

Judith laughs and pats his arm. Sisterly. Maternal.

Where *are* we going, Robert asks, peering out the window,
I've forgotten. . . . we seem to be going a considerable distance
this time.

Gezia Cemetery, says Judith.

What cemetery? Where?

The Jewish Cemetery of Warsaw, says Judith.

Oh yes of course, says Robert, of course, and I don't have my
camera, it's been stolen. Or should I say—lost. I don't want to
make trouble for anyone here.

That's right, Judith says. We don't want to make trouble.

The world is awash in visions, she thinks, and today is the
only day that matters, the day of our salvation or damnation,
this hour, this very moment. But I am not a religious woman. I
am not inclined to mysticism, however comforting or terrifying.
I don't really believe in the blood—in the rich dark unconscious
current of being—whatever it's called—whatever arcane expression: I don't believe. And the trouble with epiphanies is that
they soon cancel one another out.

Nevertheless Gezia Cemetery affects her profoundly, leaves
her rocky and exhausted and scant of breath. Spring is still with-
held, suspended; here birds call to one another with a wintry
plaintiveness; the atmosphere is rural and timeless, distant from
the city of Warsaw which in fact surrounds it on all sides. A
chill greeny-damp tranquility, hundreds of startlingly white
birch trees, grave after grave after grave. . . . Oh God why am

I here, why have I come here of all places, Judith thinks, drawing quick frightened breaths, am I testing myself. . . .

Robert Sargent is subdued at last, staring, as Judith does, at the city of graves. His childlike blue eyes are held wide, his hands are thrust into the pockets of his oversized tweed coat.

The elderly caretaker Pinchas leads Judith and Robert and their tall young Polish guide. A wide pathway of cracked pavement, beneath overhanging tree branches, between rows of graves. Pinchas is gnomelike and droll and quietly confident. His American visitors do not intimidate him. He speaks tirelessly, ceaselessly, pointing out graves, identifying the dead with a careless fond familiarity. Judith notes his leathery expressionless face, his sunken Slavic eyes, protruding ears. Kafka in caricature —grown old and sallow. He wears a shirt and tie and a soiled coat. He appears to be very much at home in this beautiful desolate place. Pinchas, is that a first name or a last name, Robert Sargent asks their guide, but when the young man translates the question for the caretaker Pinchas does not answer. He is pointing out a ruined mausoleum, speaking in low rapid Polish.

A wealthy manufacturer, Bruno translates. One of the class of Jews who made Warsaw a center of commerce.

The little procession continues. Judith hugs herself, shivering. She is wearing only the suede jump suit, her head is bare. Robert Sargent stoops to read inscriptions but of course the inscriptions are unreadable. Five hundred thousand graves, and more. Monuments of all sizes: some as high as fifteen feet, some low and squat, some mere markers half-covered by grass. Judith inquires about materials: Swedish granite (black); Polish granite (pink-gray); sandstone; marble. Here, says Pinchas with melancholy pride, at a grave site elaborately ornamental (pansies, petunias in bloom, protected by fancy iron grillwork), here, Bruno translates, the son is a millionaire in Miami Beach, the wife sends a check twice a year signed with her own name. And down here, Pinchas leads them on, pointing out a small brick tower in another fenced-off plot, here the great Mendelssohn, great in his day, secretary to Marx. Very fine people, very wealthy.

Judith and Robert happen to see a swastika scratched on a

granite monument, some distance from the path. But the swastika does not appear to be fresh.

A forest, in which the graves are tolerated. Lovely trees.
Birch, maple. Just beginning to leaf. Pale cold green, almost
translucent. Pinchas is pointing out the graves of famous Jews—
poets, writers, musicians—famous men—Bruno translates with a
quiet courtesy, expressing no doubt. Yes, says Judith, yes I see,
and over here—? Grave after grave after grave.

But these are the fortunate Jews, the Jews who died "natural"
deaths. And were buried in their own soil.

Epiphanies cancel one another out, Judith thinks, wiping her
eyes roughly with the back of her hand. Robert notices but turns
discreetly aside. He knows of course of her background: he must
have guessed: but is far too considerate to say a word.

On the way back to the cemetery entrance Robert says as if to
comfort Judith: I was fighting my way across a street in Rome
once, years ago, I was a young man then, and absurdly vulnerable, and something about the crowds struck my heart, pierced
me like a blade. *This is a lonely predicament,* I thought. I don't
know what the statement means but it applies to today.

Yes, says Judith, reaching for her wallet.

She gives the caretaker a twenty-dollar bill—hard currency—
American. And notes with a thrill of despair how the old man's
deep-sunk eyes fairly glow.

He is moved, agitated, repeats his thanks in Polish, shakes her
hand and releases it and shakes it again. Until Judith laughs,
embarrassed. And edges away.

Driving back to the Europejski Robert gently breaks the mood
by saying, with a wry laugh, You made old Pinchas's day. You've
spoiled him forever.


Adversary. Carl says, It's simply that I feel I am confronting
an adversary in you.

Judith says, I don't understand.

Carl says, I mean an adversary *in* you—inside you—a rival of
mine. He's inside you and the two of us are struggling for you.

Judith laughs sharply. Her lover's tone is so flat, his expression
so hostile. She says, But is the struggle worth it—!

He does not answer. He is sitting on the edge of his rumpled bed, a newspaper on his knees, sheets of yellow paper scattered across the bedclothes. His eyes are threaded with blood, his skin sallow. He has not yet shaved and the lower half of his face looks malevolent. There is something weary and husbandly about him and Judith thinks, He is going to ask for a divorce.

Each woke before dawn. Traffic noises, plumbing. Judith rose to her low-grade anxiety as if surfacing through a few feet of gray soapy water—no depth to it, but enough to drown in.

Last night, late, past two o'clock, an attempted lovemaking that managed to be both tender and desperate. Is it men you hate, Carl whispered, is it the species—?

Judith is a woman who believes in the body, in the life of the body. "Sensuality"—as a philosophical principle—means a great deal to her. So she could not reply. She turned away, sobbing, burying her wet face in the pillow.

Now she says quietly, You make such pronouncements as a way of not saying something else.

*Not* saying—? He looks toward her innocently, as if startled.

*I love you, I hate you,* Judith intones, rolling her eyes with the drollery of it. Things common people say. Or so we're told.

I'm not in the habit, Carl says, of making formal pronouncements regarding my emotions. You must be confusing me with someone else.

Of course, says Judith. Of course.

This adversary I spoke of, Carl says, as he assembles the newspaper, rather fussily, glancing with a frown at his ink-stained fingers, this adversary is *your* emotion. In you. A kind of shadow, a reflection. I can see it dimly at times, at other times it eludes me—it's too subtle. It occupies you and crowds me out, it's a rival, I think it's winning.

Judith says slowly, I don't understand.

Carl sighs and folds the newspaper up and tosses it onto the night table. You're not a happy woman, he says.

Is that an accusation?

A man feels a certain challenge with a woman like you—your intelligence, your quality. Your impatience. Your style. There aren't many women I can talk to as an equal—no I *won't* apologize for that remark, I haven't time for hypocrisy right now—and I think you know how much I've valued our friendship?—of

course you know. But after a while the struggle with this thing
—this adversary—*you*—becomes exhausting.

Judith stares at him. For a long moment neither speaks. Then
she says in a soft, rot-soft voice, But I don't understand, I love
you.

Oh yes do you? Carl says.

I love you.

*Do* you, Carl says. He sits on the edge of the bed, slightly
hunched over, a man of young middle age, his dark chest hair
shadowy inside his white cotton undershirt. Ten years, Judith
thinks, twelve. My lifetime. And now in Warszawa.

The other day, walking through Old Town, they stopped to
examine a display of "carved" Christs in an outdoor booth. The
Christs were mainly on the cross though there were a few close-
ups, the head and shoulders, the usual crown of thorns, lurid
droplets of paint-bright blood. All the art had the slick stamped-
out look of manufactured goods which Judith found both amusing and depressing. Shiny surfaces, dying-eyed Jesus Christ, cartoon colors. Shall I buy you one, Carl said, as a souvenir of
Poland? Judith drew away, offended. Mockery was wrong, here
—mockery was beside the point. The market square, the cob-
blestones, horse-drawn buggies hauling tourists, melodic incom-
prehensible Polish spoken on all sides, heavy shutters, iron grillwork, eighteenth-century facades of buildings. Except of course
they were not eighteenth-century, they were postwar. Everything was postwar, arisen from rubble.

Judith had drawn away, frowning and squinting, possessed by
a mood. One of her epiphanies. She felt a harsh ravening hunger
for—for what?—for understanding of this place, for sympathy,
for kinship? Carl might have been speaking to her, she didn't
hear. She was thinking with a childlike awe, But did these people despise me, then?—back then?—would they have closed
their doors to me?—their university?—their city?—their culture?

She had never felt Jewish before Warszawa.

In fact she was *not* Jewish—not really.

Carl was speaking to her, rather sharply. So she turned back.
Gazing upon him as if upon a stranger.

Now he is winding his wristwatch, now he gives it a shake beside his head. Another husbandly gesture. We should go down-stairs, he says, our guides are probably waiting.

I don't understand, Judith repeats stubbornly. *You* seem to want nothing I offer. I mean nothing—nothing—that's deep, that's genuine, that's permanent. When I'm happy you're indifferent or jealous. When things go well with my public life, my career—you draw away, you *are* jealous. Only when I'm troubled do you come to life and then you say absurd things—the sort of thing you've just said.

Carl walks into the bathroom, Judith follows close behind him.

You don't love me, she says, horrified at the words she hears, you don't give a damn about me, nothing is genuine, nothing is permanent, I hate you!—I can't tolerate this!—boxed-up in this wretched room with you!—do you think I want to be here, do you think I'm enjoying this? I hate you! Your cruelty—your condescension—

Judith, for Christ's sake—

I want a normal life with you!—I want a normal life! Judith screams. I believe in respect—mutual respect—and honesty—and fidelity—I've been willing to wait—I've been willing to sacrifice my pride—but I won't demean myself for nothing!—for you!

She begins screaming, he tries to hold her, restrain her; she pushes him away; she strikes out with her fists, sobbing like a child. It is all very amazing. It is not really happening and so Judith cannot take responsibility.

A hysterical woman, no longer young. Screaming with such rage that her face is distorted, her eyes nearly pop from her head, her throat is scraped raw with words she cannot believe she hears: You don't love me! You don't give a damn about me! You never have!

Of course I'm sorry, Carl says afterward, shaken. Of course I love you. But I'm not always certain that . . . that I know you.

You know me well enough, Judith says.

She is exhausted from the bout of hysteria. She lies on the un-made bed; her voice is flat and dull; her head hollow. Loathing

for herself, for the absurd creature Judith Horne, has taken on a
sharp tangible taste, like vomit.

It's this place, we've been poisoned by this place, Carl says
slowly. (But is he convincing?—Judith detects her own words,
even her own intonation, in his voice.) —An occupied zone, Carl
says.

Yes, says Judith flatly. An occupied zone.

The Savior. Is it Napoleon, there in the wall?—in a mural of
curlycues and clouds? Judith, bored by the soporific ceremony in
the museum, no longer quite so fascinated by the sound of Polish and not at all fascinated by the English into which it is being
translated by an earnest young interpreter, seeks out diversions
in the ceiling, in the floor, in the wall. The air is thick with
smoke, no windows are open, vodka is being served in tiny
glasses, tea Russian-style, an old woman tiptoes quietly about,
unobtrusive, annoying. Judith notes that Carl is writing something on a much folded sheet of yellow paper; a bell is ringing
in the steeple of the Jesuit Church, a high cold clear sound. Soon
they will leave Poland, at the end of the week. Soon. But Judith
does not want to leave.

She studies the mural of Napoleon. A portly cherub captured
by an adoring painter in the moment of his ascent to heaven. A
savior, another savior! A saint. (Napoleon had promised the
Poles "freedom." His armies were consequently awaited with
enormous hope.) Judith notes the laurel leaves in his hair, the ·
way his eyes turn upward in an ecstasy of heroic innocence. He
wears a freshly starched white waistcoat, a short green jacket
with red collar and cuffs and smart little brass buttons. It seems
to Judith that she has seen this painting, Napoleon in his
apotheosis, elsewhere. But she cannot remember where.

My Warszawa. A visit to a collective farm outside the city, a
visit to the village of Zelazowa Wola, Chopin's birthplace. Judith
tries to read Mickiewicz and decides the translation must be
poor. She reads publications the Poles have given her and notes
the recurring words, the history, the pathos, the sorrow, the te-
dium: *collapse, subjugated peoples, revolutionary fervor, sacrifice, betrayal, annihilation, tyrants, survival, partition, national*

*independence, clandestine organizations, secret police, Uprising, oppressed peoples, despot, oppressor, suffering, struggle.* To read about the Uprising of 1944 and the attack of the Nazis is too painful; she sets the book aside and runs her hands roughly over her face. No words, nothing to say. At lunch a young university teacher tells her in an undertone that Soviet Russia is not a nation like any other, democracy is too weak to deal with—to do battle with—such people.

Rump of boar. Duck Cracow style with mushrooms. Cabbage with nuts. Mizeria (cucumber salad) Polish style. Date mazurek, saffron baba. Very strong coffee in very small cups. —Are you Mr. Sargent's assistant, a courteous middle-aged Pole asks Judith at the banquet, totally unable to "place" a woman in this company otherwise; or Mr. Walser's assistant—?

The Jewish ghetto wasn't much of a loss architecturally, Judith overhears someone say, and it takes her too long to absorb the logic—the conversation has already moved on to another subject before she can speak. Her eyes snatch at Carl who has, yes, glanced at her, his fingers kneading his lips. But he needn't worry: she is too shocked to protest.

Gossip that might interest her: it was in the very house—the U.S.-owned house in which the American contingent met the dissident Poles—that Mary McCarthy wrote *The Group*. Does she, Judith, admire *The Group*? Is it a much read and much respected novel in the States?

So you were taken to the Jewish Cemetery, someone says. And Judith says yes. And then—uncomfortably—there is nothing further to say.

Judith and Carl puzzle over remarks made by a member of the Polish Composers' Union as he rose to give a toast the previous night. Judith thinks the remarks were friendly, Carl thinks they were ironic: in fact hostile. I can't see how you can possibly come to that conclusion, Judith says impatiently. Carl says, It was obvious—I'm not an idiot. And his handshake too, for

Christ's sake, the bastard almost broke my fingers. Judith says,
He was exuberant—he seemed rather carried away by the occasion. Carl says, with a gesture of dismissal, Shit.

Robert Sargent drifting into the coffee shop, so freshly shaven
his fair skin gleams, so sleep-befuddled his eyes appear to be
half their normal size: Judith—Carl—it's the most bizarre thing
—my toenails are growing wildly here in East Europe—I really
can't understand it, I've had to clip them for the second time
this week! The corners are wicked, razor-sharp, I really *can't* understand it.

Trying to avoid the furniture-congested corridor that leads to
the hotel's central staircase—a kind of grand spiral with a soiled
scarlet carpet—Judith seeks out the back stairs and descends
floor after floor in the half-dark, trying doorknobs (the doors are
all locked), her heart in a silly flurry. She cannot be trapped, she
can always return to her own floor, she can always scream,
pound on the doors, perhaps there is a fire alarm, she *cannot* be
trapped. Unfortunately the floors are not marked. Nothing is
marked. Unfortunately the air is very close and warm. She finds
herself in the basement—it must be the basement since she can
go no farther—turning a doorknob, throwing herself against the
door, hearing only a few yards away the voices and laughter of
strangers. It is quite dark here, and very warm. A stagnant
febrile air. Hello, says Judith, clearing her throat, hello, can you
let me out?—the door is locked on this side—
   She turns in a panic and runs up to the next floor—which is
perhaps the ground floor of the hotel?—and tries the door but of
course the door is locked. Hello, she says calmly, is anyone
there? Can you hear me? An odor of fried onions, the taste of
grit on her lips. No sound from the other side. Nothing. So she
ascends to the next floor, her heart now thudding, and then to
the next, and the next. . . . But the doors are all locked. The
doors are locked.
   She pounds on a door with her fist, does Judith Horne. Pulses
wild and desperate in her head. Help me, please, the door is
locked, isn't anyone around?—oh God please—
   It happens, then, marvelously, incredibly, that *on the floor*

*below* the door is opened. Judith hurries downstairs. Two men are backing through the doorway, carrying a stepladder; Judith rushes upon them manic with gratitude. Oh for God's sake *thank you*, oh thank you, wait, don't let the door close—

And she brushes past them, past their astonished faces, and finds herself at the far end of the corridor that runs by room 371.

An anecdote to tell Carl, someday.

Or perhaps not.

Judith jots down more names, addresses. Yes she knows someone at the University of Iowa—she will write a strong recommendation—yes she will be home at the end of June—of course she will be happy to meet with the slender youngish man who has introduced himself as Secretary of the International Committee for Unification of Terminological Neologisms. He has other interests too, he assures her; he is also a translator; he intends to translate one of her books—though he would prefer to do a book not yet published in English. Judith says, puzzled, but how is that possible?—and he says, leaning close to her, smiling a nervous insolent smile, Why I will work closely with you, confer with you over the manuscript itself, spend three–four weeks in New York City collaborating. . . . Judith says, I don't think that's very feasible, really, and the youngish man says, leaning closer still, I will convince you!—only give me a chance.

Judith is appalled at the tiny worms of dirt that roll beneath her fingertips. Between her breasts, across her thighs, her belly. Her forearms and upper arms! She has taken only the briefest, most perfunctory showers in Warsaw.

She rubs her skin hard, hard, with a washcloth. A white washcloth in which the ubiquitous word *Orbis* is stitched. Layers of grime, flakes, and near-invisible bits. Her breasts, her belly, her arms. Her legs. And oh God her feet!—especially her feet. Panting with exertion, with shame, rubbing herself and then washing herself again, hard, until her skin is reddened in ugly swaths. The ordeal takes twenty minutes. But at last—then—she is clean.

I'm turning into a beast, Judith thinks. A body.

Two of the Americans are leaving early, having come to Warsaw from Budapest. They are on a six-week tour of East Europe
for the State Department, as cultural emissaries, and Judith admires their stamina, though not their robust good spirits. We've
absorbed firsthand the tragic history of Poland, one says, and the
tragic history of Hungary. Before that—the tragic history of Bul-
garia, Yugoslavia, Lithuania, and Czechoslovakia. And do you
know where we're going next? —East Germany.

Carl, typing out the first draft of a story on the "political atmosphere" of Poland that will eventually wind up, much revised,
in a long piece on East Europe for the New York *Times Maga-*
*zine,* glances up with irritation at Judith who has been asking
him his advice: Should she buy gifts for their Polish hosts, the
ones they have become acquainted with, the nicest ones, or
should she treat them all to a dinner in Old Town; or should she
arrange for the cultural attaché to divide the money among the
dissident writers they met—since they are all so impoverished.
(It falls to Judith to be bountiful for she is the one who has
been given so many zlotys—Carl received no royalties at all.)
    Or do you think, she asks, squinting as if vexed by thought, I
should give the money in person to one of the dissidents—I
mean the one who struck me most—the one who seems most,
most—victimized—most unhappy.
    Who the hell would that be? Carl asks.
    I have his name written down, Judith says, pawing through
her purse, he's the one with the beard, Wladislaw something.
Elzbieta said he's very nice, he's a poet, a member of the Social
Defense Committee who's been arrested a dozen times—I remember thinking I felt a particular kinship with him, I don't
know why.
    You *don't* know why, Carl says impatiently, you don't have
the slightest idea, who the hell *is* the man?—a face, a handshake?—a pair of sad droopy eyes? Just because he can't speak
English and has been arrested a few times you want to give him
money.
    Judith turns her purse upside-down. There are innumerable
scraps of paper, much folded pieces of paper. Elzbieta said he

had been in Sweden for a few years publishing Polish things there, but he got so homesick he had to return, now he can't get a visa and he doesn't have a job—you must remember him—you and Marianne were talking with him too.

You've become unbalanced here, Carl says.

Because I feel sorry for these people? Because I want to help them? Judith says angrily.

You don't *know* them. A dissident isn't by definition a saint— there are anti-Semites who are dissidents—look at Solzhenitsyn. You're being ridiculous, you're being hysterical.

I don't think of Solzhenitsyn as an anti-Semite, Judith says.

He's a Russian, isn't he.

Is he an anti-Semite? Judith asks, staring at Carl.

He admired Nixon. He admires stability. What do you think? Carl asks.

Judith says nothing, staring at him. She is breathing quickly and shallowly. Carl says, For Christ's sake sit down: you look exhausted. Judith draws away. I'm not exhausted, she murmurs. I feel the strongest I've felt in days.

It's a good thing we're leaving tomorrow.

I don't want to leave, I want to *do something* for these people. Sit down. Come here.

His name, she says, snatching up a piece of paper and opening it, his name, she lets it fall and opens another, her fingers shaking, is—I can't pronounce it correctly—Barańczak?—

Barańczak, says Carl doubtfully, isn't that another man?

The embassy van is routed down a side street. On the boulevard is a royal procession—what appears to be a royal procession—limousines, army vehicles, police on horseback. The sidewalks, however, are empty.

Brezniew, it is explained to the Americans, Brezniew back in town, the Warsaw Pact, the second time this month.

Suppose he's assassinated, Robert Sargent says with an exquisite shiver. Wouldn't we be in a fix then!

Marta, her short dark hair frizzed about her face, her dark eyes wonderfully bright, smoking cigarette after cigarette, flattering Judith Horne with her spirited admiration. Of all the

American writers, of all the American writers with something profound to say. . . . And of course, Marta insists, making an emphatic gesture that Judith has come to recognize as specifically Polish—a sort of restrained jab with the flat of the hand against the air, accompanied by a look of fastidious pain—of course it is pleasing to me as a woman, I mean that *you* are a woman too, though your writing has nothing to do with—you know—the feminist issues—on the most elementary level.

What was that, I didn't quite hear, Judith murmurs; but Marta continues speaking. She is pert and bright and argumentative and almost ugly, she is clearly delighted to be sitting at a table—at last!—with the distinguished American writer Judith Horne. For days, for days, she has been begging for an interview, leaving messages at the Europejski desk, trying to telephone. . . . And now. . . . And now there is *so much* to ask.

Judith squints against the smoke, begins to gnaw on her sore thumbnail. She always dislikes flatterers, however guileless, but there is something about Marta that strikes her as offensive in any case.

Marta is Jewish, of course. No doubt about it. The eyes, the nose, the mouth, the frizzy-kinky hair—which is very much like Judith's own hair. But she is wearing a small gold cross around her neck on a short gold chain. Small but prominent. Defiant. It rides the hollow at the base of her throat, moves up and down with Marta's voice. Judith finds herself staring blankly at it as Marta "interviews" her: fires long paragraphs of incoherent questions that appear to contain their own answers; recites critical "judgments" of Judith's work on which Judith is asked to comment; asks once again—so many Poles have asked!—what are Judith's "firsthand impressions" of Poland?

Judith interrupts. That thing you're wearing—are you Catholic?

Marta's head snaps back. The reaction is almost mechanical, almost comic. Judith has the idea too that it is somewhat feigned —that the question does not surprise Marta so much as she pretends.

Of course I am a Catholic, Marta says gravely. After a pause she adds: I am a convert.

Oh yes I see, Judith murmurs, a convert, when did you convert—or when were you converted?—I don't know the correct idiom.

At the age of sixteen, Marta says, but we have not much time, Miss Horne, we must concentrate on you.

I asked you to call me Judith, Judith says.

Yes—Judith—yes of course—Judith—we have not much time: they tell me you are all leaving tomorrow—so soon! My next question is, When will you return?—and stay for a longer time?

Was your entire family converted, Judith says, or just you?—I don't understand how these things work.

I made my own decision, Marta says brightly, my beliefs are —are—She gestures appealingly, both hands prayerlike and then opening, falling limply back. My beliefs are my own, coming from within.

What about your family? Judith says.

My family, Marta says, is scattered, not in Warsaw. She pauses, sucks on her cigarette, exhales smoke. Judith irritably waves it away.

Scattered—? Judith says.

Scattered, living in different parts, Marta says with a shrug of her shoulders, some are, you know, dead—missing. After a pause she adds: My family was very wealthy. Aristocrats. My grandfather and his uncles—they had an export firm. They did business in London, Paris, Berlin, Vienna—everywhere. Leather exports mainly. Very fine leather. Expensive. The best quality.

I see, says Judith. Aristocrats.

The Jews—the other Jews—I mean the Jews here in Warsaw, in the ghetto—they could have saved themselves if they made the effort, Marta says. And also the villagers. You see, Miss Horne, they were very slow—very ignorant—filled with superstitions—lazy. Marta shakes her head, half-sorrowfully, half-repulsed. That look again of fastidious inescapable pain. —They could have saved themselves, the ones who ended up in Auschwitz. But they did not try.

They didn't try, Judith repeats.

And—Miss Horne—it is difficult to explain to an American but you must understand—they were peasants—mainly peasants.

Mainly peasants, says Judith quietly. I see.

There is a long uneasy pause. Judith stares at the tea glasses
on the table, at the lemon wedges.

Miss Horne?—Judith—I have here an important question—

In one version Judith slaps the cigarette from Marta's fingers:
it falls to the table, falls on the floor. In another version Judith
simply rises from her chair so abruptly that her interviewer is
startled, leans back, drops her cigarette. It falls to the table, rolls
to the floor. . . .

Upstairs Carl says, What happened down there?

Judith says nothing.

I wasn't watching—a few of us happened to be having coffee
—I saw you and Marta come in and you seemed to be getting
along well—the next thing I knew, you were walking out and
that poor woman was calling after you.

Was she, Judith says. I didn't hear.

The door. They have dinner alone, they excuse themselves for
the evening—though Carl would have liked to see the Poznan
Dance Theater at the Opera House—and cross the square to the
Victoria Hotel, the "international" hotel, for an expensive meal.
Polish cuisine, of course—but in elegant surroundings. (The ta-
blecloths are made of white linen, there are single long-stemmed
roses at each table, an attractive young woman in a filmy dress is
playing the harp.) I don't know why we're doing this, Judith
says nervously, I really *don't* like pretentious overpriced restaurants.

Maybe you do, says Carl, *really*.

Judith hears clearly the mild contempt in his voice but does
not respond. They have quarreled so much in Warsaw, emotion
of any kind strikes her as futile. Rage and tears and hatred; em-
braces, comforting, "love." Even when she is shouting at her
lover a part of her stands aside watching and questioning the
authenticity of the moment. Is she responding to Carl as herself,
as Judith Horne, or is she simply playing a part—screaming out
lines not her own, lines that belong simply to Woman, to anyone. Self-loathing has swollen in her like a fetus.

Carl orders wine for himself, Judith isn't drinking. Mineral
water with ice will be fine. (*Ice.* She has not seen ice cubes or

had a cold drink for a long time, except at the embassy functions, in the residences.) Carl orders a shrimp cocktail and Judith warns him that the shrimp very likely won't be fresh: after all, this is Warsaw. He orders the shrimp cocktail anyway and Judith orders borscht. The borscht should be a wise or anyway a safe choice, but it is simply liquid, and very sweet; she takes a few sips and leaves it. Carl's shrimp are tiny and taste, he says, like rubber. Perhaps they *are* rubber—rubber shrimp for tourists. I told you not to order shrimp, Judith says.

Yes, says Carl, right, you did.

The meal continues, doomed. Stringy roast beef, duck roasted so long it is impossibly dry. The black-costumed waiter brings sauces of some kind—creamy, sweet?—but neither Judith nor Carl wants any. I hate this man, Judith thinks, if we were married I would leave him, but she cannot help noting his handsome flushed face (anger becomes him, even his eyes appear darker, shrewder, lit with an intelligent watchful meanness), his movements which are no less graceful for being irritably self-conscious. If we were married I would leave him, Judith thinks dreamily. But we are not married.

The main dining room of the Victoria Hotel is fairly crowded, unlike the sepulchral dining room of the Europejski. Here people are well dressed, the atmosphere is gracious and restrained, the young woman harpist is really quite good so far as Judith can judge. (She is playing Debussy and Ravel.) At a large table to Judith's right German is being spoken, at a smaller table behind Carl two older women sit, talking in what might be Swedish. There is a French couple, there is another German table. Carl's eyes move about restlessly. What do you think, Judith says in an undertone, the Germans?—surely they can't be East Germans, here? Carl sips his wine, takes out a package of cigarettes, pushes his plate a discreet inch or two away. His expression is censorious; prim; bored. After a long time he says, Probably not.

Judith feels rebuffed. But says, These people—the Poles—hate the Germans so much, it's incredible that they would come here as tourists. I mean—*here*. It's incredible.

I suppose so, says Carl. He stares at the large table of Germans: an attractive young couple, an older couple, a single man.

Except for the language one would not have recognized them as German, specifically; they might even be Polish.

Yes, says Carl, who has been listening to their conversation, you're right, *West* Germany. It's West Germany.

How very odd, says Judith faintly.

Oh hell—why is it odd?

Judith cannot look at him. She feels her throat constricting.

*We're* here, after all, Carl says.

The remark is senseless but Judith does not contradict it. There is a spirit of childhood between her and Carl at times, childhood in the least agreeable sense: you said that, I did not, you *said* that and got it wrong, no I did *not*, I hate you, I hate you too, I *hate* you I wish you were dead.

The check for the meal is slow in coming. Carl drums his fingernails on the table. Judith yawns behind her hand. There is something brutal—brute—about her yawning, in public: such fatigue could crack the high ornate ceiling of the dining room, could crack the surface of the earth. I'll wait for you in the lobby, Judith says, I can't stand your restlessness, and she rises from the table and strides away, her face flushed, her leather shoulder bag swinging. No other woman in the dining room of the Victoria Hotel of Warsaw is wearing trousers tonight, let alone so defiantly "casual" a costume as a suede jump suit with a half-dozen oversized zippers. But then no other woman in the dining room of the Victoria Hotel has the presence, the self-possession, of Judith Horne.

She waits for her lover in the lobby. Examining advertisements for hotels in other parts of Europe—Prague, Budapest. Handsome high-rise hotels with "modern conveniences." She yawns again. In another day they will be leaving Warsaw—in another day they will be gone. The vertigo of travel, the comfort. Escape. Forgetting. They will fly out of Poland to Frankfurt Airport, to the West; immediately they will recognize the "West." Posters of left-wing *Terroristen* are prominently displayed in the Frankfurt Airport—sad sullen intelligent faces, the eyes rather like Judith's own—and young German guards stroll about in pairs, their submachine guns cradled casually in their arms. Along with signs for restaurants, restrooms, telephones, and first aid there will be signs for sex shops. The West.

Soon they will leave Warsaw, melancholy Warsaw, beautiful Warszawa, a city of fictions that has irrevocably worked a change in Judith's soul. Soon. Very soon. Judith yawns again, her eyes watering. Boredom is a mask of rage, she thinks, but rage is a mask of—?

She sees Carl approaching, through the plate glass door. He is walking quickly as usual; his expression is prim and sullen and censorious, as if he knows she is watching and refuses to raise his eyes to hers. He is putting bills in his wallet impatiently. Judith watches him without love and thinks, I don't know the man who is going to walk right into that glass door, I have never seen him before in my life.

And then, incredibly, it does happen: Carl walks into the door: his head, slightly lowered, slams against the glass with a thud that reverberates through the lobby. People look around, startled. A woman exclaims in English—Oh that poor man! And Judith has not moved. She has watched her lover walk into a glass door and she has not moved, she has not spoken, she stands frozen, staring, appalled as any stranger.

Farewell. Blaring American rock music on the plane, announcements in Polish and Russian, box lunches of cheese, cold cuts, rye bread, Pepsi-Cola in small plastic cups. The stewardesses are Russian but their fastidious self-conscious chic is international: blue suits with white turtleneck blouses, very red lips, eyes enlarged by mascara and pencil, rouged cheeks, long shining hair braided and fixed at the back of the head with silver barrettes. We have already left Poland, Judith thought, climbing into the Soviet plane.

How are you, are you all right, she asks Carl, who makes a negligent dismissive gesture in reply. The ugly swelling on his forehead does not hurt, he insists. But Judith saw him swallowing aspirin back in the hotel, two and three at a time.

Stupid accident, he says.

You could have injured yourself seriously, Judith murmurs. Her eyes flood with tears at the memory, the image: Carl walk-

ing so confidently into that glass door. Before she had had time
to call out.

What an asshole I am, Carl shrugs, it serves me right.

Don't talk like that, Judith says.

Making a fool of myself in public. . . .

How did you make a fool of yourself, don't be absurd, Judith
says, no one knows your name here.

Carl winces, as if with pain.

In the hotel room they packed quickly, carelessly. The room
was in great disorder. Judith threw things in her suitcase without troubling to fold them, she made a fumbling perfunctory attempt to sort through her papers—the farrago of names and
addresses on slips of paper, notes to herself, booklets, maps,
pamphlets printed by the state and pamphlets printed by illegal
presses—while Carl said, Never mind all that, come on, the lim-
ousine is waiting, throw it all in the suitcase or throw it all in
the wastebasket, we're late.

I don't have room in my suitcase, Judith said, there are important things here I can't throw away, please don't make me nervous, but Carl said, Come *on,* and she threw everything away
except three or four cards with names and addresses printed on
them; these she dropped in her overstuffed purse. Here, said
Carl, stooping to pick up *The Awkward Age* from the floor,
shove this in too, let's go. We aren't going to miss that plane.

Handshakes at the airport, farewells that might have been
farewells between old friends, old comrades. There is something
in Tadeusz's shy smile that touches Judith's heart—a look of
genuine loss, a look of stricken comprehension—which she will
remember for a long time—the look, the smile, disembodied—
impersonal—Polish. Thank you so much for your kindness, for
your generosity, Judith says, shaking his hand, shaking Miroslav's hand, embracing Elzbieta who is, she discovers, terribly
frail, I have your names and addresses, I will write, we'll see one
another again someday, thank you all so very much. And Carl
too shakes hands, managing to smile. Judith has noticed that he
is blinking frequently and that his right eye is awash with tears.
The bump on his forehead is ugly and, even with its ridge of
dried blood, slightly comic—a blind glaring defiant third eye.
The young Poles asked discreetly what had happened and Carl

told them with an embarrassed smile, Nothing, an accident, it's perfectly all right.

The plane taxis along the runway, exactly on time. Judith grips her lover's hand for comfort, for strength, thinking as always at such moments, *The plane crashed within seconds of takeoff, killing all passengers and crew,* but nothing happens, the plane simply rises, riding the air. Below there are squares and rectangles and long narrow strips of farmland . . . railroad tracks . . . highways . . . the long buildings of a collective farm. My Warszawa, Judith thinks, blinking, recognizing nothing. The plane ascends, banks to the left, moves into a blazing white mist. There's the collective farm they took us to, she tells Carl, who is studying a glossy booklet printed in Cyrillic—he can read Russian, with some effort—and he looks up, peers over her shoulder, squints, says, No I don't think so, I think the farm we saw is in another direction, miles away.

# VICTROLA

## WRIGHT MORRIS

Wright Morris is the author of numerous novels, among them *The Field of Vision*, which won a National Book Award, and *Plains Song*, winner of the American Book Award. *Will's Boy, a Memoir* was published in 1981. His hometown is Central City, Nebraska.

"Sit!" said Bundy, although the dog already sat. His knowing what Bundy would say was one of the things people noticed about their close relationship. The dog sat—not erect, like most dogs, but off to one side, so that the short-haired pelt on one rump was always soiled. When Bundy attempted to clean it, as he once did, the spot no longer matched the rest of the dog, like a cleaned spot on an old rug. A second soiled spot was on his head, where children and strangers liked to pat him. Over his eyes the pelt was so thin his hide showed through. A third defacement had been caused by the leash in his younger years, when he had tugged at it harder, sometimes almost gagging as Bundy resisted.

Those days had been a strain on both of them. Bundy had developed a bad bursitis, and the crease of the leash could still be seen on the back of his hand. In the past year, over the last eight months, beginning with the cold spell in December, the dog was so slow to cross the street Bundy might have to drag him. That brought on spells of angina for Bundy, and they would both have to stand there until they felt better. At such moments the dog's slantwise gaze was one that Bundy avoided. "Sit!" he would say, no longer troubling to see if the dog did.

The dog leashed to a parking meter, Bundy walked through

Copyright © 1982 by The New Yorker Magazine, Inc. First appeared in *The New Yorker*. Reprinted by permission.

the drugstore to the prescription counter at the rear. The pharmacist, Mr. Avery, peered down from a platform two steps above floor level—the source of a customer's still pending lawsuit. His gaze to the front of the store, he said, "He still itching?"

Bundy nodded. Mr. Avery had recommended a vitamin supplement that some dogs found helpful. The scratching had been replaced by licking.

"You've got to remember," said Avery, "he's in his nineties. When you're in your nineties, you'll also do a little scratchin'!" Avery gave Bundy a challenging stare. If Avery reached his nineties, Bundy was certain Mrs. Avery would have to keep him on a leash or he would forget who he was. He had repeated this story about the dog's being ninety ever since Bundy had first met him and the dog was younger.

"I need your expertise," Bundy said. (Avery lapped up that sort of flattery.) "How does five cc.s compare with five hundred mg.s?"

"It doesn't. Five cc.s is a liquid measure. It's a spoonful."

"What I want to know is, how much Vitamin C am I getting in five cc.s?"

"Might not be any. In a liquid solution, Vitamin C deteriorates rapidly. You should get it in the tablet." It seemed clear he had expected more of Bundy.

"I see," said Bundy. "Could I have my prescription?"

Mr. Avery lowered his glasses to look for it on the counter. Bundy might have remarked that a man of Avery's age—and experience—ought to know enough to wear glasses he could both see and read through, but having to deal with him once a month dictated more discretion than valor.

Squinting to read the label, Avery said, "I see he's upped your dosage." On their first meeting, Bundy and Avery had had a sensible discussion about the wisdom of minimal medication, an attitude that Bundy thought was unusual to hear from a pharmacist.

"His point is," said Bundy, "since I like to be active, there's no reason I shouldn't enjoy it. He tells me the dosage is still pretty normal."

"Hmm," Avery said. He opened the door so Bundy could step behind the counter and up to the platform with his Blue Cross

card. For the umpteenth time he told Bundy, "Pay the lady at
the front. Watch your step as you leave."

As he walked toward the front Bundy reflected that he would
rather be a little less active than forget what he had said two
minutes earlier.

"We've nothing but trouble with dogs," the cashier said.
"They're in and out every minute. They get at the bars of candy.
But I can't ever remember trouble with your dog."

"He's on a leash," said Bundy.

"That's what I'm saying," she replied.

When Bundy came out of the store, the dog was lying down,
but he made the effort to push up and sit.

"Look at you," Bundy said, and stooped to dust him off. The
way he licked himself, he picked up dirt like a blotter. A shadow
moved over them, and Bundy glanced up to see, at a respectful
distance, a lady beaming on the dog like a healing heat lamp.
Older than Bundy—much older, a wraithlike creature, more
spirit than substance, her face crossed with wisps of hair like
cobwebs—Mrs. Poole had known the dog as a pup; she had
been a dear friend of its former owner, Miss Tyler, who had
lived directly above Bundy. For years he had listened to his
neighbor tease the dog to bark for pieces of liver, and heard the
animal push his food dish around the kitchen.

"What ever will become of him?" Miss Tyler would whisper to
Bundy, anxious that the dog shouldn't hear what she was saying.
Bundy had tried to reassure her: look how spry she was at
eighty! Look how the dog was overweight and asthmatic! But to
ease her mind he had agreed to provide him with a home, if
worst came to worst, as it did soon enough. So Bundy inherited
the dog, three cases of dog food, balls and rubber bones in
which the animal took no interest, along with an elegant cushioned sleeping basket he never used.

Actually, Bundy had never liked biggish dogs with very short
pelts. Too much of everything, to his taste, was overexposed.
The dog's long muzzle and small beady eyes put him in mind of
something less than a dog. In the years with Miss Tyler, without
provocation the animal would snarl at Bundy when they met on
the stairs, or bark wildly when he opened his mailbox. The dog's
one redeeming feature was that when he heard someone pro-

nounce the word "sit" he would sit. That fact brought Bundy a certain distinction, and the gratitude of many shop owners. Bundy had once been a cat man. The lingering smell of cats in his apartment had led the dog to sneeze at most of the things he sniffed.

Two men, seated on stools in the corner tavern, had turned from the bar to gaze out into the sunlight. One of them was a clerk at the supermarket where Bundy bought his dog food. "Did he like it?" he called as Bundy came into view.

"Not particularly," Bundy replied. Without exception, the dog did not like anything he saw advertised on television. To that extent he was smarter than Bundy, who was partial to anything served with gravy.

The open doors of the bar looked out on the intersection, where an elderly woman, as if emerging from a package, unfolded her limbs through the door of a taxi. Sheets of plate glass on a passing truck reflected Bundy and the notice that was posted in the window of the bar, advising of a change of ownership. The former owner, an Irishman named Curran, had not been popular with the new crowd of wine and beer drinkers. Nor had he been popular with Bundy. A scornful man, Curran dipped the dirty glasses in tepid water, and poured drops of sherry back into the bottles. Two epidemics of hepatitis had been traced to him. Only when he was gone did Bundy realize how much the world had shrunk. To Curran, Bundy had confessed that he felt he was now living in another country. Even more he missed Curran's favorite expression, "Outlive the bastards!"

Two elderly men, indifferent to the screech of braking traffic, tottered toward each other to embrace near the center of the street. One was wearing shorts. A third party, a younger woman, escorted them both to the curb. Observing an incident like this, Bundy might stand for several minutes as if he had witnessed something unusual. Under an awning, where the pair had been led, they shared the space with a woman whose gaze seemed to focus on infinity, several issues of the *Watchtower* gripped in her trembling hands.

At the corner of Sycamore and Poe Streets—trees crossed

poets, as a rule, at right angles—Bundy left the choice of the
route up to the dog. Where the sidewalk narrowed, at the bend
in the street, both man and dog prepared themselves for brief
and unpredictable encounters. In the cities, people met and
passed like sleepwalkers, or stared brazenly at each other, but
along the sidewalks of small towns they felt the burden of their
shared existence. To avoid rudeness, a lift of the eyes or a muttered greeting was necessary. This was often an annoyance for
Bundy: the long approach by sidewalk, the absence of cover, the
unavoidable moment of confrontation, then Bundy's abrupt
greeting or a wag of his head, which occasionally startled the
other person. To the young a quick "Hi!" was appropriate, but it
was not at all suitable for elderly ladies, a few with pets as es-
corts. To avoid these encounters, Bundy might suddenly veer
into the street or an alleyway, dragging the reluctant dog behind
him. He liked to meet strangers, especially children, who would
pause to stroke his bald spot. What kind of dog was he? Bundy
was tactfully evasive; it had proved to be an unfruitful topic. He
was equally noncommittal about the dog's ineffable name.

"Call him Sport," he would say, but this pleasantry was not
appreciated. A smart aleck's answer. Their sympathies were with
the dog.

To delay what lay up ahead, whatever it was, they paused at
the barnlike entrance of the local van-and-storage warehouse.
The draft from inside smelled of burlap sacks full of fragrant
pine kindling, and mattresses that were stored on boards above
the rafters. The pair contemplated a barn full of junk being sold
as antiques. Bundy's eyes grazed over familiar treasure and
stopped at a Morris chair with faded green corduroy cushions
cradling a carton marked "FREE KITTENS."

He did not approach to look. One thing having a dog had
spared him was the torment of losing another cat. Music (surely
Elgar, something awful!) from a facsimile edition of an Atwater
Kent table-model radio bathed dressers and chairs, sofas, beds
and love seats, man and dog impartially. As it ended the announcer suggested that Bundy stay tuned for a Musicdote.

Recently, in this very spot—as he sniffed similar air, having
paused to take shelter from a drizzle—the revelation had come
to Bundy that he no longer wanted other people's junk. Better

yet (or was it worse?), he no longer *wanted*—with the possible exception of an English mint, difficult to find, described as curiously strong. He had a roof, a chair, a bed, and, through no fault of his own, he had a dog. What little he had assembled and hoarded (in the garage a German electric-train set with four locomotives, and three elegant humidors and a pouch of old pipes) would soon be gratifying the wants of others. Anything else of value? The cushioned sleeping basket from Abercrombie & Fitch that had come with the dog. That would sell first. Also two Italian raincoats in good condition, and a Borsalino hat—*Extra Extra Superiore*—bought from G. Colpo in Venice.

Two young women, in the rags of fashion but radiant and blooming as gift-packed fruit, brushed Bundy as they passed, the spoor of their perfume lingering. In the flush of this encounter, his freedom from want dismantled, he moved too fast, and the leash reined him in. Rather than be rushed, the dog had stopped to sniff a meter. He found meters more life-enhancing than trees now. It had not always been so: some years ago he would tug Bundy up the incline to the park, panting and hoarsely gagging, an object of compassionate glances from elderly women headed down the grade, carrying lapdogs. This period had come to a dramatic conclusion.

In the park, back in the deep shade of the redwoods, Bundy and the dog had had a confrontation. An old tree with exposed roots had suddenly attracted the dog's attention. Bundy could not restrain him. A stream of dirt flew out between his legs to splatter Bundy's raincoat and fall into his shoes. There was something manic in the dog's excitement. In a few moments, he had frantically excavated a hole into which he could insert his head and shoulders. Bundy's tug on the leash had no effect on him. The sight of his soiled hairless bottom, his legs mechanically pumping, encouraged Bundy to give him a smart crack with the end of the leash. Not hard, but sharply, right on the button, and before he could move the dog had wheeled and the front end was barking at him savagely, the lips curled back. Dirt from the hole partially screened his muzzle, and he looked to Bundy like a maddened rodent. He was no longer a dog but some primitive, underground creature. Bundy lashed out at him, backing away, but they were joined by the leash. Unintentionally, Bundy stepped on the leash, which held the dog's snarling head to the ground. His slobbering jowls were bloody; the small veiled eyes peered up at him with hatred. Bundy had just enough presence of mind to stand there, unmoving, until they both grew calm.

Nobody had observed them. The children played and shrieked in the schoolyard as usual. The dog relaxed and lay flat on the ground, his tongue lolling in the dirt. Bundy breathed noisily, a film of perspiration cooling his face. When he stepped off the leash the dog did not move but continued to watch him warily, with bloodshot eyes. A slow burn of shame flushed Bundy's ears and cheeks, but he was reluctant to admit it. Another dog passed near them, but what he sniffed on the air kept him at a distance. In a tone of truce, if not reconciliation, Bundy said, "You had enough?"

When had he last said that? Seated on a school chum, whose face was red with Bundy's nosebleed. He bled too easily, but the boy beneath him had had enough.

"O.K.?" he said to the dog. The faintest tremor of acknowledgment stirred the dog's tail. He got to his feet, sneezed repeatedly, then splattered Bundy with dirt as he shook himself. Side by side, the leash slack between them, they left the park and walked down the grade. Bundy had never again struck the dog, nor had the dog ever again wheeled to snarl at him. Once the leash was snapped to the dog's collar a truce prevailed between them. In the apartment he had the floor of a closet all to himself.

At the Fixit Shop on the corner of Poplar, recently refaced with green asbestos shingles, Mr. Waller, the Fixit man, rapped on the glass with his wooden ruler. Both Bundy and the dog acknowledged his greeting. Waller had two cats, one asleep in the window, and a dog that liked to ride in his pickup. The two dogs had once been friends; they mauled each other a bit and horsed around like a couple of kids. Then suddenly it was over. Waller's dog would no longer trouble to leave the seat of the truck. Bundy had been so struck by this he had mentioned it to Waller. "Hell," Waller had said, "Gyp's a young dog. Your dog is old." His saying that had shocked Bundy. There was the personal

element, for one thing: Bundy was a good ten years older than
Waller, and was he to read the remark to mean that Waller
would soon ignore him? And were dogs—reasonably well-bred,
sensible chaps—so indifferent to the facts of a dog's life? They
appeared to be. One by one, as Bundy's dog grew older, the
younger ones ignored him. He might have been a stuffed animal
leashed to a parking meter. The human parallel was too disturb-
ing for Bundy to dwell on it.

Old men, in particular, were increasingly touchy if they con-
fronted Bundy at the frozen-food lockers. Did they think he was
spying on them? Did they think he looked *sharper* than they
did? Elderly women, as a rule, were less suspicious, and grateful
to exchange a bit of chitchat. Bundy found them more realistic:
they knew they were mortal. To find Bundy still around, squeezing the avocados, piqued the old men who returned from their
vacations. On the other hand, Dr. Biddle, a retired dentist with a
glistening head like an egg in a basket of excelsior, would un-
failingly greet Bundy with the words "I'm really going to miss
that mutt, you know that?," but his glance betrayed that he
feared Bundy would check out first.

Bundy and the dog used the underpass walkway to cross to
the supermarket parking area. Banners were flying to celebrate
Whole Grains Cereal Week. In the old days, Bundy would leash
the dog to a cart and they would proceed to do their shopping
together, but now he had to be parked out front tied up to one
of the bicycle racks. The dog didn't like it. The area was shaded
and the cement was cold. Did he ever sense, however dimly,
that Bundy too felt the chill? His hand brushed the coarse pelt
as he fastened the leash.

"How about a new flea collar?" Bundy said, but the dog was
not responsive. He sat, without being told to sit. Did it flatter the
dog to leash him? Whatever Bundy would do if worst came to
worst he had pondered, but had discussed with no one—his intent might be misconstrued. Of which one of them was he
speaking? Impersonally appraised, in terms of survival the two
of them were pretty much at a standoff: the dog was better
fleshed out, but Bundy was the heartier eater.

Thinking of eating—of garlic-scented breadsticks, to be

specific, dry but not dusty to the palate—Bundy entered the
market to face a large display of odorless flowers and plants.
The amplitude and bounty of the new market, at the point of
entrance, before he selected a cart, always marked the high
point of his expectations. Where else in the hungry world such a
prospect? Barrels and baskets of wine, six-packs of beer and
bran muffins, still warm sourdough bread that he would break
and gnaw on as he shopped. Was this a cunning regression? As a
child he had craved raw sugar cookies. But his euphoria sagged
at the meat counter, as he studied the gray matter being sold as
meatloaf mix; it declined further at the dairy counter, where two
cartons of yogurt had been sampled, and the low-fat cottage
cheese was two days older than dated. By the time he entered
the checkout lane, hemmed in by scandal sheets and romantic
novels, the cashier's cheerfully inane "Have a good day!" would
send him off forgetting his change in the machine. The girl who
pursued him (always with pennies!) had been coached to say
"Thank you, sir!"

A special on avocados this week required that Bundy make a
careful selection. Out in front, as usual, dogs were barking. On
the airwaves, from the rear and side, the "Wang Wang Blues."
Why wang wang, he wondered. Besides wang wang, how did it
go? The music was interrupted by an announcement on the
public-address system. Would the owner of the white dog leashed
to the bike rack please come to the front? Was Bundy's dog
white? The point was debatable. Nevertheless, he left his cart by
the avocados and followed the vegetable display to the front.
People were huddled to the right of the door. A clerk beckoned to
Bundy through the window. Still leashed to the bike rack, the
dog lay out on his side, as if sleeping. In the parking lot several
dogs were yelping.

"I'm afraid he's a goner," said the clerk. "These other dogs
rushed him. Scared him to death. He just keeled over before
they got to him." The dog had pulled the leash taut, but there
was no sign that anything had touched him. A small woman
with a shopping cart thumped into Bundy.

"Is it Tiger?" she said. "I hope it's not Tiger." She stopped to
see that it was not Tiger. "Whose dog was it?" she asked, peering

around her. The clerk indicated Bundy. "Poor thing," she said. "What was his name?"

Just recently, watching the Royal Wedding, Bundy had noticed that his emotions were nearer the surface: on two occasions his eyes had filmed over. He didn't like the woman's speaking of the dog in the past tense. Did she think he had lost his name with his life?

"What was the poor thing's name?" she repeated.

Was the tremor in Bundy's limbs noticeable? "Victor," Bundy lied, since he could not bring himself to admit the dog's name was Victrola. It had always been a sore point, the dog being too old to be given a new one. Miss Tyler had felt that as a puppy he looked like the picture of the dog at the horn of the gramophone. The resemblance was feeble, at best. How could a person give a dog such a name?

"Let him sit," a voice said. A space was cleared on a bench for Bundy to sit, but at the sound of the word he could not bend his knees. He remained standing, gazing through the bright glare at the beacon revolving on the police car. One of those women who buy two frozen dinners and then go off with the shopping cart and leave it somewhere let the policeman at the crosswalk chaperon her across the street.

# MELANIE AND THE PURPLE
# PEOPLE EATERS

## IRVIN FAUST

Irvin Faust was born in Brooklyn, New York, and has lived
most of his life in Manhattan. He received his master's degree and doctorate from Teachers College of Columbia University. He has published seven books of fiction, the most
recent being *Newsreel*, published in 1980. Irvin Faust's stories
have appeared in a variety of magazines, including *The Paris
Review, Sewanee Review,* and *Esquire.*

"*Horse*bleep?"

Horowitz looked into the phone and was positive he could see
the thin, frowning teacher. She was even nodding.

"That's what she said, Mr. Horowitz."

"Miss Garaminta, are you *sure?*"

"I'm positive, Mr. Horowitz . . . Mr. Horowitz, if I may, I
think our Bunny Development Specialist should chat with her."

"Who?"

"Our Bunny—"

"Hold it. Just hold it." He turned away from the phone, took
three clearing breaths, returned to the phone, smiled into it.
"Not yet, okay? I'll get back to you, Miss Garaminta."

"Don't wait too long," Miss Garaminta suggested.

"I won't. Oh, I won't. I appreciate your concern, I really do."

"Thank you, Mr. Horowitz. Have a nice day."

Horowitz looks at his desk, the wall, the clock, the window.
He deep-breathes again, wads the latest interoffice nonsense,

Copyright © 1981 by Irvin Faust. First appeared in *The Atlantic
Monthly.* Reprinted by permission.

loops it toward the wastebasket. It bounces hard off the wall, drops. "Two points," he says absently. He goes back to work.

He paced the bedroom. Counterclockwise. Marcia put up with it, then removed her sleep mask, sighed. "Walk the other way, will you please? You'll make us both dizzy."

He stopped. Looked. "Aren't you concerned? *I* am. I'm paying that school goddamn good money. I'm not crazy about everything they do, but if the child's teacher calls me at work, it has to be about something."

Marcia said very politely, "Are you assigning blame because I didn't hover over the phone?"

"Why should anyone interfere with all your projects?" he asked. "Why should they do that?"

"Mel, let us not parry and thrust. I have a terrible day tomorrow."

"All right." He balanced firmly. "'Horsebleep' is not 'See Jane run.'"

"Agreed."

"Thank you." He took a step, balanced again. "Marcia, that is all she said."

"When?"

"Today."

"Wait. What did she say *before* 'horsebleep'?"

He looked down at her, shook his head. "Not a thing. Zero. She was quiet all day, until after recess. That's when she said it." He sat down suddenly. He was sweating.

"What triggered it?"

"How the hell do I know?"

"You didn't ask?"

He got up, began to pace again, stopped again, turned. "Jesus, I was too surprised . . ."

"Oh, for crying out loud." She rolled over in a neat ball, uncurled, thrust hard into the furry slippers.

"Where are you going?" he said.

"Next door."

"Wait. Don't get her up. Wait—"

The door was swinging even as he said it. He stared. The door swung again and Marcia stepped neatly back, Melanie draped on her shoulder. With easy strength she set her down in Mommy's Chair. Shook her gently. Melanie's eyes blinked wide.

"Honey," Marcia said, sitting on the bed, "did you use a sassafras word in school today?"

Melanie blinked. "I don't know."

"Reconstruct. Go back in your mind. Think about your day."

Melanie reconstructed. "I don't know."

"Honey, did you say 'horsebleep'?"

She reconstructed some more. "I think I said that."

Horowitz asked quietly, "What did Miss Garaminta do to make you say it?"

"Mel?" Marcia smiled up at him. "I don't think we should assign g-u-i-l-t."

He shrugged off the spelling lesson and said, "Please let me handle this . . . What did she do, Melanie?"

"I don't know, Daddy."

"She must have done or said *some*thing."

"Mel, too much p-r-e-s-s-u-r-e."

"*What*, Melanie?"

Melanie's chin trembled. Marcia folded into the lotus position on the bed. "What he means, Melanie, is this: Could you possibly figure out why you used a sassafras?"

". . . I don't know, Mommy."

*Bleep*, Horowitz thought.

"All right," Marcia said, "we are not driving you to the wall; everything is under control. We are not excited and neither are you. If you don't agree, just tell me."

"I feel all right, Mommy."

"Fine. Pat pat, hug hug. Now, let's all put it out of our heads and go to sleep. Let it all float away. Go inside with Daddy, Melanie."

"All right, Mommy."

Horowitz opened his mouth, but Marcia shook him off. She sank back, adjusted her sleep mask. He hesitated, then gathered up the wide awake Melanie and walked back into the yellow and blue bedroom. He walked her up and down for five minutes, felt her grow heavy and quiet. Then he eased her down under the electric blanket. He kissed her forehead, tucked her in, straightened up.

She opened her eyes, smiled up at him, and said, "Daddy, is Ed Kranepool over the hill?"

In the kitchen, after the peanut butter sandwich, he clasps both hands as if he is praying in *shul*. Then he lowers the hands in precise steps. Looks over his left shoulder, then back. Then wheels and whips toward first base. The runner is caught leaning; he's out by four feet. . . .

"Mr. Horowitz," Miss Garaminta said with quiet gravity, "I assure you that is what she said."

"Please repeat it," Horowitz said. "I have paper and pencil."

Her voice was very professional. "She said, quote, 'It's like kissing your sister,' unquote."

". . . Is that *all* she said?"

"Yes. That one phrase, all day. Mr. Horowitz, the context was somewhat bizarre."

"What . . . was . . . the . . . context?"

"Well," said the professionally concerned voice, "I had just asked her to pick up the visible boy in one hand and the visible girl in the other . . ."

"Yes?"

"And, well, she said it."

"She didn't say 'horsebleep'?"

"Oh, no, that was last Tuesday. She really hasn't communicated since then. Verbally. Until this. Mr. Horowitz, may I ask . . . would it have any . . . familial context?"

*Speak English,* he screamed silently at the wall. "I don't think so," he said calmly.

"There *is* a male sibling."

"She has a brother. Dan. He's a year and a half."

"That's a darling age. I hate to sound even remotely alarmist, Mr. Horowitz . . ."

What bleep. "Yes, go ahead?"

"I was just wondering if there might be a hint of confused sexuality . . . Mr. Horowitz?"

"No way."

"I was just wondering."

94 IRVIN FAUST

"NO WAY."

"I have to be candid with you about my perceptions."

He stopped twisting his ankle. "I appreciate that, Miss Garaminta, I really do. But it's laughable. She was flirting with her grandfather when she was eight days old. No way, Miss Garaminta."

"Well, as I said, I do have to live with my conscience . . ."

"Absolutely. I live with my conscience eight hours a day on *my* job. It isn't easy."

"Thank you, Mr. Horowitz."

"I'll be in touch, Miss Garaminta."

He swings from the heels. The ball screams in agony as it flies over the left-field wall. He walks out of the washroom feeling stronger if not better.

The next day they had a three-way conference: Horowitz, Marcia, Miss Garaminta. Horowitz listened, nodded, made good eye contact. Especially when Miss Garaminta said, "It's a bit hard to believe that she verbalizes a good deal at home."

"Believe me," Horowitz nodded, "she has a splendid vocabulary for her age. Sometimes we can't shut her up."

"Not that we're in the habit of trying," Marcia murmured.

"Well," Miss Garaminta said, "I simply have to tell you that she's very limited here. And then there's her choice of subject . . . horses . . ."

"Kids." Horowitz smiled, shrugged. "I was hung up on Hotpoint refrigerators. I thought that was crazy. Ice cubes. Hotpoint . . ."

"I don't see the analogy," Marcia said.

Miss Garaminta said quickly: "It's merely that the horse thing is rather odd in a developmental sense."

"Really?" Marcia said.

"How's that?" Horowitz said, leaning in a little.

"Well, it's generally girls who are pubeing who are into horses. This is unusually early."

"She walked very young," Marcia murmured.

"Great coordination," said Horowitz.

Miss Garaminta acknowledged with a shrug, then said, "I'm

sure that's all true. I simply raise the possibility that it's more than one of those things . . ."

The room was pregnantly quiet.

Miss Garaminta finally said, "Perhaps she *should* see our Bunny man."

"I hate to be so negative," Horowitz said, "but suppose we give her a chance." He smiled. "Maybe next week it'll be the stock market."

Marcia said, "What's your point?"

"My point is, this week, it's horses, next week it could be AT&T."

"If I may," Miss Garaminta said. "That could be overly simplistic."

"I agree," Marcia said briskly. "Let's give your man a try."

"Just an informal chat, Mr. Horowitz."

Horowitz looked at her and she nodded encouragement. He looked at Marcia.

"Why don't we ask Melanie?" Marcia said.

He thought that over. Miss Garaminta watched him.

"All right. Fair enough. But *I'll* ask her."

"Go right ahead," said Marcia.

He got up and walked next door. Melanie was stroking the shmoo in the shiny Concorde jacket instead of punching him.

"Hi, poops."

"Hello, Daddy."

"Would you like to walk inside and answer a question?"

"Sure."

"Positive?"

"Uh huh."

"Okay, we walk."

He took her hand and they walked inside and he sat her down beside him. Everyone was quiet. Horowitz looked down at Melanie, who sat with her hands folded and her toes pointing in.

"Would you like to talk to a nice guy?" he said.

Melanie looked up at him.

"His name is Mr. Sitkin. He's the Bunny Development person."

Marcia said, "He could be very relaxing to talk to."

Miss Garaminta said, "He understands your age group."

Melanie continued to look at her father. He patted her shoulder and she nodded.

"Superstiff," she said with a shrug.

Milton Sitkin had three framed diplomas on his wall and wore a beige turtleneck.

"It's a rather unusual situation, Mr. Horowitz," he said.

Horowitz kept tightly quiet.

"I've had three conferences with her, including intake."

Horowitz remained quiet.

"I'll come right out with it . . . Here it is . . . I think we're dealing with some form of glossolalia."

Horowitz finally said, "Come on."

"I've consulted the literature," Sitkin said, "to confirm my initial impression. I think that's what it is."

Horowitz tried a tiny smile. "You mean religious double-talk?" He tried a tiny wink. "We don't even talk religion with her." He smiled and winked. "We're orthodox atheists."

"I see," Sitkin said without changing his face. "Nevertheless, I feel we're dealing with some form of tongues." He bent over a spiral-bound notebook. "I quote: 'A dollar bill is the glue.'" He raised his head.

"Are you sure that she said 'a dollar bill'?" Horowitz said.

"In my notes I have the article."

". . . Could it have been plain 'dollar bill'?"

"It's possible. I use a bastardized Gregg. In any case, it's a pretty sophisticated statement for a five-year-old. Unless, as I suspect, we go back in time . . . Can we brainstorm this?"

"Sure."

"Was your family hit hard economically at some point? Say, the Great Depression?"

"Well . . . my grandfather lost everything in 1930. But I never discussed *that* with Melanie."

"Then she knows nothing of that trauma?"

"How could she?"

"Of course. How could she?"

"Look, Mr. Sitkin, she's part of a group, right? Kids discuss money, right? With me it was dimes, with them it's dollar bills."

"Of course . . . Mr. Horowitz, how about this: 'You need the mow to get an oh.'"

"How do you spell 'mow'?"

"Why?"

"Well it could be . . . say, m.o."

"Or M-o-e. Is there a Moe in your family?"

"No."

"*Moses?*"

"NO."

"I see."

They waited. Then Sitkin said, "I'll tell you my professional position. Regardless of how fascinating the tongues thing may be, it rates nowhere in the taxonomy of cognitive functions."

"I'll tell you my position as a parent. I happen to think Melanie is a pretty bright kid."

"No argument." Sitkin smiled. "Mr. Horowitz, I'm just bending over backward to play it safe. I could get one helluva monograph out of this, but *she* is my top priority."

"That makes two of us."

"Then we're all together. Frankly, I think Dr. Bimway should have a talk with her."

"Who's he?"

"Our consulting psychologist."

"I thought *you* were."

"I'm the man in the trenches. We have to take it upstairs."

Horowitz examined the diplomas. Returned to Sitkin. "I want to put that on hold for now. I'd like to discuss it with my wife."

"Of course. I wouldn't wait too long, though."

"We won't."

"Fine. To loosen up our chemistry a little, can I tell you what she said when I said good-bye?"

"Sure, you can tell me."

Sitkin returned to the notebook, flipped a page.

"That child said: 'It is not over till it's over.'" He peeled off his glasses and sat back. "Mr. Horowitz, that is positively Kierkegaardian."

"It is not EST horsemanure," Marcia said with her hands on her hips.

"I did not say 'horsemanure,'" Horowitz corrected mildly.

"Don't think for one moment I don't know what 'horsebleep' means," Marcia said.

"All right," he said. "I still don't want any EST horsebleep. Sitkin was enough." He met her eyes.

"It is not EST. I have told you a hundred times. Here's a hundred and one. It is a transpersonal approach to counseling."

"Fine. Perfect. Only let's deal with her in a more constructive way."

"And how will we do that? In front of the TV? This whole thing boils down to that, you know. Your cockamamie jockmanure, or bleep, or whatever you call it."

"I don't happen to buy that," he said calmly.

"No? Dollar Bill? Glue? Don't think I don't know. Your precious Bradley. Bill Precious Bradley."

"*Senator* Bradley."

"Don't get off the hook. Did his father's glue buy his Senate seat?"

"What the hell are you talking about?"

"'Dollar Bill is the glue.' You told her that."

"His father was a banker. He didn't even go to Princeton on a scholarship."

"Who gives a bleep?"

"Lots of people. As for glue, it so happens Bradley was the glue that held the Knicks together."

Marcia sat down hard. "Christ."

"Well, he was."

"Christ."

"Stop saying that."

She looked him over. "Maybe," she said, "you'd prefer 'You need the mo to get an O.'"

"I'd *much* prefer that. It happens to be a pretty damn good rule of life: You need the momentum to get an ovation."

"Will you please stop? You are giving me a headache."

"I'd say you were giving it to yourself."

"God. Give me strength. Or some of those aspirins your Nolan Ryan eats."

"It so happens that Nolan Ryan does not *eat* aspirins. He *throws* them. Aspirin *tablets*, to be precise."

"God."

"And kindly leave Nolan Ryan out of it. He has his own troubles; with all that magnificent smoke, he's barely above .500 lifetime."

She waited a good thirty seconds. "You should both eat it."

*He* waited, planned out the voice modulation, the spacing of the words. When he was completely ready, he said, "I thank you kindly. However, Melanie is still not going to your guru. Her karma remains intact. So does her mantra. And do not lay any EST guilt on me."

"*It is not EST*. You are so simplistic and negative I wouldn't believe it if I didn't hear it. But I did."

"Oh, you did."

"Mel, I'm getting tired. I want only one thing. I want that child to reacquire her energy awareness."

"Give her some sugar."

"Christ."

"Come on, Marcia," he said, trying a smile, "loosen up."

"I will loosen up," she said with total severity, "when the child gets the strength to surmount aspirin tablets, Dollar Bill, and the rest of your illicit world."

He leaped out of the lounger.

"Illicit? Illicit? I'll let you in on something, lady. My illicit world happens to be cathartic and therapeutic and maybe you just ought to try it."

"I'll take Ex-Lax, thank you," she said sweetly.

"So *I'm* simplistic and negative? Let us temporarily assume that, all right? But maybe, just *maybe*, this world you are rejecting out of hand is the one she prefers."

"She's five years old, *schmuck*."

"So?"

"Teach her to dance on the head of a pin."

"That's an answer?"

"Yes. Here's another. I'm taking her to Terry Meldencarver."

"I cannot accept that."

"You'd better, sonny boy, because I am."

"The hell you are."

"The hell I'm not."

She took Melanie to Terry Meldencarver.

Meldencarver lived in an apartment with low ceilings and low furniture. He had on a beautiful toupee, which he could wear in the shower, and his nose was very short and thin.

"What do you think?" Marcia said as Melanie sat in the mandala room drawing.

"I've seen it before, of course," he said in his quiet voice. "It's her oneness."

Marcia closed her eyes. "He's shattered her inner space, hasn't he?" She opened her eyes. He let the question sink in. Then he barely nodded.

"I'd have to agree," he said gently.

Marcia rocked a few times, caught herself, and said, just as gently, "I've had it, Terry."

"Easy, Marcia."

"All right, but I have. This is too much. I'm sorry, but it is."

He didn't say anything.

"What about her core, Terry?"

"I can't quite reach it."

Marcia focused on her quiet hands, then looked up, asked very firmly, "Can you do anything?"

"I'll certainly have to dissolve blame."

"Yes . . . Terry, do what . . . you have to do."

"Of course."

She examined her hands again, shook her head. "Have you noticed her body language?" she said.

"That's my business, dear."

"Oh, I'm sorry . . ."

"That's perfectly all right. Yes. She's very skewed."

"God. I know. Oh, I know. Terry . . . can you . . . restore her center?"

"I'll certainly give it my best shot."

Her hands jumped. "God, don't say that."

"Why not?"

"That's the way *she* talks now."

He reached over, touched her stiff fingers.

"Mustn't indulge in panic, Marcia."

"I know . . ."

"What else do you know?" he said, lifting her chin. She smiled and avoided the toupee and the nose.

"The universe always says yes," she answered with total repose.

Melvin:

We have a basic problem and we both know it, but I will spell it out because at times like this you lapse into your pseudo-stupidity. Here it is: I cannot and will not permit Melanie to be further trapped by your idiocy. Or to be paralyzed by it. Therefore she (and I) are going to work with Terry Meldencarver, and wipe that infuriating grin off your face. While we do, we will stay with my sister Adele. This includes Daniel. I am asking, *telling* you, not to interfere. Not now. She must get the chance, ultimately, to choose. For now, therefore, the child must give up your world or she is *forever* consigned to wondering if Red Holman can win with five *schvartzas*. This I cannot permit.

Sincerely,<br>Marcia Singer-Horowitz

He circles Holman and above it writes "sic(κ)." Then he takes his evening walk. At the corner he jabs the lamppost with three violent lefts, smashes it with an overhand right. Refuses to yell.

He came home and ate a TV dinner. Then, while soaking his right hand in hot water and Epsom salts, he turned, with the left, to a cable sports channel and watched the Wolfpack battle the Blue Devils in a dual swim meet. Then he switched to channel 10 for the Rangers and the Islanders, agreeing absolutely with all the Big Whistle had to say. During the breaks in the action, he flipped to channel 9 for the Knicks and the Nets, his head shaking at the condition of the Human Eraser's knees. During time-outs he clicked to WNYC for the CUNY tournament, where he yearned quietly for the Beavers, Nat, the NIT, the NCAA.

He maintained this routine for seven nights, coming home from work a bit earlier each afternoon so he could plunge into

the action of the Boilermakers, the Wolverines, the Redmen, the
Spurs, the Whalers, and the Flames, the Iceman, and Magic. He
also managed to pick up from the South the first optimistic stirrings of Tom Terrific and Louisiana Lightning.

On the eighth day he got up late, toughened his right hand
with witch hazel, then called in sick. He ate a TV lunch,
watched the Celtics and the Bullets on the Betamax, locked up,
and drove across town to the Green Forest Lower School. He
parked in a six-dollar garage and walked down the street to the
school. He told the security guard and the lady at the desk it
was a medical emergency.

"I hate to barge into your day like this, Miss Garaminta, but
something's come up and I have to relieve you of your top problem child."

"You've come for Melanie," Miss Garaminta said.

"Oh, yes."

"Mr. Horowitz . . . I . . . well . . ."

"Is there a problem concerning my problem?" he said lightly.

"I'm afraid there is . . ."

"Well, we *all* have problems." He waited. Then: "I *am* her father, Miss Garaminta."

She touched her cheek, her hair, her cheek again; she'd make
a good third-base coach, he thought, smiling with support.

"Oh, how I hate these family things," she said with a thin
voice.

He felt a buzz, but said, "It comes with the territory. *What*
family things, Miss Garaminta?"

She stopped with the hand signals.

He said, "You can be very candid with me."

"I know that . . . All right . . . Mrs. Horowitz gave me firm
instructions not to allow anyone to pick up Melanie except Mrs.
Horowitz."

"May I point out that marriage is a fifty-fifty proposition, Miss
Garaminta?"

"Oh, I knew this would happen. I knew it. And I'd be caught
in the middle. I told that to Dr. Meldencarver."

"Doctor?"

"Meldencarver. Melanie's therapist."

". . . Pepper-and-salt toupee? Bad nose job?"

"His hair *did* look too nice. The nose . . . was awfully thin . . ."

"Uh huh. *Doctor?*"

"That's what she called him . . ."

His hand ran through his hair. "Miss Garaminta, listen to me. A man who will change his looks will change his credentials. He's a doctor like I'm the Sultan of Swat."

"He . . . doesn't have his doctorate?" she said stiffly.

"Miss Garaminta, I don't even think he has a B.A. I'm not absolutely sure, but I know this: he is a *mister* and his major was hotel management."

She leaned against the receptionist's desk. He said quickly, "You've been candid; now I'll be candid."

". . . Yes?"

"My wife and I are having problems. Serious ones."

". . . I inferred that from . . . He studied hotel management?"

"And motel. Miss Garaminta, as a result of these problems, my wife has moved out and taken Melanie . . . Mister Meldencarver is squarely in the picture."

She stepped away from the desk.

"You *do* understand what I'm saying?" he said.

"I understand," she said quietly.

"I'm fighting a stacked deck, Miss Garaminta . . . She's probably told you things about me. She and the hotel man."

". . . *She* did. He just listened."

"What did she tell you?"

"That . . . you hit imaginary baseballs."

"What about voices?" he said evenly.

"No, oh, no, she never mentioned voices."

He leaned in. "Did your Mr. Sitkin tell you I was a nut?"

"Of course not."

"What do *you* think?"

"Why, it never occurred to me . . . A concerned parent . . ."

"Okay. Miss Garaminta, the woman who told you those things, who has really leveled some serious charges, is shacking up with a phony doctor. With phony hair and a phony nose."

Her eye contact faltered. The receptionist hunched over her *Time;* the security guard studied his keys.

Horowitz said carefully, "Melanie is smack in the middle. Between those two and her father."

". . . That man called himself 'Doctor' . . ." Her eyes tightened. She firmed up her thin chest.

"I have always been so ridiculously naïve," she said. "Mr. Horowitz, I'll get Melanie for you."

They purred south on the Jersey Turnpike. Horowitz, Melanie, the warm, cozy car. The dashboard lights glowing and out of the lights the rise and fall of a local high school basketball game. They listened without saying anything until they crossed into Pennsylvania and the game faded.

"You can turn it off if you want to," Horowitz said. She promptly turned it off.

"Where are we going, Daddy?" she said.

He nodded at his headlights picking out the road.

"Greensboro. North Carolina."

"Why, Daddy?"

"The ACC tournament."

She was quiet, then settled back.

"Big hoops, Daddy?"

"The biggest." He glanced down, then quickly back. "You haven't seen pressure till you see this tournament."

"More than Super Sunday?"

"As *much*."

She looked up through the windshield.

"Will the Wolfpack be there?"

"Of course."

"Daddy?"

"Yes?"

"Who was the leader of the Wolfpack?"

"David Thompson, naturally."

She smiled at him and they glided through the quiet glow of a small town. When they were clear of it, she said, "Daddy?"

"Yes, hon?"

"If you have David Thompson on your side, what do you have to do?"

"Alley oop."

She wiggled against her seat belt.

"Daddy?"

"Yes, doll."

"Why do the Tigers drive you crazy?"

"The slowdown, doll."

"How do you beat a slowdown, Daddy?"

"With a swarming D, of course."

She nodded, scrunched back, stared through the windshield. They were quiet in the sweeping circle around Philadelphia. When they were moving through the lights again, into Delaware, she looked up at him.

"Daddy?"

"I'm right here."

"Daddy, how do you beat a zone?"

"Outside shooting, poops."

"The ultimate weapon, Daddy?"

"Skyhook."

"What do you do with four corners, Daddy?"

"Hold a lead."

"Says who, Daddy?"

"Says the Tarheels."

". . . Daddy?"

"I hear you."

"Who needs desire?"

"Anybody who wants to win, luv."

She was silent, looked gravely up through the windshield.

"Seat belt all right?" he said.

"Uh huh."

As Washington loomed, she said, "Daddy?"

"Pit stop?"

"Not yet . . . Daddy, where did Al McGuire have Cousy?"

"Heck, in his hip pocket."

She bounced once, settled back. She was very still, but outside of Richmond she stirred.

"Daddy? Run to daylight?"

He glanced down very briefly.

"Lombardi," he said.

"Purple People Eaters, Daddy?"

"The Vikings."

"Shotgun, Daddy?"

"Roger the Dodger."

"Rockne, Daddy?"

"Go, go, go, go, go."

"What else, Daddy?"

"Fight, fight, fight, fight, fight."

". . . Daddy?"

"Yes, babe?"

"What do you have to tell Mommy, no matter what?"

He looked down at her and smiled, then returned to the road. "Eat the darn ball."

"What else, Daddy?"

"Swallow the apple."

"What *else*, Daddy?"

He nodded, tightened his mouth. "It isn't over till it's over."

She sighed.

They crossed into North Carolina and she looked up at him. "Daddy?"

"What, cookie?"

She wriggled against her seat belt.

"Daddy, if Mommy yells and screams, what do you have to do?"

He hitched up his shoulders.

"Daddy, what?"

He rolled his neck.

"Daddy?"

He pushed down on the accelerator, just a whisper.

"What, Daddy?"

". . . Give her a T," he said grimly.

"Daddy?"

"Tell her to take five."

"Daddy?"

"Sit her down for . . . a quarter."

"Daddy!"

He looked down. She smiled up and nodded. "*What*, Daddy?"

"*KICK . . . BUTT*," he said.

She sighed and said, "I'm going to take a nap now, Daddy."

She pulled the blanket up to her shoulders and leaned against him. Soon her head dropped against his arm.

He hunkers down over the wheel. He pulls out of the flow, weaves ahead, spots a Ford. He slides in behind it and picks up the slipstream. He feels the gentle pull, knows he is in splendid position. He checks the dashboard. Everything is ready. With concentration, intensity, momentum, and perfect rhythm, they race toward the checkered flag of dawn.

# JEAN-PIERRE

## ELIZABETH SPENCER

Elizabeth Spencer was born in Carrollton, Mississippi, and
was educated in Jackson and Nashville, where she attended
Vanderbilt University. She spent a number of years in Italy
and now lives in Montreal. She is the author of seven novels,
the best known being *The Voice at the Back Door*, *The Light
in the Piazza*, and *The Snare*, and two volumes of short stories. The most recent of these, *The Stories of Elizabeth Spencer*, appeared in 1981. She conducts a writing seminar at
Concordia University in Montreal, and has recently completed
a new novel. Her stories have appeared in leading American
and Canadian magazines and in many anthologies.

"My father was a car salesman out in N.D.G.," Callie told Monsieur Courtois; then, recognizing that his English was poor, she
tried out her French. "*Mon père a vendu des autos à Notre-
Dame-de-Grâce.*"

"He died, then?"

"Oh, no, he and his wife left Montreal. They moved to California about a year ago—in 1962. *Maintenant ils demeurent—*"

"I know," he cut her off. "And you stayed."

"My sister's here."

"*Votre soeur est ici,*" he said, perversely switching to French.
"*Vous habitez chez elle?*"

"*Je suis seule.*"

"*Vous êtes seule,*" he repeated, and a while later said, "*Pourquoi?*"

But by then she had forgotten the first part, and, being a little
wary of him, uncertain, she said, "*Comment?*"

Copyright © 1981 by Elizabeth Spencer. First appeared in *The New
Yorker*. Reprinted by permission of International Creative Management, Inc.
New York.

"I said why do you live alone?"

"My sister is married, so . . ."

"You work?"

"Yes, I work."

He did not seem interested enough to ask her where. The Fletchers, who had asked her along to help entertain their friend, came back from across the street; they had gone to see when the movie would start. Jean-Pierre Courtois, the friend (he was actually a business prospect), ordered another round of drinks.

After the movie, they all went to have pizza. Callie watched Monsieur Courtois while he was too intent on eating to look up and find her watching. He was dark, almost swart, with a fleshy face that could, she guessed, go sullen rather easily; his full, smooth mouth stirred with annoyance when he could not part the cheese strings from the pizza without winding them off onto his fork. He stuffed in mouthfuls that were too large, and chewed with first one cheek full, then the other. But his clothes were neat, his tie quiet, and the only thing that really set him off from the English-speaking Fletchers was the slight gleam of artificial gloss on his thick hair, and the gold he wore—cufflinks, ring, and tie clip, all very bright. Callie's stepmother, with her querulous voice, would have called him "Mister" Courtois, not "Monsieur," and said that he looked cheap, dismissing him for good and all. O.K., thought Callie, he looks cheap. I've done my duty to Kay and Bob Fletcher. I'll never see him again.

After the movie and the pizza, and after a last drink at the Fletchers' apartment out on Côte-des-Neiges, he drove her home. She lived near Sherbrooke on Saint-Marc, in an old building, ground floor, with a yard behind it. In the arch of the doorway, he stopped her. "You watched me. *Tout le temps.* Why?"

She shook her head, though he was right; she hadn't wondered why. He stepped her into the corner by the door, pressed against the whole of her, and kissed her. "*C'est ça que tu veux?*" he said roughly.

She never answered. She shook so she could hardly get the key into the lock; by the time she did, he was in the car and about to start it, which she turned back to watch him do. He drove off without a glance. Getting angry as she closed the door, she finally began to speak aloud to herself: "I'm too young for him. I can't speak his damn language. He knows all that." She whammed her bag down on the apartment table. The kiss had been an act of contempt, she thought; she had got that out of it. The French did not like English-speaking people. They did not take them out. He had been contemptuous of the Fletchers' choice for him; Bob's chance of selling him any insurance was gone. They should have asked a French girl for the evening.

Contempt, again, was what she heard in his voice when he phoned her a week later, saying his name so fast she couldn't think who he might be, and she said it was the wrong number, until he told her more clearly. Why did she agree to meet him? She didn't know; she wished she hadn't.

He sat across from her, in a booth in a place that advertised steak from Texas steers, and he looked at her—this time it was she who was watched while eating—and smoked, and asked her questions. Sometimes he was silent. "I like your hair," he told her suddenly. She got angry again, and couldn't eat another bite.

Her hair was pale, fine, and straight. It hung down evenly on either side, and was a little longer in the back, where it dipped down into a V. He must be thirty years old, she thought, and probably married. She did not even try to talk to him. She was still so young, scarcely turned twenty, and given to quietness. Since her mother's death she had endured a bitter family life, prone to fights and festering. She had studied French to get the voices out of her head.

But then she began to think of what the French went through here, treated as inferior by the English, called names they resented (she didn't blame them); they preferred a life unmarred by violating eyes and scarring comments—such regard, such words as her stepmother had gone in for. So, as she remembered this, her humor improved and she said kindly, "*Merci.*"

"What?"

"I said thank you. For dinner. For saying you liked my hair."

"*Bienvenue,*" he answered. Bad French, she knew, but she let it go.

It was her hair he touched at the door, and this time he came inside to kiss her. Departing, his car made its accustomed skidding noise at the corner. The scene just past was a still spinning disc, and she clung dizzily to its center, thinking, I've never got into things like this before.

But then maybe it had to happen sometime, with somebody. And maybe, she thought, it was why she'd stayed on in Montreal alone rather than going to California, why she'd moved out of her sister's house and asked her not to tell their father, for fear of starting all sorts of family worrying and suspicions—those quarrels now grown silent.

That was in May. In June, she married him.

Her sister had her out to Notre-Dame-de-Grâce when she heard the plan, and sat her down at the kitchen table with coffee in a ceramic mug covered with yellow daisies. "You can't do this, Callie. He's one of those awful Quebec people. They left France so long ago nobody there knows they exist. We met somebody from Paris the other day who still couldn't understand a word of their French after two weeks here. You'll wind up with fifteen brats and not even good French. Why didn't you just get rid of him?"

"You know somehow," said Callie, "when someone is permanent in your life. You can marry them or not marry them; they're always there just the same."

"That's the most childish thing I ever heard of," her sister said. "Unless you've got in trouble and won't tell me."

Her sister's name was Beatrice, but she cultivated an English tone and liked people to call her Bea. To save Callie from defending herself against the charge of childishness—or not defending herself—the phone rang. It was Bart, her brother-in-law, wanting to speak to her.

"I knew Bea was going to talk to you today, but I don't know if she'll tell you what I said. In my opinion, I think you don't believe any of us loves you, Callie. Well, whatever you think, that's not true. We do love you."

"Thank you," she said.

"Will you just remember that one thing? We love you."

She said she would remember.

"And then," said Bea when Callie returned to the table, "there's your social life, for instance. What kind of husband image is he going to be? Bart and I make an impression, I know

that. Even our names go together—you have to think of everything. But 'Jean-Pierre and Callie,' how does that sound?"

"Terrible," said Callie.

"And then the financial side. At least, you must have talked it
over."

"He makes a good living. He told me so."

"He owns property—"

"He owns two apartment houses," said Callie, though she
knew Bea had informed herself of that already, just by the way
she stopped. "They're out in East Montreal."

"Have you seen them?"

"No, have you?"

"Don't be ridiculous," said Bea. "Of course not. Why would I
go there? Nobody lives over there but—oh, you know,
plumbers." She always doubted whether Callie ate enough, and
whacked off a wedge of coffee cake for her now.

"They must exist," said Callie, "because Bob Fletcher wanted
to sell him insurance for them."

"What did Bart want?" asked Bea.

"He said he thought I thought you didn't love me."

"That's ridiculous," said Bea. "Why do you think I wanted to
talk to you?"

"I don't know," said Callie.

"You'll never see his money," said Bea. "I'm certain of that."

"I guess he'll buy the groceries," said Callie, getting stubborn.
She had not, to tell the truth, discussed finances. She had found
out the simplest way—by going there when invited—that his
apartment was in midtown and that he could afford anything he
wanted; he didn't have to think twice.

To Callie, the real question was not why she wanted to marry
Jean-Pierre, with whom she felt she belonged, but why he
wanted to marry her—this English-speaking girl, so much
younger, with nothing to offer him. Because he liked her, he
said. His first wife had died. The family had blamed him. He
brought the confidence out reluctantly, like information it was
dangerous to share. It seemed he had got a bad name in the
French community—the strict side of it. He could move into
other French circles, but they would find out eventually. Be-

sides, since he was Catholic, Callie was never sure that he
thought he was really marrying her, in the final, true sense, at
all. They had a ceremony in the office of a French Protestant
church, down in the shadow of the Pont Jacques-Cartier. There
were some dusty green textbooks on theology on glass-fronted
shelves; a desk, a lectern, and a rug worn colorless. The
witnesses were Jean-Pierre's uncle and Callie's former landlady,
who left soon after—she had an appointment. Bea and Bart
were away, she supposed because they disapproved. They had
invited her and Jean-Pierre to dinner at the Beaver Club before
they left, and given them a Waterford fruit bowl and a check.
But their absence stung her, even though the excuse was plausi-
ble: Bart had an interview for a high position in a Cincinnati
brokerage firm, and it could not be postponed.

Jean-Pierre gave a wedding luncheon for some of his friends,
relatives, and business connections and their wives, girlfriends,
and mistresses. One even brought along a cousin of his own.
Jean-Pierre smoked a lot and paid Callie little notice. "Died of
blood poisoning in the hospital," she overheard him saying at
one point. "She got it there. In the hospital. Some doctor her
family knew. Why blame me? I wasn't with her every hour,
every minute. I had to keep food on the table. What they said
was 'But did you have to be in Quebec City?' 'I was where I had
to be,' I said, 'even if it was Miami, Florida.'"

He went on in French to another man: "Stay out of hospitals
—the best thing is take care of yourself. . . . Her mother never
talked to me again. 'Look, Madame,' I told her, 'you lost your
daughter, but me, I lost my wife. Which is worse?' 'She lived
with me all those years,' she says. 'That's a stupid question.'
'O.K.,' I told her, 'but you have to admit it's a stupid idea to
think I killed her.' 'Where were you when she died?'—she must
have said that a hundred times. If she were here right now she'd
be saying that—'Where were you when my daughter died?' My
God, those women . . . Big, strong . . . She'd cry; O.K., you'd
expect that, but every tear so fat and swollen! That's enough.
Let's drop it."

From across the table, a friend, perhaps another uncle, raised
a champagne glass and clinked it with Jean-Pierre's. He lit a
cigar. They had yet to drink to her. In fact, they never did,

though in parting they all kissed her hand. *"Bonne chance,"* they kept saying. *"Merci,"* she said. They assumed she knew no French. Yet she understood them well enough. Alone with Jean-Pierre, she spoke to him in his language.

They drove over the border to Burlington for the weekend, ate at a good restaurant, went to the Holiday Inn, and everything was the same as ever. For some reason, they cared about each other. He said that it would be *une union heureuse et éternelle*—she would see.

Jean-Pierre had thick dark hair, darker than most of his friends', and gray eyes nearly as dark as coal. He looked almost Spanish, she told him once or twice. He said she didn't know what she was talking about: he was altogether French; his family had come over in *mille six cent quatre-vingt trois*, among the first settlers.

"I'm sorry your wife died like that," Callie ventured the first evening. "I didn't know it was like that."

"Why mention it?" Jean-Pierre asked.

All the second day he was laughing and gay. He told her funny stories, one after another. She ate a lot for lunch and dinner, and felt happier than she ever had before. I did the right thing, she thought. Nobody would know that but me. The next day, driving back to Montreal, something went a little wrong with the car—the gas line clogged—and Jean-Pierre was unhappy and silent all the way to the Champlain Bridge.

Jean-Pierre took her over to East Montreal to see his two properties: dark brick buildings, of forty-five apartments each, he said, with doorways made of yellow stained oak set with mottled glass, and painted in slanting gold letters: "Les Tuileries," "Le Trianon." It was a close, humid day, misting rain, and narrow iron balconies along the sides of the buildings were crammed like rush-hour buses with sweating people in shorts, T-shirts, and sandals. Smoke rose from a barbecue. The windows all seemed dull. Somebody looked over a balcony railing and noticed Jean-Pierre and threw something down—maybe just an empty carton. Another person yelled at them. "Would you like to go inside?" he asked her. *"Non, merci,"* said Callie, and that night she had a dream of the buildings, windows crowded with painted, shouting faces, the people all fat and too big for the small rooms behind them, all sweating and smoke-stained and complaining of noise.

What did she know about it? If she tried to ask too much he would brood—a brooding so deep and thorough that his eyes seemed to peer beautifully into her soul's depths. A mystery so deep couldn't be just about business. Perhaps it was his dead wife haunting him; perhaps he felt guilty about her. Had he known some other woman, who was unkind to him? Was he in debt? Had a friend betrayed him? Was he bored with Callie and regretting that he had married her? She asked him. *"Mais non, ma p'tite . . . pourquoi tu parles comme ça?"*

They moved from his old apartment into a larger place and furnished it through a cousin of Jean-Pierre's—a dealer in Saint-Laurent—who had given them a discount price. Most of the pieces were imitation Danish modern, but the wood was real.

In early June, when they had been married for nearly a year, Jean-Pierre disappeared.

She had come in from grocery shopping and found a note on the dining table, weighted down with the Waterford bowl: "I will be gone for a while, *c'est nécessaire.* There is money in the bank two thousand." After a week she thought about notifying the police, but something put her off that. She thought of calling the building superintendent of Les Tuileries and Le Trianon. She was afraid of actually knowing. He might be in some sort of trouble. But maybe it wasn't his fault. Phone calls came in French for Jean-Pierre. *"Il est hors de la ville,"* she said. *"C'est impossible. . . . Je ne sais pas. . . . Je n'ai aucune idée."*

Then she had a call herself from Bob Fletcher. "Excuse me, Callie," he said, "but I heard Courtois is about to sell those apartments on Rue Rachel."

"I don't know about his business," said Callie.

"We insured them, you know. He was having some trouble getting coverage—it wasn't clear if they were residential or offices. We wanted the account, at first. I was trying to expand to the French. That first evening, remember? Sure you do. Later I pulled off from it. I'd have dropped it, but Bart insisted. Bart

was worried, because he thought you might be getting hooked
up with the wrong guy. Who's to say? Anyway, I went ahead
with it. You're getting on O.K., I hope."

"He isn't here," said Callie. "I'll tell him. I'm fine."

When she hung up, the phone rang again, and a woman's
voice asked in French for Jean-Pierre. It was something to do
with money from Trois-Rivières which was expected in some
other town, in Rimouski, and Callie thought she heard the words
"*son fils.*" (His son? Impossible! But maybe it wasn't.)

"Find him yourself!" she said in English. This provoked a long
eruption, but she couldn't make out the words and she began to
cry. That was wrong—the wrong thing to do.

The weather was hot. From the apartment windows she often
looked down on the area in back of a shabby house—one of a
row of old houses that, on the street side, had steep stairs up to
the front doors, each topped by an ornate second-floor balcony
with a triangular roof, no two quite alike. Behind this house
there was a small garden with a lounge chair, where a woman
sunned herself on weekends. Callie had bought a new bathing
suit and some white sandals she especially liked. Having no
place now to wear either, she went one twilight and talked to the
woman in the house, asking if she could use the chair on week-
day afternoons.

"You can keep it from being stolen," the woman said. "I had
one stolen last year, and now I've chained this one to the fence.
But I think somebody is going to take it anyway." And she gave
Callie the key to the back gate.

So for a week Callie sunned in the chair, latching and
unlatching the new sandals and soaking the sun into her fair
skin. A cat, its white fur stippled in silky gray, marched back
and forth on the back steps from time to time. It also climbed
the board fence between that yard and the next, and, finding a
post and a wooden ledge to balance on, curled tail around feet
and sat regarding her. She made some contact with the steady
slate-blue gaze; a current ran from the sun to her, from the cat
to her, from her to the cat. She had felt alone and anxious, numb
and half dead, but now there was a joining, a new sense of life.
When she looked up, she expected to see herself on the narrow

back balcony of her apartment, looking down. The weather held. On the third day, when she went inside the cat followed her.

All absences are mysterious. Whether the absence is understood or not, the absent person is, somehow, not really gone. "Not gone," Callie wrote down on her grocery list. Not being physically present, his thoughts became all important. They filled the sky; they overweighed the world. But what were they? "Thinks of me," she wrote next, then added, "But what?" Sometimes she could hear him talking, clearly, in her head, but to someone else: *"J'ai un mal de tête effrayant."* . . . *"Les gens sont fous."* . . . *"Elle est trop jeune . . . une enfant . . . presque."*

To stop these conversations she took several sleeping pills— over-the-counter things that did very little good. All weekend, the cat slept on the foot of the bed and purred. That Monday she had to acknowledge that the money had shrunk, that bills, bills, bills kept coming in, that the rent was due. She went to a library out in N.D.G. where she had worked before she married —what seemed an age ago.

In the spacious, book-scented room, its windows open on a warm overcast day, Mrs. Gentian was still behind the desk. She gave Callie a toothy, affectionate smile. She was a hurrying, eager soul, anxious for things to run right and for people to be happy. She believed that books increased the happiness of the human race. She imagined that Callie had come back because she liked her, and missed her, and wanted to say hello. Callie knew this and hated to disappoint her, but she had to.

"Can I help out with anything during the summer, Mrs. Gentian? I just need to make some extra money."

"Well, my dear, I don't know. . . . Somebody told me you got married."

"I did. He's away right now. For the summer."

"Tell me. Is he English or what?"

"French—Quebec French."

"Well . . . they're different," said Mrs. Gentian, and she looked away, resetting her glasses. She said that Callie could come in part-time, and gave her the record collection to handle. But it took very little time to sort and rearrange and recatalogue them, and check them in and out for the few habitués who wanted to go sit at a record player in a windowless cubicle on a

green summer day, so Callie was mainly at Mrs. Gentian's beck
and call for minor errands and duties. And sometimes she just
sat and read.

It was poetry she kept looking at now. She'd tried to talk
about poetry to Jean-Pierre; he had mentioned Saint-Denys Gar-
neau, whom he'd heard of but never read, and Mallarmé, whom
he'd studied in school but could not remember.

Callie sat and read Emily Dickinson. She read it line for line.
A whole book lay before her, and she thought it might just last
all summer; poetry went much more slowly than a novel. She
learned that nature was marvellous but cruel, that death was in-
exorable, that to lose your love was another sort of death, that
God was somebody whom, if you had any sense at all, you had
to argue with. Montreal was muggy, overcast, and dirty that
summer. The trees in the residential streets looked cool and full,
but downtown near her own apartment, along Sainte-Catherine,
vomit dried in various shades of green all day outside the
*tavernes,* and all dogs seemed afflicted with diarrhea. She went
back and forth to N.D.G. on the bus. Like filling a bucket in a
mountain lake, she tried to fill her mind with the poems of
Emily Dickinson and the concerned kindness of Mrs. Gentian,
who had sensed that something was wrong and had quit asking
her about her husband. But the comfort leaked away during the
night, and every dawn she woke in a dry-tongued fright, wondering, What can I do? Whom can I go to? Sooner or later she
would have to tell someone. The concierge's wife kept asking,
*"Quand est-ce qu'il revient?* Is he gone forever?" and Callie kept
saying, "Next week, I think," and gave her a check for the rent.

My life closed twice before its close.

She wasn't going so far yet as to say she was dying. It was just
that, except for the cat, the lounge chair, and the sandals, she
felt alone. If she told Mrs. Gentian, she would have sympathy,
but the feeling would not end. If she called Bea and Bart in Cincinnati, Bea would say I told you so, you ought to have had
more sense. Bart would worry, and call Bob Fletcher, or maybe
fly in, and they would start managing things. When the English
managed things, who cared about the French? She knew that
much. She wrote to her father and stepmother in California that

everything was fine. The slanting script of her letter looked too small for the page, so she drew happy little climbing vines up either side to frame it. At the table in the library, with moist air leaking some water against the windows ("spotting," the English called it; *"maussade,"* said the French), she thought about nature in New England, perhaps still full of tall elms—the elms that were sick and dying in Montreal, some already chopped down and hauled away. Full, too, of hummingbirds, and berry bushes growing up the slopes of hills, of robins dining on fat worms, of swarms of butterflies dancing in inexhaustible sunlight. Well, she guessed the Laurentians were nice, too—she could take a bus up there some Sunday and see things like that; it was just that nobody had written about them that way, nobody she knew of. And there was all this thing about life, love, hurting, that wound through everything this woman was thinking about or looking at.

> My reason, life,
> I had not had, but for yourself.
> 'Twere better charity
> To leave me in the atom's tomb.

"What's 'the atom's tomb'?" she suddenly asked the young man across from her at the library table. He had come there for four days in a row, had sat facing her each time, and read, after parking a baby in a stroller at his side. The baby usually slept; the young man read magazines. He had uncontrollable curly dark hair, shabbily cut, and gnawed fingernails, and he wore a short-sleeved beige shirt and no tie. Why did he always sit opposite her? All the other tables were empty. Might as well ask why the cat had put its head up over the fence.

"You're still reading those same poems," he said.

"They're about New England," she said.

"I read different things," he said.

"Different how?"

"I try to vary my reading."

She did not reply. She got up to help Mrs. Gentian sort through some new periodicals and put them on the racks, replacing the older ones, which she brought in a stack to the desk for filing. She was wearing the sandals, a wraparound skirt, and a faded coral blouse. She felt the young man watching the sandals. He was like someone approaching a door.

When she returned to the table, he asked, "Why do you like New England?"

"Because of what I'm reading about it," she said, and laughed, the answer having led him in a circle, as she knew it would.

He did not smile. "'The atom's tomb' would be what you were still in if you'd never become human or been born, I guess. I think I read that, too, once."

She observed him with more tolerance. He looked intelligent in a harried way; she thought he was probably Jewish. "Why do you bring that baby every day?"

"Where else would I leave her?" he asked.

"I don't know," she said, and began to read again, having (all roads led to Rome) come close to the subject of wives and husbands.

"My wife works," he pursued anyway. He was the kind of library reader who sat down on his backbone instead of on his hips, legs stretched out (sidewise, to miss her own), feet crossed at the ankles, elbows spread on the tabletop to their farthest reach, his face nearly dipping into the book. He was arranged like a geometrical design. He seemed to be speaking to her through a magnified web of the print he was just reading from. "I'm out of a job. I got fired. My wife works. I have to mind the baby."

> I measure every grief I meet
> With analytic eyes;
> I wonder if it weighs like mine,
> Or has an easier size.

"Are you scared?" she asked him. She hadn't meant to say that.

"Of course," he said breathlessly, and the sense of contact made her dizzy.

"The brain is just the weight of God," Callie read. What on earth did that mean?

"This morning," he said, "I fell over the stroller on my way for the mail. I knew it was there, but I fell over it."

"Oh," she said, and remembered a nightmare she had had the

night before—Jean-Pierre driving by on Sherbrooke Street and laughing at her while the light changed. Somebody she'd met once, somebody she'd married in a dream he hadn't had.

"I've watched you every day," the young man said. "Something's the matter with you, too. Nobody reads poetry the way you've been doing unless something is the matter."

She didn't answer—any more than if he had addressed the white cat. Thinking of the cat, she put out her tongue's tip and then drew it in again. Thus would the cat have done, adjusting one paw. Finally she said, in a careful way, not wishing to add to troubles by the weight of a feather, "What's that matter to you?"

"I don't know," he said, after considering the question. "I have this feeling that something's happening to both of us, that we're having the same sort of struggle about whatever it is. I'm worried, you're worried. I'm scared, you're scared."

"Then maybe," she suggested, "we'd do better to be around somebody who didn't feel that way."

"That may be true," he replied. "But I wonder if we wouldn't be better able to get along with a likeness than a difference, at this point. I mean, if you're sinking in the ocean you need somebody to pull you out. But if you're falling through space, a companion in flight is about the best you can hope for."

"I don't know which it is," she said, and went back to her book.

> The Carriage held but just Ourselves
> And Immortality.

That was company of another kind. Closing the book, she got up to help Mrs. Gentian at the desk. The young man was watching her as she moved. He was watching her sandals walking. The cat, she recalled, watched in a different way, yet this regard, too, cut through the stifling web of her anxiety.

In August, the library closed, and she and the young man, whose name was Simon Weill, drove down to New England for the day in a car he had borrowed from his Uncle Stan. It was a fine, clear, sky-blue fresh summer day.

They went south to Swanton, in Vermont, then turned east

into beautiful farm country over little known roads that led
through green-and-white villages. Uncle Stan's car was a blue
Volkswagen with a tick in its noisy motor. The fenders were
splotched with maroon paint to cover the rust.

"There's a farm down a road near here," said Simon. "My
mother knew a lady who lived there. She rented a room from
her for a while once, when she was getting over an operation. I
can't think of her name. It's a pretty place. You'll like it. We'll
get some food and go there." He stopped at a grocery in the next
town. He said the farm was five miles from there, but it seemed
more like ten.

Later, all she remembered of the farm was the quarry, out of
use, deserted, at the end of a small road that ran beside the
farmhouse. At the house they stood and called, then knocked,
but no one answered. There wasn't even a dog. Callie thought
someone was inside just the same.

In the quarry, they split up the food from the grocery sack and
ate it—cheese and crackers, salami, ham, and bread, a box of
cakes, Cokes, and beer. The sun was hot. The rocks were flat
from having had other rocks cut away from them; their surface
was smooth in places, hot, and almost comfortable. Callie lay
down and dozed. But as though the walls of the farmhouse had
dissolved to let her see through into its rooms, she believed she
saw the woman who owned the house—stretched out on a
chaste, white-painted iron bed, her plain head resting on a white
pillow, her eyes closed, with the comfortable sounds of insects,
birds, and an occasional passing car floating through the window. Soon she would get up and bake banana bread.

Callie opened her eyes, and all around her the squares, rectangles, and trapezoids of the outcropping rock towered or dropped
away, like a ruin. Over the tops of the rocks, high and low,
sumac was growing, peering out like Indians. It was a wild
shrub with long-angling branches, lozenge-shaped leaves, and
squat, strong candles of dark brown, with the look of thick wax
drippings. After frost, these would turn bright and the leaves
would burn red. They were waiting for that to happen, she
guessed, as the woman on the bed upstairs in the house was
waiting for her napping hour to pass so she could get up and
bake. And she, Callie, was waiting, but waiting for Jean-Pierre

was not to be compared to other kinds. Everybody and everything, she thought, was waiting, in one way or another. Now she was waiting for Simon Weill as well, because he had gone somewhere, too.

Callie stood, and wandered farther down through the quarry, which deepened. The path through its center slanted downward, and its chopped-out walls rose higher on either side. A turn to the left and she saw him, standing with his back to her at the edge of a pond. The pond had rocky sides, sloping up out of the water, and she thought the water was from rain, for there was no movement in it, no exit for it. Simon was a waiter, too—she saw that; just by the way he was standing, she saw he was waiting for her.

"Did you go to the police about your husband?" he asked her.

"No, I called up some of his friends, people I had met with him one way or another."

"What did they say?"

"One gave me an address of some relatives up near Trois-Rivières, and another said, 'Oh, Jean-Pierre. But he always come back. *Pas de problème. Vous allez voir!*'"

"My father used to sell religious statues, rosaries, crosses, missals, all that stuff, to all the orders—the French Catholics, that is. Every place with a convent, a shrine, a hospital—Lac Saint-Jean, the Beauce, the Gaspé, Kamouraska—there he was: 'Very good rosaries, blessed by the Pope, hot from Rome.' Jews get into everything. He said the Québécois, if they get in trouble or get scared, they take to the bush. *Coureurs des bois.* They go to places like Chicoutimi, Rimouski, Rivière du Loup, from there upriver, downriver, into the woods. It was just his idea."

He saw that she was worried—he was troubling her. "You are too gentle for this. All summer it's you I've waited to see. Shiksa. One time at the dinner table, I said out loud, 'The gentle Gentile.' Shana—that's my wife—she heard me. 'A book I'm reading, nothing important,' I said. Now the summer's running out. I can't stop it. I've got no job still. Nor money. My wife works. I live in shame. Yesterday I thought, She likes New England, so take her to New England. What else?"

"The sumac," Callie said. "It's looking at us. Branches, candles, leaves."

He looked around, as if noticing for the first time. "It must remind you of Jean-Pierre. You think he's followed us?"

"Why do you say that?"

"Everything you see. Everything reminds you of Jean-Pierre." She kicked off her sandals.

"Have you ever read Toynbee?" he asked.

"No, why?" She tested the water with her foot.

"Something he said about societies finding identity, about processes of testing, this way and that way, what to do? The French here might be doing that. Scared, but they have to try. You think so?"

"I don't know." She waded in. The water, being whitish with a chalky suspension, hid the rocks it lay over. The rocks were uneven, some slippery, and toward the pond's center they suddenly dropped away. She drew her foot back, feeling it actually elongate in the pull of an iciness that meant depth at the least, maybe something bottomless. Simon tried to follow her out, but he cut his foot on a rock and sat on the edge with his trouser legs rolled up, washing off threads of blood until they stopped appearing. She waded back, sat near him, and shivered.

"I am disappointed in life," said Simon. "So far, at least, I am disappointed in it. How about you?"

"Hush! Look!" said Callie.

Standing at a good distance, just at the bend of the path between the rocks, was a tall woman in a plain, straight-cut dress, with dark hair. On the instant of their looking, she turned and walked away, vanishing.

"I think that's her," said Simon.

"The one your mother stayed with?"

"I think so, but I can't remember her name."

"I think it's Emily Dickinson," said Callie.

They gathered their things together: time to go. The last savage glare of the sun shot at them from the high cut of the quarry's cliff, where a single frond of sumac, like an outspread hand, sprang up at it. Then the light calmed. The sky was clear, the blueness of the air continuing downward, blue almost to the milky surface of the pool. Callie walked with him, remembering the water, its thickness and sudden cold. The quarry grew larger around them, and they a small pair passing from it. When they passed the farmhouse, a voice called out from inside, "Laura, don't take your brother down there anymore."

"I won't," Callie called back.

"I asked you before, do you remember?"

"I just forgot," she called.

"He was the one that brought those girls and all that beer."

"I'm sorry, I forgot," she answered, but to him she said, "If she's your mother's friend, don't you want to go and talk to her?"

"I wonder if this is the place," he said, walking on. "I don't remember any quarry."

"You'd have to remember that," she said, thinking of its awesome finalities—the silent, stony walls, the path that ended at the dead pool's edge, the watchful sumac high and low. "That was 'the atom's tomb,'" she said.

"So now we know."

Back in Montreal, she made him let her out a block from where she lived.

"You didn't know it, maybe, Callie," said Simon, gnawing a fingernail that was already fractional, "but down there in the quarry I wanted to love you. It was very much on my mind. When that woman appeared, the feelings got away."

"It's O.K.," she said, and took his hand from his mouth and held it.

"That damned Emily," he said. "Let's go back again."

"They're expecting you, aren't they? Your family and all."

"I know it's late. Time to go."

She got out, promising to call him. It was almost dark.

When she rounded the corner into her own street and looked up, she saw the apartment windows, and a light inside, toward the back. Frightened, she stopped for a moment, considering. Some other waiting was going on up there.

Just over the threshold—lobby, elevator, and corridor all passed—her forward motion failed her. She stood where she was, the door still ajar at her back, as if on the edge of a forest she did not dare to enter. The arched spring of the cat out of a closet was so startling she cried out. Its back seemed to stand for a moment in the air, the cool silver the color of fear. It landed right in the middle of the living room rug. It must have been crouched on a high shelf, hidden in the dark. It let out a small noise and trotted toward her, raising its face in a voiceless cry. Coming into the room, she bent to pick it up, but its heart was beating all over it, much like her own. It raced to her shoulder, clinging, its claws coming sharp into her skin, and sharper still when a step sounded from the kitchen and Jean-Pierre walked in. He saw them both, the cat and her, and stopped dead still.

At a wary, Indian distance, the two of them stood in silent confrontation.

"Where were you?" he finally asked, speaking English.

"I work in a library. I have all summer. Where were you?"

*"Une grosse question."* He turned aside, made to do so, she thought, by the cat, who had reared up on stiff paws above her head and spat at him. He had not changed at all, Callie thought, extravagantly relieved, for her dreams had brought him to her hurt and broken. He looked tired and was wearing a suit she'd never seen, that was all.

"Where did you get that cat?"

"I didn't get him. He just came here after you left. He wanted to stay with me. I don't know why."

"He stays because he belongs to you," said Jean-Pierre. *"Il est à toi. Il le sait bien."*

She did not answer.

"If he left, he would come back," he pursued in French. Then, in English, "He knows his place. *Et sa maîtresse.* He knows."

*"Et toi?* What is it you know?"

He spread his hands. "All that I know, *mon ange,* I'd like to tell you. *C'est une histoire assez longue."*

"You went back to your people. Down the river. Around Quebec."

He was looking at her with anxious desire, at the long hair the cat guarded. Her own desire was a gravid body sleeping. She went past him into the bedroom. Once alone with her, the cat jumped down but stayed close. She washed her face and hands, changed her blouse, and brushed her hair. Rimouski, Chicoutimi, she thought, steadying her breath against the strange names. Kamouraska, Rivière du Loup. . . . They fell through her thoughts as thick as snow. Tadoussac . . . Lac Saint-Jean . . .

Saint-Gabriel. . . . Why did you go? What did you learn? He had promised to tell her. When he told her, would she know?

The moment when I turned back, she wanted to say to him, was in a deserted quarry, beside a stone-dead pool, with another man's voice talking, sumac looking down; where, when you turned, were you? She imagined his secret face, most private in that instant, and knew she would seek out the moment under his words, hidden in the thicket of whatever he would talk about.

The cat still hung about her ankles. "I won't leave you," she knelt to say. "It's only Jean-Pierre. He lives here too."

# IF A WOODCHUCK COULD
# CHUCK WOOD

### W. D. WETHERELL

W. D. Wetherell was raised in Garden City, New York, and
currently lives in New Hampshire. An earlier story, "The
Man Who Loved Levittown," appeared in *Prize Stories 1981:
The O. Henry Awards.* His first novel, *Souvenirs,* was published later that year. The recipient of a National Endowment
for the Arts creative writing fellowship, Mr. Wetherell is
currently at work on another novel.

They had lasagna for Thanksgiving dinner that year. The meat-
less kind. From a can.

"Nothing like the smell of a good bird in the oven," Mike Senior announced, scraping his boots on the doormat, inhaling.

"Uh, Pop?" Janet whispered.

"Yes, ma'am?"

"Never mind. Happy Thanksgiving, Pop. Let me help you
with your coat. There are a few things in the kitchen I've got to
see to yet. Mike should be back any minute. I'll leave you and
Shawn to get reacquainted."

He smelled it all morning. He smelled it when he woke up in
the cramped, stuffy bedroom he rented near the school in South
Boston where he worked as a custodian part-time—fresh,
brought in from the woodshed where it had been kept during
the night to keep it moist. He smelled it as the bus crossed the
state line into Maine—skin turning brown, the first drippings
running down the sides. He smelled it at the rest stop where he
bought Shawn an Indian tomahawk made in Taiwan, smelled it

Copyright © 1981 by The Virginia Quarterly Review. First appeared in
*The Virginia Quarterly Review.* Reprinted by permission.

during the walk from the abandoned railroad bridge where the
bus let him off—almost done now, the gravy bubbling in the pan,
its aroma taking him past the boarded-up stores of the old mill
town, the overgrown orchards, the brief view of the lake which
meant he was halfway there . . . a rich, fragrant distillation of
sixty Thanksgivings past, so strong that none of the changes in
the house could stain it; not the plastic stretched tight over the
windows to keep out drafts, not the towels stuffed against cracks
the plastic missed, not the ugly black woodstove jutting out from
the fireplace, appropriating all the space near the couch . . . not
even the garlic and parmesan cheese Janet was sprinkling over
the top of the casserole dish in a last desperate attempt to make
it all palatable.

"And just how heavy is it this year, Shawn?" he asked, playing
to memories and traditions he felt it was his duty to impart.

"Seven. Seven and a half in May."

Shawn was busy chopping up the coffee table. He thought his
grandfather had asked him his age.

"Seven pounds, eh? Kind of on the scrawny side, isn't it? By
the way, Shawn. That's a real Indian scalping hatchet you've got
yourself there. Never point it at anybody unless you mean business."

Mike got home around one. He didn't say where he had been.
He went into the bathroom to wash his hands.

"I was just admiring your stove there," Mike Senior said when
he came back. "Clever the way it fits in so snug."

"Eats wood."

Mike Senior nodded, as if Mike had said something profound.

"That so? Well, guess it's nice to have the trusty furnace to
fall back on. You can say what you want about the good old
days but give me a nice tight burner every time."

"We shut it off, Pop. Eats oil."

Mike Senior nodded again, pursing his lips this time, as if his
son had just topped his previous insight with an even truer one.

"That's an idea. Hey, you know, talking about woodstoves. . . . We used to have one when I was a boy. A real pot-
belly, too. At least my grandfather did. He was quite a piece of
work, my grandfather. Your great-grandfather, Mike. Shawn's

great-great-grandfather. It was my job to fill the stove every night before I went to bed so it wouldn't go out."

"Did it?"

"Did it what?"

"Go out. This one's always going out. That's what it does best. Goes out."

"Well, naturally. You've got to. . . ." He tried to remember what his grandfather had said in 1918. "You've got to spit on it first. You've got to make sure your tinder is dry."

Mike sat on the couch nursing a beer. His face had hardened since the last time Mike Senior had seen him. There was something reproachful about his prematurely gray hair, his tired eyes.

"You never showed me, Pop. You never taught me about woodstoves when I was small."

This took Mike Senior off guard. The frowning. The green work pants he hadn't bothered changing out of. He wished Shawn could come back from wherever he was hiding.

"Well, no. Of course, because we didn't have one. We had a furnace, Mike. I remember showing you where the oil went in. Remember, Mike? It was through the spigot underneath your mother's rhododendron."

"Was that the same grandfather whose brother starved to death on his way out West?"

"He didn't starve," Mike Senior said angrily. "At least he did, but it wasn't his fault. The wagon train lost its way. Their scout was drunk. It was an unusually bad winter."

He didn't like the direction the conversation was heading. Not at all. He waited until Janet came in, then . . . following the ritual . . . sniffed at the air like a bird dog, glanced significantly at the pocket watch he had bought at Woolworth's to someday leave to Shawn, pushed himself up off the couch.

"Guess it's time I started working on the old gobbler," he said, stretching. "Got my favorite knife all sharpened up for me, Janet?"

"Uh, Pop."

But it was too late. Before Janet could stop him he had gone into the kitchen.

"Please, Pop. Don't say anything to him about it, okay? He's super uptight about things right now. He's discouraged, Pop.

You would be too if you were in his shoes. Let's just have a nice quiet dinner for a change, all right? All right, Pop?"

He heard Janet whispering all this over his shoulder, he saw the casserole dish cooling off on the counter, saw the rubbery noodles the color of slugs, the blistered tomato sauce, the black stains in the empty oven, but it still didn't register. He stood there rubbing his nose in disbelief.

"What's this?" he finally managed to choke out.

"It's called lasagna, Pop. It's Italian food. We thought we'd try something different this year."

"Something cheaper you mean," Mike said. He was in the kitchen now, pushing Shawn out in front of him. "Shawn wants to see Grandpop carve."

But Mike Senior had recovered himself now. He started digging away at the middle of it with Janet's spatula, ignoring his son's sarcasm.

"Who wants an end piece? Shawn? Nice crispy corner going to waste here. Nothing like variety I always say. Variety is the spice of life. Nice dark piece okay for you, Janet?"

He carried the dish into the dining room, trying to hide his disappointment. It was one tradition down, but there was another yet to go. All during the bus drive he had rehearsed saying grace, going over different words, trying them out on the bus driver who was glad for the company and helpful in suggesting phrases of his own. It was a special prayer for the occasion, traditionally reverential but timely, too, showing Mike he understood after all. He was too shy to tell him so face-to-face, but with their heads bowed he thought he might just bring it off.

"I think we're ready to start now, Mike," he said, interrupting the celery before it could be passed any further. "Heavenly father. . . ."

But Mike missed his cue—whether deliberately or accidentally Mike Senior couldn't tell. He was talking to Shawn, jabbing his fork at the casserole dish like a teacher pointing to a map.

"We can't have turkey anymore, Shawn. Why not?"

Shawn didn't answer.

"Because it's too expensive, that's why not. It costs over a dollar a pound and lasagna feeds the four of us for only a buck. Understand that, Shawn?"

"Why bother him with it?" Janet said. She had seen her father-in-law fold his hands, then quickly unfold them, and she felt embarrassed.

"The boy has to learn," Mike said defensively, putting his fork back down. "The sooner he does, the easier it'll be."

They finished dinner in silence. Mike Senior wondered if it would be possible to slip grace in before dessert, but as it turned out there wasn't any dessert, only coffee. By the time they finished and washed the plates off . . . they didn't use the dishwasher anymore, Janet explained . . . it was still only three. Janet said something about Parchesi. Mike said something about needing more wood.

"That's the best idea I've heard all day. Mind if an old man tags along?"

Mike went to find Shawn who was hiding again, this time in the bathroom. He stood over him while he buttoned his coat. He made him leave his tomahawk behind on the kitchen counter.

"This isn't a game, Shawn. If you work hard you can play with it later."

Janet was watching the three of them get ready from the sink. He turned to her, heading off her protest before it was made.

"Well, it isn't, you know. Not anymore. The boy has to learn."

They went through the door in chronological order—Shawn in a hurry to be outside, Mike Senior hanging back to fasten his hood, Mike . . . dressed in the army jacket that had always been too short for him, even in the army . . . caught somewhere in between, needing to free himself of the house, feeling reluctant to face the cold. It was below freezing now. The sun had lost its strength in nagging its way westward through the iodine-colored clouds which had clung to it since morning; what yellow was left was wasted on the roof of the corrugated iron shed where he kept his tools. He crawled in on his hands and knees, then shoved out what they would need. An oil can and some rags. The chain saw. Almost as an afterthought, the ax.

"Let me give you a hand with that, Shawn."

"Don't, Pop. He can manage."

"Yeah, but it's awfully heavy, Mike. I just thought. . . ."

"I know what you thought, Pop."

There was no use arguing with him. Mike Senior gathered up what was left, then hurried after them, his irritation soothed away by the ax. He felt it only fitting that he should be the one to carry it. When Mike first handed it to him, he had swung it back and forth to check its balance, then held it outstretched in front of him to sight down the shaft.

"Good ax," he announced at last, running an appreciative finger along the blade. "Damn good ax."

The path crossed a culvert, then merged into an overgrown dirt road the construction crews had used in putting up the summer homes around the lake back in the fifties. There were No Trespassing signs here, the remains of a wire fence once rumored to be electrified. Mike stepped over it into the trees, or at least what was left of them. A worm had gotten all the pine. There were still some birch but not many. The summer people cut them down to decorate their fireplaces.

"Up here!"

He saw the two of them cross the stream in the wrong direction, then swerve back toward the road. His father had caught up with Shawn now. He was saying something to him, helping him with the saw. He carried the ax the wrong way, propped over his shoulder like a rifle. Trip over a stone and it's good-bye ear, Mike thought, lighting a cigarette. He wondered what he was telling Shawn.

There was a dead tree on the edge of the woods. Maple, possibly oak. He couldn't tell without the leaves. He had discovered it the same afternoon he lost his job—rotten, tilting, but not yet down. It hadn't meant much to him at first. Something noticed through the bitterness, nothing more. But as October went by and his walks became longer, he began to feel the tree was deliberately mocking him by staying upright, the same way the neat, unused woodpiles of the summer people mocked his own empty shed, his stove that ate wood, then went out. Finally, the night before, lying next to Janet unable to sleep, he heard a distant thump up near the lake, as if a giant had suddenly drummed his fist against the frozen ground. He nodded—for the first time in weeks he allowed himself to smile.

"Whew. You set a pretty good pace there, Mike," his father

said, swinging the ax off his shoulder, missing his ankle by a
hair. "This is our baby, eh? Nice sturdy elm from the looks of
her. Where shall we dig in?"

Mike ignored him. He took the chain saw from Shawn and
opened the gas tank to make sure it was full. He pushed the
prime in twice, then yanked the starter cord out much harder
than was necessary.

"Damn."

Mike Senior was breaking off some branches near the tree's
base. Shawn was straddling the trunk, kicking his heels up and
down like a cowboy. Neither one had seen him.

"Get off of there, Shawn!" he yelled automatically, wondering
what in hell could be wrong. He pulled it again, breaking the
cord this time, the little knob on the end flying backwards into
his face.

The saw burped—there was a gratifying cloud of blue smoke,
then a roar. He was shouting for them to get out of the way . . .
he was fighting to hold the saw steady, bracing it against his
thigh the way the salesman had showed him in the store . . .
when it burped again, throwing sparks out from beneath the
handle, kicking loose from his hands, and somersaulting across
the dead tree onto the ground. It spun violently around the un-
derbrush for what seemed like minutes, sending branches and
pine needles and pebbles into the air in a miniature whirlwind
before conking out against a rock.

None of them said anything. In the distance Mike could hear
a small plane.

"Goddammit!"

It was Shawn who said it. Shawn who hadn't opened his
mouth since they left the house. Mike Senior's face turned red—
Mike drew back his hand as if to hit him. But he put it off for
the time being. He squatted down next to the chain saw, prodding at it with a stick like someone checking to see whether a
fierce animal was still alive.

"He picks it up at school," he said with a shrug once the safety
was on. "Shawn! Say anything like that again you're going to get
slapped, understand?"

The dead tree looked bigger now. There were branches pok-
ing out he hadn't noticed before, goiter-like knots where old

limbs had broken off during storms, twisted vines that still held parts of the trunk dangerously high off the ground. With the chain saw he had thought it manageable, even puny. But now, unarmed, it was if the tree were mocking him again—his broken saw, his joblessness, his son's mysterious silences and abrupt shouts.

"You pay a hundred bucks for something you'd think it would work," he said without much conviction.

Mike Senior nodded. "Good thing we have the ax."

He was swinging it back and forth like a batter limbering up on deck, the eagerness on his face contrasting dramatically with the sullenness on Shawn's, as if the two generations' usual roles had been reversed—Mike Senior the excited boy, Shawn the jaded old man.

"They didn't bother with fancy gizmos in the old days. All a man needed was an ax and a rifle and he was set for whatever came his way in life. They opened up a continent that way, Shawn. They made us the nation we are."

"Like Uncle whatshisname, right?" Mike said. "The guy who starved."

The stove ate kindling, not just logs. He showed Shawn what kind to look for and started him off through the trees with a little shove. He looked very small against the gray sky. Every now and then he would stoop down to pick up a stick, but it was obvious his heart wasn't in it. For a moment Mike was tempted to call him back.

"First you make sure you got plenty of room to swing her. . . ."

His father had taken his coat off. His father was rolling up his sleeves.

"Then you hold her nice and tight. Nice and tight, Mike. My grandfather had hands like a blacksmith. He'd take a tree like this and have it in toothpicks inside of a minute."

"Don't you think you better start further up?"

But he didn't listen. He spat on his hands, wiped them off on his pants, then brought the ax down with all his might against a huge knot in the tree's base. The blade glanced off without biting in, knocking some dirt loose, flaking off a few pieces of scabby bark.

"Nice and tight. I see what you mean."

Mike Senior shook his head in disbelief, staring at the ax like something must be wrong with it. He went over to the oil can and squirted some over the blade, then swung it again closer to the spot Mike suggested. This time the blade bit into the wood with a satisfyingly resonant whonk, but when he bent down to pry it loose for his next swing the ax refused to budge.

"It's stuck," he finally decided, after examining it from all angles. "Uh, your ax is stuck, Mike."

"So I see. What happens now?"

"I think it's your oil. They used to have this special kind years ago. I remember it came in a red, white and blue can. It had Teddy Roosevelt's picture on the side. If we had some there'd be no problem."

"I thought you said you knew how to do it."

"I do. Only it's been a while, Mike. My grandfather wanted to show me, but my father wouldn't let him. He wouldn't let me go out in the woods once I was Shawn's age, Mike. He thought that was old-fashioned. People were ashamed to use wood in those days. We had a furnace. My father threw the ax out the day the men came and put it in."

He was still talking when Mike kicked the ax loose. Apologizing, explaining, making excuses for them both. But it was too late for that now—all Mike could think of was his own bitterness. He would hear his father's voice behind him as he brought the ax up, lose it beneath his own grunt as he slammed it back down, pick it up again as the hard, biting cut echoed off toward the lake.

"Things will get better, Mike. It might be kind of tough right now but you've got to keep the old chin up, roll with the punches."

He swung the ax harder, swinging it less at the tree than at all the frustration that had been building inside him for so long. Harder and harder. Deeper and deeper into the wood.

"Things always look darkest before the dawn, Mike. Things are bound to get better soon. I can feel better days in my bones."

The bosses. The unemployment office. The applications for work. The maybes. The next weeks. The sorrys. The nos. The staying home. The game shows. The walks. The Salvation Army store. The food stamps. The day-old pies. The making do, stretching out, diluting. Janet's own bitterness. The pipes that froze. The rags stuffed against drafts. The doctor's bills. The gas. The bare tires. The lottery tickets. The part-time jobs. The patches. The cutting back. The cold. The stove. The wood. The goddamn wood.

"It's free, Mike. That's the great thing about it. I heard the man say so on the radio this morning when I was getting ready to come."

Mike stopped to catch his breath. The sweat was rolling down his forehead, stinging his eyes. His wrist hurt—there was a pain in his back below his left shoulder. As tormenting as it was, his anger had made no visible impression on the dead tree. He was still less than a third of the way through.

"What?" he mumbled, feeling defeated.

"Energy from the sun, Mike. It's the energy of the future, the man said. It's our only renewable source of energy that's free."

Mike laughed.

"Free, right? That's a good one, Pop. That's the best one I've heard in years. The sun, right? Somebody's already got a plan to slap a meter on it. They've probably got a patent on the thing right now. They're going to put it in a pump or a can and it's going to cost us plenty, you wait and see."

And when he turned to watch the sunset that's exactly how it looked—appropriated, sold, fading behind the ridge near the lake like all the other missed opportunities in his life, appealing only when gone. He was standing there watching it vanish when Shawn appeared from the same direction, blotting out his last glimpse of it, emerging from whatever faint light remained.

"Here he is!" Mike Senior yelled, happy for the distraction. "Our lumberjack, Mike. Look and see how much he's brought back."

"Too small."

"Here, take a look, Mike. He's got himself half the forest."

"Too small!"

Mike grabbed the branches from his son's arms and threw them toward the road.

"Go back and find bigger ones, Shawn."

"Mike, for Pete's sake, he's only a . . ."

"Move!"

Shawn wiped his nose off on the sleeve of his coat, then started robot-like in the opposite direction from the one he had come, pushing his way through the briars until he disappeared. Mike watched him go, then . . . grabbing the ax . . . swung it blindly at the dead tree with all the strength that was left in him. The bark flew up past his head . . . the tree shivered, writhed, began to split . . . the ax bit deeper, deeper . . . the overstrained shaft shattered apart into splinters, leaving a piece the size of a pencil sticking through his right hand.

"Mike!"

Without screaming, without saying a word, he dropped what was left of the broken ax and started running up through the woods toward the lake.

"Mike?"

Mike Senior went over to the tree to sit down, feeling drained, wondering whether he should wait for them there or go back to the house for help. It was dark out now. By squinting he could just make out the road, but not much further. He wasn't sure if he could find the way by himself—Mike wouldn't let Janet turn on the back spotlight anymore. He had just made up his mind to wait another ten minutes before shouting for them, when something small and square and silent separated itself from the black behind the tree.

"Shawn!"

He put both hands over his chest. He started shaking his head.

"You gave me quite a start there, Shawn. Not good for the old ticker getting surprised like that. You could have been an Indian and what would I have done then?"

Shawn's arms were full. He came to a stop near the abandoned chain saw—mute, gloveless, staring up at his grandfather as if he had never really looked at him before.

"Uh, your Daddy's gone wee wee."

Shawn could tell his grandfather was embarrassed to be alone with him. He was fidgeting with his hands, clasping them together, then unclasping them, sliding his false teeth in and out with his tongue in a way he never did when Shawn's parents were around. At the same time he seemed on the point of saying

something but not sure how to begin. He made Shawn come
over and sit down next to him. He patted his knee, then his
shoulder. He pointed to the broken ax, mumbled something
about wagon trains and grandfathers and not giving up. He
made Shawn bow his head like he did in Sunday school. He
started reciting something in a hoarse voice, like a frog's.

"Heavenly father. . . ."

The words were too big for Shawn—he was too busy studying
his grandfather's face to pay attention. He kept his eyes closed
most of the time, but every so often he would stop mumbling
long enough to look nervously over his shoulder toward the lake,
reminding Shawn of a squirrel.

". . . and for our health which has been pretty good all things
considered, and for this thy produce of thy table . . ."

On and on. Louder and louder. There was a dab of spit on his
lips. There was a little gray froth churned up when they moved.

". . . we await thy assistance, thanking you serenely for
pitching in to help like you have, bestow . . . upon . . ."

He lost his way, doubling back over words Shawn knew he
had already said, stopping, shutting his eyes even tighter as
though he was trying to squeeze them out.

"Bestow . . . Grateful, Lord . . . thy humble servants . . ."

He was mumbling again when Shawn's father came back. He
was in one of the intervals where his eyes were closed so he
didn't see what Shawn saw—that his father's right hand was
wrapped in a dirty handkerchief, that his father was carrying an
armful of wood.

"Where are they?" he demanded.

Six logs. White, evenly cut. Six logs of magical white birch.

"Too green," he said, kicking apart Shawn's pile of kindling
with his boot. But he said it halfheartedly—the kick was mis-
directed, more like a shrug than a kick. He seemed in a hurry,
glancing back toward the lake the same way Shawn's grandfather had in saying his prayers.

"The boy has to learn," he said to no one in particular, hand-
ing Shawn one of the birch logs, then another, then a third. It
was all Shawn could do to hold them. He felt his knees give way
under the weight—he bit his tongue to keep from crying.

"Let's get out of here."

His father grabbed the chain saw and started running down toward the house.

"I'll help you," his grandfather whispered, holding back. "He can't see us now. Here, let me take this heavy one off the top."

They made their way through the woods as best they could, tripping over stones, sliding on the dead leaves. His grandfather kept whispering words Shawn couldn't understand, his breath feeling hot and tickly, stinking of garlic. Shawn tried to block it out, slapping at his ear like it was a mosquito which wouldn't go away, thinking only of how much he hated the wood he carried in his arms. How he hated the scabby feel of it. How he hated its smell when it burned—the way its smell associated itself with everything in life he had learned to detest.

"I promise, Shawn."

He wouldn't listen now. The dark. The cold. It seemed he had always been tumbling through it this way, arms aching, wrists scratched and bleeding. It seemed he always would be, too, forever trying to catch up, unable to escape a future consisting entirely of heavier logs, even thicker, more acrid smoke.

"Things will get better, Shawn."

His father was waiting for them by the house, the spotlight turned on after all, throwing his shadow out across the lawn like a giant's.

"Things will get better!" his grandfather hissed as they stepped clear of the woods, piling the third log back on top of the two he already carried so his father wouldn't know. But it was too much for Shawn. The weight. The unfairness. From all the frustration and fear he finally found the word he had been groping for all afternoon.

"Liar!"

He spun around to face his father, throwing up his arm to protect himself from the inevitable slap. But his father's expression never changed. His father was looking down at the ground pretending not to have heard—his father was falling down onto his knees, gathering in the logs Shawn had dropped like a beggar scooping up precious coins. In that one glimpse Shawn knew that he had won—that his father would never stop him now, that he could yell at his grandfather again.

"Liar!" he screamed, hating him. "Liar!"

# THE CITY

## JOHN UPDIKE

John Updike was born in Shillington, Pennsylvania, in 1932,
and attended Harvard College. He is the author of some
twenty-five books, mostly of fiction, and presently lives in
Beverly Farms, Massachusetts.

His stomach began to hurt on the airplane, as the engines
changed pitch to descend into the city. Carson at first blamed
his pain upon the freeze-dried salted peanuts that had come in a
little silver-foil packet with the whiskey sour he had let the stewardess bring him at ten o'clock that morning. Fifty, he did not
think of himself as much of a drinker, but the younger men in
kindred gray business suits who flanked him in the three-across
row of seats had both ordered drinks, and it seemed a way of
keeping status with the stewardess. Unusually for these days,
she was young and pretty. So many stewardesses seemed, like
Carson himself, on second careers, victims of middle-aged restlessness. A long-divorced former mathematics teacher, he
worked as a sales representative for a New Jersey manufacturer
of microcomputers and information-processing systems. Late in
life, after twenty years of driving the same suburban streets
from home to school and back again, he had become a connois-
seur of cities—their reviving old downtowns and grassy industrial belts, their rusting railroad spurs and new glass buildings,
their orange-carpeted hotels and bars imitating the interiors of
English cottages. But always there was an individual accent, a
style of local girl and historic district, an odd-shaped skyscraper
or a museum holding a Cézanne or a medieval altarpiece that
you could not see in any other city. Carson had never before

Copyright © 1981 by The New Yorker Magazine, Inc. First appeared in
*The New Yorker*. Reprinted by permission.

visited the city into which he was now descending, and perhaps
a nervous apprehension of the new contacts he must forge and
the persuasions he must deliver formed the seed of the pain that
had taken root in the center of his stomach, just above the navel.

He kept blaming the peanuts. The tempting young stewardess,
tanned from West Coast layovers, had given him not one but
two packets in silver foil, and he had eaten both—the nuts tast-
ing tartly of acid, the near engine of the 747 haloed by a rain-
bow of furious vapor in a backwash of sunlight from the east as
the great plane droned west. This drone, too, had eaten into his
stomach. Then there was the whiskey sour itself, and the time-
squeeze of his departure, and the pressure of elbows on the arm-
rests on both sides of him. He had arrived too late to get an aisle
or window seat. Young men now, it seemed to him, were so cor-
pulent and broad, with the mixture of exercise and beer the culture kept pushing. Both of these wore silk handkerchiefs in their
breast pockets and modified bandit mustaches above their prim,
pale, satisfied mouths. When you exchanged a few words with
them, you heard voices that knew nothing, that were tinny. They
were gods but without timbre. Carson put away the papers on
which he had been blocking in a system—computer, terminals,
daisy-wheel printer, dual-drive disks, optional but irresistible
color-graphics generator with appropriate interfaces—for a pros-
pering little manufacturer of electric reducing aids, and ran a
final check on what could be ailing his own system. Peanuts.
Whiskey. Being crowded. In addition to everything else, he was
tired, he realized: tired of numbers, tired of travel, of food, of
competing, even of shaving in the morning and putting himself
into clothes and then, sixteen hours later, taking himself out of
them. The pain slightly intensified, as if a chemical jot more had
been added to its tarry compound. He pictured the pain as
spherical, a hot bubble that would break if only he could focus
upon it the laser of the right thought.

In the taxi line, Carson felt more comfortable if he stood with
a slight hunch. He must look sick, he was attracting the glances
of his fellow-visitors to the city. The two young men whose
shoulders had squeezed him for three hours had melted into the
many similar others with their attaché cases and polished shoes.
Carson gave the cabdriver not the address of the manufacturer

of reducing and exercise apparatus but that of the hotel where
he had a reservation. A sudden transparent wave of nausea, like
a dip in the flight of the 747, decided him. The cool autumnal
air beat through his suit upon his skin. As he followed the
maroon-clad bellhop down the orange-carpeted corridor, not
only were the colors nauseating but the planes of wall and floor
looked warped, as if the pain that would not break up were
transposing him to a set of new coordinates, by the touch of
someone's finger on a terminal keyboard. He telephoned the exercise company from the room, explaining his case to an answering female and making a new appointment for tomorrow morning, just before he was scheduled to see the head accountant of
another booming little firm, makers of devices that produced
"white noise" to shelter city sleep. The appointment-squeeze
bothered Carson, but abstractly, for it would all be taken care of
by quite another person—his recovered, risen self. The secretary
he had talked to had been sympathetic, speaking in the
strangely comforting accent of the region—languid in some syl-
lables, quite clipped in others—and had recommended Maalox.
In the motion pictures that had flooded Carson's childhood with
images of the ideal life, people had "sent down" for such things,
but during all the travelling of his recent years he had never
come to believe that this could be done; he went down himself
to the hotel pharmacy. A lobby mirror shocked him with the
image of a thin-limbed man in shirtsleeves, with a pot belly and
a colorless mouth tugged down on one side.

The medicine tasted chalky and gritty and gave the pain, after
a moment's hesitation, an extra edge, as of tiny sandy teeth. His
hotel room also was orange-carpeted, with maroon drapes that
Carson closed, after peeking out at a bare brown patch of park
where amid the fallen leaves some boys were playing soccer;
their shouts jarred his membranes. He turned on the television
set, but it, too, jarred. Lying on one of the room's double beds,
studying the ceiling between trips to the bathroom, he let the afternoon burn down into evening and thought how misery itself
becomes a kind of home. The ceiling had been plastered in
overlapping loops, like the scales of a large white fish. For varia-
tion, Carson stretched himself out upon the cool bathroom floor,
marvelling at the complex, thick-lipped undersides of the porce-

# 144 JOHN UPDIKE

lain fixtures, at the distant bright lozenge of mirror. Repeated violent purgations had left the essential intruder, the hot tarry thing no longer simply spherical in shape but elongating, undissolved. When vomiting began, Carson had been hopeful. The hope faded like the light. In the room's shadowy spaces his pain had become a companion whom his constant interrogations left unmoved; from minute to minute it did not grow perceptibly worse, nor did it leave him. He reflected that his situation was a perfect one for prayer, but Carson had never been at all religious, and so could spare himself that additional torment.

The day's light, in farewell, placed feathery gray rims upon all the curved surfaces of the room's furniture—the table legs, the lamp bowls. Carson imagined that if only the telephone would ring his condition would be shattered. Curled on his side, he fell asleep briefly; awakening to pain, he found the room dark, with but a sallow splinter of street light at the window. The soccer players had gone. He wondered who was out there beyond the dark whom he could call. His ex-wife had remarried; of his children, one, the boy, was travelling in Mexico and the other, the girl, had disowned her father. When he received her letter of repudiation Carson had telephoned and been told, by the young lawyer she had been living with, that she had moved out and joined a feminist commune.

He called the hotel desk and asked for advice. The emergency clinic at the city hospital was suggested, by a male voice that to judge from its briskness had just come on duty. Shaking, lacing his shoes with difficulty, smiling to find himself the hero of a drama without an audience, Carson dressed and delicately took his sore body out into the air. A row of taxis waited beneath the corrosive yellow glare of a sodium-vapor street light. Neon advertisements, stacked cubes of fluorescent offices, red and green traffic lights scratched at the taxi windows, glimpses of the city that now, normally, with his day's business done, he would be roving, looking for a restaurant, a bar, a stray conversation, a possibility of contact with one of the city's unofficial hostesses.

The hospital was a surprising distance from the hotel. A vast and glowing pile with many increasingly modern additions, it waited at the end of a swerving drive through a dark park and a neighborhood of low houses. Carson expected to surrender the burden of his body utterly, but instead found himself obliged to carry it through a series of fresh efforts—forms to be filled out, proofs to be supplied of his financial fitness to be ill, a series of waits to be endured, on crowded benches and padded chairs, while his eye measured the distance to the men's-room door and calculated the time it would take him to hobble across it, open the door to a stall, kneel, and heave vainly away at the angry visitor to his own insides.

The first doctor he at last was permitted to see seemed to Carson as young and mild and elusive as his half-forgotten, travelling son. The doctor's wife, it somehow came out, was giving a dinner party, for which he was already late, in another sector of the city. Nevertheless the young man politely, circumspectly gave him time. Carson was, he confessed, something of a puzzle. His pain didn't seem localized enough for appendicitis, which furthermore was quite unusual in a man his age.

"Maybe I'm a slow bloomer," Carson suggested, each syllable, in his agony, a soft, self-deprecatory grunt. There ensued a further miasma of postponement, livened with the stabs of blood tests and the banter of hardened nurses. He found himself undressing in front of a locker so that he could wait with a number of other men in threadbare, backwards hospital gowns to be X-rayed. The robust technician, with his standard bandit mustache, had the cheerful aura of a weight lifter and a great ladies' (or men's) man. "Chin here," he said. "Shoulders forward. Deep breath: hold it. Good boy." Slowly Carson dressed again, though the clothes looked, item by item, so shabby as to be hardly his. One could die, he saw, in the interstices of these procedures. All around him, on the benches and in the bright, bald holding areas of the hospital's innumerable floors, other suppliants, residents of the city and mostly black, served as models of stoic calm, which he tried to imitate, though it hurt to sit up straight and his throat ached with gagging. The results of his tests were trickling along through their channels. The young doctor must be at his party by now; Carson imagined the clash of silver, the candlelight, the bare-shouldered women—a festive domestic world from which he had long fallen.

Toward midnight, he was permitted to undress himself again

and to get into a bed, in a kind of emergency holding area. White curtains surrounded him, but not silence. On either side of him, from the flanking beds, two men, apparently with much in common, moaned and crooned a kind of blues, and when doctors visited them pleaded to get out, promised to be good henceforth. From one side came a sound of tidy retching, like that of a cat who has eaten a bird bones and all; on the other side, internes seemed to be cajoling a tube up through a man's nose. Carson was comforted by these evidences that at least he had penetrated into a circle of acknowledged ruin. He was inspected at wide intervals. Another young doctor, who reminded him less of his son than of the legal-aid lawyer who had lived with his daughter and whom Carson suspected of inspiring and even dictating the eerily formal letter she had mailed her father, shambled in and, after some palpating of Carson's abdomen, sheepishly shrugged. Then a female doctor, dark-haired and fortyish, with a Slavic accent, came and gazed with sharp amusement down into Carson's face and said, "You don't protect enough."

"Protect?" he croaked. He saw why slaves had taken to clowning.

She thrust her thumb deep into his belly, in several places. "I shouldn't be able to do that," she said. "You should go through the ceiling." The idiom went strangely with her accent.

"It did hurt," he told her.

"Not enough," she said. She gazed sharply down into his eyes; her own eyes were green. "I think we shall take more blood tests."

Yet Carson felt she was stalling. There was a sense, from beyond the white curtains, percolating through the voices of nurses and policemen and delirious kin in this emergency room, of something impending in his case, a significant visitation. He closed his eyes a second. When he opened them a new man was leaning above him—a tall tutorial man wearing a tweed jacket with elbow patches, a button-down shirt, and rimless glasses that seemed less attachments to his face than intensifications of a general benign radiance. His hair was combed and grayed exactly right, and cut in the high-parted and close-cropped style of the Camelot years. Unlike the previous doctors, he sat on the edge of Carson's narrow bed. His voice and touch were gentle;

he explained, palpating, that some appendixes were retrocecal; that is, placed behind the large intestine, so that one could be quite inflamed without the surface sensitivity and protective reflex usual with appendicitis.

Carson wondered what dinner party the doctor had arrived from, at this post-midnight hour, in his timeless jacket and tie. He wished to make social amends but was in a poor position to, flat on his back and nearly naked. With a slight smile, the doctor pondered his face, as if to unriddle it, and Carson stared back with pleading helpless hopefulness. He was as weary of pain and a state of emergency as he had been, twelve hours before, of his normal life. "I'd like to operate," the doctor said softly, as if putting a suggestion that Carson might reject.

"Oh yes, *please*," Carson said. "Great. When, do you think?" He was very aware that, though the debauched hour and disreputable surroundings had become his own proper habitat, the doctor was healthy, and must have a home, a family, a routine to return to.

"Why, right *now*," was the answer, in a tone of surprise, and this doctor stood and seemed to begin to take off his coat, as if to join Carson in some sudden, cheerfully concocted athletic event.

Perhaps Carson merely imagined the surgeon's gesture. Things moved rapidly. The sheepish legal-aid look-alike returned, more comradely now that Carson had received a promotion in status, and asked him to turn on one side, and thrust a needle into his buttock. Then a biracial pair of orderlies coaxed his body from the bed to a long trolley on soft swift wheels; the white curtains were barrelled through; faces, lights, steel door lintels streamed by. Carson floated, feet first, into a room that he recognized, from having seen its blazing counterpart so often dramatized on film, as an operating room. A masked and youthful population was already there, making chatter, having a party. "There are so many of you!" Carson exclaimed; he was immensely happy. His pain had already ceased. He was transferred from the trolley to a very narrow, high, padded table. His arms were spread out on wooden extensions and strapped tight to them. His wrists were pricked. Swollen rubber was pressed to his face as if to test the fit. He tried to say, to reassure the masked crew that he was not frightened and to impress them with what a "good guy" he was, that somebody should cancel his appointments for tomorrow.

At a point and place in the fog as it fitfully lifted, the surgeon himself appeared, no longer in a tweed jacket but in a pale-green hospital garment, and now jubilant, bending close. He held up the crooked little finger of one hand before Carson's eyes, which could not focus. "Fat as that," he called through a kind of wind.

"What size should it have been?" Carson asked, knowing they were discussing his appendix.

"No thicker than a pencil," came the answer, tugged by the bright tides of contagious relief.

"But when did you sleep?" Carson asked, and was not answered, having overstepped.

Earlier, he had found himself in an underground room full of stalactites. His name was being shouted by a big gruff youth. "Hey Bob come on Bob wake up give us a little smile that's the boy Bob." There were others besides him stretched out in this catacomb, whose ceiling was festooned with drooping transparent tubes; these were the stalactites. Within an arm's length of him, another man was lying motionless as a limestone knight carved on a tomb. Carson realized that he had been squeezed through a tunnel—the arm straps, the swollen rubber—and had come out the other side. "Hey Bob, come on, give us a smile. *Thaaat's it.*" He had a tremendous need to urinate; liquid was being dripped into his arm.

Later, after the windy, glittering exchange with the surgeon, Carson awoke in an ordinary hospital room. In a bed next to him, a man with a short man's sour, pinched profile was lying and smoking and staring up at a television set. Though the picture flickered, no noise seemed to be coming from the box. "Hi," Carson said, feeling wary, as if in his sleep he had been married to this man.

"Hi," the other said, without taking his eyes from the television set and exhaling smoke with a loudness, simultaneously complacent and fed up, that had been one of Carson's former wife's most irritating mannerisms.

When Carson awoke again, it was twilight, and he was in yet

another room, a private room, alone, with a sore abdomen and a
clearer head. A quarter-moon leaned small and cold in the sky
above the glowing square windows of another wing of the hospital, and his position in the world and the universe seemed
clear enough. His convalescence had begun.

In the five days that followed, he often wondered why he was
so happy. Ever since childhood, after several of his classmates
had been whisked away to hospitals and returned to school with
proud scars on their lower abdomens, Carson had been afraid of
appendicitis. At last, in his sixth decade, the dread enemy had
struck, and he had comported himself, he felt, with passable
courage and calm. His scar was not the little lateral slit his classmates had boasted but a rather gory central incision from navel
down; he had been opened up wide, it was explained to him, on
the premise that at his age his malady might have been anything
from ulcers to cancer. The depth of the gulf that he had, unconscious, floated above thrilled him. There had been, too, a certain
unthinkable intimacy. His bowels had been "handled," the surgeon gently reminded him, in explaining a phase of his recuperation. Carson tried to picture the handling: clamps and white
rubber gloves and something glistening and heavy and purplish
that was his. His appendix indeed had been retrocecal—one of a
mere ten per cent so favored. It had even begun, microscopic in-
vestigation revealed, to rupture. All of this retrospective clarifica-
tion, reducing to facts the burning, undiscouragable demon he
had carried, vindicated Carson. For the sick feel as shamed as
the sinful, as fallen.

The surgeon, with his Ivy League bearing, receded from that
moment of extreme closeness when he bent above Carson's
agony and decided to handle his bowels. He dropped by in the
course of his rounds only for brief tutorial sessions about eating
and walking and going to the bathroom—all things that needed
to be learned again. Others came forward. The slightly amused
dark Slavic woman returned, in her white smock, to change his
dressing, yanking the tapes with an, he felt, unnecessary sharp-
ness. "You were too brave," she admonished him, blaming him
for the night when she had wanted to inflict more blood tests
upon him. The shambling young doctor of that same night returned, no longer in the slightest resembling the lawyer Carson's

daughter had spurned in favor of her own sex, and there appeared a host of specialists in one department of Carson's anatomy or another, so that he felt huge, like Gulliver pegged down in Lilliput. All of them paid their calls so casually and pleasantly that Carson was amazed, months later, to find each visit listed by date and hour on the sheets of hospital services billed to him in computer printout—an old Centronics 739 dot-matrix printer, from the look of it.

Hospital life itself, the details of it, made him happy. The taut white bed had hand controls that lifted and bent the mattress in a number of comforting ways. A television set had been mounted high on the wall opposite him and was obedient to a panel of buttons that nestled in his palm like an innocent, ethereal gun. Effortlessly he flicked his way back and forth among morning news shows, midmorning quiz shows, noon updates, and afternoon soap operas and talk shows and reruns of classics such as Carol Burnett and "Hogan's Heroes." At night, when the visitors left the halls and the hospital settled in upon itself, the television set became an even intenser and warmer companion, with its dancing colors and fluctuant glow. His first evening in this precious room, while he was still groggy from anesthesia, Carson had watched a tiny white figure as if taking a sudden great stitch hit a high-arching home run into the second deck of Yankee Stadium; the penetration of the ball seemed delicious, and to be happening deep within the tiers of himself. He pressed the off button on the little control, used another button to adjust the tilt of his bed, and fell asleep as simply as a child.

Normally, he liked lots of cover; here, a light blanket was enough. Normally, he could never sleep on his back; here, of necessity, he could sleep no other way, his body slightly turned to ease the vertical ache in his abdomen, his left arm at his side receiving all night long the nurturing liquids of the I.V. tube. Lights always burned; voices always murmured in the hall; this world no more rested than the world beyond the sides of an infant's crib. In the depths of the same night when the home run was struck, a touch on his upper right arm woke Carson. He opened his eyes and there, in the quadrant of space where the rectangle of television had been, a queenly young black face smiled down upon him, a nurse taking his blood pressure. She had not switched on the overhead light in his room and so the oval of her face was illumined only indirectly, from afar, as had been the pieces of furniture in his hotel room. Without looking at the luminous dial of his wristwatch on the bedside table he knew this was one of those abysmal hours when despair visits men, when insomniacs writhe in an ocean of silence, when the jobless and the bankrupt want to scream in order to break their circular calculations, when spurned lovers roll from a soft dream onto cold sheets, and soldiers awake to the taste of coming battle. In this hour, she had awakened him with her touch. No more than a thin blanket covered his body in the warm dim room. She pumped up the balloon around his arm, relaxed it, pumped it up again. She put into Carson's mouth one of those rocket-shaped instruments of textured plastic that have come to replace glass thermometers, and while waiting for his temperature to register in electronic numbers on a gadget at her waist she hummed a little tune, as if humorously to disavow her beauty, that beauty which women have now come to regard as an enemy, a burden and cause for harassment placed upon them. He thought of his daughter.

Though many nurses administered to him, and as he strengthened he came to develop small talk with them even at four in the morning, this particular one, her perfectly black and symmetrical face outlined in light like an eclipsed sun, never came again.

"Walk," the surgeon urged Carson. "Get up and walk as soon as you can. Get that body moving. It turns out it wasn't the disease used to kill a lot of people in hospitals, it was lying in bed and letting the lungs fill up with fluid."

Walking meant, at first, pushing the spindly, rattling I.V. pole along with him. There was a certain jaunty knack to it—easing the wheels over the raised metal sills here and there in the linoleum corridor, placing the left hand at the balance point he thought of as the pole's waist, swinging "her" out of the way of another patient promenading with his own gangling chrome partner. From observing other patients Carson learned the trick of removing the I.V. bag and threading it through his bathrobe sleeve and rehanging it, so he could close his bathrobe neatly.

His first steps, in the moss-green sponge slippers the hospital
provided, were timid and brittle, but as the days passed the
length of his walks increased: to the end of the corridor, where
the windows of a waiting room overlooked the distant center of
the city; around the corner past a rarely open snack bar and into
an area of children's diseases; still further to an elevator bank
and a carpeted lounge where pregnant women and young husbands drank Tab and held hands. The attendants at various
desks in the halls came to know him, and to nod as he passed,
with his lengthening stride and more erect posture, his handling
of the I.V. pole soon so expert as to be comically debonair.

His curiosity about the city revived. What he saw from the
window of his own room was merely the wall of another wing of
the hospital, with gift plants on the windowsills and here and
there thoughtful bathrobed figures gazing outward toward the
wall of which his own bathrobed figure was a part. From the
windows of the waiting room, the heart of the city, with its
clump of brown and blue skyscrapers and ribbonlike swirls of
highway, seemed often to be in sunlight while clouds shadowed
the hospital grounds and parking lots and the snarl of taxis always around the entrance. Carson was unable to spot the hotel
where he had stayed, or the industrial district where he had hoped
to sell his systems, or the art museum that contained, he remembered reading, some exemplary Renoirs and a priceless Hieron-
ymus Bosch. He could see at the base of the blue-brown mass of
far buildings a pale-green bridge, and imagined the dirty river it
must cross, and the eighteenth-century fort that had been built
here to hold the river against the Indians, and the nineteenth-
century barge traffic that had fed the settlement and then its
industries, which attracted immigrants, who thrust the grid of
city streets deep into the surrounding farmland. This was still a
region of farmland; thick, slow, patient, pious voices drawled
and twanged around Carson as he stood there gazing outward
and eavesdropping. Laconic phrases of resignation fell into place
amid the standardized furniture and slippered feet and pieces of
jigsaw puzzles half assembled on card tables here. Fat women
in styleless print dresses and low-heeled shoes had been called in
from their kitchens, and in from the fields men with cross-

hatched necks and hands that had the lumpy rounded look of
used tools.

Sickness is a great democrat, and had achieved a colorful cross
section. Carson came to know by sight a lean man with regally
dark Negro skin and taut oriental features; his glossy shaved
head had been split by a Y-shaped gash now held together by
stitches. He sat in a luxurious light brown, almost golden robe,
his wounded head propped by a hand heavy with rings, in the
room with the pregnant women and the silver elevator doors.
When Carson nodded once in cautious greeting, this apparition
said loudly, "Hey, man," as if they shared a surprising secret.
Through the open doorways of the rooms along the corridors,
Carson glimpsed prodigies—men with beaks of white bandage
and plastic tubing, like those drinking birds many fads ago; old
ladies shrivelling to nothing in a forest of flowers and giant face-
tious get-well cards; an immensely plump mocha-colored woman
wearing silk pantaloons and a scarlet Hindu dot in the center of
her forehead. She entertained streams of visitors, thin dusky delicate men and great-eyed children; like Carson, she was an hon-
orary member of the city, and she would acknowledge his passing with a languid lifting of her fat fingers, tapered as decidedly
as cones.

On the third day, Carson was put on solid food and discon-
nected from the intravenous tubing. With his faithful, docile
pole removed from the room, he was free to wave both arms and
to climb stairs. His surgeon at his last appearance (dressed in
lumberjack shirt and chinos, about to "take off," for it had become the weekend) had urged stair climbing upon his patient as
the best possible exercise. There was, at the end of the corridor
in the other direction from the waiting room, from whose windows the heart of the city could be viewed, an exit giving on a
cement-and-steel staircase almost never used. Here, down four
flights to the basement, then up six to the locked rooftop door,
and back down two to his own floor, Carson obediently trod in
his bathrobe and by now disintegrating green sponge slippers.

His happiness was most intense out here, in this deserted and
echoing sector, where he was invisible and anonymous. In his
room, the telephone had begun to ring. The head of his com-

pany back in New Jersey called repeatedly, at first to commiserate and then to engineer a way in which Carson's missed appointments could be patched without the expense of an additional trip. So Carson, sitting up in his adaptable mattress, placed calls to the appropriate personnel and gave an enfeebled version of his pitch; the white-noise company expressed keen interest in digital color-graphics imaging, and Carson mailed them his firm's shiny brochure on its newest system (resolutions to 640 pixels per line, 65,536 simultaneous colors, image memory up to 256K bytes). The secretary from the other company, who had sounded sympathetic on the phone so long ago, showed up in person; she turned out to be somewhat younger than her voice, and comely in a coarse way, with bleached frizzed hair, the remnant of a swimming-pool tan, and active legs she kept crossing and recrossing as she described her own divorce—the money, the children, the return to work after years of being a pampered suburbanite. "I could be one again, let me tell you. These women singing the joys of being in the work force, they can *have* it." This woman smoked a great deal, exhaling noisily and crushing each cerise-stained butt into a jar lid she had brought in her pocketbook, knowing the hospital discouraged smoking and provided no ashtrays. Carson had planned his afternoon in careful half-hour blocks—the staircase, thrice up and down; a visit to the waiting room, where he had begun to work on one of the jigsaw puzzles; a visit to his bathroom if his handled bowels were willing; finally, a luxurious immersion in a week-old *Newsweek* and the late innings of this Saturday's playoff game. His visitor crushed these plans along with her many cigarettes. Then his own ex-wife telephoned, kittenish the way she had become, remarried yet something plaintive still shining through, and with a note of mockery in her voice, as if descending into a strange city with a bursting appendix was, like his leaving her and ceasing to teach mathematics, one more willful folly. His son called collect from Mexico the next day, sounding ominously close at hand, and spacey, as long awkward silences between father and son ate up the dollars. His daughter never called, which seemed considerate of her. She and Carson knew there was no disguising our solitude.

He found that after an hour in his room and bed he became

homesick for the stairs. At first, all the flights had seemed identical, but now he had discovered subtle differences among them—old evidence of spilled paint on one set of treads, a set of numbers chalked by a workman on the wall of one landing, water stains and cracks affecting one stretch of rough yellow plaster and not another. At the bottom, there were plastic trash cans and a red door heavily marked with warnings to push the crash bar only in case of emergency; at the top, a plain steel door, without handle or window, defied penetration. The doors at the landings in between each gave on a strange outdoor space, a kind of platform hung outside the door leading into the hospital proper; pre-poured cement grids prevented leaping or falling or a clear outlook but admitted cool fresh air and allowed a fractional view of the city below. The neightborhood here was flat and plain—quarter-acre-lot tract houses built long enough ago for the bloom of newness to have wilted and dilapidation to be setting in. The hospital wall, extending beyond the projecting staircase, blocked all but a slice of downward vision containing some threadbare front yards, one of them with a tricycle on its side and another with a painted statue of the Virgin, and walls of pastel siding in need of repainting, and stretches of low-pitched composition-shingled roof—a shabby small-town vista here evidently well within the city limits. He never saw a person walking on the broad sidewalks, and few cars moved along the street even at homecoming hour. Nearest and most vivid, a heap of worn planking and rusting scaffold pipes, and a dumpster coated with white dust and loaded with plaster and lathing, testified to a new phase of construction as the hospital continued to expand. Young men sometimes came and added to the rubbish, or loudly threw the planking around. These efforts seemed unorganized, and ceased on the weekend.

Drab housing and assembled rubble, what he saw through the grid of the cement barrier that permitted no broad view nevertheless seemed to Carson brilliantly real, moist and deep-toned and full. When he had first come to this landing—still unable to climb stairs, the I.V. pole at his side—just shoving open the door had been an effort, and the raw true outdoor air had raked through his still drugged system like a sweeping rough kiss, early fall air mixing football and baseball, stiff with cold yet damp and not quite purged of growth. Once he heard the distant agitation of a lawnmower. Until the morning he was released, he would come here even in the dark and lean his forehead against the cement and breathe, trying to take again into himself the miracle of the world, programming himself, as it were, to live—the air cool on his bare ankles, his bowels resettling around the ache of their healing.

The taxi took him straight to the airport; he saw nothing of the city but the silhouettes beside the highway and the highway's scarred center strip. For an instant from the air a kind of map spread itself underneath him, and was gone. Yet afterward, thinking back upon the farm voices, the far-off skyscrapers, the night visits of the nurses, the doctors with their unseen, unsullied homes, the dozens of faces risen like bubbles to the surface of his pain, it seemed he had come to know the city intimately; it was like, on other of his trips, those women who, encountered in bars and paid at the end, turned ceremony inside out, and bestowed themselves without his knowing their name.

# WHEN THE LORD CALLS

## GLORIA NORRIS

Gloria Norris was born and grew up in Holcomb, a small town in northern Mississippi. She graduated *magna cum laude* from the University of Southern Mississippi and received a master's degree from Ohio State University. She has worked as a writer and editor in Chicago, New Orleans, and New York and is now a publishing executive. "When the Lord Calls" is the first of a trilogy of stories she is writing. The second, "Revive Us Again," will also appear in the *Sewanee Review.*

When the Lord calls you—BAM—it comes like a bolt out of the blue. I was winding up that guest pastorate down in south Mississippi, and the wife was serving us nothing but buttermilk and cornbread on what the congregation was still giving when He looked down and decided He would help. I wasn't expecting that letter one bit when I went down to the little store that has the post office at the back behind a little wire-mesh booth. I only went every other day because old Jackson behind the counter would every time ask me when was I paying up what I owed him—imagine that, after all I'd did for this town. And believe me, I'm just one lone preacher, not a whole tribe like that Angel Martinez that needs a whole bus to haul around his group. Do you know that Angel takes around one feller that does nothing but play a trumpet number to inspire the congregation before Angel gets up to preach? No, I'm just serving God alone. But He picked me for His call, although I am short and fat and all that's left of my hair is a band of gray running around a bare round bulb of a scalp shiny as a china doorknob.

Copyright © 1982 by Gloria Norris. First appeared in the *Sewanee Review,* Vol. 90, No. 1 (Winter 1982). Reprinted by permission.

"I guess it's a good thing the other feller put the stamp on this letter for you," says old Jackson, sourpussing through the mesh window. "You'd of asked me to put the three cents on your bill too."

"God loves the cheerful giver, Brother Jackson. It's all in the hands of the congregation to pay their minister." And I took my letter and walked out slow, not letting his glare hurry me. I doubt his salvation very much.

I open up the letter and this Mr. Harvey Giles is writing Would I come up to a place called Alcoma to hold their meeting the very next day. "We've heard a lot about you and are real anxious to hear your message, which we hear has inspired so many and call collect because we need you right away." I wonder how in the world they heard about me when I ain't even heard of that town. But he put in only two dollars for traveling. He must have thought I had wings and was going to fly; the two dollars was for a place to piss on the way. So I tuck the letter in my pocket and don't know that I would go.

Then the Lord hit me with another sign. I was walking along that hot street, when one of the church deacons, Lamson, he's got the Chevrolet agency, new and used cars, comes out of the bank and grabs my arm. "Brother Benson, looks like you just about wore out that Ford car of yours."

I laugh and say: "Yes, the Lord has put some mileage on that old car."

He says: "Well, I got a nice little used Chevy down on my lot, just about 50,000 miles on it, and I tell you what, you drive your old one in today and drive that one out, and I'll take care of the difference."

I couldn't believe it. You couldn't get five dollars for my old car, a 1932 sedan, seventeen years old. When I start to tell him what a man of the Lord he is, he cuts me off. "No, it's not anything like what you deserve because you have done more than any man I've known in my fifty years to bring Jesus alive and walking the streets of this town. You come on down and get your car." Now I never realized it but he's a man that's really got Jesus in his heart. My old car had a carburetor that's about to go, tires wore down thin as a dime, and the lights and back doors not either one working.

So I come in home at the guest parsonage, knowing now I would go; I've already called them and I got this shiny black Chevy, and I tell the wife to get the kids packing, the Lord's called me to north Missippi.

Then she acts up the way she did. She starts pulling her hair and turning all colors. I don't know what started her off. Everywhere we've lived they say she's a good preacher's wife, never raises her voice. But she screams out at me in the kitchen. "*Why you need to drag us off again? You don't need us when you got all the deacons' wives and their innocent little daughters to run after and lick over like a dog. You don't need me when you got the choir soprano to take in the back of the church every afternoon.*"

"What's the matter with you?" I said. "Have you ever known me to turn my back when the Lord calls me? Here they've heard about me and need me to come hold their meeting. You expect me to say no?"

"Oh the *Lord* calls you," she commences to scream. I don't know to this day what got into her. Maybe the female change starting. She rolls her head back with her eyes squeezed shut and the neck veins all popped out. "*The Lord calls you to save the soul of every little gal that's got hot pants.*"

I slapped her then. She was insulting the Lord's call in me. I figured she would shut up in a little while, but she went on all night crying.

The next morning I go in the kitchen where she's getting breakfast all red-eyed and quiet as a beat horse and I say brisk, pretending I've overlooked her acting up: "I'm ready to go serve my Master, are you?"

Well, she commences screaming again and throwing things at me. The upshot is that around ten o'clock I'm in the black Chevy with my black suit and two dress shirts driving up the highway alone. And after I done nothing but be a good husband for twenty-eight years, she's gone off to her mother's with the five kids and left me. I was so riled I was driving too fast. I says as I barrel over those red-clay hills We'll just see who will crawl back. We'll just see. It sure won't be me that does the crawling, I got the Lord's work to do and I can't stop for any woman's devilment.

Whoo-wee, it was a hot trip; by noon I was getting mighty hot. But I didn't stop even for a cool drink of water, just kept going up the blistering highway over the red-clay hills with their longleaf pine, sweating like I'm plowing a mule in that August heat.

I hadn't got far when I realize that Lamson's car give off too much heat. It ran okay but it give off more heat than any car I ever saw. And when you carry around a little weight like I do, you suffer with the heat. I passed through Jackson around two, but I still didn't let myself stop.

By four-thirty I hit Grenada and pull in at a City Service station to get seventy-five cents' worth of gas. I figured that would get me there and I would get the rest of my gas free from Giles. I drink two Co-Colas and a Orange Crush and feel a little better, but I hustle on to get on the back roads to Alcoma, cause you don't get on those after dark without getting lost.

It was around five-thirty I set to wondering was I on the right road. I was bumping slow down a old gravel hill road, winding around so you meet yourself coming back, the dust pouring out behind me. Lucky I met a old man walking down the road.

"Howdy, I'm Brother Benson and I'm on my way to Alcoma to preach the Baptist revival, am I going the right way?"

He looks at me like I just broke out of the penitentiary. It's like pulling teeth but I drag out of him that I'm totally out of my way. I have to go back several miles, turn at a mailbox that says Brown, go to a forked oak tree and turn right, go on for two or three miles, past a negro church and several miles more I'll hit the road that'll take me on into Alcoma.

Just past that mailbox I feel it. *Thump, thump, thump.* I brake it easy but the car nearbout pulled off into the ditch. I barely rassled it back. It was the right front tire, flat as a pancake, and not a soul in sight when the dust died down in that sun that was still beating down so it could fry your brains.

I jacked the front up and rassled the old bolts off and just about got the spare on when a colored boy come along, walking barefoot in the dust. I stand back and wipe my face while he finished it up. He says: "You ain't gone use that tire again." Says: "It wadn't nothin' but a recap tire anyway. Like the rest of um you got. You not gone run long on any of them."

That Lamson never told me the car had recaps. I could have taken the tires on my old car; they were better. Now how in the world am I gonna buy tires, the prices they are nowadays? I wonder about that Lamson's salvation.

When I get back in, I'm so wore out and fried down that I almost forget to thank the boy, but I say I'll pray for you, son, and he says Yassuh. Looking after me like he expected to get paid for that little bit of work.

Then the road gets narrower and hardly any gravel left on it, the yellow bitterweeds growing up from the side ditches and leaning in to slap the sides of the car like a curtain parting and then around a bend and up a hill and I'm to the Alcoma Baptist Church.

What there is of it. I get out and look at it, old and leaning in like it might collapse any minute, set up on high concrete triangles. And bitterweed growing right up and around the church steps like nobody set foot there for years. Out back in the cemetery they'd growed wild and high as your thigh.

I come all this way while she ran off to her mother's, and this is what I come for. I will be lucky to get my eats. I sit on the steps mopping my head. It's just a couple of miles up the road to Alcoma and Giles' house where no doubt they'll have some ice tea for me and I can get cooled off, but right then I can't go on. I was wrung out like a dishrag.

But the Lord gave me a third sign. He took pity on this sick and weary pilgrim. I watched the sun setting down behind the treetops, slanting through gold in the trees He made, turning them gold on top over the green, the trees making a long shade now, creating a cool spot on the earth for His creatures. God shows Hisself in shade trees. And His exaltation filled my weary heart. I know He is here watching over me. I praise Him for His being. Without which this mortal life of pain would be worse than nothing. I praise Him and He fills me with joy in my heart. Everything else drops away—her and being wore out and the heat and the recaps and the disappointment of Alcoma Baptist Church—it is all nothing. I feel it just the way I felt when He first came into my heart. The whole world dropped away and I cried to the rafters *God lives, Jesus is my Savior, lucky me.*

After that came a call stronger, frightening, but impossible to

deny. I was bald since I was twenty-five and I carry around a lot
of weight and most women can look over the top of my head.
But He chose me. It's me that brings the light to them. They must
listen to me. Yes, she must put away her personal feelings about
the choir soprano and, yes, I will admit it was not always singing we were doing in the back of the church, but she is flaunting
God not to realize that in sum I am doing His will. And it's not
just her; there are those in the church that are misguided, that
cannot heed the light I bring them. I must gird myself and force
God's light on them. It cannot be like this all the time. Many
times I must force myself to preach, not feeling it, but must
force the words out, carrying on His work blindly, as the mule
must plow for his master, to the end of the row till he says stop.
But I have faith He sees into my heart and when I have reached
my limit, He gives me exaltation, so I can go on with His work.

So when I got back in the car, I swear I will show her I am on
God's bidness. Who knows, I might prize some money out of
these cheap farmers and make them build a new Alcoma brick
church, with me as permanent minister. And no fooling this
week with any choir soprano, I promise her.

It was like a confirmation after I drove on through Alcoma's
one street of stores facing the railroad track and got to Giles' big
brick house at the edge of town. Had nearbout a acre of yard in
front and another acre in back. And that back was just lined up
like a John Deere army with shiny new green tractors and
seeders and discers. His garage had a pickup and a big blue
Buick for the wife. And he's the man that's the head deacon of
that old rundown church.

Giles hisself comes to the door. He's a red-faced man, short
and big-bellied. "Well," he says, "we been expecting you since
five o'clock, Brother."

"Well," I says smiling and sticking out my hand, "I didn't have
anybody but the Lord to help me get here. How are *you*, dear
lady," I says to Mrs. Giles, a little thin lady in a flowered dress
hurrying up to greet me.

"Welcome, welcome," she says, making up for Giles. "We're
just so thrilled to have you. Why, where's Mrs. Benson and your
childrun? We were expecting them too."

"Oh, her dear mother," I say quick, "was taken sick sudden. She had to go nurse her mother; she was heartbroken at not getting to come."

She runs off to the kitchen to get me that ice tea and Giles and I sit down in his big living room.

He says several polite things about how happy they are to have me and it was him that insisted they bring me up.

But I let him know I'm not any deacon's preacher. I tell him I was expecting a church in much better repair. I tell him about those bitterweeds needing mowing first thing in the morning. And I say seems like there's a lot of reviving to be done here.

Mrs. Giles comes in with my tea, but it's no time to relax. I say we should start off by praying.

They bow their heads and I pray, finishing up ". . . and let those that have no obligation to You be brought into Thy fold, and let those that already *have* a obligation *see* it. Amen."

Giles' face looks redder when he raises his head and says to Mrs. Giles, "Hadn't you better go see about supper?" "I sure *had*," she says, jumps up, her flowered dress sailing behind her. "I sure hope Brother Benson likes oven-smothered pork chops," she calls, smiling back at me.

"There's nothing I'd rather eat," I say, "short of heavenly manna."

Giles looks so mad, I better back down. "Now," I say reasonable, "I'm sure you deserve a lot of credit just for holding this old church together. You must have a idea of who in the community we should see, who we should concentrate on bringing into the church and who has backslid as well."

He names off some, and I listen close. "Well, that sounds like a good start. But I have often found that the action of one man is what gets a good revival started. Is there one man in a *position* to start the revival off big?" I ask, naturally meaning him, he could give five hundred dollars if he would.

"Yes," Giles says, "there is. A old high-school buddy of mine, a well-to-do drunkard."

I decide right then not to wear myself out on Giles. You'd do as well to get up a running start and butt your head into his brick house as to make him see the light. I passed on to this drunkard.

"Was he a Baptist before he fell away?" I ask.

"No, he's Presbyterian. But they give up on him years ago."

"Is that right? No one at all concerned about his soul. You won't find that among us."

"I've been right concerned about him," Giles says. "Went to school with him. His daddy was the druggist here and his mama was from a fine family. Gene Paul has the drugstore building and a big piece of land alongside the railroad he could sell any day for a big price. But he don't care about nothing. Been drinking for thirty years. I wouldn't be surprised if he was to be found dead any morning. It gets you to worrying about your duty when you see somebody that was a school friend walking around in danger of Hellfire."

"Well," I says slow, like I might, and I might not, agree with him. "It would be the thing for us to visit him. It's more than one drunkard I've been graced to bring to God. And sounds like he would be a good addition to the church as far as its cash needs go."

Giles clears his throat. "About your pay, Brother Benson, there's a lot of members who aren't able to give much . . . We'll have to see how much we can give you when we see how much collection we get during the revival."

Uh-oh. I been waiting for this. They all want salvation but they want it cheap. I would preach for nothing but I got a family to think about. And now some tires too.

"That's between you and your conscience. But I normally get three fourths of the week's collection and a guarantee of one hundred dollars."

He turns it off as best he can. But after supper we talk some more and settle it: if I can get this drunkard in the church I'll get two hundred and fifty dollars. If I don't I will only get seventy-five dollars. But he knows hisself that is so little that I make him tag onto it that either way he'll throw in a set of tires from all those he's got laying around in his backyard.

I have rarely preached better. Right that first night when I stepped up to the pulpit a charge went through me. That very night a bunch that had been away from God yielded and came down to the altar and received Him through me. The next night a bigger crowd, and people joining right and left. The third night the church was about to bust with the crowd and Giles was counting that collecting plate. I was filled with joy, His power running through me. I even told Giles I could get this drunkard if only he would produce him.

He was downright apologetic because he couldn't get hold of him for me to visit for three straight days. Finally he come rushing in and says Gene Paul promised to see us this afternoon around three after I've taken dinner with one of the church families. And that's when this durn little Rachel got in to mess me up.

I was taking dinner with one of the deacons that's got a farm a few miles north in the reddest, poorest hills, not much to be got out of without breaking your back. Johnson's a good man, one you can count on to do his share in the church, however little his tithe may amount to, and I was glad to partake of their Christian companionship before taking on the drunkard.

We were sitting in the front room while his wife worked on the dinner, me and Johnson and his married daughter and her young husband that lived with them. They all praised my preaching and then a young girl with long black hair come in.

"Brother Benson, this is my baby girl Rachel," Johnson says. "She's the apple of her daddy's eye."

I noticed her the night before out in the congregation. Short skirts and knees pointing opposite directions, a little devil's workshop.

Seeing her up close, she is pretty as a movie star—white skin and long black hair and big brown eyes with long, curly lashes like a doll's. She's thirteen, fourteen, just turning into a woman. Her arms still slender like a little girl's and her face still has baby fat in the cheeks. But her body is all swollen out in the breasts and hips and behind like a grown woman's. Naturally she's in between, don't know what to make of her body changing and consequently acts like she's mad at the whole world, looking at me with this little frown and her lips poked out pouting. But I know what she's waiting for if she don't.

I take her hand and say: "Honey, I can see you've got Jesus in your heart just by your pretty brown eyes."

Her married sister, over to one side, cuts in: "We hadn't noticed Jesus in her that much ourselves."

The girl cuts *her* eyes around furious at her daddy and he
shifts around and looks at the young husband, Alvin. He turns
red like he just swallowed a whole chili pepper.

Johnson swallows his big red Adam's apple. "Preacher, we got
. . . uh . . . a problem in our family, and I reckon we *need*
some counsel from a man of God—"

Right then Johnson's wife rushes in—she's still holding a bowl
of hot rice straight from the kitchen—shouting "It's all on the
table now, y'all come and eat, *come and eat!*", hustling the two
gals to the table and smiling big at me and when she gets near
her husband she hisses: "*You keep your big mouth shut, don't go
telling one word of that.*"

Well, I'm used to wrought-up situations, called upon as I am
to counsel the dying and troubled, so I didn't let it worry me.
The two girls sit on opposite sides of the table looking away
from each other so there's no chance of one having to use the
same eyespace as the other. They push their food around, not
even pretending to take a bite. I sit alongside Rachel, Betty sits
by Alvin, and the Johnsons at each end.

Everybody stays quiet as the dead except Mrs. Johnson who
keeps passing me things and saying "Now do try some of my
peach pickles, Brother Benson," and "We sure would be grateful
for some rain." Old Johnson is bending over his plate eating like
a horse.

The young husband across of me is a big strapping fellow,
two heads taller than me, big wide shoulders and hips skinny as
a fencepost. Slate-blue eyes and light-brown hair in little curls
that dips down on his forehead. A fine figure of a man to the
ladies no doubt. But he hadn't got nothing to say for hisself. I
could talk circles around him.

I carry on with Mrs. Johnson like nothing is wrong. I'll be
glad to give my help, but meanwhile I'll enjoy my dinner. It was
fried chicken and some right good gravy for the rice and biscuits, nice and hot, and tomatoes and greens just picked that
morning from the garden.

We hadn't got all the way to dessert, I was just on my second helpings, when Rachel busts it up. She jumps up with tears in her big brown doll's eyes and shouts, "Oh, Daddy, I love him, I *love* him!"

Betty jumps up and shouts back, "But he's *my* husband and if you ever do again what you did yesterday out by the woodpile I'll snatch you baldheaded!"

Rachel runs acrying to the bedroom and Betty skitters out to the kitchen, her eyes boiling with tears.

It's Mrs. Johnson I feel sorriest for. She'd rather her house burn down as for scandal to come out before the visiting preacher. She looks at me like a drowning person. Old Johnson glares at Alvin like he's ready to shoot him for meddling around with his baby girl.

I'm not going to get that dessert. I sit Johnson back down and ask him what happened at the woodpile.

"Maybe it's my fault, Brother Benson; I won't let Rachel go out yet with boys. I can't see any of them being good enough for her."

"I see, and she's bucking against that?" The more he stammers out, the more I say Oh, brother, it sure is your fault. Old Johnson won't let Rachel even go to church with a boy. So what does that leave for a young girl, discovering herself, but look around at home? And she sees this big handsome older man that pets her and teases her and generally acts like she is God's gift to the world, just like her mama and daddy do.

And she's no doubt caught sight of him kissing Betty in the kitchen when he pretends to go get something, and seen those sick-calf looks he gives his wife those nights when he says he's so tired he's going to bed early and asks does she want to too. And no doubt she and this Betty have always fought over things like sisters do and Rachel can't stand the idea of her sister having something she don't.

Rachel had been trailing Alvin, giggling at little private things they talk about. The day before, when Rachel came home from school, she shoots out to the woodpile where Alvin's got his shirt off chopping wood. She worms closer and closer, him with his muscles rippling over his chest while he chops. All of a sudden she grabs him around the neck and kisses him right on the lips.

I can bet what this Alvin would of done next, but Betty is

looking out the kitchen window. She screams like a rattler bit
her and hollers her mother out in the yard and the whole house
has been screaming and crying ever since.

"We don't know what to do," says Johnson, patting his wife
that's crying into a dishtowel. "I can't turn my daughter and her
husband out. But I'm not going to see Rachel unhappy or taken
advantage of."

"You're lucky," I says, "because I've run into just this situation
before, and I appreciate all sides of it. You leave it to me to talk
to Rachel."

I go back to her bedroom and ease the door open. She looks
up from the bed she's crying on, her eyes spitting fire, her long
black hair tumbling all over her breasts. When I sit down and
scold her a little, Miss Spitfire comes right back.

"I don't care what you say, I love him," she sasses me and
tosses that hair back from her breasts all heaving up.

"But does *he* love you?" I cut back. Her lips goes to trembling
and she crumples up. I know how to handle these little gals.

"Now you're not only in the wrong coveting your dear sister's
husband, but you're embarrassing yourself as a woman running
after a man that don't care about you."

Rachel fires her eyes. Oh, I can't help but feel a urge.

"I don't have to listen to you," she snaps at me. Now ninety-
nine percent of the people you let me talk to them two minutes,
and they'll be respecting me and Yes, Preachering. This little
Rachel could use a lesson.

I close my eyes and pray loud: "Lord, help this little girl to
see she is putting herself in danger of Hellfire."

I move over and sit by her on the bed and take her hand. I
talk to her soft about how God loves her even though she's
doing wrong. She lets me hold her hand but looks down at the
pillow. I can see the curliness of her long dark eyelashes against
that soft baby-fat cheek and the swell of her blouse and Lord-
amercy my breathing sounds loud in this little gal's bedroom.
Just then Johnson barges in, looking at me hard on the bed.

"Rachel and I are having a good talk, Brother Johnson," I
says. "I believe she's feeling sorry for what she done."

"Is that right, honey?" says Johnson squatting down, patting
his old work-calloused hand on her little soft white one.

"It's him talking, not me," she shrills out. "I didn't ask him to come meddling around."

I wait for Johnson to bring this little gal in line for talking disrespectful to the preacher, but he's spoiled her rotten. He just herds me right out of there. But Mrs. Johnson is apologizing all the way out the door, and I say "I just hope I helped *some*" before Johnson thanks me too. I drive back to Alcoma and all the way this little gal's got me thinking what I shouldn't. Oh the devil can hide in the prettiest little face.

Giles drives me over to the drunkard's in his big Buick, him in fresh work clothes he's put on for the visit and me still in my morning tie and carrying my Bible. We bounce up this dirt road that goes by a closed-up big two-story house to a old cookhouse at the back. Gene Paul is sitting on the porch tilted back in a cane chair, a shriveled drunk's face he has and a big shock of white hair. I could see that face behind a bank president's desk; he was born to wealth.

Coming up the walk with Giles I boom out: "I've come to bring you the Lord's word, Mr. Wescott."

"*Prescott*," hisses Giles.

Well, that was the way it went. My mind couldn't focus on this Wescott-Prescott. It was wandering off to eyelashes just when I should be focusing on him.

This drunkard looks like he's already had a drink for the day. He looks sly at Giles.

"So you're running the Baptist Church, Harvey. I bet you got it all down on your books as a tax deduction."

Harvey looks like he spit on his mother. "You can say what you like to me, Gene Paul. The fact is, I done brought this preacher to see you out of concern."

I open up my Bible and pretend like it just fell to the place where I'm reading from. "Here is a message I didn't select, but God selected for you. *And the day shall come when he shall separate the lambs from the goats, the lambs on one side, the goats on the other.* I don't want you to do nothing right now, Mr. Wescott, I just want you to give us a chanct by joining us tonight for some Christian companionship. Open yourself up and let God Hisself speak to your heart.

"Nobody cares for you like God, and you're shutting Him

out," I says. "And He loves you better than a mother." Wescott
sits back and tears all of a sudden swell in his red drunk's eyes.
If I hadn't had that durn little Rachel on my mind, I would have
talked mother more—maybe he's lost his recent. But I close off
too fast. "Won't you just come tonight?"

He don't say he will or won't, and when we are bouncing back
out in the Buick Giles says sharp: "Well, I guess *that* was a waste
of time. I don't know about giving you those tires after all."

"You just aren't trusting enough in the Lord," I snap back. But
I was feeling as low as ever I have. My mind wandered from
His task after all those signs.

Gene Paul doesn't show up that night. But afterward old
Johnson asks me if I'll come out the next afternoon to see
Rachel. She's setting in her room and won't touch a bite to eat.
Oh, I know these tricks. I tell him I got too much of the Lord's
work to do. But the next afternoon when I'm preparing in my
room at Giles' for the last night of the meeting and one last
blowout sermon, praying Gene Paul shows up, I keep thinking
on that little gal. Like somebody else is inside me, I get up and
go to my car and drive out to Johnson's.

The pa and ma greet me like I'm their long lost son and take
me right to Miss Rachel's bedroom. I tap on the door and call
out sweet: "It's Brother Benson, can I come in?"

"No. I told you the other day I don't want your meddling."

"Well, I'll just step in anyway, because your mama and daddy
are worried sick and somebody's got to talk to you."

I close the door on Johnson's face. She's sitting in a green chenille bathrobe in the middle of her bed, a pout on her pretty
lips, black hair hanging long and loose.

"Your mama's worried you not eating."

"Not going to eat. I'm going to run away."

"All by yourself?"

"No. None of your business."

"You not running away with your own sister's husband?"

She shoots me a look like she could sizzle me in a frying pan
and pour me out to the dogs. "I will if I want to."

"You mean he's told you he'll run away with you?" I say real
soft and understanding. If he has, she won't tell me.

"You leave me alone!" She throws herself on the pillow and

busts out crying. So I know Alvin is innocent, all the mooning's on her side alone. I feel sorry for the poor man, his wife mad as hell at him.

I put my hand on her back and she don't move it. Lord-amercy, it's been a long time since I've had my hand on such a pretty girl.

I am getting hot as a pistol. I don't know what I'm doing but I know I got to get us out of there. "Now Rachel, I'm going to leave and let you get dressed and I'm going to drive you into church myself. The Lord may show you the error of your ways there."

"I'm not going anywhere," she sobs.

"I'll just put a nice hot sandwich in my car and you eat it while I drive you in and we'll talk on the way about how you're grieving the Lord mooning after your sister's husband."

Her sobs slow down. I know these little gals—they can't go without more than three meals. I can feel her thinking this would be a good way to eat without losing face in front of Betty and still keep her ma and pa and Alvin all worrying about her.

I don't even wait for a reply. "She'll be out soon and ride into church with me," I tell Mr. and Mrs. Johnson. And sure enough she comes out dressed. But going out the door she shoots this at me: "Daddy, I guess you don't care if I ride by myself with the preacher. He's too old and ugly for even you to worry about."

She oughtn't to said that last. It makes me so mad I lose what judgment I have left. I got to have her, no matter my promise to the wife. She eats up that sandwich like a hungry dog and driving along I eye those little roads that run off to nothing but a cow pasture all along the winding hill road.

"Rachel, tell me, is Alvin the only man you're sweet on?"

She looks furious out at those dark little roads to nowhere we're passing.

"I bet there's lots of cute boys in your class at school. Bet they're all sweet on a pretty little gal like you. Idn't there one of them you like too?"

"They're all wormy sapsuckers."

I can't help busting out laughing. This Rachel may be only thirteen years old but she is already some woman. I can see

those poor wormy sapsuckers, all of them too green to know
how to treat this beauty of beauties that keeps them all squeezing their pants under their desks and blushing and acting like
young goats, too dumb to know how to treat a woman. Let me
show you how this old and ugly man can talk to make a woman
hot.

"Rachel, you are just on your way to becoming a beautiful
woman, but you're not there yet. Let Brother Benson tell you
what he knows you do at night."

"I go to sleep."

"But not before you take off your clothes and look in the mirror at that pretty body naked. That's natural for a little girl
that's going to grow up and be a beautiful woman, one that
makes men sick just to sidle up to her."

She looks over at me, interested. How did I know that? "And
sometimes you touch yourself, on your breasts and elsewhere because they are so new to you, and you like to make those little
shocks go through you."

"What kind of preacher are you?" Rachel asks, but her voice
ain't mad anymore. She is awed.

"I know what you think about at night. When you're lying
there touching yourself. And I know you want to go dancing
with boys, but we Baptists don't hold with that."

"I don't see no harm in it," she says, still awed. "A lot of girls
do."

"Why, Rachel, if you was to dance with a boy, your breasts—
excuse me for using the word, but I'm speaking as your minister
—your breasts would rub up against that boy and excite him.
And you would want to rub some more and some more. Idn't
that what you think about every night?"

"O Lord," she screams, "I can't stand it, I can't stand it, kiss
me, I want a man to kiss me."

She set me on fire. I reached over with the car still going over
those hills and I set my hand right under her dress between her
white thighs and squeezed like the whole world was there.

She screams and throws herself against me, throwing her arms
around my neck and kissing me, and the car is already slipping
on the shoulder. "Get off," I squeal, "get off—I can't see!" but it
is too late. I rassle the car all the way down to the bottom of the

ditch where it rams against the gully wall and throws me against the wheel like my lungs was knocked out. And I jump out of the car and it hits me what folly I've done.

She busts out of the car and charges over to me. "Oh, you dirty old man. You reached under my dress," she squeals out.

"What are you talking about?" I said. "You are lucky it was me you met tonight instead of some other man. A man of God that could ease you natural but in God's way."

"You dirty old man! I'm going to tell my daddy on you!"

Whatever heat I had wilts right inside me. This is one of the worse situations I been in. I cain't even jump in my car, stuck in the bottom of a gully, and hightail it out of Alcoma and north Missippi.

"My daddy's gonna get you!" She's crying and scrabbling up the gully bank to get up on the road. I grab her arm and try to pull her back.

"Don't you know *you're* the temptation!" I scream out desperate. "You're a vessel of the devil, girl, with your skirts raked up and your pouting lips." She kicks backward and hits me in the stomach, and I feel like heaving, but I hold on. I can already feel that Johnson's buckshot in my belly.

"You got to see you are a creature in *sin*. You are lucky it was me you met. I can show you you are disgusting in God's sight, and that you must repent."

She jumps almost to the top of the gully, but slips back down the side and falls on her knees, wore out and her head drooping. I clamp my hand on her head, desperate and talking automatic: "O Lord, show this little girl that she must learn what it is to be a godly woman. Show her You gave her natural desires, as You did to us weak men, but she must learn to express them in a way pleasing to You."

She lets out a scream: "O Jesus, I want Your holiness. Make what You will of me!"

My heart surges out. I can't believe I am being graced so easy. She has felt God's power and grace. And, yes, He has given it to me. My flesh is weak like other men's, I was tempted. If it just happened a little different I'd be the one kneeling on the ground begging God to forgive the old Adam in me.

"O holy Jesus," she cries out, "wash me white as snow, it's You I love."

I have seen this before, a little gal just full of womanhood coming on, and the right minister turning it into the proper love of Jesus. Sometimes the gal backslides right away, but I believe I've turned this spitfire for life. It's me she'll remember, not Alvin. She wears herself down crying and thanks me, wiping away her tears, for showing her God's truth. Then she gets down with me in the ditch—she's a real strong little girl—and we push that car right back onto the road.

Well, it seems like my night. Just like I knew in my heart he would, this drunkard Wescott sashays right into church. I preach hard, giving 'em my man dead in Tennessee and all I got, and I get him right up at the final invitational hymn, *Just As I Am*, but something happened and in all the crush of folks coming down to devote their lives to Jesus as I've revealed Him, Gene Paul slips away. A lost soul. I saw Giles looking all around for him and I figured he was going to try to weasel on even the seventy-five dollars and the tires, but I kept on smiling and blessing them all, including Rachel who was kissing Betty and still looking pretty as a doll, and old Johnson thanking me and saying is there anything I can do for you, and I think fast and say "Yes, I need some tires bad," and he says "You got 'em." So the next morning I left Alcoma with my new tires knowing the revival didn't come out just like I wanted, but I didn't feel bad over it because you learn that's just the way revivals are, sometimes they lift you up, and sometimes you just have to take them as they come. *Amen.*

# MY LIFE AS A WEST AFRICAN GRAY PARROT

Leigh Buchanan Bienen is a criminal defense attorney and advocate for women. She has written books and articles on the law, and her fiction has appeared in *Panache, The Mississippi Review, US 1 Anthology,* and *The Ontario Review.* She lives in Princeton, New Jersey, with her husband and three daughters and is completing a novel.

## I

The dark, I am in the dark. They have put the green cloth over my cage. I am in the dark once again. I smell the acrid felt. I smell the green of transitions, the particles of dust in the warp of the fabric which remind me of forests and terror. I am in the dark. I shall never fly again. Even my masterful imitation of the electric pencil sharpener will not pierce the dark. My master and mistress are talking in the corridor. "That will shut it up," she says, knocking the aluminum pan against the porcelain sink and causing me, as she knows, pain.

My cage sits on a squat wooden table in a room facing the kitchen. The smell of roasting pig sickens me, although the odor of tomatoes and basil reminds me of my duty to God. My mistress does not recognize my powers. She calls from the kitchen, "What do you know, plucked chicken?" A visitor thoughtfully suggests the parrot might like the door shut while she sniffles her way through the cutting of onions. Worse, they leave open the water-closet door, shouting things to one another from within. The animal odors do not offend me, but my master sprays a poi-

Copyright © 1981 by Leigh Bienen. First appeared in *The Ontario Review.* Reprinted by permission.

sonous antiseptic on the fixtures which irritates my sensitive nostrils and threatens my divine coloration. The red of my tail will
fade in fumes of ammonia or chlorine.

Like blood, the color of my red tail has its own startling quality. This extraordinary color makes my red feathers magical. The
red is a vivid crimson which glows from across the room. The
red is the source of my power, my beauty, which I possess only
briefly. The red is set off by its contrast to the pearl gray of my
breast. The ivory white skin around my eyes, and the gunmetal
gray of my chipped beak. The feathers on my back shade to
light gray at the root, leaving a line of charcoal along the knife's
edge of my wing feathers.

It is difficult to remember how beautiful I once was. The
silken gray feathers falling over a young, full breast in layers as
delicate as the tracery of a waterfall, each hue of gray, each
smudge of crimson in subtle harmony with the rest. Now only
the surprising crimson remains, the purest blue-red of my tail
and the hints of the same crimson in my remaining wing
feathers. Now to my mistress's distress I have plucked my breast
almost clean. Pink dots appear where the oval pinfeathers were.
Tiny blood flecks materialize from my pores like crimson tear-
drops, but not like the crimson of my tail. This urge to destroy
myself and my unbearable beauty comes over me in spurts and
impedes my progress. In a rush I grab five, six or seven feathers
and pull them out in a flurry. The pain is delicious. The mistress
shrieks at me from the kitchen when she catches me at it: "Stop
picking, filthy bird." But she cannot separate me from myself.
Only I possess the engine to destroy my own beauty.

My master and mistress purchased me because they had been
told I could talk. The owner of the pet store, a fat Indian with
one milky blind eye, pulled out my red tailfeathers and sold
them one by one. He told my master and mistress I could talk,
not because he believed it but because recently I had bitten his
finger through to the knuckle. He believed a parrot's bite was a
curse. This same fat Indian failed to mention the magical quali-
ties which caused my feathers to be valued by those who bought
and sold in windowless back rooms. My master and mistress
praised my beauty with awe while the Indian, slumped in a

small wooden chair in the back storeroom, wondered if he would catch a vile infection from my nasty bite.

The master and mistress proudly carried me home and installed me in a large cage on a table in the dining room, on top of a figured blue carpet and beside a tall window which let in the creamy winter light through white silk curtains. The cat came and curled up in a puddle of sunlight beneath my cage. At first the master and mistress fussed continually over my placement by the window. When the sun went down, at a remarkably early hour every afternoon, the master would jump up and pull the curtains shut. "The breeze will kill the bird," he shouted at his wife, as if she were not in the room. In reply she insisted that cold was no worry. She had seen pictures of parrots in the Jardin des Plantes shaking snowflakes off their wings. "But the draft, the draft, there must not be a draft," she shrieked. As the winter days shortened and became increasingly pale, this exchange was repeated. A small machine was installed in the dining room. Its angry red coils created a suffocating dryness which by itself almost catapulted me into my next incarnation. The heat radiating from those disagreeable wires bore no resemblance to the warmth of sunlight in my African jungle.

In those days a perch stood alongside my cage. On some afternoons, at the time when the winter light was strongest, my mistress would open the cage door allowing me to climb out onto the wooden perch, where I could stretch one wing then another slowly downward towards the floor. If the master was out, my mistress would sit down at the dining room table and recite speeches at me. The same sonorous words over and over. Her diction was beyond reproach on these occasions. Once she taped her voice and played it beside my cage for the entire day. I added to my repertoire the sibilant sounds of plastic across metal as the tape rewound itself on the white disc. Instead of her cultured tones I preferred the syncopated accents of the immigrant cleaning lady who muttered lilting obscenities as she scoured a shine into the inlaid tabletops in the living room.

During this early period I often whispered aloud, laughed, or simply whistled. The master and mistress were amazed when my laughter coincided with their amusement. They did not under-

stand that laughter is a form of crying, that we laugh to keep
our perception of the world from crumbling. My own laughter is
a hollow chuckle, a sinister and frightening sound, recognizable
as a laugh by its mirthlessness. When humans laugh they add
wheezes and croaks to mask the sadness of laughter. My master
and mistress do not yet understand that the highest form of
communication is wordless, achieved by a glance upward or a
bestial grunt, by the perception of a change in the rhythm of
breathing, or by a blink of an eye, in my case the flicker of a
brown membrane between lashless lids.

When visitors came into the dining room they used to remark,
to the pleasure of my master and mistress: "Look! How it stares
back at you." Meaning, they were surprised. My yellow eye
pierced through whatever image they had manufactured of
themselves, images of purpose and the aura of an imminent, important appointment which was constructed by a high, excited
tone of voice. My yellow eyes can see behind a necklace of
stones to the throb at the throat, behind thick tweed to the soft
folds of the belly, to the dark roots of hair which has been falsely
hennaed to a color which is a poor imitation of the red wings of
the Amazonian parrot.

The guests were always amazed. At dinner advertising men
and women in public relations were encouraged to speculate
upon whether my mobile and bony throat (not yet exposed by
picking) or my knobby, black tongue produced such extraordinary sounds. The mistress asked pensively: "Imagine how the
bird speaks." The master replied with gravity: "The consonance
between words and meaning is illusory."

At her urging they called in an expert in the field of Parrot
Linguistics, a spectacled man who wore a Russian suit with
wide, waving trousers. The mistress served him tea in a glass
with a slice of lemon on the saucer. The man removed his thick
glasses and examined the white papery skin surrounding my
beak and nostrils. My beak was chipped, but he only commented, "I see nothing unusual about the beak or throat of this
parrot."

"His tongue," my mistress urged, "look at his tongue. The bird
has an exceptionally long and globular black tongue."

The expert had already donned his baggy jacket and removed

his spectacles. "Yes," he said, "it is unusual for a bird to encompass such a wide range of laughter."

My imitations of the human voice exactly reproduced individual intonations. The precision of my imitation of the Polish servant rendered my mistress speechless with jealousy. Erroneously, the copywriters concluded mimicry was the source of my magic, and they congratulated my mistress on acquiring such a rare and amusing pet. In those early days of enthusiasm my mistress would wipe her finely manicured fingers upon a paper towel and scratch my skull, murmuring, "Now Polly, poor Polly, here Polly." In those days they both fed me tidbits from their table, corners of roast dripping with honey, a half-eaten peach with chunks of amber flesh still clinging to the pit, or the thigh bone of a chicken, a treat of which I remain inordinately fond. I would sidestep over, slide down the metal bars of my cage with my head lowered, and take the tidbit in one curled claw.

The mistress carefully saved all of my red feathers in those days, picking them out from the newspaper shreds with her long red fingernails. She put them in a box of tooled leather and closed the lid so that the incandescence of red would not startle a stranger who happened to walk into the room. Later they became so alienated from the source of my beauty, and so quarrelsome, they no longer took pleasure or strength from the color of my tailfeathers. They even forgot to lock my cage and sometimes carelessly left the door open after shaking a few seeds hastily into my dish. During the earlier phase they were proud to possess me. They purchased bird encyclopedias and left them open on the table turned to pages with pictures of parrots. The painted drawing of the yellow-headed Amazon intrigued me and greatly contributed to my education. Feathers of the palest lemon cascaded down from the top of the head ending in a ring of creamier yellow around the neck. The white cockatoos also inspired envy, especially for the flecks of fine pink and light yellow which tinged their wings. I admired their crests, feathers as a flag to the world, and the white back feathers which had the sheen of ancient silk. Another source of wonder were the many-hued black parrots from South America, so advanced in beauty they are rarely glimpsed even by their own kind.

Now when they stand beside my cage, my master and mistress

only discuss the price I will fetch. "Is it eight hundred dollars?"
he asks. "The last advertisement in the paper had one listed at
eight hundred dollars."

My mistress is greedier, but also more practical. "It will fetch
more at an auction," she answers, "when people bid against each
other in competiton."

The refusal to acknowledge my sexual identity is a special humiliation. I laid an egg to announce my essentially female nature. Now that she hates and fears me, my mistress always refers
to me in the impersonal third person. I have long since been
moved away from the dining room, into a small dark room no
bigger than a closet. The tiny unwashed window faces a bleak,
blank wall of brick, and the door to a dark and dusty closet
stands open behind my cage. The mistress uses my room for
storage. The abandoned wire torso of a dress frame is a cage
shaped in the outline of a woman. A broken vacuum cleaner lies
coiled in permanent hibernation in one corner. Portraits of forgotten ancestors, who willed their property to other branches of
the family, stand facing the wall. My cage is now cleaned only
once a week. The room is too mean even to serve as an adequate
storage facility. The fat, neutered gray cat no longer likes to visit
me because there is no rug on the floor and the room is
unheated. She curls herself in front of the refrigerator, where a
small warm exhaust is continuously expelled from the motor. We
exchange remarks about the deplorable spiritual condition of our
custodians. The striped gray cat and I together speculate upon
whether or not the master and mistress will in their next incarnation understand the power of red, as distinct from the power
of blood, the sole power which now strikes fear in their hearts.
Both the master and mistress show a measurable anger when the
tiny flecks of blood appear against my gray skin. My blood is either light pink or a droplet of burgundy, both distinct from the
singing crimson of my tail. When my mistress concluded that
the picking was going to continue she began to think of ways to
get rid of me. But she would not consider letting me go at a loss.

II

It is difficult for me to remember the jungle, the sun in Africa,
or my days in the dark pet shop owned by the blind-eyed In-

dian. My journey must be almost finished, for only the young command memories. In my native jungle parrots are caught by blindfolded boys who climb to the treetops and rob the nests of their chicks. The mothers swoop down, diving with their gray and white heads tucked under, as they shriek their protest. They will attack and tear the flesh as the bald chicks disappear into a knotted cloth held in the teeth of a boy who shimmies down the trunk as fast as he can. The parrots beat their red-flecked wings around the heads of the nest robbers, biting an ear, frantically flying from branch to branch as they accompany the marauders to the edge of the forest with high-pitched screams. The village boys are blindfolded because they believe they will be struck blind if they look into a parrot's nest. To these people we have long been recognized as magic birds, lucky birds, or birds which carry a curse. And now we are almost extinct.

With six other featherless shivering chicks who died within a week I was brought to a pet shop in the middle of the urban sprawl which constitutes a city outside the jungle. The owner placed me in a cage on top of a teetering pile of small cages. One contained a banded snake with a festering hole in his side, another held a monkey with a crippled arm. There were also green parrots and yellow ones from neighboring forests.

Eventually I became an ornament in the compound of a king, living in a gilded cage on a vast veranda shaded by a roof of woven rattan. Every evening a servant boy peeled me an enormous rainbow-colored mango. My cage was a tall cylinder, large enough to fly across and decorated with tin bells and wooden totems. Visitors came especially to admire me from a distance. They did not press their faces within inches of my nostrils, oppressing me with the odor of skin. They stood back to gaze at my feathers and offered me meat. Like worshipers, they came in formal dress. The women were wrapped in cloth of bright blue, and the men wore flowing gold-embroidered gowns which swayed and brushed the floor as they walked rapidly towards me across the veranda. Another parrot was resident in this royal household. She taught me bearing, demeanor and style. She had been the property of kings through three generations. She remembered kings who had been forgotten by their heirs and successors, and her beautiful piercing whistle caused all those within earshot to stop talking and listen to her call. When she was found dead at the bottom of her cage one morning they buried her with incense and incantations, mourning her loss with ancient, certain ceremonies.

The royal family also had a dog, a brown cur with an extraordinarily long and ugly hairless tail. The dog had to be locked inside the royal compound, or he would have been eaten by the many hungry people outside the walls. The cur was fat, and the urchins who roamed the mud streets in packs would have snatched him for roasting or stewing. The animal was so dispirited and envious of the esteem in which parrots were held that he spent hours lying beside our large golden cage discussing philosophy. The youngest daughter of the king occasionally came barefoot onto the veranda and held his head on her lap while she fed him morsels of goat. Finally he became so fat and arthritic he could not climb the steps to the veranda. His view was that the vicissitudes of fate he suffered in this epoch were haphazard. In the next generation—he expressed this opinion while lying panting on the cool clay floor—it would be dogs with long tails, instead of birds with red feathers, who would be offered raw meat and worshiped for their wisdom. Who knows, he remarked with a supercilious snarl, whether or not the privileges you now enjoy because of your divine coloration will not be given to those with visible ears? He often called attention to his long, bald tail as if the tail by itself should have entitled him to all that he envied. On drowsy tropical afternoons my partner and I humored him by appearing to take these notions seriously.

### III

It is true that when I strike I wound. I bit the finger of a small dirty boy to the bone when he poked a yardstick through the bars of my cage. His mother and my mistress were whispering in the kitchen, and they both ignored my shrieks of warning. The boy ran squawking in pain to his mother, and my embarrassed mistress banged the metal bars of my cage with a metal fork, shouting reproaches. The startled mother held her son to her breast and pressed a linen handkerchief of my master's to his limp finger. Furred tentacles of crimson stretched out along threads of cotton and silently eliminated the white between. The sniffling boy looked at me, where I was shivering in the farthest corner of my cage, and signaled his triumph.

I miss the treats, especially the blue-red marrow of chicken bones, which my mistress used to give me in an attempt to make me recite her name. In those days I used to climb upon the back of her hand. She held out her fist with the painted nails curled under, and I could feel her wince when I placed one gray claw and then the other against her skin. I uncoiled my talons to avoid cutting into the flesh of her hand and balanced myself by hooking onto the cage with my beak. She feared I would turn and strike for no reason, and her wrist would stiffen. At such times I was swept away by the sense of her as another living creature, myself at an earlier stage of development. This involuntary response filled me with sadness, for I thought of the generations and generations which remained before her, and I moved away from her hand and huddled on my perch, mourning as she soaped her hands at the kitchen sink. I no longer try to reach her, except with whistles and catcalls, for I know she has come to hate me. Sometimes I receive a reply. She will turn on the radio or rustle the newspaper in an answer.

If nothing else a cage has walls to climb. When my mistress enters the room I take my hooked beak and spill the seeds out of my plastic dish and onto the floor. I can spill almost all of my food in one angry gesture. My beak along the railings makes an insistent, drumming sound which never fails to evoke a click of annoyance from my mistress. When she leaves I slide down the bars and pick out sunflower seeds, the tiny grains of millet, and especially those very small twigs from among the shreds of newspaper. Sometimes my mistress and master discuss my fate in the corridor, using sign language. I can hear the faint rustle of sleeves as they gesture in the hallway. But I rarely listen. I am dreaming of my next life now. The cat curls up in front of the vent of the icebox. We plan together. She licks her paw, passes it over one ear, then her eye, softly.

I can still not resist music, especially the soprano tones. The high notes bring back memories of the sadness of being human. Until the music plays I can convince myself that I have reached a point where memories could no longer overcome me, a point where my feathers offer complete protection. But at the height

of a melodic line I hide in the farthest corner of my cage, as-
saulted by emotions. The beauty of singing strikes home, into
the depths of my parrot's heart. I relive my human life, the fears
and promises of childhood, the exhilaration of striving, and the
limited peace which settles in the breast on rare occasions. I sur-
pass the highest notes with my own high-pitched shriek.

At first my mistress was delighted with these performances,
calling the neighbors to witness. Later she shut the door when
the radio played music, as if to keep me away from something.
The music which I heard faintly from behind the closed door inspired me to dream, and when I sang I swooned, losing my foot-
ing on the perch, falling fluttering to the iron grate at the bottom of my cage. The music transported me back to the high
trees of the rain forest where parrots flew from limb to limb high
above the shrieking of monkeys, never leaving the shadowed
protection of branches.

IV

The Attack. It came so startlingly that my screams of pain and
fright escaped without thought. A large rat had crawled from
the alleyway, through the old crumbling walls of our city house,
into a crawlspace in the closet of my dark room. The door of my
cage had been carelessly left open. The gray beast with brown
ferret eyes slithered his soft fat body up the table leg and into
my cage. He stuck his black snout into my food, spilling the
seeds, and proceeded to stalk me with a cold-blooded ruth-
lessness born of generations of experience. In spite of his
aged, spoiled softness, the beast struck swiftly, efficiently, with
one bite after another, striking my wing, my leg, my throat, then
pulling away from my reach. His rat snout twitched and the
small dappled spots on his back quivered as he flattened himself
to pounce once again at my neck, my throat. Shrieking, bleeding, I beat my wings helplessly against the inside of the cage.
Feathers were everywhere. Blood splattered on the unclean
walls from a bite on my chest, an open wound in my leg, and
from a hole in my wing. In two bites he had pulled out all of my
red tailfeathers. Aiming for the eye of the lumbering beast—in
spite of his waddling gait, I could not place a fatal blow he was

so insulated with fat—I bit the soft rubbery flesh of his nose. I dug my claws into the well-fed muscular shoulder until he turned his head and with bared buck teeth bit off one talon and a large part of the toe above it. Wounded, he went into retreat, his hairless tail threading its way around the door frame of the closet.

The attack must have been brief although my wounds were many. The vision of relentless, reasonless destruction remained: a fat waddling beast baring rodent teeth as he came to trap me in the corner of my cage. Hours later my mistress returned and found me shivering and barely alive, crouched on the bottom of my cage. At the sight of the blood, the scattered red and gray feathers, my mistress was distraught, especially when she realized her personal carelessness had exposed me to a danger which neither of us realized had been ever present.

For days and nights I was only aware of the electric light clicking on and off at intervals. My mistress, perhaps only regretting the loss of her financial investment, sat beside my cage and wept with a depth of feeling which kindled surprise even in my semiconscious state. Other visitors came and peered at me anxiously through the bars. Those who had marveled at my feats of imitation came now to stand silently in front of my cage, disapprovingly clucking their tongues over the pity of it.

My bite wounds stopped bleeding almost immediately, but the shock to my spirit had been profound. Worse, a silent, raging infection daily gained upon me. Soon I could only rest my beak on the bottom rungs of my cage. Finally I could no longer stand. I simply crouched in a corner at the bottom of my cage and rested my head against the bars cursing the demon beast of destruction. I could no longer sing, speak or whistle. Every red feather was gone, and my wing and chest, where the feathers had been pulled out, were bare and covered with festering sores.

In the middle of the night my mistress took me to the veterinarian's hospital in the heart of the city, a large facility associated with an old and famous zoo. Although I could no longer raise my head, I felt no localized pain. A young man with a beard and a white coat picked me up in a towel, held me under a bright light, and put a stethoscope to my heart. With my last quantum of strength I flapped my mutilated wings in protest. Then the blessed darkness, my cage left on an antiseptic stainless-steel table, as the doctor switched off the bright light overhead behind him.

In the hospital it was impossible to distinguish night from day. The veterinarian in the white coat, his soft black eyes and his black beard made it difficult to determine his age, treated me with injections, ointments, and powerful medicines, monitoring my blood every few days. My leg was put in a splint and photographed. A milky white substance was applied to the open sores on my breast and wings. The veterinarian sat in front of my cage and talked softly to me as he wrote his day's reports in soft, smudgy pencil on a mimeographed form. When he looked up at me, so clinically, after scratching something on a paper attached to a clipboard, the vision of gray destruction was momentarily dispelled. Under his care I slowly began to regain my strength.

My mistress came to visit on occasion, although she hardly spoke or looked at me when she came. While I limped gingerly to the edge of the cage door, she would talk to the young girl whose function it was to inform the doctors of any unexpected events in the ward. In this large acrid room with concrete floors and row after row of cages, crises were frequent. Not all could be saved. My immediate neighbors were a white cat with cancer whose stomach had been shaved bare to expose a line of cross-stitches like teeth marks across her pale, pale pink skin, a dog whose back leg had been amputated so skillfully that if he stood in profile on his good side his silhouette looked whole, and a one-hundred-year-old yellow crested cockatoo whose anemia had been caused by a diet of nothing but sunflower seeds for over fifty years. She had been sent to the zoo for an evaluation by the heirs to an estate when she passed hands after the death of the old couple who bought her on their honeymoon in a pre-war London flea market.

During the latter part of my recuperation I was placed in a green-domed aviary in the zoo along with other tropical birds. The domed enclosure imitated the wild, which did not, I thought, properly prepare the displaced birds for spiritual progression through containment. Their instincts to fly, to be free, were inappropriately encouraged. Attitudes of confinement and limitation, required for passage onwards, were thwarted. In spite of my condition, I myself was overcome with a memory and desire for flight when I entered the dome, even though it had been years since I had been let out of my cage. The memory of flying overcame me with an exhilarating rush of recognition. To fly, to be free, to soar on a current of wind, seductive memories took over before I was able to re-establish the distance I had learned to impose at great cost to my spirit. The sunlight filtered through the green glass dome and through the imported foliage. I was unused to the soft, almost liquid light, unlike the dark chill of my room.

The tropical birds in the zoo immediately recognized that, unlike them, I had not been born in captivity. I was taken from the wild. Some had ancestors who were wild, but most, the exception being one all-black Amazonian parrot, were born in zoos, pet stores or aviaries. They could not hope to compete with my heritage as the idol of kings. Two other members of my own species displayed themselves on a palm branch near the top of the green glass dome, showing that even in these circumstances they had learned to restrain from flight. One had a fine assortment of red flecks in the wing he stretched downward for my inspection.

I continued to hop away on my good leg, flap my wings and shriek at the touch of a human, but I knew I owed my resuscitation to the skill and expertise of the dark-eyed doctor. Those gentle educated fingers had deduced what was needed to make me well. His knowledge was the opposite of mine, gained measuring things outside of himself, mine the mastery of the mysteries within.

The creamy chill of winter passed into the shy green of spring. The doctor considered me well enough to go home. My mistress came and carefully listened to his instructions. The doctor never commented upon the cause of my injury, but upon arriving back in the apartment I saw the hole in the closet wall had been hastily covered over with a piece of plywood and a few nails.

After my stay in the hospital my mistress began covering my cage at night, perhaps because my laughter in the dark unnerved her, perhaps to protect her investment. Those occasional shrieks at midnight, attempts to discover if there were kindred spirits in the neighborhood, might have been frightening. One evening the mistress bustled into my small room with a large piece of green felt. It was an especially unusual occurrence because she rarely came close to my cage now, asking the master or even a casual visitor to sprinkle a few seeds into my dish. The first time she walked in with the cover she threw it without warning over my cage as I hissed and flapped my wings. Then she slammed the door shut.

My age, my great age weighs heavily upon me when the cover floats down over the cage for the night. The cover stills my voice, blocks out my vision of even this closet where I will be confined for the rest of my parrot life, unless I am rescued by a stroke of fortune or sold again. If another epoch is coming when parrots are worshiped and fed mangoes and red meat, I do not think I will live to see it. My fate will be to die in this tiny cage, surrounded by my own filth, without love, and reliant upon a natural enemy for conversation. The snow outside makes the wall behind my cage as chill as the marble of tombstones, and I long for the damp warmth of the jungle. What joy have I except the joy of my own whistle? Sometimes the city birds answer my imitations of their calls. Soon I shall be beyond the need to communicate, at a level where I recognize that the attempt to pass messages between living things is as foolish as words. In my next life I will live for five hundred years in a form which is incapable of development or destruction. Perhaps then the dog with his long tail will have assumed my position as teacher, scholar and despised pet, and the cat will be left to sleep undisturbed in the limbo of sunlight.

The master and mistress are huddled together in bed now, happy to know I am temporarily silenced. I hear the creak of the springs, a cough, the single click of the light switch, which I answer perfectly. I shut one yellow eye and wait for the morning.

# SHARDS

## DAVID JAUSS

David Jauss, a native of Montevideo, Minnesota, teaches
creative writing and edits *Crazy Horse* at the University of
Arkansas at Little Rock. Story Press will publish *Crimes of
Passion*, a collection of his fiction, in 1983. "Shards" received
first prize in the 1981 *California Quarterly* short story contest.

Struck by sun, anything's beautiful. A dead cat, calico when I
got up close, was fool's gold from across the street. There were
maggots more than a few. I was six. I got sick. Even now, I love
the sun more than what it strikes.

Light's the only thing to love. First, it lasts. And it's the kiss
that stings the eyes closed. To open your eyes means tears. The
trick's to keep them open while they're shut, Father says. That's
the murderer's code.

The first time I saw a corpse it was night. My eyes were open
wide, always are in the dark. My pulse goes up, I swear, when
the sun goes down. I see everything *clear*, like a cat.

No moon, nor star. Everything dark. The county road rainblack, snakeskin slick. When I saw the cars I swerved, skidded in
the ditch. Stepfather's DeSoto was all right—muffler damage,
nothing more—but I was sick. I *knew* someone was dead. I was
sixteen and still I felt sick.

Nausea never passes, only changes form. I waited till it turned
to numbness, then got out and climbed up the ditch through
shin-high weeds so wet they soaked my Levi's. The Pontiac's left
turn signal was still blinking. Its reflection in the asphalt: red,
black; red, black. For some reason, that light made me sadder
than I'd ever been. I couldn't take my eyes off it.

Copyright © 1982 by The Regents of the University of California. First
appeared in the *California Quarterly*. Reprinted by permission.

Sometimes the night's a palpable weight. It shoved me to my knees: I still carry a shard of windshield glass just under my right kneecap. It floats, like an injured athlete's bone chip. Me, I'm an athlete of death.

But kneeling's not praying. I wasn't praying, though the highway patrolman thought so. A hand shook my shoulder as if waking me. I looked up: the maroon-and-tan uniform, the gold braid around the brim of the hat. "I'll need your help, son," he said. "There'll be plenty of time to pray later." I hadn't even heard him drive up.

The patrolman opened the Pontiac's door with a yank, but we had to crowbar the Ford's. Both drivers, one no older than I, one Stepfather's age, were dead. No doubt about it. The patrolman didn't even bother to check their pulses. Just pushed his hat up his pale forehead. Whispered "Jesus" like a sigh.

I nodded, but I was barely listening. All I could think about was the statue of St. Christopher on the Ford's dash. The car was totaled, the driver's face crushed, but the statue was unharmed. Not a chip in the paint. Unperturbed, St. Christopher was still toting the Christ child across the blue waters of the suction cup.

The second the patrolman looked away, I jerked the statue off the dash and stuffed it in my jacket pocket. I still have it, too, at least what's left of it. The morning after the accident, I took it to the quarry where the Tyler Rifle Club shot clay pigeons Sunday afternoons and I blew it into slivers of plastic from a hundred feet with my 30-06. I'm a crack shot, have been since I was twelve. The Army didn't know what they were losing when they turned me down.

I would have been a good soldier. Death doesn't bother me, unless it's accidental. That car accident shook me up a whole summer. That was seven years ago, but sometimes I still dream about it and wake so scared or angry or something in between that I've got to go out and do something. Not drink. Bourbon blurs the eye and makes me dream awake. What I need, those times, is to talk, and at 3 AM, no one'll listen but prostitutes. I pay my money, but all I do is talk.

But if a death is planned, it doesn't bother me. At least *some-*

*body's* in control. Accidents belong to God, Father says; murders, to us.

No killer likes to kill; we do it to prove we're free. As a boy, I used to pray to have this burden lifted from me, but something made me hunt the bottomland along the Minnesota near Stepfather's farm. Killing made me sick to my stomach at first, but it cured my hunger. When I wasn't in the woods, I was always hungry. I ate and ate, but stayed lean. Even without exercising, I burned everything up—still do. But when I was hunting, I never ate anything from sunrise to sunset, and never got hungry. I was that free.

I'd pretend I was hungry, though. All hunters know nature's a conspiracy of beauty: cottonwood leaves flash scatterfire silver in the sun, and your eyes close from seeing so much. That's when the buck comes down to the stream to drink, but by the time your eyes are open again, he's vanishing into poplars, white tail a mock flag of truce. Hunger's the only way to keep your eyes open once beauty's shut them, so I always pretended I'd starve if I didn't kill something. I crouched in my duck blind or stalked deer tracks for hours, thinking about nothing but translating the slow squeeze of a trigger into food. And when I brought something down, I felt like I'd saved my life.

Mother always said I spent too much time hunting and not enough dating. But I never felt free with women: I couldn't keep my eyes open. A simple kiss could fire my gunpowder veins. There was Marcie, skin fawn-tan summer and winter. And Veronica, all bracelets and silk. But mostly, Ellen. Her green eyes were always bright as if she'd just been weeping. The first time we made love, something crashed in me and lights flared behind my eyelids. And when I woke, my stomach was roiling and my lips numb as after Novocaine. As soon as I could, I washed myself off.

Father says sex is just another kind of accident, like a car crash. There are never any survivors. I knew that even before Mother's death, but still I made love to Ellen every chance I got. The night Mother died, I was waiting for her and Stepfather to go to a party in town so Ellen and I could make love in my bedroom. While Stepfather dressed in his room and Mother put on her makeup in the bathroom, I sat downstairs in the den and imagined Ellen beneath me. Eyes closed, lips parted. The sudden shudder of her orgasm. Then I heard Mother cough, three or four times, hard, as if she'd swallowed something wrong. The last cough almost a gasp. And then the boneshuddering thud. I stood up so quickly I felt dizzy. Stepfather was already at the door. "You all right, Mother?" he was saying. "Are you all right in there?"

That time I did pray. I didn't kneel, just stood there, head swirling, and swore to God I'd never sin with Ellen again if only He would let Mother live. I don't know how I knew she was dying, but I knew. Perhaps it's a killer's gift. Or perhaps Father had already begun his whispering.

Some prayers are answered no. The others are ignored. Who knows which kind this was? It doesn't matter: either way, Mother was dead. But I want it known I hold God personally responsible for her death. Women her age don't die of heart attacks, nor die, of all places, in a bathroom, wearing a slip, face half made up, one lip coral pink.

Stepfather, in black trousers and undershirt, stood beside the bathroom door, gulping air. "Help me," I said, but he didn't move.

"You shouldn't—move her," he said. "She might have—broken something."

"Help me!" I said, but he did nothing. He was hanging onto the doorjamb with both hands now. So I lifted Mother myself, hoisted her over my shoulder and, legs shaking under her weight, carried her to her bedroom and laid her on the yellow chenille bedspread. Her eyes were half open, so I shut them with my fingertips.

Father, help me tell this part.

I tried to bring her back with artificial respiration. I tried but it didn't work. I tilted her head back and began to blow. Her mouth smelled like Listerine and her lipstick tasted like wet chalk. My brain swung, dizzy. I tried to forget the smell, the taste, even her, and lose myself in the breathing; blowing; breathing; blowing. A kind of ventriloquism, breathing for another body. It's unnatural, maybe even wrong. But I tried to save her. I breathed myself into her until my head was light, ringing, my stomach cramping. A diver down too deep, I swam toward the sky until my lungs clenched like fists. That's when I started to breathe the killing water. I haven't stopped since.

Breath chuffing, Stepfather paced behind me. "You're not—doing it right," he said. I was, but he shoved me aside and took my place over her still body. I watched him, fat and trembling, pinch her nose and blow into her mouth. Under his closed lids, his eyes moved like a dreamer's.

That was the second time I saw a corpse. It shook me up worse than the car accident by far. I dream it night and day.

One night, awake, I dreamed I saw her ghost. I knew it was her, though I couldn't see her face: the nimbus was too bright. Since then, I've seen with her light. Every glance sears.

When I said *ghost,* the Army doctor took his glasses off and looked at me as if it took astigmatism to see me clear. Doctors don't believe in ghosts. They know a dead star shines for centuries; why not a soul? But I knew I couldn't persuade him so I didn't bother to tell him about the things Father's told me about death.

A squint's to make you small, to fit you, square peg, in a round hole. That doctor squinted me to a molecule and asked if I was afraid of ghosts. I'm not, and I wasn't. What scared me then were ordinary things, the things of Mother's I'd found everywhere after she died. Under a sofa cushion, the opal earring she'd spent days looking for. Hidden beneath a sweater in her dresser, a snapshot of Father in his Army uniform, the last one ever taken. A brush with some of her meringue-blond hair still in it. To touch them hurt.

Two weeks after the funeral I left home. I revved the Chevrolet to wake Stepfather, then sped down the dark driveway onto the country road, tires churning gravel, gearbox growling. I kept my eyes on the road, but felt Stepfather at his window, parting the sheers to see my taillights, my only farewell. I could hear him saying, "No. Don't leave. Not now." Above me, the star-slung sky hung like a spider web around the fat moon. Shifting into fourth, I fishtailed onto the highway, going sixty.

That was five years ago. Since then I've lived everywhere, been everybody. In Minneapolis, I was Roger Holman, night janitor at Berman Buckskin Leather Goods. At the Olympia

Brewery in Seattle, I was Alex Carey. In Denver, when I tried to
enlist, Burt Loomis. And so on. Outside of a ticket for speeding
on the Ventura Freeway, I had no problems with the law, yet I
felt like a wanted man. Even before I was, I felt that way. That's
why Father gave me the aliases. He said I needed re-christening.

The only time I used my real name was the fall I took
freshman philosophy and physics courses at Berkeley, and I was
so afraid of being arrested (again and again I imagined the sudden click of handcuffs, the gruff voice and pistol in the back) I
almost broke down. My thoughts were riddled with dark; they
rose in spasms, fragments I couldn't assemble. Even my vision
was splintered, cubist. There was something in me like a prism
that broke light into too many colors to decode.

I took physics to study light. A killer's a student of light, Father says. What I learned was this: light's schizophrenic. Sometimes it acts as if it consists of waves; other times, corpuscles.
Most people don't know the difference, light's light, but I can
tell when it shifts from waves to corpuscles, when it starts to
dance like blood gone mad.

I took philosophy to learn to be good. But the more I read,
the more I heard death's dull monotone. Peeling syntax like the
skins of an onion, I found tears all the way down to the nothing
at the core. After an hour or two, the forked vein in my forehead
would start ticking like a bomb. Then everything in the room—
desk, lamp, chair, bed, walls, everything—seemed wrenched,
warped, or shattered into fragments by the skewing light.

I was so scared and confused I went to see the student counselor. Silver hair, pulled back. Glasses on a chain. I couldn't talk
to her; I just sat there, sweating in her air-conditioned office, and
looked out the window. There were dozens of women walking to
classes in high heels and tight blue jeans. I closed my eyes,
imagining the darkness where they tucked their shirttails. When
I looked back at the counselor, she was staring at my face like it
was an X ray. That afternoon, I moved on.

I moved to keep up with time. Sometimes time warps into
space the way outside warps into inside in a Moebius strip. So
when time's moving too fast, you have to move too. Only then
can you slow it down.

I don't know why I went back to Minneapolis after leaving

Berkeley. When I threw my duffel bag into the Chevy's trunk, I thought I was heading for Phoenix. But once I got out on the freeway, the hum of tires was a mad Gregorian chant. It made me drive. I drove all that day and the next. At gas stations I talked nonstop with attendants. Argued politics, religion, weather. I was not in good shape. At night, the sky was so vast and black, it seemed gravity was not strong enough to keep me from being sucked into space.

I'm a weak person, and I admit it. According to the legend, St. Christopher felt the strange child on his shoulders grow heavier until he was supporting the weight of the world's misery, but he never buckled, never sank under the river rush. That's why he's a saint and I'm a sinner. But remember: he's only a legend, a fairy tale, and I'm real, I'm the evening news. And I've learned to make my weakness my strength.

My first week back in Minneapolis, time slowed and I was all right again. The reason was Cindy. According to the *Star*, her last name was Rasmussen, she was twenty years old, and a recent divorcée. The paper didn't say anything about her profession. Cindy was the first one, and the only one that mattered. It wasn't the same with the other three. With them, I was practicing an art. They were faces chosen at random in theatres, museums, department stores. I never read about them in the papers the next day.

But Cindy was different. She chose me as much as I chose her. There was something in her that demanded I kill her. Father recognized it too. He knew it even before I did.

The night I met Cindy, I had a dream. I dreamed I'd run into the cars that blocked the rainblack county road. I was dead, my face caved in, and yet I was outside too, trying to open the door with a crowbar, and the patrolman, fat and trembling, was pacing behind me, saying, "You're not doing it right; let me do it." When I woke, my mind was a snarl of darkness; I had to think carefully, slowly, one thought at a time, so I wouldn't get caught in the tangle. What I needed was air, sharp slapping night air, to clear my head, so I pulled on my brown cords and gray sweatshirt and went for a drive. Even though it was December, cold, soot-gray snow flanking the streets, I rolled the window down so I could *breathe*.

The drive ended at the Strand. It was the first time I'd been there in over four years, but Henry, the skinny Scandinavian with acne scars who runs the house, recognized me. "Hey, Slim, ya been out of town?—or did ya get married?" He smiled and puffed on his cigarette. The smoke wound around his neck, a noose.

"Out of town," I said. "Been in the service."

"Yeah?" he tapped his cigarette on the ashtray. "What'll it be? A single or a double?"

"A double," I said, and set a twenty and ten on the counter.

Henry took the bills and smoothed them out with his yellowed fingers. "Right this way, General," he said, then led me up the short flight of worn stairs into the mildew of the dim hallway. At the end of the hall, he stopped. Hanging upside down on the door, a gilt number seven.

"One of our new girls," he said with a nod at the door. "Cindy." A quick one knuckle rap. "Miss Lucinda?" he asked. "Gentleman caller to see you."

I couldn't make out what she answered, but I could tell it was a curse.

Henry laughed and puffed on the cigarette. "Go on in, Ike," he said. "She's all yours."

I opened the door and stood there a moment. A black underwater light. Shadows shifting amorphous as fish and anemone along shoals. Cindy, sitting on the edge of the narrow bed, pale, wan-faced, small-chested, wearing only a black slip. Her hair black, too, and in the blue-black light, iridescent, like a starling's wings. Coughing a little. The sound, the scrape of sandpaper on wood. Delicate, as if a sharp cough could shatter her like glass.

I didn't think I knew, then, what I would do, but I must have because I started to tremble. I couldn't control myself. It was the kind of trembling you do when you fall in love, but it wasn't love I felt. I didn't know what it was. All I knew was that I would do something, and then my bad dreams would be over. Father knew too. *Soon, soon, it will all be over.* His whisper was almost a song.

Cindy crossed her arms and legs and shivered. "Hurry up and close the door, for Christ's sake," she said. "There's a draft."

I closed the door. It shut on everything I had been. I was

someone else, breathing new air. Air so pure it burned my lungs like ground glass.

"Calm down," she said. She glanced at her wristwatch. "You wanna get started?" she asked and, standing, began to pull her slip up over her shoulders.

"Stop," I said.

White skin bruise-blue in the black light.

She lowered the slip and looked at me. "What," she said. Not a question, nor the beginning of a curse. Just "What." Whenever I think of her, I think of the way she said that word. As if it had nothing to do with language.

"I only want to talk," I said. The light revealed her skinny body through her slip. I stared past her at the cobweb cracks in the wall.

Her hand on my wrist. "Listen," she said, "there's nothing to be nervous about. You're a good-looking guy, and it's all natural. I'll help."

I stepped away, turned my back to her. The hiss of the radiator. The tick of my pulse.

"Look," she said. "I'm no shrink. If you need to talk to someone . . ."

Out the window, across the street, a tavern's red neon blinked on and off, staining the sidewalk.

When I looked back to her, she was saying something about how some doctor had helped her once during a bad time. With a delicate white hand, she pushed back a strand of hair that had fallen onto her cheek.

"You're very beautiful," I found myself saying.

She stopped. "Listen, if you're changing your mind . . ."

"No." I shook my head. "Really. I just want to talk." And, trembling, set ten dollars on the edge of the bed.

She looked at the money, then tilted her head at me, as if trying to see me straight. "You're really unhappy, aren't you?"

"Yes," I answered. "I am." My voice distant, an underground thrum.

"I feel kind of weird sitting here in my slip if we're just going to talk," she said. "Do you mind if I put on my dress or something?"

I shook my head and she took a dark dress off a hook, stepped into it, and zipped it up.

"There," she said, and sat back on the bed, her hands folded onto her lap.

I wanted to kiss her then, she looked like such a little girl. But what I did was cry. It surprised me as much as it surprised her: I hadn't felt like crying at all.

I stopped crying almost the second I started. Eyes stinging, my face in my hands, I began to tell my story. I told her everything, but I didn't tell her the truth. Instead of telling her about Mother's death, I told her Ellen had died, killed in a car accident when a drunk sideswiped our car late at night. I told her, too, that Father disowned me after Ellen's death, saying I was responsible because I had kept her out past curfew to sin with her. And I told her I was thinking about killing myself. By the time I was done confessing, I was crying again.

"Now I know why you're so unhappy," she said. "I wish I could help you, but like I said, there's nothing I can do. You really ought to talk to a doctor or a minister or somebody like that."

I stopped crying. I had imagined her crying with me, putting her arms around my shoulders, kissing my cheek. But she was just looking at me like I made her nervous, like she wished I'd leave.

"You can do something," I said. "You can sympathize."

"I feel sorry for you," she said. "I do. And I'll give you my doctor's name and number if you want. But there's nothing I can do to solve your problems."

"What makes you so sure?" I said. I was surprised at how loud I said it: almost a shout.

Cindy looked at me, her forehead furrowed. "I think you'd better go now."

I stood up. I felt dizzy, as if I'd been drinking. "You haven't earned your money yet," I said.

"What're you saying?"

I thought of the dark gash between her legs. Now I wanted her beneath me, I wanted to hurt her, make her weep.

"You know what I mean," I said. "I paid my money."

She stood and moved toward the door.

"Listen," she said, dead quiet, "you're scaring me. If you don't get out of here this minute, I'm yelling for Henry." She put her hand on the gilt doorknob.

Then I started to tremble again, but not because I was afraid, though that's what Cindy must have thought. I was trembling because Father had given me his blessing. *You know what you have to do,* he said. And I knew.

"I mean it," Cindy said. "I'll yell."

I left. If I'd stayed any longer, I would have told her, and that wouldn't have been good. So I left. Driving home, I sang, every song I knew. I sang as loud as I could, until my lungs were raw, my throat throbbing. Sang to the splintered legs and wave-blue suction cup stuck to my dash. Sang to the stars carved in black ice. Sang. Sang.

The next three weeks, I slept when the sun was up and stalked Cindy at night. I parked outside the Strand until she left, usually around five. Sometimes she left with another girl, a short muscular blonde in a rabbit-fur coat; once with a man in a navy parka, probably one of her johns; but usually, alone, in a taxi. Whatever, I kept strict records: dates, times of departure, routes taken, times of arrival. Lights on low, I followed her to her home, a two-story brownstone converted into apartments on Malcolm, just off Seventeenth. In my Spiral notebook, I wrote: *Quiet neighborhood. No dogs. One streetlight dead. The moon over her roof like Bethlehem's star.* And drew: diagrams of her house, front, back, and sides; approach and escape routes; bullet trajectories. After her lights had been out for a while, I stepped off the distance from her door to the curb, the curb to the various places I might park my car, and recorded all the figures before going home.

Always, I made it home before sunrise. For three long weeks, I pulled my blinds on the sun. When you love light, its sleights of sun, you have to kill it. A penance. Each day, a bead on a black rosary.

The penance made me free. My hunger was gone: somedays I ate only one meal, a bowl of corn flakes or a can of tomato soup, nothing more. The longer I stalked her, the less I needed to eat.

And since her death, I've done nothing but stalk. That's why I'm so lean now, almost invisible. You could walk past me on the street and never see me. My victims never do.

One night, after I'd stalked Cindy for more than two weeks, I woke to minus thirty wind chill and a landscape lunar with snow. That cold air is pure adrenaline. Father said the time had come, so I cleaned and loaded the Springfield. The smell of oil and metal, so familiar, comforting. That night, I waited three hours across from the Strand, watching snow drift across my windshield. Then, suddenly, Cindy, loden camel's-hair coat and upturned collar, hurrying into a yellow cab. The Springfield's muzzle lay cold on my lap. I followed her home.

From the curb to her door: eighteen steps, maybe twenty in the ankle-deep snow. I'd count to ten, then fire. Already I'd imagined, time and again, her tumbling slowly into the snow as if into an embrace. The cab pulled away from the curb, and she started up the walk. I counted to six, then sighted down the scope, hung her on its cross, counted seven; eight; nine.

But I didn't pull the trigger. *It's not right,* Father suddenly said. *A rifle's too impersonal.* I lowered the Springfield, let Cindy walk to her door, climb the stairs to her room, switch on the yellow lights. And tumble into sleep.

I couldn't sleep, though. I didn't even lay down for the next three or four days. Day and night, I wrote letters. A long one, to Stepfather, asking for forgiveness, never sent. One to Ellen, hinting at marriage, sent, later returned unopened. Several to old employers, demanding back pay or compensation for injuries. One to the U. S. Army, attacking their biased enlistment policies. An anonymous note to Henry, warning him that one of his girls was in danger.

And then, knowing I'd never sleep until it was done, I went back to Cindy's house, this time with a Charter Arms .44 caliber handgun. You probably think you know this part of the story, but the papers didn't tell this part, never could. There's nothing factual about a murder; murder's fiction, an escape from the fatality of fact. Destruction is a form of creation, after all. Each murder's a way of saying "Let there be light."

That night the sky was stone. So heavy I could hardly walk without staggering. I'd been running on empty so long, I was out of breath, an old man, by the time I walked the two blocks from my car to Cindy's house.

The night before, I'd counted her footprints in the snow from the curb to the hedge that fronted her yard: eight. Crouched behind the hedge, waiting for her and my breath, I tried to see through the tangle of leaves and twigs. Nothing. All I could see, if I turned and craned my neck, was her house and, above it, the cusped moon, curved like a machete. I'd have to rely on hearing alone; I'd count seven steps, stand, and shoot.

I must've waited twenty minutes hunched in the snow: Cindy was late. Every now and then, a car slid by on the icy street, but never stopped. Occasionally, the blare of their radios, even through closed windows.

I was freezing, almost ready to go home. Then the taxi drove up. Cindy's voice, wordless, a wind chime heard through blowing snow. The cabby's, heavy, flat, ringing like iron on pavement. Then the engine's cold surge, the tires spinning a second on a patch of ice before catching. I looked through the tangle of leaves but saw nothing.

She started up the walk. The click of her heels on the slick ice. One, two. A cough. Three, four.

Though I'd planned to kill her for weeks, somehow I didn't realize I was going to do it until that moment. I felt a spurt of joy sudden as a struck match.

At six, I stood up and stepped in front of her.

"Oh!" she said and jerked back. In the dark, her mouth was red, lipstick a running wound.

Then she saw the gun. My hand had raised it. I looked at my hand. It was trembling but I was perfectly calm.

"*No,*" she said, her breath a blossom in the cold, and put out her hands like a shield. Her mouth kept moving, but no words came out.

Suddenly her legs buckled and she fell to her knees. I thought, at first, she's begging me not to kill her, then no, she's praying, she's asking God to save her. But when she fell, face first, on the ice, I knew I had already shot her. There'd been no noise, I hadn't felt my finger squeeze the trigger, but I had done it. Father said, *Now your suffering is over, now you are free, now you are death.*

How long I stood over her, I don't know. Time had warped so completely into space that all that existed was me, Cindy, and the bloodstained ice. I stood there, staring. There was a halo around her body, an aureole like that you see around everything after you've looked at a light too long. Kneeling, I wiped a bubble of spit from her mouth with my handkerchief.

I wanted to stay, to be with her forever, but Father said I had to go. Lights were coming on all up and down the street. Men and women in nightclothes dialing the police.

*Run*, Father said; my legs refused. I walked, underwater, slow, down the street, all memory of escape routes gone. All happiness gone too, left with Cindy's body. I wanted to go back to her, to sit beside her in the snow, alone, forever, to live in the light her body gave off. *You'll be captured*, Father warned. But I didn't care, still don't: if I'm ever caught, I'll be happy, I'll be able to rest, I won't be free anymore. I didn't care, but I kept on walking. My legs were not my own.

My hand wasn't mine either. When I reached the corner, it suddenly aimed the gun at the streetlight and shot it twice, square in its heart, before I knew what it was doing. The light burst into a thousand shards that fell like shivers of snow. My hands over my head, I walked through that snowfall. I am still walking through it.

# THE ONLY SON OF THE DOCTOR

## MARY GORDON

Mary Gordon was born in Far Rockaway and brought up
in Valley Stream, New York. She now lives in New Paltz,
New York. She is the author of two novels, *Final Payments*
and *The Company of Women*. Her stories have been published in *Ms., Redbook, The Atlantic Monthly, Antaeus, The
Southern Review,* and other journals. She is married to Arthur
Cash, the biographer of Laurence Sterne. They have one
daughter, Anna.

Louisa was surprised that she was with a man like Henry, after
all she had been through. She liked to tell him that he was the
best America could come up with. She told all her friends about
his father, who had built half the houses in the town where
Henry lived, who had gone broke twice but had died solvent;
about the picture of his eighteenth-century ancestor, dumb as a
sheep but still a speculator; about his mother, who had founded
the town library. And she told them—it was one of her best stories now—that when she had agreed to go to bed with him, he
had said to her, "Bless your heart."

It was to expose him that she had wanted to meet him in the
first place. There had been a small piece about him in the
*Times,* and she had not believed that he could be what he
seemed, a country doctor who ran a nursing home that would
not use artificial means to keep the old alive. The story said he
was in some danger of being closed down; the home was almost
bankrupt.

If things looked simple, Louisa's genius was to prove that they
were not. She wrote to the doctor about his home, hoping to

Copyright © 1982 by Mary Gordon. First appeared in *Redbook* magazine.
Reprinted by permission.

unmask him and his project. The *Times* had been almost idola-
trous; they described reverentially his devotion to the aged.
They described the street where he lived as if they had dreamed
of it over the Thanksgiving dinners of their childhood. Louisa
drove the hundred and twenty miles from New York hoping to
see behind the golden oaks a genuine monstrosity, hungering to
discover, in the cellar of the large farmhouse the doctor had converted, white skeletons behind the staircase, whiter than the
Congregational church that edified the center of the village. At
the very least, she hoped to find the doctor foolish, to catch him
in some lapse of gesture or language so that she could show the
world he was not what he seemed.

When he opened the door to her, she saw that his face was
not what she had expected. The eyes were not simple: blue, of
course they were blue, but they were flecked with some light
color, gold or yellow, warning her of judgment, of a severeness
at the heart of all that trust. And she knew he was a man who
was used to getting whatever woman he wanted. She could tell
that by the way he closed the door behind her, by the way he
led her into the living room.

"Tell me about yourself," she said, pressing the button of her
tape recorder. "Tell me how you came to such work."

His voice was so perfectly beautiful that she felt she had suddenly stepped into a forest where the leaves were visible in
moonlight. He said he was devoted to stopping the trend of
prolonging agony. That was what had made her love him first:
those words "the trend of prolonging agony." It made change
sound so possible; there was such belief implicit in that construction: that life was imperfect but ordinary, and not beyond
our reach.

He had thought he would be an actor, he said, after college.
He said his dream was to play light comedy; he had wanted to
be Cary Grant. But she could see his gift was not for comedy.
His gift was for breaking news. She knew, sitting in his living
room, that his was the voice she would have preferred above all
others to speak the news of her own death. He said he had decided to take up this work, after years of practice as an internist
in Boston, because he had seen how impossible it had been for
his mother to die well. So he had come back to his home town,

where his father had built half the houses, where his mother had
founded the library, to start an old-age home.

He asked Louisa for her help in keeping the home alive, for it
was, as the *Times* had suggested, in danger of bankruptcy. The
piece she wrote about him and his work brought floods of contri-
butions. She talked her friends into helping him with a fund-
raising campaign. His own efforts had been small, and local, and
hopelessly inefficient. He wrote all the fund-raising letters himself, at a huge black manual typewriter. He was always writing
letters, always meeting with the board of directors. The board
was made up of townspeople: the lawyer, the minister, the prin-
cipal of the high school. When she came up from the city to
speak to the board, to advise them on the first steps of their
fund-raising campaign, her differentness from them made her
feel like a criminal. Later she would be able to sit with them at
the doctor's table and joke or help them peel potatoes. But that
first meeting of the board made her think of the city
mouse–country mouse tales she had read as a child. Sitting
around her at the doctor's table, all those people made her feel
edgy and smart-alecky and full of excessive cleverness suspi-
ciously come by. She felt as if she were smoking three cigarettes
at once. They turned to her with such trust; they were so
impressed by her skills; they were so sure that she could help
them. Their trust made them seem very young, and it annoyed
her to be made to feel the oldest among them when in fact she
was the youngest by fifteen years. The night of that first meeting
of the board, she went to bed with the doctor because he
seemed the only other adult in town.

By the time the campaign was over and the committee had
raised its money, she had got into the habit of spending her
weekends with him. They never said that she would do this; she
simply called on Thursdays to say what train she would be taking Friday. And he would say: "This is what I've arranged for
us. We'll have the Chamberlains on Saturday; Sunday we'll take
a picnic lunch to the river."

It was partly his voice that made her love doing these things.
His voice made everything simpler; it could reclaim for her pleasures she had believed lost to her forever. Her first husband had
told her she was a disaster with tools. The doctor (his name was

Henry; she did not like his name; she did not like to use it, although she admitted it suited him) taught her simple carpentry.
He made it possible for her to ask questions that were radically
necessary and at the same time idiotic: "When you say joist,
what exactly do you mean? How does a level work?" He made it
possible for her to work with things whose names she understood.

She had learned, particularly in the years since her divorce,
when people had invited her for weekends out of kindness, that
it was impossible for a person living in the country to take a city
guest for a walk without reproach, implied or stated. She could
see it in the eyes of whatever friend she walked with, the
unshakable belief in the superiority of country life. People in the
country, she thought, believed it beyond question that their lives
had been purified. They had the righteousness of zealots: born
again, free at last.

This had kept her out of the country. The skills she prized and
possessed were skills learned in the city: conversation, discrimination. She remembered a story she had read as a child about a
princess who had to go into hiding on a farm. How she suffered
at the hands of the milkmaid, who set up tests that the princess
was bound to fail: the making of cheeses, jumping from hayloft
to haycart, imitating the call of birds. The milkmaid took pleasure in convincing the princess of the worthlessness of the princess's accomplishments. And she did convince her, until a courtier arrived. The milkmaid was tongue-tied; she fell all over her
feet in the presence of such a gentleman, while the princess
poured water from a ewer and told jokes. Louisa saw herself as
the princess in the tale, but the courtier had never come to acknowledge her. Always she was stuck in the part of the story
that had the princess spraining an ankle on the haycart, unable
to imitate the cry of the cuckoo! On the whole, she had found it
to be to her advantage to decline invitations to any place where
she would be obliged to wear flat shoes.

But she loved simply walking in the country with Henry. He
had a way of walking that made her want to take month-long
journeys on foot with him. He did not spend time trying to get
her to notice things—bark, or leaves, or seasonal changes. He
would walk and talk to her about his mother's father, about his

days in the theater, about his work with the aged. He would ask
her advice about the wording of one of his letters. Always, when
they were walking, he would soon want to go home and begin
writing a letter. So that for the first time in her life it was she
who begged to stay outside longer, she who did not want to go
indoors.

And his house was the most perfect house she had ever
known. It had been his family's for generations. The living room
had thirteen windows; he kept in a glass-and-wooden cabinet his
great-grandmother's wedding china. But his study was her favorite room. He had a huge desk that he had built himself, and on
the desk was a boy's dream of technology: an electric pencil
sharpener, a machine that dispensed stamps as if they were flat
tongues, boxes for filing that seemed to her magic in their in-
tricacies. He had divided his desk by causes; it was sectioned off
with cardboard signs he had made: nuclear power, child abuse,
migrant workers. He never mixed his correspondences. But the
neatness of his desk was boyish—not an executive neatness, but
the kind of neatness that wins merit badges, worried over, somewhat furtive, somewhat tentative, more than ɾ little ill at ease.

And he had pictures of ships on the wall of his study. Ships!
How she loved him for that! It was impossible that any other
man she had ever known well—her father, her husband, any of
her lovers—would have had pictures of ships. All the men in her
life had doted on the foreign, which was why they were interested in her. Why, then, was Henry interested? Sometimes she
was afraid that he would realize he had made a mistake in her,
that he would wake up and find her less kind, less generous, less
natural, than the women he was accustomed to loving. She was
afraid that he had misunderstood her face because he liked it
best after sex or early in the morning. He liked her best without
makeup, and he didn't notice her clothes. Other men had loved
her best when she was dressed for the theater or parties. Henry
preferred her naked, with her hair pulled back. This disturbed
her; it made her feel she was competing in the wrong event. She
could never win against girls who dashed down to breakfast
after taking time only to splash cold water on their eyes. She
had some chance against women who invented their own
beauty. But he would dress her in his shirts; he would kiss her

before she had washed her face. Now she did not wear makeup
when she was with him—he had asked her not to so simply.
How could she refuse such a desire, spoken in the voice she
loved? But she was afraid that she could lose his love, in some
way she could not predict, if he loved her for herself the first
thing in the morning.

And it troubled her that she could not predict in Henry the
faults that would cause her one day not to love him. Would she
one day grow tired of his evenness; would she long for storms,
recriminations? She felt she had to ask him about his wife; they
had gone on for months saying nothing about her. What kind of
woman would leave such a house, such furniture? Henry said
only that she was living in New Mexico, she had a private income, they wrote twice a month. He said nothing that would
allow her to look into herself for the wife's faults, to see in
Henry the wife's objections. In time she grew grateful for his
reticence. She was, for the first time, safe in love. He did not
look, for example, at other women in restaurants. He did not see
them. Perhaps it was because she and Henry spent so much of
their lives away from each other. It made her gentler, that lack
of access. It made him, she thought, less curious.

She asked him once if he had ever thought of asking her to
come and live with him. He looked at her strangely; she could
tell that he had not thought of it. That look surprised her, and it
embarrassed her deeply. And then she began to feel that look as
an extreme form of neglect. They had been together for six
months; they had been in love. And he had not thought of living
with her. He said (one of those truths he thought there was no
reason not to tell), "I just don't think of you as making much impression on a house. I don't think of you as caring about it."

"Of course I do. I like having a beautiful place to live."

"Yes, but I mean you don't become attached to a house itself.
You become attached to the things in it."

There was no way she could prove him wrong. She would
have to do something so extreme that everything in her life
would have to change utterly. She would have to build herself a
house in the woods and live in it for years to prove to him that

she cared about houses. And she was ready to do it; she awoke next to him at four in the morning and she thought that that was just what she would do. She would quit her job; she would stop seeing him. She would build herself a house to prove to him that she cared about houses. In the morning she laughed to think of herself writing a letter of resignation, buying lumber, but she was frightened that because of him she had entertained, even for a moment, such a fantastic renunciation. She saw that loving someone so calm, so moderate, that being loved so plainly and truthfully, could lead to extremes of devotion, of escape.

He accused her of being unable to resist the habit of separating sheep from goats. It was a loving accusation, for he loved her for falling in love with old women in restaurants, for wanting to send gas station attendants to chain gangs. He told her that her habit of sheep and goats had lifted from him a burden; he did not have to look so clearly at people when he was with her. She made a list of the phrases he used to defend the people she criticized: "good sort," "means well," "quite competent at his job," "very kind underneath it all." He put the list on the corkboard above his desk. He said he kissed it every morning that she was not there. He touched it for good luck, he said, before writing a letter.

One Thursday in August when she called he said, "My son is with me." She had made his son one of the goats. Partly it was an accident of their ages; his son was nearly her age and she resented him for it. But it was a class resentment as well, and a historical one. Henry's son—with, she thought, using a phrase her mother might have used, all the advantages—had gone the way of the children of the affluent sixties. He had dropped out. Dropped out. It was such a boring phrase, she had always thought, such a boring concept. Dropped out. And yet she resented his hitchhiking through Denmark while she was working as a waitress or in the library to support her scholarship, resented him for not carrying on his father's line, for not having an office by this time, with pictures of ships. And she did not comprehend how he could resist all this. All this: she meant the house with all the windows, the attic full of old letters, the grandmother who was named for her great-aunt, killed during the Revolution. Before Louisa met him, she decided the boy was thickheaded. She could not be sympathetic to this boy who had left his father. When his father was the man she loved.

On the train up, she tried to remember what Henry had told her about his son. There had been the same reluctance to talk about his child as there had been to talk about his wife, and she had been as grateful. He had said something about the boy's hitchhiking through Denmark. And there was something about a fight. She remembered now that there was some reason for her wanting to forget it. She had not liked Henry's part in it.

The family had been vacationing in Europe and Henry's son had refused to return home. He was fifteen at the time, and he wanted to spend the year in Scandinavia, hitchhiking around, earning money at odd jobs. Why Scandinavia? she had asked, searching for some detail that would make the boy sympathetic. It simply took his fancy, Henry had said. He had, of course, insisted that his son come home and finish high school. His son had refused. Finally, after a week of silence, the boy had said, "Well, there's only one thing to do. We'll have to go outside and fight."

"What did you do?" Louisa had asked, with that combination of thrill and boredom she felt when she watched Westerns.

"I let him go."

Of course. What had she wanted him to do? Arrange some display of paternal weapons? He would not be the man she loved if he had forced his son to succumb to his authority. But why was she so disappointed? How would her own father have acted toward her brother? Her brother, a lawyer now with three children, would never have had the confidence for such defiance. He would have known, too, physical anger at his father's hand. Such knowledge would have prevented risk. Louisa resented Henry's son for knowing, at fifteen, that he could survive without the sanction of his parents. She wanted to tell that boy what a luxury it was—that defiance, that chosen poverty. She wanted to tell him that with less money and position, he could never have been so daring. She wanted to tell him he was spoiled. By the time the train pulled into the station, she was terribly angry.

She realized that she had ridden for miles with her hands clenched into fists.

She was exceptionally loving in her embrace of Henry. He told her, with some excitement, that Eliot had spent the last few days painting his barn. He said, with a gratitude that touched and frightened her, that his barn was now the most beautiful in the county. He told her what good stories Eliot had to tell, about Alaska, about South America. She closed her eyes. Nothing interested her less than stories about men in bars, and fights, and roads and spectacular views, and feats of idiot courage. She knew she would have nothing to say to his son. Would this make Henry stop loving her? By the time they were in front of the house, she knew she was wrong to have come.

He was sitting at the kitchen table with his legs spread out, at least halfway, she thought, into the room. Henry had to step over his son's legs to get to the table. She followed behind Henry, stepping over his son's black boots. She hated those boots; there was something illegal-looking about them. They were old; the leather was cracked so that it looked not like leather but like the top of a burned cake. It was an insult to Henry, she thought, to wear boots like that in his house.

"Eliot, I'd like you to meet Louisa Altiere. Louisa, my son, Eliot Cosgrove."

"Hey," said Eliot, not looking up.

Louisa walked over and extended her hand.

"I'm very glad to meet you," she said.

He did not take her hand. She went on extending it. With some aggressiveness she thrust her hand almost under his nose. He finally shook her hand. She wanted to tell him that she had got better handshakes from most of the dogs she knew.

"Why are you glad to meet me?" he said, looking up at her for the first time.

"What?"

"I mean, people say they're glad to meet somebody. But, like, how do you know? You're probably really a little ticked off that I'm here. I mean, you don't get to spend that much time with Henry, here. And here I am cutting into it."

"On the contrary, I feel that knowing you will enable me to know your father better."

"Watch out, Eliot," said Henry. "Watch out when she says things like 'on the contrary.'"

The two men laughed. She felt betrayed, and excluded from the circle of male laughter. Henry had put his feet up on the table.

"I'll go and unpack," she said, feeling like a Boston school-teacher in Dodge City. She wondered if Henry had told his son what she was like in bed.

She looked at the barn through the window of Henry's bed-room. She used to like looking at it; now it bulked large; she resented its blocking her view of the mountains. She kept walking around the bedroom, picking things up, putting them down, putting her dresses on different hangers, anything so that she would not have to go downstairs to the two men. My lover, she was thinking, and his son.

Henry had a drink waiting for her when she did go down. He stood up when she walked into the room. How much smaller he was than his son. It did not have to do entirely with Eliot's being born after the war and having more access to vitamins. She had loved Henry for being so finely made that his simplest gestures seemed eloquent. Once she had wept to see him taking the ice cubes out of the tray. She remembered his telling her that when Eliot was a child they called him "Brob," for "Brob-dingnagian."

While Henry talked to her about his work on the Child Abuse Committee and the letter he had received from a prominent U.S. senator, Eliot sat at the table, whittling. It distracted Louisa so much that she was not exactly able to understand the point of Henry's letter. She stared at Eliot until he put down his knife.

"I thought whittling was something that dropped from a cul-ture when people became literate," she said.

"What makes you think I'm literate?" said Eliot, throwing the pop top of his beer can over her head into the garbage.

"I assume you were taught to read."

"That doesn't mean I'm still into it."

Henry put his head back and laughed, a louder laugh than she had ever heard from him.

She spent the rest of the afternoon shopping and making dinner. Bouillabaisse. She was glad of the time it took to sauté and to scrub; it meant she did not have to be with Henry and Eliot. And the dinner was a success. But while Henry praised Louisa, Eliot sat in si'ence, playing with the mussel shells. Then Henry turned his attention to his son. They spoke of old outings, old neighbors. They laughed, she was disturbed to see, most heartily about a neighbor's wife who had gained a hundred pounds. They imitated her foolishness in clothes, her walk that forgot the flesh she lived in. They talked about their trips to Italy, to the Pacific Northwest.

She saw there was no place for her. She cleared the table and washed the dishes slowly, making the job last. They were still talking when she rejoined them at the table. They had not noticed that she had left.

Henry mentioned the meeting he would have to go to after supper. He was the chairman of a citizens' committee to stall a drainage bond. Louisa was annoyed that Henry had not told her he would be away for the evening, had not told her she would be alone with Eliot. Perhaps he had guessed she would not have come if she knew.

"I think it's good that you and Eliot will have the time alone. You'll get to know each other," said Henry when he was alone with her in the bedroom, tying his tie.

After Henry left, she took her book down into the living room, where Eliot sat watching a Country-and-Western singer on television. She was embarrassed to be sitting in a room with someone at seven-thirty on a Saturday night, watching someone in a white leather suit who sang about truck drivers.

"When did you first become interested in country music?" she asked.

"A lot of my friends are into it."

She opened her novel.

"You don't like me much, do you?" he said, after nearly half an hour of silence.

His rudeness was infantile; no one but a child would demand

such conversation. All right, then, she would do what he wanted; she would tell the truth, because at that moment she preferred the idea of hurting him to the idea of her own protection.

"I don't think you deserve your father."

The boy stopped lounging in his chair. He sat up—she wanted to say, like a gentleman.

"Don't you think I know that?" he said.

She turned her legs away from him, in shame and in defeat. How easily he had shown her up. He could work with honesty in a way that she couldn't. He reminded her that he was, after all, better bred; that she was what she had feared—someone who had learned the superficial knack of things but could be exposed by someone who knew their deeper workings. She did not know whether she liked him for it; she thought that she should leave the house.

"I'm sorry," she said. "I had no right to speak to you like that."

"The real secret about my father is that nobody's good enough for him. But he keeps on trying. His efforts are doomed to failure."

Did he say that? "His efforts are doomed to failure." Of course he did. He was, after all, the son of his father. And she saw that he had to be what he was, having Henry for a father. She saw it now; such a moderate man had to inspire radical acts.

"Forgive me," she said. "I was very rude."

He was not someone used to listening to apologies. She wanted to touch his hand, but she realized that for people connected as they were, there was no appropriate gesture.

"Once I was in Alaska, riding my bike through this terrific snowstorm. And I had a real bad skid. I fell into the snow. I think I musta been out for a couple of minutes. I thought I was going to die. When I came to, I could hear the sound of my father's typewriter. I could hear him at that damn typewriter, typing letters. I was sure I was going to die. I was sure that was the last sound I'd hear. But someone came by in a pickup and rescued me. Weird, isn't it?"

She could see him lying in the snow, wondering whether he would survive, thinking of his father. Hearing his typewriter. Was it in love or hatred that he heard it? She thought of Henry's

back as he wrote his letters, of the perfect calm with which he
arranged his thoughts into sentences, into paragraphs. And what
would a child have thought, seeing that back turned to him, listening to the typewriter? For Henry needed no one when he was
at his desk, writing his letters for the most just, the most worthy,
of causes. He was perfectly alone and perfectly content, like
someone looking through a telescope, like someone sailing a
ship. She thought of this boy, four inches taller than his father,
fifty pounds heavier, wondering if he would die, hearing his father's typewriter. But was it love or hatred that brought him the
sound?

She began to cry. Henry's son looked at her with complete dis-
interest. No man had ever watched her tears with such a total
lack of response.

"I'll say good night, then. I'm taking off in the morning. Early.
I'll leave about four o'clock," he said.

"Does your father know?"

"Sure."

"And he went to the meeting anyway?"

"It was important. And he's going to get up and make me
breakfast."

"What about tonight?"

"What about it?"

"Don't you want to stay up and wait for him?"

"He'll be late. He's at that meeting," said Eliot, climbing the
stairs.

"I'll wait up for him," said Louisa.

"Far out," said Eliot—was it unpleasantly?—from the landing.

She read her novel for an hour. Then she went upstairs and
looked at herself in the mirror. She took out all the makeup she
had with her: eyeshadow, pencil, mascara, two shades of lipstick, a small pot of rouge. She made herself up more heavily
than she had ever done before. She made her face a caricature
of all she valued in it. But it satisfied her, that face, in its ex-
tremity. And it fascinated her that in Henry's house she had
done such a thing. Her face, no longer her own, so fixated her
that she could not move away from the mirror. She sat perfectly
still until she heard his key in the door.

# THE PONOES

## PETER MEINKE

Peter Meinke is Director of the Writing Workshop at Eckerd College in St. Petersburg, Florida. His stories have appeared in *The Atlantic Monthly, Yankee, Redbook, The Virginia Quarterly* and other magazines. He has also written two books of poetry, *The Night Train and the Golden Bird* and *Trying to Surprise God,* both published by the University of Pittsburgh Press. Last year he was The Jenny McKean Moore Lecturer at George Washington University in Washington, D.C.

When I was ten years old I couldn't sleep, because the minute I closed my eyes the ponoes would get me. The ponoes were pale creatures about two feet tall, with pointed heads and malevolent expressions, though they never actually said anything. What they did was to approach me, slowly, silently, in order to build up my fear (because I knew what they were going to do); then they would tickle me. I was extremely ticklish in those days, in fact I could hardly bear to be touched by anybody, and the ponoes would swarm over me like a band of drunken and sadistic uncles, tickling me till I went crazy, till I almost threw up, flinging my legs and arms around in breathless agony. I would wake up soaked, my heart banging in my chest like the bass drum in the school marching band. This lasted almost an entire year, until the Murphy brothers got rid of them for me. Because the ponoes would come whenever I fell asleep, I hated to go to bed even more than most children. My parents were not particularly sympathetic; ponoes did not seem that frightening to them, nor were

Copyright © 1982 by Yankee Publishing, Inc. Originally published in *Yankee* magazine under the title "Getting Rid of the Ponoes." Reprinted by permission.

they sure, for a long time, that I wasn't making them up. Even my best friend, Frankie Hanratty, a curly-haired black-eyed boy of unbounded innocence, was dubious. No one else (including myself) had ever heard of them; they seemed like some sort of cross between elves, dwarves, and trolls. But where did I get the name? I think my parents felt that there was something vaguely sexual about them, and therefore distasteful.

"Now no more talk about these, um, ponoes, young man. Right to bed!"

"I'm afraid!" That year—1942—I was always close to tears, and my bespectacled watery eyes must have been a discouraging sight, especially for my father, who frequently would take me to the Dodger games at Ebbett's Field, and introduce me to manly players like Cookie Lavagetto and Dixie Walker. I had a collection of signed baseballs that my father always showed to our guests.

Because I was terrified, I fought sleep with all my might. I read through most of the night, by lamplight, flashlight, even moonlight, further straining my already weak eyes. When I *did* fall asleep, from utter exhaustion, my sleep was so light that when the ponoes appeared on the horizon—approaching much like the gangs in *West Side Story*, though of course I didn't know that then—I could often wake myself up before they reached me. I can remember wrestling with my eyelids, lifting them, heavy as the iron covers of manholes we'd sometimes try to pry open in the streets, bit by bit until I could see the teepee-like designs of what I called my "Indian blanket." Often I would get just a glimpse of my blanket and then my eyelids would clang shut and the ponoes were upon me. It is possible, I suppose, that I only *dreamed* I was seeing my blanket, but I don't think so.

Sometimes I would give up trying to open my eyes, give up saying to myself, *This is only a dream*, and turn and run. My one athletic skill was, and remains still, running. There were few who could catch me, even at ten, and today, premature white hair flying, I fill our game room with trophies for my age bracket in the 5,000- and 10,000-meter races along the Eastern seaboard. Often, toward the end of a race, I hear footsteps behind me and

I remember the ponoes; the adrenaline surges again, and the footsteps usually fall back. But in my dreams the ponoes would always gain and my legs would get heavier and heavier and I'd near a cliff that I would try to throw myself over but it was like running through waist-deep water with chains on, and I would be dragged down at the edge. This, I suppose, with variations and without ponoes, is a common enough dream.

My mother was more compassionate to me because at that time she was also suffering from a "classical" recurring dream: the empty room. She would be in a large hotel, walking down a long corridor where all the doors were exactly the same, and un-numbered. She would go along, fear bubbling in her throat, looking at the doors until she stopped in front of one that she knew, for some reason, was hers. Slowly, inch by inch, she would open the door, see the empty room, and scream in terror, waking herself up. Sometimes she would scream only in the dream and sometimes she would scream in actuality as well. But since her dream would only come once a week, or even less frequently, she didn't have the problem with sleeping that I did. Even she would lose patience with me, mainly because my schoolwork, along with everything else, suffered. Mother was very high on education and was determined—as I was a reader —that I was going to be the first member of our family to go to college. Norman Vincent Peale preached regularly at a nearby church and the neighborhood was awash with positive thinking.

During this year, since I scarcely slept in bed, I fell asleep everywhere else: in the car, at the movies, even at dinner, a true zombie. In the winter I liked to curl up on the floor near the silver-painted radiators, whose clanking seemed to keep the ponoes away. I constantly dropped off at my desk at school, once actually clattering to the floor and breaking my glasses, like some pratfall from The Three Stooges, whom we would see regularly on Saturday matinees at the Quentin Theatre. Eleven cents for a double feature, it was another world! But Miss McDermott was not amused and would rap my knuckles sharply with her chalkboard pointer. She was a stout and formidable old witch and when she first came at me, aiming her stick like an assassin from *Captain Blood,* I had thought she was going to poke

my eyes out and leaped from my seat, to the delight of my classmates, who for weeks afterward liked to charge at me with fingers
pointed at my nose.

We had moved from the Irish section of Boston to the Irish
section of Brooklyn, and my father, Little Jack Shaughnessy, liked
to hang around the tough bars of Red Hook where—he told me
—there was a cop on every corner looking for an Irish head to
break. My father was Little Jack and I was Little Jim (or
Littlejack and Littlejim) because we were both short, but he
was husky, a warehouse worker at Floyd Bennett Airport.
Though he was not a chronic brawler, he liked an occasional
fight, and was disappointed in my obvious fear of physical vio-
lence.

"Come on, Jimmy, keep the left up." He'd slap me lightly on
the face, circling around me. "Straight from the shoulder now!"

I'd flail away, blinking back the tears, the world a blur without my glasses, like a watercolor painting left in the rain. To this
day, when I take off my glasses, I have the feeling that someone
is going to hit me. Oddly enough, it was fighting that made me
fall in love with the Murphy brothers, Tom and Kevin, though
love may not be exactly the right word.

I was a natural-born hero worshiper. Perhaps I still am, as I
believe unequivocally that our country has gone steadily to the
dogs since President Kennedy was shot in 1963, despite all the
revelations of character flaws and administrative blunders. When
I was young, most of my heroes came from books—D'Artagnan,
Robin Hood—or movies: characters like the Green Hornet and
Zorro, or real actors like Nelson Eddy whose romantic scenes
with Jeanette MacDonald made my classmates whoop and
holler. I would whoop and holler too, so as not to give myself
away, but at night, fending off the ponoes, I would lie in bed in
full Royal Canadian Mountie regalia singing, in my soaring
tenor, "For I'm falling in love with someone, someone . . ."
while Jeanette would stand at the foot of my bed shyly staring
down at her incredibly tiny feet, or petting my noble horse,
which was often in the room with us. This fantasy was particularly ludicrous as I was unable to carry a tune, and had been
firmly dubbed a "listener" by Miss McDermott in front of the

whole music class, after which I spent the term moving my
mouth to the words without uttering a sound.

The Murphy brothers were tough, the scourge of P.S. 245; ex-
torters of lunch money, fist fighters, hitters of home runs during
gym class, they towered over most of us simply because they
were older, having been left back several times. Tom was the
older and meaner; Kevin was stronger but slow-witted, perhaps
even retarded. Tom pushed him around a lot but was careful not
to get him really mad, because there was nothing that Kevin
would not do when in a rage, which became increasingly evident
as they grew older. Pale, lean, black-haired, they wore white
shirts with the sleeves rolled up and black pants and shiny black
shoes: for brawlers they were very neat dressers, early examples
of the Elvis Presley look, though they never looked so soft as
Elvis. Most of the rest of us wore corduroy knickerbockers, whistling down the halls as we walked, with our garters dangling
and our socks humped around our ankles. Small and weak, I
wanted nothing more than to be like the two fighting brothers,
who seemed to me to resemble the pictures of tough soldiers,
sailors, and marines that were posted everywhere.

The Murphys had strong Brooklyn accents (they actually
called themselves the Moifys), but the whole neighborhood was
heading that way, and the schools fought valiantly against it: accents were bad in 1942. I still remember the poem we all had to
recite:

> There once was a turtle
> Whose first name was Myrtle
> Swam out to the Jersey shore . . .

Tom Murphy would get up in front of the class (like many of
the others), grinning insolently, scratching obscenely, ducking
spitballs, and mutter:

> Aah dere wunce wuz a toitle
> Whoze foist name wuz Moitle
> Swam out to da Joizey shaw . . .

We would all applaud and Tom would clasp his hands above
his head like a winning prizefighter and swagger back to his

seat. Miss McDermott never hit the Murphys, but tried to
minimize their disturbance (distoibance!) by pretending they
weren't there.

But there they were: they had the cigarettes, they had the
playing cards with the photographs that made us queasy, they
wrote on the bathroom walls and the schoolyard sidewalks. Of
course they must have written obscenities but in the fall of 1942
they mainly wrote things like KILL THE KRAUTS and JAPS ARE
JERKS: they were fiercely patriotic. I thought of the change when
I recently visited my daughter's high school: painted on the
handball court was YANKEE GET OUT OF NORTH AMERICA.

And, suddenly, Tom Murphy adopted me. It was like the lion
and the mouse, the prince and the pauper. Like a German submarine, he blew me out of the water and I lost all sense of judgment, which was, in 1942, a very small loss. Perhaps it was because I was so sleepy.

On rainy days, when we couldn't go outside to play softball or
touch football, we stayed in the gym and played a vicious game
the Murphys loved, called dodge ball. We divided into two sides
and fired a soccer-sized ball at each other until one side was
eliminated. The Murphys, always on the same side, firing
fastballs the length of the tiny gymnasium, would knock boys
down like tin soldiers. I was usually one of the last to go as I
was so small and hard to hit, but no one worried about me because I was absolutely incapable of hitting anyone else, and
eventually would get picked off. But one rainy September week,
while our Marines were digging in on Guadalcanal and Rommel
was sweeping across Egypt, they had to call the game off twice
in a row because the brothers couldn't hit me before the next
class started. They stood on the firing line and boomed the ball
off the wall behind me while I jumped, ducked, slid in panic,
like a rabbit in front of the dogs, sure that the next throw would
splatter my head against the wall. Even when the coach rolled
in a second ball they missed me, throwing two at a time. The
truth was, I suppose, that the Murphys were not very good ath-
letes, just bigger and stronger than the rest of us.

The next day was a Saturday, and I was out in front of our
house flipping war cards with Frankie, who lived next door,
when the brothers suddenly loomed above us, watching. Kevin

routinely snatched Frankie's cap and he and Tom tossed it back and forth while we crouched there, waiting, not even thinking, looking from one brother to the other.

Finally, Tom said, "Littlejim, go get me a licorice stick," and stuck a penny in my hand. "Fast, now, get a leg on." Mostroni's Candy Store was three blocks away, and I raced off, gasping with relief. The thought had crossed my mind that they were going to break my glasses because I had frustrated them in dodge ball. I'm sure I set an East Thirty-second Street record for the three-block run, returning shortly with the two sticks: two for a penny, weep for what is lost. Tom took the sticks without thanks and gave one to his brother, who had pulled the button off Frankie's new cap. Frankie still squatted there, tears in his eyes, looking at the three of us now with hatred. He could see I was on the other side. I sold Frankie down the river and waited for new orders.

"Can you get us some potatoes?"

"No," I said, "I don't think so." Tom glared at me. "Maybe one."

"Make it a big one," he said. "I feel like a mickey." Mickeys were what we called potatoes baked in open fires; all over Flatbush you could smell the acrid aroma of charred potatoes.

"My cap," said Frankie. Kevin dropped it in a puddle from yesterday's rain and stepped on it. Ruined. Frankie picked it up, blindly, holding it with two fingers, and stumbled up the steps to his front door. We lived in a row of attached two-story brick houses, quite respectable, though sliding, with a few steps in front (on which we played stoop ball) and a handkerchief-patch of lawn, usually surrounded by a small hedge. In front of our house was the lamppost by which I could read at night, and next to it a slender young maple tree, which my father would tie to the lamppost during strong winds.

I went through the alley to our back entrance, and found my mother working in our Victory Garden of Swiss chard, carrots, radishes, beets. My father went fishing in Sheepshead Bay every Saturday, a mixed blessing as he would come back loaded with fish but in a generally unstable condition so we never knew what to expect. Today I was glad, as it would make my theft easy.

My mother looked up as I passed. "Littlejim, are you all

right?" My mother has always been able to look right into my heart as if it were dangling from my nose, a gift for which I frequently wished to strangle her.

"Of course," I said with scorn in my lying voice, "I'm just thirsty."

"Well, have a nice glass of milk, sweetheart," she said, wiping her forehead and looking at me closely. I trotted into the kitchen and looked in the potato pail beneath the sink. There were around ten left so I took a large one and a small one, stuck them in my shirt, and went out the front door. The Murphys were waiting down the street by the vacant lot, the fire already going.

Thus began my life of crime, which lasted almost eight months, well into 1943, for which I showed natural gifts, except temperamentally. I was always trembling but never caught. I graduated from potatoes to my mother's purse, from packs of gum at the candy store ("that Nazi wop," said Tom) to packs of cigarettes at the delicatessen: the owners watched the Murphys while my quick hands stuffed my pockets full of contraband. Under the protection of the Murphy brothers, who beat up a German boy so badly that he was hospitalized, who dropped kittens into the sewers, who slashed the tires of cars owned by parents who tried to chastise them, I collected small sums of money from boys much larger than myself. Like Mercury, god of cheats and thieves, I was the swift messenger for Tom and Kevin Murphy.

I loved them. They needed me, I thought, not reading them very well. What they really needed was temporary diversion, and for a while I provided that. Kevin was virtually illiterate, so, beginning with the Sunday comics one afternoon, I became his official reader. He read (looked at) nothing but comic books— *Plastic Man, Superman, Captain Marvel, The Katzenjammer Kids; Sheena Queen of the Jungle* was his particular favorite because of her lush figure and scanty clothing.

"Get a load of that," he'd squeak (Kevin, and to a lesser extent Tom, had a high nasal whine). "What the freak is she saying?"

" 'Stand back,' " I'd read, " 'There's something in there!' "

"Freaking A!" Kevin would shout. He got terrifically excited by these stories.

It was not long before I was talking like the Murphys, in a

high squeaky voice with a strong Brooklyn accent, punctuated
(in school) by swear words and (at home) by half-swear words
that I didn't understand. My mother was horrified.

"What the freak is this?" I'd shrill at some casserole she was
placing on the table.

"Jimmy! Don't use language like that!"

"Freak? What's wrong with that?" I'd say in truly abysmal ignorance. "Freak, freaky, freaking. It doesn't mean *anything*, everyone says it." This is 1943, remember.

"I don't care what everyone says," my father would shout,
turning red. "You watch your lip around here, and fast!"

On weekends we sat around a fire in the vacant lot, smoking
cigarettes I had stolen (the Murphys favored the Lucky Strike
red bull's-eye pack, which showed through the pockets of their
white shirts) and eating mickeys which I had scooped up from
in front of Tietjen's Grocery. About six of us were generally
there—the Murphys, myself, and two or three of the tougher
kids on the block whose faces have faded from my memory.

One spring day, when rains had turned the lot into trenches of
red clay among the weeds and abandoned junk—people dumped
old stoves, broken bicycles, useless trash there—Tom Murphy
had the idea for The Lineup. This was based on a combination
of dodge ball from school and firing squads from the daily news.
The idea was to catch kids from the neighborhood, line them up
like enemy soldiers against the garage that backed on to the lot,
and fire clay balls at them. They would keep score and see who
was the best shot.

"Go get Frankie and his little brother," Tom told me. To Tom,
almost everyone was an enemy. "They're playing Three Steps to
Germany in front of his house. Tell him you want to show him
something."

Since the cap incident, Frankie had become much more alert,
darting into his house whenever the Murphys appeared on the
block. He often looked at me with reproach during the past
months, but never said anything, and I simply dropped him like
a red hot mickey, though he had been my only real friend.

"He won't come," I said. "He won't believe me."

"He'll believe you," Tom said. Kevin stepped on my foot

and pushed me heavily into the bushes. It was the first time he
had turned on me and I couldn't believe it. I looked at Tom for
help.

"Go get Frankie and Billy," he repeated. "We'll hide in the
bushes."

I walked miserably down the block, sick at heart. Shouldn't I
just duck into my own house? Shouldn't I tell Frankie to run?
Somehow these alternatives seemed impossible. I was committed
to the Murphy brothers. While my childhood went up in flames,
I spoke through the blaze in my head and talked Frankie into
coming to the lot for some mickeys. I was bright-eyed with innocence, knowing full well what I was doing, cutting myself off
from my parents, my church, selling my friend for the love of
the Murphy brothers, whom I wanted to love me back.

"My ma gave me two potatoes. They'll be ready in a couple of
minutes. You and Billy can split one."

Frankie wanted to believe me. "Have you seen Tom or Kevin
today?"

"They went crabbing," I said, glib with evil. "Their Uncle Jake
took them out on the bay. They promised they'd bring me some
blueclaws."

The walk down the block to the lot, maybe two hundred
yards, was the longest I've ever taken. I babbled inanely to keep
Frankie from asking questions. Billy was saved by suddenly deciding to go play inside instead—he didn't like mickeys, anyway,
a heresy admitted only by the very young. I didn't dare protest,
for fear of making Frankie suspicious. The lot appeared empty
and we were well into it when Kevin stood up from behind a
gutted refrigerator; Frankie whirled around right into Tom, who
twisted his thin arm and bent him to the ground.

"Lineup time!" shouted Kevin, "Freaking A!", as they carried
the kicking boy over to the wall. There, they threw him down
and tore off his shoes, making it difficult for him to run, over the
rusty cans, cinders, and thorny bushes. They had made a large
pile of clay balls already, and the three other boys began firing
them mercilessly at the cowering figure, their misses making red
splotches on the garage wall. This was the first Lineup in our
neighborhood, a practice that quickly escalated so that within a

few months boys were scaling the lethal tin cans their parents flattened to support the war effort. The Murphy boys held back momentarily, looking down at me.

"Where's Billy, you little fag?" Tom asked.

"He wouldn't come. He doesn't like mickeys." I was wincing at Frankie's cries as a clay ball would strike him.

"Maybe you ought to take his place," Tom said. "One target's not enough." Kevin reached from behind and snatched off my glasses, plunging me into the shadowy halfworld in which I was always terrified. Without my glasses I could hardly speak and I said nothing as they pushed me back and forth like a rag doll.

"You see that hoop there?" one of them said. "Bring it over to the garage and stand in it, you four-eyed freak." Squinting, I could barely make out a whitish hoop lying near the fire. I bent down and grabbed it with my right hand and went down on my knees with a piercing scream that must have scared even the Murphy brothers. They had heated the metal hoop in the fire until it was white hot and my hand stuck briefly to it, branding me for life. The older boys whooped and ran off, firing a few last shots at Frankie, Kevin not forgetting to drop my glasses in the fire, where my father found them the next day.

I knelt doubled up, retching with pain and grief while Africa was falling to the Allies and our soldiers battled through the Solomon Islands: the tide had turned. I went home and had my hand attended to—third-degree burns!—and slept dreamless as a baby for the first time in years.

# PUTTING & GARDENING

WILLIAM F. VAN WERT

William F. Van Wert teaches courses in film and creative
writing at Temple University. He has published two books on
film and a collection of short stories, *Tales for Expectant
Fathers,* was recently published by Dial Press. He was born
in Midland, Michigan, and is the father of three boys.

"Looks like rain," my father says with a mixed stare of genteel
benevolence and childish malice. As with most things at his age,
rain is a mixed blessing: good for the garden, bad for golf.

My father has been retired for twelve years, but he still eats
his businessman's breakfast of poached egg and grapefruit at 7
A.M., then works on the house and the yard, then "clocks out" at
two to play golf. He makes lists for himself the night before of
things to do, then crosses them off with the gold Cross pen his
employees gave him when he closed the appliance store. He
changes lightbulbs, he fixes the toilet that won't flush, he makes
wooden shelves for the shanty or devises yet another clothesline
for my mother. His clotheslines have been looking more like
Calder mobiles in recent years, but he takes no pride in them
nor in any "indoors" work. For he is still a farmer in his heart.

He is a farmer who hasn't farmed since he was sixteen. His father died of a heart attack when my father was only thirteen and
the last of six children left on the farm. My grandmother kept
him on the brand-new Oliver my grandfather bought but never
got to use. She watched him going up and down the rows of
wheat and corn and beans until sunfall when they would eat together their simple Dutch supper of half meat and double
starch. He would eat only half of his roast beef, saving the rest

Copyright © 1982 by the University of Northern Iowa. First appeared in
*The North American Review.* Reprinted by permission.

for his sandwich the next day at school. But he would eat double helpings of corn and mashed potatoes, something he still
does. And he would drink a cold beer, before and after supper,
falling asleep in his father's rocking chair promptly after the latter beer. And my grandmother would yell at him in Dutch to
wake up and do his lessons and go to bed. She insisted on the
lessons even then, knowing that she would sell the farm as soon
as he graduated from high school. Perhaps she also knew that he
would make his way from Bay City to Midland, selling tomatoes
to passing cars.

"Let me check the garden and then we'll clock out fast, okay?"
he says with a wink. He doesn't have to ask. I know it's my cue
to get the golf bags from the shanty and put them in the trunk
of the car.

"Make sure the tees aren't broken and pack a few practice
balls for four and seven," he adds. Four and seven are the par
3-holes at the Clare golf course, and they have water traps in
front of them. You have to use a five-iron or a three-wood, you
have to elevate your tee a little and you have to get the ball up
in the air, pop-up fashion, or you go in the woods on the right,
into another fairway on the left or into water front and back. I
prefer the water, even though it costs my father a ball every
time. I like to see the water jump like gunshot in the afternoon
sun and hear the "plop" like frog-talk around the green.

My father still has a drink before and after supper, but now
it's a manhattan before and a Bourbon-and-soda after. And he
promptly falls asleep, only now it's a black felt recliner instead
of the old wooden rocker. And sometimes my mother blames it
on the golf . . . and sometimes on the drinks.

"Jim . . . ?" my mother says, as though she were taking his
pulse.

"Let him sleep, mom," I coax, "he's had a long day."

I know I'm not exaggerating, for my feet are tired too after
eighteen holes, front and back, plus four more, a practice four
for me to straighten out my drives and for him to practice his
putting. I suppress a yawn as I say this, knowing that I would
never go to sleep at seven in the evening. My mother and all
seven of her children were born night owls. My father is still a
farmer. He can't keep his eyes open after ten o'clock.

"But he promised to make a bonfire tonight."

It's true. He likes to light up the sky on these summer evenings. He does it for his children and their children, the marshmallows half eaten, the cigarettes smoked to keep the mosquitoes away and then thrown into the fire, the last looks at the lake and its flat blue ripple like a worried forehead. And my father relaxes as he eases the logs into the pit and watches the flames dance up at him. His worried forehead cannot keep its frown, the money ledger in his mind, his Dutch farmer's respect for habit, the forty years he kept the books. His mouth goes slack with the breeze through the birches behind him. He looks off and surveys the lake with the look of a man about to drown. He eases the spring on his sadness, the firm jaws of silence and too tight control of a lifetime. And sometimes he laughs at nothing or tells a joke that's not funny or curses or swings an imaginary number one-wood into the lake. But mostly he surveys the land, sometimes as an alien might. He doesn't swim or boat or sit on the dock. Sometimes he likes to fish at night when one of his sons will go along. Sometimes he makes one go along . . . to have a chat. But these are not flatlands of ploughed fertility, this is not God's soil for growing, and these white birches will never put food on the table.

"Nice night," he says softly, as much to himself as to me. We both have hands in pockets, and I realize that my gaze goes where his does, my body stretches when his does, involuntarily. Perhaps this is what is meant by being my father's son.

"Jim . . . ?" my mother says again, this time more insistently.

My father turns slightly in the recliner, still snoring and mumbling softly in his sleep.

"Damn . . ." he whispers, "I could have parred that baby."

"I'll par you one, you ole bloater," my mother says, mock-sternly.

It's not the sleep she minds. It's the snoring, the look of lax pleasure around the corners of his mouth, the jaws going gentle, his usual look of kind but unswerving purpose going to putty, the deep lifelines puffing out again, as though his face were up for grabs, an invitation to sculpt. My mother is tired at this time of night. It's too early to play cards and too soon after dishes to do much else but sit. The evening news is just finishing on TV.

My mother likes the game shows in the morning, the soapers in the afternoon and the "family" shows at night, especially "Little House on the Prairie," "The Waltons" and "Eight is Enough." This is the only time she doesn't watch TV, because she doesn't like the news. My father puts the news on at six and eleven. He wants to catch the weather, he wants to hear the sports and know what the next day will be like for the garden and the golf. But he often misses the weather on the six o'clock news, because he's asleep, and then he has to stay up for the eleven. If he gets the weather at six, he can go to bed at ten.

My mother has known these habits for forty-some years, and still she objects every night. Yet even her objections are comfortable now, more by rote than by passion, familiar and perfected, a little like the way an Olivier recites his Shakespeare, having recited it a thousand times already.

"Well? What is it, dear?" my father asks finally, some ten minutes after my mother has stopped prodding and begun her sewing in the other room. During the day my parents both act as though I were their honored guest, someone to laugh with and cater to and look lovingly upon, one of their flesh grown up. But at night they revert, they can't help themselves; they act, I'm sure, the way they act when they are alone with no more children left in the nest.

And when there were no more children left, almost seven years ago now, my father did as so many men from Michigan have done: he bought a winter home in Florida. He was like a little peacock for the first few years. It was as though he had bought the entire state of Florida. He began to wear sunglasses and white belts and short-sleeved flower shirts with the top buttons undone, so that his chest hair peeked out like the tuft of a woman from an x-rated movie. He even grew a moustache for a time and looked Jewish and Italian at the same time. He announced that he would never shovel snow again.

"I never realized you hated Michigan winters so much," I told him. "Have you always felt this way?"

He just smiled and that was his answer. I never knew what he had felt all those years of supposed white Christmas and winter wonderland. But he really retired with grace and for good when he bought up Florida. That's when he began to play golf and grow his gardens. The fruit trees brought forth at least twice a year in southern Florida. It reminded me of having read somewhere that women in and around the Amazon menstruate twice and sometimes three times a month, dying of "old age" at thirty. I wonder at that kind of climate where things grow in double time, while the people, those suede faces that look like immigrants or outpatients from the geriatric ward, the endless midwestern Mayflower, those people come to retard the harvest of their own spoiled skin.

And my father thrived in that climate. He ate the grapefruit off his trees for breakfast, put on his gloves and went out to mow the lawn, spray the trees, spread mulch and prune the shrubs. He would lay the sticks around his tomatoes that looked so big and gaudy-bulbous, like the insides of watermelons. And he would fondle his limes, the good green smell of photosynthesis all about them, overbig and awkward on the branch, the size of avocados. He spent hours in his yard, chatting with the neighbors who were in their yards, all retired and all watering the lawn.

And my mother would wince at noon and take off her blouse, close the curtains and turn on the air conditioner. She would iron clothes and watch the afternoon soaps and never peek outside. She missed her children, she missed her sisters and brothers, she missed the Michigan friends who shared cups of coffee with her in the mornings. She adjusted, after a fashion. She baked brownies for the sick, and there were always the sick in their new trailer park. She joined a poker club and went to that every Tuesday night. She started quilting and putting the several hundred photographs of all of us as children into albums. She longed for summer and the cottage in Michigan. She did a lot of waiting, especially at times when her children couldn't get away from their jobs and come down for a visit. She stopped writing letters about this time. She said we were too old now and she was too lazy. She started taking naps in the afternoon, and she began to call us long-distance once or twice a week. And at the same time that she stopped going to church, she began to say "pray to God" in the middle of many of her sentences.

"I don't know," she would giggle, the prerequisite self-denial every time she was about to say something serious, "but I pray to God he don't die before I do. I mean, he loves it down here. He tends his trees and gets down on his knees and plays in dirt for hours. He makes his little visits to the neighbors, brings their mail to them, cuts their lawn for them. If it's finished in our yard, he looks for someone else's yard. And you should see the living dolls down here. Looks like someone erased their faces years ago, but they're still ready, and do they ever love your father. Pray to God I don't ever look like that, live long enough to look like that."

"And what about you, Mom?"

"Oh, I'm fine. It's okay. You know me, I like to complain a lot."

"Tell the truth. What about you?"

"I guess it would be okay, honest, if it weren't so stinking hot down here. I itch all the time. I go to scratch a mosquito and it's only heat. I hit myself all the time for nothing."

We both laugh and hang up. That's the way the calls have gone for seven years.

Then she got cancer.

My father called in January, the week after New Year's. Classes had just begun, I was teaching again, I was in the middle of a writing binge.

"Your mother went in for a test last week . . ."

I waited, even though I already knew the rest.

". . . and, well, they found something."

He choked up. He could barely finish his sentence.

"She didn't want to tell any of you, but I said to her, 'We have to tell the kids.'"

They found something. My poor father couldn't even name the thing, couldn't say that word, couldn't bear that thought. It was his way, this honesty so indirect that the listener had to fill in the blanks. When he told me the facts of life, he called it "intercourse" and "copulation." I was ten years old. I didn't understand a thing he said. I had heard about "screw" and "lay" and "go down" and "all the way," but I had never heard of copulation. He couldn't name the thing.

Something in his voice denied emotion while calling S.O.S. in baby screams. I couldn't sleep, I couldn't think. I took the next plane to Florida and met the man without his mask. My mother was to be operated on the next day. He had just come back from twelve hours at the hospital.

He looked fit and trim in his blue panama suit. He looked ready for Mass, but his eyes were bloodshot and the drink in his hand showed only ice, for the third time in thirty minutes.

"How are you, Dad?"

He tried to say "Fine," he tried to hug me and play host and make me a drink, but he couldn't. He just collapsed in my arms, big bear-man of Dutch silence, his body too shrieked to control and his sad need to control, to fall back into fatherly silence, to hold it all in, the patterns I learned so well from him. I held his body in my arms, his chest expanse so big I could barely lock my fingers around his back. I held him and whispered to his cheek that he could let down now, and he never said a word about that, not then and not after. But he broke down and sobbed and our bodies, standing near the Bourbon bottle, our bodies rocked back and forth, like slow dancers in the smoke of public places. How they look as though they've melted into each other, or maybe just holding each other up, still swaying to the music, even with the band on break.

And when he broke from my hug, he made himself another drink and cursed and cried for another hour. Trying to be sensible, philosophical, jovial, he kept begging that it be him instead of her. My sister, who had just arrived that afternoon, couldn't stand to see him that way. She kept telling him he had to be strong, and his eyes flashed dark sparks at her, but his head bobbed up and down in mute assent. He shut it up and said no more.

He told me in the car the next day that it did no good to pour forth. It made him weak and tired, so much so that he couldn't "hold his cheer" when he was with my mother. And so he had resolved to shelve the emotions and make the rest of her time some kind of circus of smiles and crackerjacks, worry-free.

He let me sit alone with my mother in her hospital bed. We didn't look at each other much. We just held hands and talked about the weather in Philadelphia and, the few times our eyes met, we tried to laugh but it came out tears. She looked so old and shorn like a bald crow, hunched up like my grandmother and scared and proud, still too proud to complain for herself. I gave back the letter she had written me two years earlier, the one marked "personal" that scolded me for loss of faith, the one that reminded me that I was a "cradle Catholic." Her eyes filled up with wet thanks, but her throat caught, the bandaged throat where they took the lump, it squeaked, and it looked like she wanted to spit on me.

My father paced the floor of the hospital and he sat like a mannequin in the recliner at home. He felt guilty that he couldn't take it away from her and give it to himself. He felt guilty about not showing us a good time, but he felt guilty about going out.

"Let's go hit some golf balls," I urged.

He smiled and nodded no.

"Dad, let's go hit the balls," I commanded.

"I can't do that. What would anyone think, seeing me play golf while she's like that?"

"To hell with what they think. You need to get it out. You need to kill some balls."

He just got up and walked out the door and waited for me in the car. It was the only time that he didn't preach to me on the golf course. No lessons about keeping my left foot on a line with the tee, taking my practice swing, keeping my left arm stiff and not going any further than my shoulder on the arc. He dribbled his first few drives. He was still trying to play good golf.

"Dad, we aren't here to break forty today. I want you to wind up and cream that sucker. I want you to put all your anger into it and rip the cover off the damn ball. Pretend it's the lump they took out."

He wasn't used to such a reckless swing. He wound up high and far behind his neck like some Tarzan reaching overhead for a vine. The silver stick held for a moment behind his neck, looking like a brace for polio. And then he swung through, wild and Babe Ruth striking out. He missed it all and found himself on the seat of his pants. He just put his head into his hands, and I thought I ought to crouch and cradle him. But he came up laughing like a mystic, pray to God, cocked to the eyeballs with root anger and fear. And we just banged away all day, like terrorists. Some holes we didn't even bother to putt out. We just picked up our battered balls and went around the green to the next fairway to swing as hard as we could one more time. We lost about twenty balls between us that afternoon in water and woods and bunkers of quicksand. The balls were flopping like pigeon droppings in the air and skittering helter-skelter through the high grass. And then we went home and got sudden-drunk, so drunk we laughed through the evening news of hurricanes and hijackings, record interest rates and police brutality. After cancer, it was all a joke, a belly-buckle bottle-sucking mother lode of gold humor. It was good to hear that other people were dying.

I went to Florida to hold it in, like my father, to hold it all together and heal them both. To give back what they had given, wasn't that what a son was supposed to do? To make them laugh. Scold them. Take care of the essentials, like meals and laundry and groceries. I went down there to touch my mother, the untouchable one now, and to talk with my father, the silent master of mind control. But instead I ended up hugging my father and being with him in his silence. I ended up talking a lot with my mother and asking her to ask for herself.

"What's the lesson in all of this, Mom? What does it mean for you?"

"Hell if I know," she said casually, eyes off on the floor somewhere, biting her lip.

She had what was called the early superivenicaval syndrome, and what it meant was the choking off of blood, the puffed cheeks and collapsed right lung and vessels on her neck like bean sprouts. Before I left she had begun her cobalt of five thousand rads, a little Hiroshima at a time, in the squat aluminum hovel with the sign on the door: WARNING: DO NOT PLAY ON ROOF.

"Looks like rain," my father would say, driving to the treatments. It rained every afternoon in Fort Myers, and the rain whipped up the royal palms that usually looked like sculptures of cement, it whipped them up and made them look like helicopter blades, and then it all dried up just as predictably as the fast food huts and the endless excursions to Winn-Dixie for the "sales." Rain was not the enemy here. It came and went every day, and my father gardened before it and golfed after it. And in between, during the downpour, we would go for the treat-

ments, the traffic bumper to bumper, slow-mo and excreting exhaust so thick the houses shimmered in the sun and the pampas
grass looked like a cheap cowboy movie.

"Hot," my mother complained. "Hot as Dutch love."

We watched the other patients come in and go out, some
bandaged and some burned, all of them making weak gestures
of good luck to each other, the modern-day lepers. My mother
got nauseous looking at them, the treatment more hideous than
the disease, all those people with red-beet noses, wigs on and
wobbly, their lips looking green and withered like the pulp of
the lime.

I tried but I could not go gentle into that good night. I had
the most pornographic dreams every night, as though the savage
sexual mutilation of babies, the sweet surrender of my brother's
wife, the hind-end humping with any and every woman I have
ever known were the antidote, the only cure for cancer and this
helpless hopeless feeling of standing still and watching my
mother turn into a prune. It reminded me of the whores I used
to see in Thailand, their imperious eyes of yellow peril and their
sweet, noxious breath between pale-pink teeth from the betel-
nut juice, asking me the passerby:

"Hey, honey, you want fucking or sucking?"

And it was true now. I thought of every last one of them in
my dreams, and it was true. That was all I wanted out of life.

We all went to Florida to be with my mother. Some brought
their children, and there was no way to predict behavior, before
or after. Two of my brothers went down and spent their days on
the beach, unable to cope, to look at her without breaking down.
My sister began to act like my mother, look like her, scolding my
father for drinking and falling asleep and playing golf.

Where was the lesson in all of this?

I went down there again in March during our spring break.
My mother had just finished the cobalt treatments and was
about to begin chemotherapy, biting her nails and looking a little unkept, derelict, taking bird-bites of despair for breakfast
and lunch, a piece of old toast and twenty cups of black coffee.
The grapefruit on my father's trees were in their second bloom,
fresh and plump and pink inside, somehow so sexual that this
pink pulp be the first thing the tongue should touch in the morn-

ing. By contrast, my father's golf balls looked a little smaller, a little bruised from bad contact and off-center chipping.

My mother was still alive, even though the doctors said she might not last beyond April. Carcinoma and metastasis. Even the doctors couldn't name the thing, and my father felt so guilty because he couldn't understand them. He kept dropping by their office, kept calling on the phone, and he couldn't form a picture in his mind for the words they told him.

My mother stayed alive, because my little sister was still anything but little, unmarried and over two hundred fifty pounds. She stayed alive because the summer was coming, and that meant the cottage in Michigan. My father tried to suggest that maybe they should stay in Florida, not risk a long drive, stay with the doctors they already knew. My mother wouldn't hear a word of it. She wanted the cottage now more than she had ever wanted any of her seven children.

"I'm still alive, because you kids keep praying, that's what. I don't see how I can die with all that interference," she smiled.

And when I left, she winked at me, the silent sign that this would not be the last time. She still had not come to grips with the cancer. She just offered it up to God, merits for one of her children every time she threw up or went dizzy or got depressed and put her head under the pillow. My parents had buried my Aunt BaBa of cancer two years before. My mother had sworn then that she would never want to die of cancer. My father took out two cancer insurance policies.

They told me about the difficult visits with BaBa in the hospital, how she begged them to take her up to the cottage to die, how they washed their hands after every visit, because they still thought cancer could be caught like a common cold. They talked about wishing friends well who got cancer and about avoiding those people. Now my mother could separate her friends into distinct categories: the ones who called but didn't name the thing; the ones who sent cards with spiritual quotes or Rod McKuen poems; the ones who never got in touch with her and the very few who came in person right away and kissed her on the forehead.

"Ain't life cruel?" she said, with the tone of a blackjack dealer, as though you had to expect the unexpected.

238 WILLIAM F. VAN WERT

My father kept stroking his chin and wondering if he had a lump of his own.

My father taught me how to gather the topmost grapefruit first, the ones that get the most sun. He taught me the time of the day when one could spray; how to tell the quality of an orange by the firmness and shadow at the umbilicus, the place where it was attached to the tree; how to crate tomatoes for best weight and least bruising, the smaller, unripe tomatoes on the bottom and the big red ripe ones on top, separated one from another by little cardboard cutouts.

He wiped the dew-line of sweat from his bald head and smiled.

"Sometimes I wonder why I ever did anything else."

"Because you had seven kids . . ."

"Perhaps. But if you work the ground, I mean, if you really work it every day, my mother used to say you'd never get dizzy. You'd always know where you were."

"Is that why you do it?"

"Huh? Oh, not really."

"Why, then?"

"I don't know if there are words for that sort of thing."

"Come on, Dad. Why?"

"Well, it teaches me the love of the body. Especially at my age."

I didn't say anything.

"I told you there weren't any words."

And he went back to digging.

My mother's cancer had devoured everything: the worry, the attention, the prayers. My father was a forgotten man. Nobody asked how he was. He stopped getting on the phone when anyone called.

And when I left, she winked at me, her silent promise that this would not be the last time. And my father waited until the last minute, hugged me quickly, the usual fast feeling between grown father and son. But then he kissed me. He did it so quickly that I had to wonder on the plane going back if it had really happened. I cannot remember a single other time that my father has kissed me. I cried, and maybe the crying was somehow assurance that, yes, it actually happened.

"Looks like rain," my father says with his mixed stare of the green thumb and the imp. "We'll go anyway, huh?"

I nod and go to pack up the golf bags in the trunk of his car. And then I walk down to the dock, while he tends his garden. I stare at the lake and wonder why it is that I can never get enough of this clean air and quiet lake. It's more than nostalgia, the remembrance of a good childhood, the carefree swims with my brothers and sisters, the only time my father ever got out his movie camera, some twenty years of cryptic film, from kindergarten to college, of kids that looked like any kids but got to look like him, doing belly-smackers off the end of the dock.

I take a mental snapshot this time, something to develop and return to the next time winter in Philadelphia oppresses me. I like this lake in the morning and at night, lit up or in shadow. I step on the dock and stare for miles, wondering as I walk across the boards why it is that people don't live in the place that speaks to their heart, that feeds their passion. There is no money to feel in my pockets, and of course I know the answer. But maybe the cottage offers me the chance to ask the really foolish questions. I wear my father's sweatshirts and baseball hats, I stop shaving and waste time, I actually take time to stare again. First foot on the dock and I become a character out of Dr. Seuss, a Zanzibar Buck Buck McFate fishing for Doubt-Trout in the cool pool of Nool. I compete with everyone and everything in the city, but here I talk back to crickets and wonder what else these big Dutch hands of mine were made for, besides driving a car and moving a typewriter.

I turn and look at my father, who is throwing up his hands at someone higher than these thunderclouds overhead. My father is two men, the man in Florida who can make anything grow, who can eat what he grows. Because his garden is always green down there, his golfing is a luxury, something he does as much for the companionship with other men from the park as for his own passion, something he does deliberately, with flair and style. Here in Michigan, there is only this lake and the beach sand that is as barren as it is beautiful. He has imported the grass, which goes bald each summer, the sand swallowing up the little blades of green. He plants no fruit or vegetables in Michigan. Here it's flowers, flowers whose seeds he has bought in a store. He gives them dirt, he waters them and watches over them, even though he doesn't even know their names. The pine trees grow on either side of his flower boxes, the birches swing freely behind them, but the boxes are coffins. His flowers die as quickly as he can plant them.

"Damn," I hear him mutter, unaware that I'm that close, "woman's work . . ."

And he turns to me with that look I've noticed recently, the twisted look of the Feeble in his eyes, the look of drunk driving, delirium tremens. My stomach sinks to see that look of no-care in his eyes. The cancer policies have their limits. My mother is neither dead nor cured, and my father has taken to calculating the cost of the future. I look away at the flowers and understand his despair and their lesson: they bloom and die outside of any-one's control or calculations. Like children. The lesson here is something other than the love of the body, something beyond bad dirt and fallen petals, shriveled stems and bees that have to look elsewhere to drop their pollen. You can't eat the flowers.

So the golf is his business and passion. He goes alone or he goes with the neighbor, but he goes for the golf, not the camara-derie. I go for something else.

Not one of his five sons wanted his appliance business and neither of his two daughters wanted to learn how to type and be a secretary. Now nobody wants to golf with him. But I have consented, at first as a way to be with just my father, this man I have loved all my life and never known. My father goes through a complete personality change on the links. His old shoulders straighten up and he walks with a bounce again. He laughs and jokes, winking and whistling at the women golfers, exchanging quick repartees with the men, these other retirees with the hard knocks of their working days written all over their faces, includ-ing the eighty-five-year-old crustacean with the craggy cheeks and the twinkle in his eyes, who comes up to tell a joke as stale as the seat of his baggy pants.

"Hey, Jim, you hear the one about the geezer who passed gas in this public place? His friend says, 'Hey, Ed, not with a lady present,' and Ed, he says, 'I didn't know we was taking turns.'"

My father laughs, because respect is required on the golf

course. It's a private world of old fools acting young again, and my father admires them because they play eight hours a day. I go along, because it's my only chance to see the boy in my father, and he's happy I've come with him to share his passion. He doesn't care if I lose the balls or if we have to wave the hard hitters through while we look for my errant drives. And when I really peg one, he watches it go its three hundred yards and stands transfixed, as though before a miracle.

"Gee, if I only had your power. You don't have to whack it hard, see? It just goes and goes."

I ask him what would have happened if he had discovered golf before he was sixty-two. He shrugs his shoulders in such a way that I know he's asked himself this same question a thousand times.

"I might have spent everything we had," he says with a mock-horrified look on his face.

"Would that have been so terrible?"

"I couldn't have bought in Florida," he says, and this time he's serious.

On my first drive I get to within a hundred yards of the green. The closer I get to the green, the worse I get. I takes me seven more shots to put the ball in the cup. My father, whose drives rarely go more than a hundred and fifty yards, has put it in with four shots. He comes close to par on every hole, usually missing with his bad putting.

"It's the chip shots and the putts that separate the men from the boys," he says from someone else's sermon. "Who takes the time to learn how to putt?"

He has taken to hacking the weeds around the cottage with his nine-iron and putter, so that these clubs are as much an extension of his hand as the watch around his wrist. So far, it hasn't helped.

He teaches me the etiquette of golf, all the polite positions of where to stand while someone else swings, what happens if your ball hits someone else's ball, when to take a mulligan and when not, how you can't touch the sand on your practice swing in the sand traps. And we talk golf from the tee to the green. Only on the green and only after we've both put our balls in the cup do we talk about our personal lives. The time it takes to walk from the green to the tee-off mound for the next hole is the allotted time for any real talking.

I have come this time just to be there and be healed as much as to heal. In the nine months from January to August, my marriage has gone bankrupt. One brother and one sister have already left their marriages in these nine months. And, because my parents never talk about the cancer, they have taken on the burden of these marriages as their concern, their worry, their sorrow.

On the green for number three, after my father has put his putt in for par, he asks me:

"Are you compatible?"

"What do you mean?"

"You know. Are you sexually compatible?"

"I don't know how to answer that. I'm turned on all the time. She's turned on almost none of the time."

"But is it something that can be helped? In time? Or therapy?"

"I don't know, Dad. We used to think we saw it the same way."

"Do you need money?"

"Yes. But not from you, thanks."

By then we've reached the mound for teeing off on number four and have to wait another four hundred fifty yards before we can talk about anything but golf again.

Something has shown up in my mother's blood test for the week. The new oncologist is afraid that it has spread to her liver.

"As long as it's not my brain," she jokes, for she is most afraid of someone irradiating her brain, of becoming a vegetable. But she's also worried about her liver, her lungs and all those organs she can't see and can only feel by the poison of the cytoxin in her chemotherapy.

"Can we say a rosary together?" I ask. It's something we haven't done as a family for at least twenty-five years. Mary insists that she has to do the dishes and Jo goes to the toilet, so the "family" consists of me and my parents. I can scarcely remember

the sorrowful mysteries—the scourging at the pillar, the crown-
ing of thorns, the carrying of the cross, the crucifixion—all those
necessary steps toward the resurrection of the body. My father
and I take turns saying the "Hail Mary" and my mother says the
"Holy Mary."

I ask my mother to stop saying novenas for my marriage and
to start praying for herself. I suggest that the "lesson" to her cancer can only come when she feels worthy enough to pray for
herself.

"I'll think about it," she says.

I massage my father's feet as I have done every night of my
visit. The knotted feet with corns and calluses and bulging veins,
gnarled as a hunchback from so many years of steel arch sup-
ports, have actually straightened out and lost some of their
"crystals," their pus and their stink. And because we have just
said the rosary, I begin to feel a little like Christ doing Peter's
feet. There are so many questions I want to ask this man, so
many things he could tell me, but talk never comes easily. So I
massage his feet and let that be enough.

When he has gone to bed, my mother and I talk. With her the
talk comes freely, the jokes and sidelong glances as codified as
traffic signs. We know when to start and stop. And I rub her
aching shoulders, she who resists any kind of touching. I realize
that I can give to them separately, but I am confused by them as
a couple. I revert to stupor, to being their son, to letting them do
for me. And I realize why I am a writer: verbose, like my
mother, but on paper, preserving the silence of my father.

The next day we go to the hospital and she is proclaimed an
N.E.D. (non-evaluative disease): clean scans, remission time.
There's no overt joy or celebration that night at supper, only this
sense of pause in the eye of the storm.

"The lesson," my mother confides that night when we're alone,
"is that I have been too proud. I had seven children, they were
all whole and healthy, and I bragged them up too much. God is
punishing me for that."

It's not the answer I expected after nine months of living with
this auto-cannibalism. But it was surely the only way that my
mother could rationalize the Book of Job all around her, the only

way she could hold the cancer and the broken marriages in the same perspective. One thing about prayer: you always get what you ask for and it never looks like you thought it would.

The next day, my last day at the cottage, my father pleads sheepishly to clock out early and take me golfing.

"Again?" my mother says, irate.

"Honey, what have you got in mind?"

"Not a thing, Jim. Go on, both of you."

We go with her cursed blessing. In the car, his hands so hard around the steering wheel that his knuckles look like polished piano keys, my father starts to sob, the Feeble dancing in his eyes, and he begs for himself.

"It's the only time I don't have my mind on it. I thought she understood that."

I don't say anything. I have no idea of the bargains and compromises they have struck to stick together for forty-two years. But I shudder, involuntarily, for the bare fog of what this body has been through in its lifetime passes over me, this body born on the farm before there was any pollution, this body now strapped in a Buick LeSabre on cruise control, and only the golf course is left to remind one of what the "natural" world must have been like.

"The bitch," he whispers.

I had to hear that whisper to know she was safe with him, to know that he still loved her after all these years.

The greens are separate from everything else on a golf course. They are alone their named color, green and carpet-soft. And my father has a special reverence for putting on these greens. I have watched him walk more softly when he approaches the greens. I have seen him tiptoe around a ball and measure the distance between him and the hole. I still swing too hard on my putts, and today on this, the ninth hole, I have hit grass before ball, so that the ball skipped right over the cup like a stone thrown sideways across the surface of the lake: bump, bump and bump, without ever dropping. My father flicks the ball with his putter, so that it has topspin, and the ball backs its way into the hole. His ball says "caution" and mine "abandon," and I wonder if we wouldn't be better off, this beloved stranger and I, at our ages, to trade

styles for the sake of those who live with us. What do they say?
Rage is to age what truth is to youth?

I'm thinking these things when I realize that my father is not
walking with me to the car. I turn to see him on hands and
knees, lovingly replacing my divot on the magic carpet, this es-
sence of green, the only garden that is left for him.

# FEASTING

## ELIZABETH BENEDICT

Elizabeth Benedict was born in Hartford, Connecticut, grew
up in New York City, and went to Barnard, where she won
poetry and prose prizes. She published a poem in *The Paris
Review*, and *Seventeen* magazine recently published one of
her stories. Ms. Benedict now lives in Washington, D.C., and
is writing a novel.

We have spent only a week of nights together in the year that
we have been lovers, but for every one of those seven nights, we
have spent ten times that many hours on the telephone—calls
between New York and Los Angeles, Kansas City and Fort
Worth, a bar in Jackson, Mississippi and the Senate Press Gallery, defying sleep, time zones, deadlines, his wife and my husband.

Our livelihoods are connected intimately to the telephone. We
are both reporters and could no sooner survive without the telephone than we could without each other's long-distance affec-
tions. Yet the first sound of Patrick's voice on the phone, at any
hour, in any city, even when I am expecting a call from him, still
goes right to my knees, as if I had just heard of a death. "Don't
be nervous," he said once, when it was I who had called him,
"it's just me."

We spent three months in the same city earlier this year at hotels on opposite sides of town, and only three of those ninety-
odd nights together—and about half of them on the telephone,
once from midnight to dawn. We are sometimes drunk together
on the telephone, or if he is when he calls me, back late from a
business dinner, I start a new bottle of wine and take it and a

Copyright © 1982 by Elizabeth Benedict. First appeared in *The Massachusetts Review*. Reprinted by permission.

glass and the telephone into bed with me and talk to him until I no longer make sense.

It was during one of those late, lavish phone calls that we first exchanged fantasies. I wanted him to kneel on the floor as I lay at the edge of the bed with my legs wrapped around his head. He wanted, he said, for me to touch myself while we were making love. "It would be erotic for you to be solicitous with your body."

He has had other fantasies and fascinations and has relentlessly sought my permission to explore them in phone call after phone call, as if my willingness, halfway across the country, made any difference. He has wanted me to wear black, lacy underwear and to take it off of me in elaborate, ritualistic stages and make love to me wearing only a black garter belt. It entered early and oddly into our conversation. One of the first nights we were together, I said, "I'll miss you tomorrow."

"Do you have any black underwear?"

"What?"

"Do you have any black underwear?"

"I just said I'll miss you and you said do you have any black underwear. Did I miss something?"

"No. Do you?"

"No. Just pastels."

He has never said and I have never asked whether he asks his wife to wear black underwear as well. My husband has never mentioned black underwear or anything remotely like it to me. My husband is tender and dependable and ordinary in his lovemaking—except on the rare occasion when he has had too many martinis—and I would be surprised if he wanted anything more of his lovers.

When I think of it, though, I remember that it was I who made the first mention of unusual sexual interests to Patrick. And now I am sure that his wife does not wear black underwear to bed with him or indulge him in another taste we danced around and talked around for months. I told him, the first night we were together, that one of my lovers had spanked me, that it had been his idea. Patrick said he had never done that and wanted to know what it was like.

"Demeaning."

"Did he hurt you?"

"No. He was almost meek when he spanked me. The *idea* was demeaning."

"Not erotic?"

"Maybe for him."

"You didn't do it to him?"

"He didn't want me to. I think he thought it was a male prerogative."

Patrick patted my behind lightly. "Like this?" he said.

"Harder."

He patted harder.

"I haven't given you permission to do that."

"Is that part of it?"

"Yes."

"Who makes up the rules?"

"The players, I guess."

"Should we change them?"

"No."

"How many times did he hit you?"

"Just a few."

"With his hand?"

"Yes."

"Will you give me permission?"

"No."

"Why not?"

"I didn't like it."

"But you let him."

"I said yes to see what it was like and I didn't like it." I was emphatic, exasperated.

"You want to stop talking about it." A statement, not a question. I said yes.

There is a blunt charm to his curiosity but sometimes he does not know when to stop. I suppose that is part of the appeal, his shamelessness. When we were planning to meet in Chicago, he said, "Will you bring your black underwear?"

"I told you, I don't have any."

"Why don't you just stop off at Marshall Field on your way from the airport and pick up a garter belt?"

"Because I don't want one."

"Why not?"

"I guess I'm embarrassed."

"Just try it once."

"I don't want to."

I was tempted to call his bluff, greet him in lacy black things when he came to my door at the Palmer House, champagne glass raised into the air. But my assignment was changed at the last minute and I spoke to him that night in Chicago from a pay phone at a bar in Memphis.

The day after Christmas we spoke for several hours on the telephone, each of us in our offices, thousands of miles apart, about black underwear and spanking. We lay in bed one night several months after that, half undressed, my skirt pulled up around my waist and my underpants dangling on my ankles. He rubbed my behind over and over in smooth, careful circles and as I felt my spine loosen and curve against the grip of his arm, I heard the clap of his palm hard, really hard, against my buttock and there was a second in which the sound and the pain were separate and when I understood what he had done I recoiled and whimpered and went to him and said "hold me" and felt a thick knot in my throat. For a moment I was dazed, a child harshly, unexpectedly punished. He should have asked.

There were other things wrong that night, wholly separate from that humiliation—he said he wanted me and he didn't, he wanted his wife and he didn't, he wanted me to be simple and I am not. I left, annoyed at his indecision, at four in the morning. Walking out the door of his room I felt released and oddly chipper. I turned and said blithely, "I owe you a spanking," which I did not remember until he told me about it months later. "I thought it was a great parting line," he said.

He is unpredictable: expansive as spring in the morning and stingy and abrupt at dinner; curious at eleven and hostile at midnight. When sudden street noises make me jump, he holds

me tighter and says, "It's okay, I'm here." But I have a dim
memory, either a dream or a moment I want to forget, of his
saying, "Don't be so frail. It's just a fire engine." He has shut me
out and sent me away and asked me back again, all within minutes. In one phone call he said, "I don't want to see you again,"
and in the next he said, "I need to see you before I leave town."

"Need. Don't you mean want?"

"No, need. I need one of your hugs."

But he left town, after all, without one. "I'm going home tomorrow," he said, "and I can't take you back there with me."

"Can't we just—"

"Please don't make me say no to you."

He is not distinguished by his sense of humor. He is neither a
comic—adept at puns, stories, one-liners—nor a straight man—
capable of skillfully and subtly making another's witticism his
own; getting the last laugh. He is moved by suffering, injustice,
small children. He remembers everything. Often our conversations are weighted, somber, the earnestness of graduate students or very young lovers. He is humorous only incidentally,
without design. I'm sure he has missed some of his finest moments. "We never do anything together but eat in restaurants
and screw," he said once.

"That's not true," I stammered.

"Then why is it that the only images I have of you are across a
table or on your back?"

Had it been my line, that last one, I'd have said it with a
deadpan that looks for a laugh and waited until I got mine. But
Patrick was deathly serious, just making pronouncements on the
truth, with emphasis.

I do not know for a fact that my husband has other lovers.
Nor, I imagine, is he certain that I do. It is ironic that we spend
most of our working lives collecting facts—my husband is a lawyer—yet are content to proceed in our personal life on nothing
more final than assumptions, and even those are largely unar-
ticulated.

If all of this sounds stilted, stiff, it is because our marriage is somewhat that way. We observe professional courtesies with one another; we are cordial; we enjoy one another; we "get along"; we laugh together. Perhaps that is what we do best. Like smart aleck boys in high school, we exchange affectionate insults. "Talk a little louder, I can't hear you—not that I was listening in the first place." My husband is aggressive in his profession and sure of his pleasures: tennis, Chinese food, good causes. I am one of his pleasures too, but he cares for me as he does for his sports, sincerely but with reserve, as if there are rules, speed limits. He is rarely amazed. I didn't know it bothered me until Patrick pointed it out.

I do not know whether Patrick caused my stirrings of discontent or whether he was just there to receive them. There had been a few other men before him who, like myself, worked odd hours in strange cities and lived out of suitcases. A handful of times I ended up in bed with someone I did not know very well. I was not particularly troubled by my behavior. At the same time, I did not want to make a habit of it.

But Patrick took me off guard. He was not casual. He asked me questions I would rather not have answered and repeated my answers back to me fifty phone calls later. When he asked me about my marriage—what was at its core—all I could think of to tell him is that my husband and I laughed a lot and went bicycle riding together and we were not as happy as we once were. Our life together, I realized, had been as flat as a map and the flatness obscured by the excursions, the detail, the dependability.

Yet I did not leave my husband and have no intention of leaving him. He is my anchor and my escort. He will pick me up at the airport and fix the water heater and beam when he introduces me at parties. It is not ecstasy; it may not even be happiness. There may not be a single word, a simple phrase, to describe whatever it is that holds us together. And as for marrying Patrick? We discussed it once, where we discuss most matters of consequence—on the telephone.

"I would love to be married to you," he said. "I would take care of you and cook for you and have babies with you. They would be so wonderful. Why are you laughing?"

"What time is it where you are?"

"Two-fifteen."

"I give you until the sun comes up to change your mind."

"Why then?"

"Don't you remember that line from *Guys 'n Dolls?* 'People do strange things in the night—I know because I live in it.' "

"You're probably right." He paused. "In fact I know you are."

It was soon after that that I gave him permission. We had both been working late and drinking and later, as he lay under me, inside me, I said as calmly as I would ask for a glass of water, "I want you to hit me." He expressed neither surprise nor pleasure. He grazed the surface of my buttock with his palm, moving his hand in circles over my skin, so lightly that his calluses felt like feathers against me. For a moment his hand was gone, held above me and then lowered again with a resounding crack, the sound of a door slammed shut in an empty room.

He changed hands and stroked me again and slapped me again, his palms gossamer, then hard leather against me. He pressed further and further inside me until I felt for a moment, until I started to say so—and realized my error as the words formed in my mouth—that I was inside of him. When I began to tremble, he slapped me again and the noise and the smart, as sharp as a pinprick but wide as an ocean, rode through me like a wave and I quivered and froze and collapsed on top of him, like a puppet whose strings have been cut, and my arms fell against his shoulders and my face into the sweet curve of his neck, and it was only then that I realized he had been holding me as tightly and carefully as you would a baby from the second his hand left my bruised buttock.

We dozed, we talked, we showered. We stood locked together and dripping wet on the cold bathroom floor and there was an urgency, not of lust but of affection in our embrace that made me think he would surely change his mind about marrying me. "It'll take me days to stop thinking about you after I leave," he said.

"Maybe you should stay."

"No. I was thinking of something else. The opposite."

"Oh, that. You've said that before."

"I guess it's time to say it again."

It was the last time we spoke for months. There was no animosity in our silence; nor was there a longing I would easily admit to. But some nights when I was traveling and had had a few drinks, I wanted badly to call him. I wanted to tell him I was afraid and had made a lot of mistakes and that some of them were irrevocable. It was just as well I didn't know where to reach him; I was always better in the morning. I could go for days without thinking of him, except when I was at large airports where newspapers from around the country are sold. I would find his and race through it, oblivious to the news, looking only for his name and the dateline of his story to find out where he was. Then I was sent abroad to cover for a reporter who had become ill. I thought of Patrick only fleetingly during the month I spent in Asia and North Africa. I could not wait to sit down in the afternoon and write about what I had seen and return the next day to see what I would write about. But I could not sit down at my typewriter and write in the dateline at the top of the story—Bangkok, Cairo, Tangier—without thinking: when Patrick reads this, he'll at least know where I am.

I had been back in the states for several weeks when I was sent to Washington for a story. On my way to the airport, I called my office for messages. There was one from Patrick. The number he left had the Washington area code. He could have no idea I was on my way to Washington. I decided to surprise him, not call until I got there.

On my way from the airport to town I stopped at Garfinkel's and bought a black bra and black bikini underpants. They were out of garter belts in my size.

At ten o'clock that night he was not in his hotel, up the street from my own. I put on my black underwear and stood in front of the full-length mirror on the closet door, feeling more that I should feel sexy than I actually did feel sexy. So I turned off the overhead light. Perhaps some sultry music. I laughed at the idea

of seducing myself and discovered there wasn't a radio anyway.
I turned on the small light on the night table and in the gray
light the skin in my reflection turned a dark brown and the
black patches that covered me became luminescent, my circles,
my triangle. I pressed my palms against my stomach and rubbed
them over my dark, lacy breasts until my fingers met at my nipples. I moved my hips in a circle, then another and my hands
against my hard nipples and as I watched my lips open, my eyes
begin to become glassy, more from the idea of myself in this attitude than from its effects on me, I laughed again. I put on my
high brown boots. That added something, but not enough. Patrick was right—I needed a garter belt. I called him again, sitting on the edge of the bed, my legs crossed, only my boots and
my crossed thighs visible in the mirror. I wiggled my foot, hung
up after six rings, put on a flowered dress and went downstairs.

I called him several times more and finally walked up Six-
teenth Street to the Hilton. It was late spring but still chilly and
I felt full of mischief and glee when I reached the main entrance
of the hotel and saw Patrick going through the revolving door in
front of me. I followed him and entered the lobby a second before his line of vision left the huge wall of mirror in front of us.
We stood like mannequins in front of the glass and a smile came
over his face.

"What a surprise," he said, "the world traveler is back."

We stood in the foyer of his room and I let him pull my dress
off over my head and watched him looking at my body as my
black underwear came into view in stages. "Wonderful," he said
over and over and leaned down to kiss my stomach as he
dropped my dress to the floor. He knelt before me and licked my
stomach voraciously, holding his hands tightly over my black,
silky buttocks. He took several steps with his knees and moved
me with him to the edge of the bed where I lay down, letting
my legs hang over the side while he buried his head between
them, licking the black lace between us until he pulled the underpants down my thighs and over his head and his tongue and
my lips met completely now as I wrapped my knees around his
back.

I arched my back and my neck and behind me, above the

dresser, was a mirror and in it I could see the top of his head and his full, fully dressed shoulders, his hands now moving up my stomach and under my bra to my breasts. I unhooked the bra and fell into his warm, waiting hands.

When we were naked, we watched ourselves in the mirror, I on top of him, the muscles in my stomach undulating against him. I was conscious of watching myself and of watching him and of watching us together, as if I were making love to two, maybe three different people. He pressed my breasts together and bit them lightly when they were full and wet from his tongue and then harder as my hips pressed closer to him and we moved together this way, our hips apart for an instant and locked together for another, until everything inside me became electric and I turned my face away from our reflection to his real face which was thick with sweat and anguish and I thought until I no longer thought, god, I thought, god, what a feast.

# SLOW-MOTION

## STEVEN SCHWARTZ

Steven Schwartz was born in Chester, Pennsylvania, in 1950.
He received an M.F.A. from the University of Arizona, and
now teaches English at the University of New Orleans. His
stories have appeared in *Cimarron Review, Columbia, Epoch,
Mid-American Review,* and elsewhere. He has recently completed a novel.

For Gordon, everything important began with the letter "H":
hormones, hirsute, height, hope . . .

"Heredity," he mumbled when Loni walked in amidst the
peals of welcome. She was fifteen, but important. He and Mora
(Moran was his full name), having found their spots at the
party, watched her squeal hello to her friends.

She winked at Gordy.

He had spoken with her on the phone this afternoon. She
wanted to know about his friend Mora, "the athletic guy,"—did
he ever say anything about her, would he be at the party tonight?

Mora winked back at her, shamelessly, like a train signal.
"Enough," Gordon said. "You're making a spectacle." What a
predictable beast he had for a friend. If a garage door went
down, Mora would wink at it.

Last week, Gordon had overheard one of the senior girls say
that she liked the way Mora moved—his bottom half. Gordon
relayed the information to Mora just for something to talk about,
regretting the words immediately. "So she likes me from the
waist down," Mora said at the gym locker he shared with Gordon. He breathed expansively. "Not bad for ninth grade, huh?"

Copyright © 1981 by Steven Schwartz. First appeared in *Mid-American
Review*. Reprinted by permission.

"Give me the soap," Gordon had said.

"You? Take a shower?"

"Just give me the damn soap."

It was true that he avoided showers; or when he did take one, if he met somebody in the aisle, he'd cover his crotch with the bar of soap. He even considered carrying a notebook in front of him, a little studying while his back got wet. He was one of three in his gym class who hadn't reached puberty yet. One kid had skipped two grades, so he didn't count. The other boy was like him, clean as glass, not a manly hair on his body. Except this kid didn't seem to mind: he danced around the locker room like a party host, stayed in the shower until he shriveled up, and would have strolled through the halls in a diaper if the dress code had permitted it. But Gordon—how many times Gordon had sat in class breaking out in a rash from putting on his mohair sweater after gym without first having taken a shower. The world was divided into two groups: those who had and those who hadn't. Endlessly, he speculated on whether someone had, and one boy who he was positive hadn't, switched to his gym class and Gordon saw within a miserable second that the kid had. They all strutted around the locker room with their new badges of manhood, their hairlines changing, their pectoral muscles becoming chiseled padding, and their voices cracking in midair as obscenities and insults were lobbed from one side of the room to the other. And he took cover. Dressed secretly behind the locker door. "Hey, what you hiding there?" Mora had asked. "You taking a piss or something in our locker?"

Why was he friends with such an ignoramus? He asked himself this question often, and answered aloud, while stretching himself from a chinning bar with cinder blocks on his feet. "Because Mora *is* a sub-cretin." He could ask Mora any question without him suspecting a thing. He once asked Mora about masturbation. Mora gawked at him, astonished: "You don't know what masturbation is?" Gordon realized that he should, so he said it had something to do with the rate at which the body processes food. But even to Mora this sounded a little wide of the mark. The big fellow raked his nails across his chest, as he always did when burdened by the demands of an academic explanation, and asked: "You never touched yourself before—you know, down there?" and he nodded at Gordy's crotch. And Gordon thought that he had or convinced himself he had, because, after all, he had to—whenever he soaped himself in the shower. "Of course I have. Is that all you mean?" "Yeah, that's what it is. I've been doing it for a couple of years." And they both felt relieved, especially Gordon who had been doing it for much longer than Mora, but then suddenly became a little worried that he had.

"Why don't you call her over?" Mora asked. "She's your cousin, isn't she?"

"She's not my cousin. Our mothers are just good friends. That doesn't make us cousins, Mora."

"Call her over anyway. Go ahead, she's looking at you."

He had known Loni since he was five. Their families belonged to the same swim club. They had communicated by cannonballing each other, until junior high when there began a verbal flood, via the phone, where she would confess her latest crush, ask him for advice, listen patiently while he explained why people felt she was shallow (he was deep), and then gratefully include him on her list of most desirable men. Having matured, last summer, Loni browned herself for hours at the pool. She would spread herself out on a towel near the lifeguard, and when changing shifts, the one going off duty would chuck her into the pool. She'd emerge, furiously pleased, little globules of water careening over the baby oil that coated her copper breasts. Gordon would glare at her as she hung over the edge of the pool, her small breasts tightly curved, as if the water had smoothed her shape perfect over a million years just so she could step out and strut down the concrete with her chest swept up like the surf. "You don't have to keep reminding everyone your tits are on straight," Gordon had lectured. They had that kind of brother-sister relationship, although he despised it. Without having the physical equipment for desiring her, he nevertheless did. It was with much regret and frustration that every time she made a flirtatious gesture toward him he acted aloof or bothered.

"Listen, Gordy, you going to fight Sipple or not?" This was Sipple's second asking. Mora was Gordon's second. It had been tradition for as long as Gordon could remember to rank the neighborhood kids according to fighting prowess. For years, Gordon had ranked second right behind Mora, and the ratings had gone unchallenged since seventh grade. Gordon hoped he would go down in history as the final occupant of the number-two slot. Unfortunately, Sipple was number three and demanding a match. He had badgered Mora, as Gordon's second, to make Gordon fight or forfeit, which under the rules meant a public declaration at the lunch table that Sipple was the stronger, the braver, the more fearless . . . an admittance designed to make backing out impossible without severe disgrace.

Gordon had become quite a scrapper over the years—a frequent bloody mouth and nose, but escaping with no broken bones. Sixth grade had worn him out, though. He fought constantly. He couldn't stop thinking about whom his next opponent might be. He provoked people and when no one would fight him he got headaches. His parents bought him glasses, but when that didn't help, he was sent to a psychiatrist, and when that fizzled, he came home one day and challenged Mora.

At first Mora ignored him as being crazy (no one had ever challenged Mora) and went back to building his model ship; but when Gordon kicked the aircraft carrier to pieces, Mora knocked him around the room for ten minutes until Gordon saw the old South. From then on the pressure lessened somewhat. That was the end of the sixth grade, about the same time the need to be best at everything diminished for him. He no longer cared about being first with the best Arbor day poem, the best science project, the best grades; now he was second, a well-rounded second.

He had agreed to fight Sipple once before. On the designated day, Sipple and his second and Mora and a few others came to Gordy's house, but he pretended to be sick. Which was an acceptable excuse once, but only once. The trouble was that Sipple, who had been ranked very low at one time because he was such a puny kid, was now filled out and way over the hump of puberty. After a good dinner, with his books in hand, boots on, and holding his rock collection, Gordon might break a hundred and twenty. Sipple, meanwhile, looked like a rack of winter coats. Nor were they children anymore; whatever blows were to be exchanged would hurt, really hurt, irreparably perhaps; stitches,

busted teeth, oozing eyes, dented skulls, cauliflower ears . . .
anything could happen when you lived on borrowed glory.

"I'll fight him sometime," Gordon said. "On a weekend."

"Tomorrow is Saturday," Sipple's second pointed out. "What
about after slow-motion?"

"No, I have a drum lesson then."

"Well, make up your mind or you'll have to forfeit. I think
you're making excuses myself." The second skirted away, mostly
because Mora drew himself up to his full six feet two, an
awesome height for a ninth grader, especially since Mora never
showed the slightest anger unless pressed to the extreme. He
was so dumb, a swamp cabbage, an extra thick one, Gordon
thought, for having such faith left in him. Mora believed Gordon
couldn't lose, and it baffled him why Gordy didn't shut Sipple up
with a few left hooks to his scrambled brains. Such statements
convinced Gordon that Mora's bull neck extended right through
to the roof of his skull. Gordon had never socked anyone in the
face in his life. He won every brawl by working away at the
body, weakening his opponent with sharp blows to the arms and
stomach. Mora's confidence was total because he never watched
the fights, yawning with boredom while they were going on, and
never mentioning them once they were over. He just *expected*
Gordon to win, that was the way things are: some people are
first, some are second. Some never are. "I'll be back," Gordon
said. "I'm going to the can." He could feel the pressure settling
on the dome of his head, sluggish, lazily at first, like the work
crew coming on for the dawn shift. He'd find an aspirin.

"Hey! Hold up!" Loni called when she saw Gordy leaving the
room. She came bouncing over from where she was dancing, still
wriggling her hips and singing along with the music. She
slapped her hands unsteadily on his shoulders and then
stretched backwards, arching up until her tennis shirt slid to the
middle of her taut chest, dropping finally on her rear in a heap
of giggles. She reached up to him with a paper cup of Scotch.

"Where'd you get this?" Gordon demanded.

"Rebecca brought it. We've been drinking all night!"

She jumped up, her green eyes wide, her breath a wave of liquor breaking an inch away from Gordon's face. On her tiptoes
she was taller than him. She cupped the Scotch to his mouth, a

gesture which reminded him too much of a baby being fed, and when she tried to drink from the other side, he pulled away. "Stop it, will ya, don't be obnoxious. Nothing's worse than a fake drunk."

For a moment she pouted, but quickly became animated again with a few smudges of chapstick across her lips. She clicked the cap back on, and her hands, forever busy, rooted in his pockets until they found a pack of gum. "You *always* have gum, Gordy," and she unwrapped two pieces, folding one in his mouth and one in hers, and then pulling him out of the room, whispering that she had something to tell him in private.

In the kitchen they met the mother of the girl who was giving the party. Loni made a hasty and confusing explanation about why she and Gordy had to use the upstairs bathroom, and the mother, preoccupied with her own daughter who was outside with a married man, let them go. Loni leaped up the stairs, and Gordon followed cautiously. She was crazy—so forward! When they went shopping she'd make a lunch out of sampling cheeses at the Swiss Shop and then have the nerve to ask for a drink of water. Or she'd ride backward on the escalator, reading aloud a sex book that she'd swiped from her parents' night table.

She got to the bathroom ahead of him and waved him to hurry up. He had stopped to study a print of an Andrew Wyeth painting, not sure if he was stalling to prolong the excitement of whatever she had in mind or hesitating to avoid a catastrophe. She's nuts, he thought again, while moisture started to seep into his shirt; she probably wants to burn the house down.

"Hurry!"

He meandered down the hallway papered with thorny-stemmed roses that looked like tufts of red hair. Every few steps he glanced back at the Wyeth painting, pretending to enjoy a last look.

In the bathroom, the scented soap, the odor of Loni's hair, and the liquor on her breath settled over him like a pungent lilac cloud. With her eyes closed, she gripped his shoulders and pushed him down on the hamper. She curled her tongue up in concentration as she pried open his knees with hers. A cool breeze from underneath the window pierced an opening between his back and the wall, and he breathed in a small space behind her ear. The smells, sweet and fleshy odors, piled over him like brightly colored blankets until he was afraid of being smothered in fragrance.

"I've got to go!"

"Wait! I'll leave!" Gordon offered. But she had already said no by locking the door and switching off the light; and he heard her pants unzip and the toilet seat bonk down and a full bladder breaking over the water's surface, followed by the efficient conclusion of a tissue roll whirling to a stop.

He sat rigidly while his eyes got used to the dark and he could see her feet turned out to the sides. Stepping out of the pile of clothes at her feet, she slid over on her knees to where he was sitting and laid her head on his lap. When it appeared she might have fallen asleep, he touched her shoulder lightly, and she stretched up to him. Her smooth stomach curved against his legs, and the cushion of hair at her center, half the size of his palm, brushed over his thigh, riding up the muscle, until he could feel his veins glowing beneath the path.

She kissed him awkwardly on the side of his mouth, then parted that tight line with her tongue. He had always imagined her lips would be perfect to kiss, two tiny cushions softer than his often cut ones. But how different it felt: rubbery and salty and wet, a gummy, hungry clam sucking out his tongue. Her lips fell on his neck, not gently or secretly as he had hoped, but slippery and hard, a slick, clumsy feeling, like trying to twist two wet balloons together. She lifted her shirt and compressed her chest against his. His neck braced against the tile, his arms formed a hoop around her, and everywhere the minute rustlings of clothing ticked away. Not lying still for a moment, her hands worked at his belt, unbuckling it finally, until the pressure on his neck and the pounding in his heart and the hammering in his head made him jump up as her fingers slid beneath the band of his underpants.

Loni knelt on the shaggy purple bath mat, breathing heavily, her hair stringy with sweat, her perky chin sagged in befuddlement. "Put your pants on," Gordon hissed. "I hear somebody." She crawled over to them and tugged them on, just before a light knock intruded. Gordon tried to answer as anyone would annoyed at being interrupted in the bathroom: "It's occupied."

"It's Mora. What are you doing in there?"

"This and that."

"What?"

"What do you want, Mora?"

"Sipple says it's now or forfeit. I made all the arrangements for tomorrow. After slow-motion."

"I told him I have a drum lesson then. Make it for some other time."

"When?"

"In a couple of months." That would be a good time. He was scheduled to get braces on his teeth and could certainly use this as an excuse for not fighting.

"I don't think he'll go for it. Are you by yourself?"

"Are you?"

"What?"

"Go away, Mora. I'll be out in a few minutes. Tell Sipple that tomorrow is definitely out, okay?"

"I don't know, I'll try. You want me to wait for you out here? There's not much happening downstairs."

"I'll be down in a few minutes."

"There's a court out back if we want to play some Pig."

"Not now, Mora."

"Horse?"

"GO AWAY!"

And when the sound of Mora's heavy footsteps on the stairs began pounding inside his skull, he glanced sideways at Loni, who was staring intently at him, and he knew it would be a long while before he could face her fully again.

Slow-motion was a game somewhere between rugby and square dancing. More precisely it was a form of football where each team had two players and no running was allowed. Other rules included no kickoffs, no punting on fourth down, and no laterals. On the other hand, straight-arming and headhunter tackles were encouraged, and players were not officially down until they were flat on their backs or faces. Mora at this very moment was crawling on his knees toward the goal line, while Sipple and his teammate, Robert, hung from the tall boy's shoulders and head like bunches of grapes. A minute before, Mora had stood erect, dragging them around his ankles. And shortly before that, he and Gordon had formed a wedge, holding the ball together (the square dancing part) and split open a hole until Gordon was felled by Sipple's resounding cross-body block. The tackle knocked the wind out of him and left in its place the conviction that Sipple was growing progressively brutal in trying to instigate something. Mora, being the loyal hulk that he was, shot the trunk of his arm into Sipple's forehead, momentarily stunning him, and plodded on.

This was the fourth game of the day, the match that would decide the final rankings for the season. Gordon could remember when after a game he'd leave without a scratch. Now he went home a pure casualty. Sitting on the edge of his bed, he'd gradually unbend his legs until they were straight enough to carry him into the shower. Once there he'd hang on the knobs, while the water—cold or hot, it didn't matter—gushed over him, and he could examine the mural of bruises on his skin. But what else was there to do? When he wasn't playing, he would mope around the house waiting for Mora to come home from varsity practice, or for Loni to finish with gymnastics or candy striping or whatever else she blazed through her freshman year doing. His parents pestered him to join the school band or a "combo" or the photography club or get involved in a theater group or if nothing else just study a little more, activities which bored him to the point of headaches when he thought about them long enough.

This morning when Loni called, he begged his mother to say he wasn't home. And after she did, an argument ensued about why he was so rude. In between telling him to finish his cereal and to cut the lawn, she scolded him for his arrogance until he couldn't stand it anymore and flipped over his oatmeal, the desecration of food a more terrible taboo in his home than murder, and he ran outside. Undoubtedly he would be grounded again. As it was he had to be in at night before anyone else, he wasn't allowed to ride around in cars yet, or God forbid, smoke cigarettes, and he still had to accompany his parents on boring one-day vacations to historic places. If they went out to eat and he refused to go, there would be a terrible quarrel. Sometimes he'd just stand in his room opening and banging shut his door, wailing obscenities at them about his headaches. What made matters worse was Loni bicycling over to his house on a school night, often as late as eleven o'clock, with the blessing of her parents, only to be told that Gordon was grounded. When she pressed for the reason why, invariably his mother would say—and it was like a dry razor slicing off the hair of his eyebrows—because Gordon wouldn't grow up. And he'd watch Loni's peppy hips twist back and forth as she pedaled away.

Maybe it was better to be grounded than face her. After an incident like last night's, he was more convinced than ever that she was a dangerous pest, nagging him to grow faster, to catch up with everyone. What did she see in him anyway?—a temperamental, overly critical, sour-dispositioned young man, as his parents were likely to point out during their arguments with him. In other moods, he accepted that she liked him for some unknown reasons he could never appreciate. And still other times, he would blast his stereo and punch the bed, rebuild his bike or run laps until he dropped, anything to keep from thinking about what she expected of him. And when he wasn't racking his brain over his importance to her, he wondered if his parents were preventing him from reaching puberty by treating him like a child.

"Okay, now," Mora said, sketching the play with his finger on Gordy's chest. "Same as last time, straight out, buttonhook left at the hedge and I'll hit you low. Stay here for a second, though, so they think we're making a new play." Gordon looked over his shoulder, not being able to resist a glance at Sipple's menacing stare. Sipple's whole face was gums and teeth, and when he stretched back his lips, he looked every inch a beast in dungarees. And always that sinister leer.

"Come on! Time's up!"

I'll crush you it said to Gordon, and he was scared because Sipple's hatred had grown more obsessive in the last year. Mora had offered a two-word explanation: "He's jealous." Sipple's father was an alcoholic and rarely home, and when he was there, the chilling screams that came from the house kept stray animals and kids away like an electrical fence.

"Ready!"

Sipple was kicked out of the house with the same regularity

that Gordon was grounded. He had been known to walk the
streets all night and now lived most of the time at his aunt's
house. Last summer he had been caught breaking trolley windows and when he came out of detention after a night, he went
straight for Gordon. When Gordon's mother said he wasn't at
home, Sipple cursed her and ran off.

"Set!"

The incident passed and it wasn't until recently that Sipple re-
sumed his offensive, never missing an opportunity to taunt Gordon about everything from the quality of his lunch ("you
could've cut off its head at least") to the sound of his voice
("you squeal like a little girl"). Gordon ignored these comments
civilly, with Mora intervening once or twice by stretching himself out in the middle of a gaping yawn and knocking Sipple's
books off the table. Today, Sipple was tenacious, out for blood.
He dogged Gordon every play, even though by rights of his size
he should be covering Mora and letting Robert guard Gordy.
And with each tackle or block, he jammed an extra elbow or
knee into Gordy as a substitute for the fight Mora had success-
fully canceled. Gordy was getting it in pieces, slivers of glass
stuck in his skin, ready to shatter.

"Hike!"

He pivoted at exactly the spot Mora had told him, ditching
Sipple for a moment, and when he reached down, the ball stung
his hands. He felt Sipple lunging from behind and he tried to
sidestep him, but was too slow. Hands cracked across his back
like a wild swing with a crowbar, and he was down, his jaw rap-
ping twice on the ground when Sipple dove on him. Half conscious, he was aware of two things: that he had fumbled and
that Sipple, ignoring the loose ball, was still on top of him. A
punch in the kidneys, which was supposedly Sipple helping himself off, triggered in Gordon the idea that not maturing was
somehow directly related to not fighting Sipple. Lying there
with what felt like a broken back and jaw, he listened to the frantic clicking in his head that signaled the solution: he had to
fight; the cowardliness was keeping him from growing. Somehow
things had gotten twisted up in his life so that this fight was
inevitable and puberty only a possibility. The inevitable had to
be faced in order to earn the possible; nothing, not even anat-

omy, was given free . . . and Gordon's head began to ache trying to figure all this out. He stood up, brushed himself off, took a deep breath to straighten his spine, waited patiently until Mora pounced on Robert who had recovered the fumble, and then slid a few steps in front of Sipple and rammed a fist into his grinning opponent's navel.

Sipple toppled over, partly from Gordon's punch, and partly from what appeared to be sheer pleasure—because he leaped up with a rodeo yell and tore into Gordon. If there was one thing Gordon had, it was wind. He danced and sputtered around, making all sorts of threatening jungle sounds. Afraid to hit anyone in the face, he was not above a few rabbit punches to the kidneys. The tactic stalled Sipple, but not for long. One after another, he landed punches against Gordon's head, building up a slow, hammering rhythm that was more painful than anything Gordon remembered from his younger days. Gordon's teeth snapped shut several times and he wrapped his lips around them, giving that up when he tasted blood. He kept his face covered, barring the blows with his thin arms, listening with surprising calm to his limbs being slapped like hamburger patties.

Sipple stuck out his face, boxing low and sucker-style from the waist, and finally Gordon took the bait and swung wildly, missed, and then, opening his eyes, swung again, connecting this time on the ear. Sipple smiled and said, "Now you've done it." He backed Gordon up against a sticker bush, punching him deeper into it so he was being pummeled from in front and clawed greedily from behind. His shirt ripped and the scratches on his arms began bleeding. Sipple, out of control, pumped away at Gordon's nose until blood spurted. Under the rules, no one was allowed to stop the fight; no one ever had. The loser had to concede, and for some reason, even though Gordon knew he was looking worse than some of the meat-cleavered faces in *Ring Magazine,* and even though a panic was rising in him that Sipple had snapped and lost all sense of reason, he couldn't surrender. The same odd thought kept running through his head, propping him up: he'd have to fight harder to lose than to win. He'd count off the punches in rounds of five: one for Mora, one for Loni, two for his parents, and one for himself, until there were no punches left, nothing more to expect. Punched out.

Then he would open his fists and nothing would be there, absolutely nothing but air.

Resting his head on Sipple's shoulder, pawing and slapping at his opponent's pudgy sides, he saw Mora and Robert step into the circle and shake Sipple to stop. When Sipple's response was a knock against Gordon's head that sent the ground spinning like a game wheel, Mora kicked Sipple's legs out from under him. And Sipple left, slowly, along with Robert and the other spectators who had gathered, until it was just Mora and Gordon.

Gordon stood in a peculiar pose, as if he were trying to remember something important. He cupped his nose and not feeling anything poked wildly for the flat opening of a nostril, withdrawing a thimble of blood on his finger. What food there was in his stomach rose up against a gate in his throat and then down again when the ground rushed up, as if stomach and ground were weights on a seesaw: the ground receding, the bucket in his throat rising. . . . He flopped on the grass, holding it steady, rolling over on his back and shutting his eyes against the shapeless clouds. Mora asked: "You gonna be all right?"

"Fine." Blue pulsated less than green, maybe because the position was good for his nosebleed.

"You ought to come home with me and wash up," Mora said. "My mom will take care of you. You know her, she won't mind. I could make you a cherry coke."

"Christ, Mora."

"I'll put some rum in it! Come on, it's not good for you just to lie there. You'd better get up."

"What if I can't? I think there might be something wrong with my head." The pain bothered him in a different way than his ordinary headaches: sharp, dense, and black; and then numb, airy, and porous. He pictured his brain as one of those huge underwater sponges, the thoughts dropping in the holes like wishes, himself listening for the plunk. . . .

"Let's go," Mora said. "I'll give you a hand."

Gordon pulled himself up with Mora's help, and once standing confessed he felt dizzy, so he hooked an arm around Mora's shoulder. Swamp cabbage, Gordon thought, I'm less than Jell-O and the idiot wants me to sip cherry cokes with him. When they went a little further, Gordon stopped thinking about things. The throbbing in his head urged him to hurry up and decide—before it was too late. But he felt himself drifting away from the frantic little voice, amused by its desperation. He really did feel light as air, a gust of wind. And had he opened his eyes, he would have seen that his feet no longer touched the ground, and that he was being rushed along in the arms of his friend.

# HEARTBEAT

## LINDA SVENDSEN

Linda Svendsen was born in Vancouver, Canada, and now
makes her home in New York City. She has been the recipient
of a Stegner Fellowship in Fiction, the Mary Ingraham
Bunting Fellowship, and a Canada Council grant. Her fiction
has appeared in *The Atlantic, Prairie Schooner, Best Canadian
Stories 1981* and *1982, Cosmopolitan,* and other magazines
and anthologies. She is working on a collection of stories.

I met Bill when I was studying urban anthropology at Hunter.
He was studying galaxies. I loved him for his vision and ability
to see the distance; I wasn't sure what he saw in me. After living
together for eight months, we seldom enjoyed the peace or lust
we'd known before splitting the rent.

One night in April, when Bill and I fought about his long
hours spent sitting in a topless bar, I gathered all the fruit in our
apartment. Anything juicy, easily bruised: apples, bananas, a
lemon. I threatened to quit college and spend nights at International House until I could find a ride and return to Canada.

"Why are you taking all the fruit, Adele?" Bill sat at the
kitchen table, his feet propped on a chair. He wore sweat pants,
a turtleneck, and a fuzzy toque, all of which kept him warm on
cold evenings. A biography of Galileo was open on his lap. Bill
looked reliable: a man for home and yard.

"In case I get hungry. It's a long drive north," I said.

"I don't believe you."

"I don't care."

The truth was, Bill and I often shared fruit after making love,
and I didn't want him sharing this intimacy with anybody else. I

Copyright © 1981 by Linda Svendsen. First appeared in *The Atlantic
Monthly.* Reprinted by permission.

could imagine myself skulking away and another woman arriving. They'd make rigorous New York love and, afterward, Bill might feed her the firm Bings we'd so carefully picked. (Even though cherries were scarce, my imagination easily supplied them.) Or they'd share a plush wedge of watermelon and she'd spit the little black seeds onto his stomach in her casual way, aiming for his belly button, missing. Incautious, they'd nibble the white on the rind. He'd never notice my absence.

"Why aren't you packing your underwear? Or a toothbrush?"

"Because, Bill." I tossed an apple from one hand to the other. "I don't want you eating any of it with anybody else."

Bill looked down at his lap, then back at me. He seemed very tired. "Please trust me," he said.

I closed the door behind me and intended to walk into the night. I ended up in the communal laundry down the hall. Nobody else was there; it was after midnight. I sat cross-legged on a dryer and listened for the reassuring scuff of his flip-flops along the corridor. But heard only soft laughter, the striking of a match, from somebody else's rooms.

I bit into the apples and chewed faces: eyes and lips of red peel, oddly pared smiles. I watched the pulp surrounding these strange features turn brown. Then I went back.

Bill still sat at the table. His book was turned to the same page. "Come sit on my knee, Adele," he said, and I did.

When my mother and stepfather called long-distance, the next morning, to invite us to join them in Florida, Bill and I had made old promises again and were toasting bread for BLTs.

They believed it was the best graduation gift they could offer —two weeks with the three most important people in my life in a state I'd never visited. Their other reasons: I deserved a holiday after college, before the future; they hadn't seen me in ages. In other words, they hadn't ever seen my boyfriend, Bill. Except in snaps.

From my chattering letters, they didn't guess that Bill and I argued definitions of fidelity. They knew about the weekend jaunt to Martha's Vineyard, how it hadn't rained, how we steamed our own mussels on the beach facing Chappaquiddick, and paced widow's walks. They didn't know about our real life, and how I worried that Bill was meeting a lover at the library near certain call numbers. Or how pensive I was when he danced salsa, two songs in a row, with the ecstatically married secretary of the Astronomy Department.

What they didn't know wouldn't hurt them. Sometimes I was sure Bill thought that about me. I hoped Florida would effect a cure: the sun and sleep and privacy.

My mother and Bill burned on the very first morning. Bonded, they compared noses, shoulders, and kneecaps, and trudged back to the rooms for cold tea bags. "Takes the sting out, Bill," my mother said.

My stepfather, Robert, and I continued to tan silently on the beach; the scent of coconut hung like a net. I listened to the Gulf of Mexico and heard the children shouting, angrily, far away. I stretched in the direction of Texas.

"So." Robert's voice seemed to come from nowhere, from the Gulf. "Bill studied astronomy."

"That's right."

"And what's he going to pursue?"

I considered answers. Then chose to say, "Research. He wrote his final paper on asteroids and the atmosphere."

He didn't say anything for a while. I glanced at him, and he was staring out at the water, and I saw, from the angle of his head, that he was watching a small trawler.

"So he's serious about space, eh?"

"Yes."

He nodded, then looked at me. "You should turn."

I shifted onto my stomach, and felt the cool wind brush my back and legs. The conversation seemed over; Robert decided to go into the water. He shuffled his feet in the shallow depths to intimidate any drowsing devilfish. Then he started a strong crawl toward some point he had fixed upon.

Later that afternoon, the four of us drove in a rented car to the J. N. "Ding" Darling National Wildlife Refuge. The car smelled of Noxzema and Robert's skin bracer. Too late for the escorted tour, we drove miles on dirt roads through mangroves, stopping at outlooks.

"What are we looking for?" my mother demanded. "There's a bird," she said, pointing at the sky.

My stepfather, wearing binoculars and a movie camera, read all the signs. "There are alligators here."

"I'm waiting in the car," my mother said, then vanished. I heard her call from a rolled down window, "Watch where you're going, Adele."

We explored the swamp for almost half an hour. Every alligator we discovered was a drifting stick. But Bill spotted eleven geckos, and we saw a spoonbill grubbing under a gumbo-limbo tree.

Tired and hot, I hiked back to the car.

"This will cool you off," my mother said, turning on the air conditioning.

"Do you think Bill is having fun?"

"He's having a great time," I said.

"Are you?"

"I'm having a wonderful time, Mum. I like Sanibel."

And I was having a wonderful time. After a dinner of lobster and key lime pie, we noticed children roller skating near the restaurant. They wore hats of straw and waved sparklers. A boy in a Scout uniform passed one to Bill, who lit it and spelled my name against the night. I watched the letters disappear, each before the fiery completion of the next.

Our bedroom was only an earlobe away from my parents', and this embarrassed us. We tried not to leave the living room at the same time, hoping staggered departures would conceal our eagerness. I stood, then my mother stood and invented a yawn, and we both said good night. Bill lingered with Robert and water polo highlights on television.

In our bathroom, I washed and approved my tan lines in the mirror. Then I started a mystery on top of the fresh sheets. I heard the announcer chanting penalties in the other room, Robert's and Bill's polite murmurs. I heard the waves, only inches outside the window. I wanted to throw a rock into the dark and hear how ominously close it would splash.

Bill came in. He slipped out of his cutoffs and pulled me down beside him on the bed. "All right," he whispered. "Let's play Scrabble." He folded my page corner. "Let's play Go."

We laughed and, as it turned out, didn't play anything. His skin was very sensitive. But I rubbed him with salve and he gripped my toes in his hand and named some after stars: Sirius, the dog-toe, Nova-toe, and White Dwarf.

The day before leaving the island, we crossed the causeway at Punta Rassa and drove to Fort Myers. Robert wanted to exchange the Cougar, because its tires were dangerously bald. This done, we stopped for lunch and discussed doing something else on the mainland. I mentioned the swimsuit factory; Bill, the giant water slide. My stepfather announced we'd visit Edison's winter home.

Our guide was Naomi, from Land's End. She wasn't beautiful, but her English accent was charming. She said "spot of trouble," "bloody awful nights in the laboratory," and "a wee bit fou." Her skirt was polka-dotted and above her knees, and she told the group she respected scientific methods. I felt Bill smile.

My parents confided in her immediately, saying "us three"—indicating themselves and me—were Canadian. They said we were in the Commonwealth together with her, and shared the same constitution. She shook hands with them, but looked at Bill and asked where he was from.

"New York," he said. "The city."

We strolled through Edison's botanical gardens and learned about banyan trees, their roots dropping from the sky, tall bamboo, and goldenrod. Naomi showed us Mrs. Edison's walk, with flagstones donated by Ford and Firestone. We saw the swimming pool of Portland cement. We heard about Edison spitting on the floor, Edison sleeping standing up, Edison proposing to his second bride in Morse code.

Bill kept Naomi's pace, and asked questions. She cited Edison's experiments to increase the life of the light bulb, his efforts at submarine detection. They seemed to be enjoying history.

I imagined them together. I was no longer slowly measuring my parents' steps and inspecting grounds. I saw Bill and Naomi in Cornwall: the cottage with a thatched roof; smoke circling the chimney; Naomi in a scanty apron, and nothing else, near the hob. They'd sip Guinness and eat shepherd's pie together under quilts.

She would be a better lover than I. The way she enunciated vowels and consonants, her choice of verbs, the way she moved her mouth, were proof. She would call him different names at night, names he'd never heard before. She'd kneel and say Beast, Master William.

My mother touched my shoulder. "Are you all right?"

"I'm fine."

"Why don't you go up there with Bill? You're missing the talk."

"I can hear," I said. "I'm not missing anything."

Bill turned and waved, urging me closer to him and Naomi and the rest of the engrossed crowd. I shook my head and gestured toward my mother. "No," I mouthed.

By the time we entered Edison's laboratory, I hadn't pictured their children, but had named them: Clarissa and Cyril and little Daphne. Even Robert had remarked upon the friendliness of the British. Bill and Naomi were at the front of the group, and when she stopped to comment on exhibits, Bill gave all his attention. I stared at him and willed another glance backward to where I stood with my parents.

Finally I walked away. I said something to Robert, "Sunstroke," maybe, and started running down the narrow aisle past Edison's sockets, fuses, and primitive telegraphs. I passed a model of the Black Maria. I ran by the glow of incandescent light and then was outside.

In the car on the way back, Bill marveled at Edison. The phonograph and the deaf man: how the subtleties of music escaped him, but not sound. My mother agreed that Edison was brilliant and wondered which Canadian could match him. Robert suggested that Canada was known more for humanitarians than for inventors. Then he asked if we should buy ice for my head.

That evening my parents played marathon croquet on a torchlit lawn.

"At last alone," Bill said.

We ate on the balcony, a supper of tossed greens, and admired our sixth sunset. Bill perched on a pillow and I leaned

backward against his chest. He twisted my hair into two pony-
tails and tied them with strips that usually secured celery.

"The sun sinks faster here," I said.

"Seems to."

"Is that because we're near the equator?"

"I can't remember."

"I always forget that the sun never sets." I turned to look up
at Bill. "That it's the earth turning away from the sun."

He rested his chin on my head and placed his arms, light as
sleeves, over mine. "Still a 'jolly good show' for free."

Hours later we were still arguing.

"Where do you get these ideas?"

"You!" I yelled.

"I asked you to move up."

"You didn't want me to."

"Next time I'll send a wire."

"Look," I said firmly. "You liked her."

"Smiling doesn't mean I want to lay somebody. I've told you
this before."

"You're a liar," I said.

Bill grabbed my hair. I was pulled onto my feet and backward
into our bedroom. When he finally let go, I scrambled toward
the closest wall and faced it. I was ashamed that the two of us—
joyous wrestlers during sex—were now fighting deliberately to
hurt. I thought of pets, confused by the familiar hand that feeds,
strokes, then unexpectedly slaps.

"I don't know what to do, Adele." Bill sounded serious and
sad. "I don't know how to make you believe me." I knew he was
looking at me, waiting; then he went out.

I lay down on the bed and closed my eyes.

When my parents returned, after one, Bill was huddled on the
balcony.

"Is he watching for satellites?"

"I doubt it," Robert said.

"Is he asleep?" I heard my mother open the sliding door.
"Bill?"

"Maybe he's in the doghouse," Robert said.

They didn't say anything for seconds, and I guessed the exchange. My mother's referential eyes.

I suddenly heard Bill say hello, who won, too bad, good night. He came into our room without flipping on the lamp.

"Adele?"

I didn't answer.

"I think we should talk about giving notice when we get home. I don't know what's keeping us together anymore."

Next door, my parents undressed. I listened to the scrape of hangers in their closet and I heard them complain about their scores. I heard our names spoken, more than once.

We divided Florida by east and west. The second and last reservation was at a Fort Lauderdale motel on North Atlantic Boulevard, the east coast. Robert told us we were now off-season, and rates were very reasonable.

The trip across Alligator Alley, Route 84, took five dull hours. Robert asked Bill if he cared to drive; he was delighted to, and my mother assumed his place in the back with me. Bill and I had barely spoken to each other over poached eggs, so it was doubtful we could have maintained enough backseat small talk to amuse my parents, or fool them.

My mother talked about the tournament the night before, how hustlers had tampered with the mallets. "Nothing's sacred anymore," she said. "What did you two do last night?"

"Nothing, Mum."

"You both took it easy?"

"Yes. We ate supper and watched the sun go down." I looked out the window at a truck speeding in the other direction. It carried long palm trees, adults, on their sides. "Did you see that?"

"What?"

Bill braked needlessly and often. When a pelican swooped across the road, he applied his foot. When a car signaled left, station wagons away, Robert had to grip the dashboard. "I'm not used to power brakes," Bill said.

I noticed his strong hands on the wheel, and remembered my scalp, how it had stung.

"So these are everglades!" Robert said.

The land was flat, the slash pines short and not exotic. It occurred to me that we might be in a different hemisphere, that we'd ventured farther south than intended. Nobody lived there: no undershirts stiff on washlines; no dogs on porches, dead in sleep. Nothing to joke about or judge. But there were tourist attractions—six, three, one mile ahead.

"Do you want to go on an airboat?" Robert asked.

"Not really," I said. "Bill, do you?"

He resisted looking at me in the rearview mirror. "Doesn't matter." He glanced at Robert. "But if you and June want to?"

"I'm not getting my feet wet," my mother said.

"Who knows when we'll be down here again." Robert folded a map of the southeastern states. "Probably never."

I realized that Bill and I were casting a pall over their trip.

The new suite, decorated in an avian motif, had only one bedroom, and my parents claimed it. Bill opened the couch in the combination kitchen, hallway, living room. I found the linen, shook pillowcases spattered with parrots, and tucked in a blanket of faded blue wings and beaks.

"One more week," said Bill, not conversationally.

"That's right," I said. "Seven days."


Bill's younger brother, Donnie, worked summers at the Magic Kingdom, in Orlando. Bill had written him from New York, listing dates and addresses, and he arrived before brunch on the third day of gloom at Fort Lauderdale. My mother noticed his face, and thought he'd been in a motorcycle accident.

"I know," he said. "I stayed too long under the sunlamp." The skin was blistered and peeling; his swollen nose threatened his upper lip.

My parents loved him. He was familiar with Canadian sports and talked curling with Robert; he sliced crudités for my mother; he was fun. They invited Donnie to stay as long as he wished. And Bill and I were, if not congenial, more considerate of each other with the buffer of his company.

While Bill soaked in the bathtub, Donnie and I talked on a shaded patio and identified hookers pouting on the sidewalk. I picked out two.

"Three," Donnie said.

"Two."

"I'm not kidding, Adele."

"I'm not kidding either, kid. Look at her bag." I'd heard that prostitutes favor purses the size of chipmunks.

"She *is*."

"I'm not going to ask how you can tell." I loved Donnie too. He was shorter than Bill, more muscular, more fair. He'd once knotted a cashmere sock around Bill's neck when he was suffering from a sore throat. He'd knocked out a college buddy who killed some dragonflies in the microwave for kicks.

I wanted to ask him about Bill. But Donnie was young; he still believed in the rewards of a suntan. I couldn't burden him.

Bill, in a white motel towel, called from the door, and we tiptoed back to the room over hot concrete. Donnie bent to pluck the bottom leaf off a shrub.

"What's that?" I asked.

"Aloe." He straightened and showed me the lance-shaped shoot. "The juice is good for insect bites, rashes, burns—I'm going to use it on my face."

"You're an optimist." I hopped on one singed foot, then the other.

"Not really," he said. "Everything gets better eventually, anyway."

"That's optimistic," I said.

"Things can only get better. Right?" He held the aloe to his nose.

"Right."

"Some things get better faster if you just let them be." Donnie went on to describe the quick knitting of a kitten's broken leg, and how the vet had never been near it.

That night I encouraged Bill and Donnie to go out alone. "I'm going to stay here and write letters," I said. I also thought it would be a chance for them to talk and possibly review my virtues.

Bill kissed me on the top of my head.

They said they wouldn't be late.

By three they weren't back, and I made a tarot spread of postcards on the coffee table. I asked the cards whether I should stoop to follow. A fisherman hugging a marlin, deep-sea charter boat boldly advertised behind him, pointed into my past; a lady water-skier, wearing a bikini the color of bright persimmons, crowned me; a pale and bored flamingo anticipated my future; the final outcome was oranges. This card appeared twice. I couldn't fight the provocation of fruit. I borrowed Bill's kangaroo jacket and pulled up the hood.

The first bar I checked had held a wet-nightgown contest earlier in the evening. The runners-up, in baby dolls and lace, still drank. The jukebox played Lesley Gore and they shouted the chorus, "It's my party and I'll cry if I want to." I ordered a Florida Key and, strangely, relaxed. I'd intended to be thorough: I was going to case every club, pizza nook, and parked car on the North Atlantic strip and catch them at seduction. But as I watched the other women swaying in flannels and satin, I recalled slumber parties where my girlfriends had been accomplices in love: giving advice, keeping secrets. For a while, I forgot about Bill and the woman he was probably with.

A tractor driver from Gainesville introduced himself and offered me the world.

"Thank you anyway," I said.

On the way back, I passed unlit motels. I walked around a few courtyards and parking lots and counted room numbers. I wanted to pause and listen by each dark window, expecting to hear panting in a rhythm I would recognize. As if expecting to hear my own name in another's whispered.

When I unlocked the door in daylight, at our place, they were both dressed and asleep on the opened couch. Donnie wore one thin moccasin. I slipped it off, spilling sand on the blanket. I nudged Bill. He moved closer to the middle; I accepted his warm edge.

"There was a full moon last night." Donnie talked softly.

"I know."

"Bill and I got sick of bars and walked on the beach."

"That's romantic," I said. "What time was that?"

"About three."

Donnie, Bill, and I were in bed. It was early morning, and I'd brewed coffee to lure us into the day. Bill still slept between us.

"We were across from the Crab Shack when Bill spotted

something floating on the tide." He sipped his coffee. "It was a turtle. With a shell three feet wide."

"That's big."

"She crawled onto the beach and started digging a hole with her back flippers."

"Laying eggs," I said, and wished I'd been there.

"Right." Donnie was impressed. "But we weren't sure. We'd heard about whales beaching themselves, dying, so Bill ran to a phone and called the SPCA."

"And they came?"

"Eventually. We'd already watched her lay the eggs and drag back to the ocean. She was incredibly weak." Donnie looked at Bill, his eyes slightly open even in sleep. "He called her 'Mama.' 'Come on, Mama,' he said. 'You can make it, little Mama.' I thought he was going to pick her up and carry her."

I ran a finger along Bill's shoulder, over the slope and along the arm, until I reached his matching finger, its nail and tip. I wanted to cry for that gentle side of him I'd missed.

"We showed the Turtle Patrol—they're the ones who came— where the eggs were buried, and they took them for incubation. They should be turtles in sixty days."

With heat and luck, I thought.

"The guy said this one wouldn't hatch." He reached over and lifted an egg out of his other moccasin. I touched it. It was leathery, gray, heavier than a hen's. I thought of rolling it on Bill's pink chest.

"Where were you this morning?" Donnie asked.

"Turning tricks," I said, and winked. "What else?"

"Bill was worried." Donnie took our mugs into the kitchen for refills.

I watched Bill sleep and wondered what would have happened if he and I had discovered the mother turtle in the moonlight. We might have talked about the mate she swam with only once, imagined conception off the Ivory Coast or Togo, offspring never to be seen. Witnessing this event might have made us kinder to each other.

We could have entered the Atlantic with her, then watched until she was our sorrow, out of sight beneath the waves.

Donnie headed back to Disney World that evening. He kept vigil in a haunted house, comforting terrified kids and pointing out "spirits" to the nearsighted, and had to go to work early the next day.

My parents stuffed French bread and gouda into his rucksack and shook hands with him. Bill and Donnie embraced, then Donnie pivoted to face me; he lifted my chin with his forefinger. "Take care of the bro."

"I will."

"Don't think so much," he said.

He climbed onto his bike and raced the motor. He shouted thanks again; Robert said it was a pleasure, anytime. Donnie turned to the north, his face glazed with aloe, one hand held steady in the air.

That night Bill and I slept together, by ourselves. We took turns rubbing. Bill asked for percussion and I steadily drummed with the sides of both hands up and down his spine. Then he scratched me, almost roughly, all over.

We were kissing when we heard my parent's door open and Robert squeezed by our bed. He turned on the stove light, six feet away from us, poured a glass of water and sipped it. My vision was partly obscured by Bill's arm, but I caught the eerie gleam of Robert's white pajamas. I saw his tired face. He looked at the window and seemed to study his own reflection. Then he placed the glass in the sink, turned off the light, and groped the same way back. It was so quiet I couldn't hear our hearts. Bill and I waited in the new dark.

My mother and I got drunk in a bar named The Plucky Duck. She was buying; it was the last whole day of Florida; she'd quarreled with Robert.

"Men," she said, over gin.

Robert and Bill had driven to Flagler Dogtrack to gamble on greyhounds. My stepfather, after research, anticipated returns on Silver Streak, Cat's Meow, or Bite. Bill, against all odds, was betting on Jupiter.

"A good fight clears the air." My mother tried to convince herself.

They had disagreed about the maid. My mother said the

rooms didn't need tidying, since we were checking out soon. Robert said we were paying for the service, so they should be cleaned. If we were already paying, she said, why had he over-tipped the Cuban girl every single day? Robert replied that he had felt sorry for her and told my mother to drop the subject.

My mother now sat, swinging her legs, on a tall stool beside me. Young boys shot melodramatic pool behind us. One of them sank the eight on his break, and swore.

"Do you know how to play?" she asked me.

"Nope."

"Does Bill?"

"He's good."

"I like Bill," she said. "Remember some of the fellows you used to go with? The one who used to sleep in his car in front of the house? What was his name?"

"I forget, Mum."

"He used to brush his teeth in the birdbath."

"He did not."

"He did. I saw him one morning when I drew the curtain."

"He never owned a toothbrush."

"He drove you to work every day until his car was repossessed." My mother pushed my hair behind my ear. "I think Bill cares for you very much."

"I think so." And with that I admitted, to myself, what I'd always known. I was Bill's only lover; I would measure every other woman with his eyes: could it be her? We had jogged on Riverside, in winter, and his eyes had loved a stranger's round ass and stride. I remembered snow and how cold the day had been. I remembered ice, pale as fingernails, arresting the Hudson.

Robert and Bill treated us to the movies with their winnings from the track. My mother chose the retrospective festival at Hialeah Drive-In: *An American in Paris* and *Gigi*. The cashier's hut displayed a historical plaque, and Robert held up the line to read it.

"This was once a grove," said Robert. "Ruby-red grapefruit. And then it was the biggest farmer's market in the Sunshine State."

My mother surveyed the paved lot. "It doesn't look as though anything ever grew here."

Robert parked behind the projectionist's booth. A Volvo pulled in, on our right, and the two Schnauzers of an elderly couple barked at us and scrambled from front to back side window.

"Somebody shoot them," I said.

Nobody parked on our left.

"I don't think it's ever going to get dark tonight," my mother said. "I heard it hailed in Toronto today." She still felt the liquid afternoon.

"It's spring," Bill said.

The cartoon began, Robert turned up the volume, and we watched faint figures against twilight—dropping from cliffs, freezing, drowning, reappearing and asking for more.

"Can you two see?" she asked. My mother was far away from Robert; she practically sat on the arm of the door.

"We see fine." Bill's finger tightened on the belt loop of my short shorts, pulled me closer.

During the first feature, my mother fell asleep. So did the dogs.

Bill asked me to walk to the playground with him during intermission. We filed, hand in hand, past rows of cars, and heard the speakers answering each other across the lot. There were no children under the huge screen. We climbed the monkey bars and Bill hung upside down, by his knees, until he heard the jingle of coins falling. Then we searched for his lost change by the reflected light.

The second feature started. Bill and I stretched out on the bare ground and looked up.

"Bill," I said. "I want to tell you something."

He slipped his arm under my shoulders and pressed his nose against my cheek.

I told him about Donnie squeezing juice from spikes of aloe, believing a plant could cure his burn. And how if it didn't, he had faith in time, the powers of his own skin. I told Bill what we already knew. Nothing would alter the green beat of my heart. Not nature, time, or love.

"I love you always," he answered. "We'll be unhappy forever."

# POOR BOY

## LYNDA LLOYD

Lynda Lloyd was born in Lindale, Georgia, but has lived most of her life in Atlanta. She is a graduate of Antioch College, where she studied under Nolan Miller. She has earned her living as a free-lance writer (broadcast television, advertising) since 1972. "Poor Boy" is her first published fiction.

I have lain here for nearly two weeks now, where my murderers left me.

It's a good hiding place. You go a few yards off the road into the woods and you have lost the civilized world completely. It is one of those frightening pockets of wilderness that you find in the South, even near big cities.

When I got out of the car, when I still thought that they were just going to strand me out here in the backwoods, when I still thought it was just some kind of hardnosed joke almost, I smelled pine needles. I felt how hot and damp the night was and saw a steep downward bank in the spill of the headlights. The bank was covered with thick vines and dropped away from the road into looming trees. When the headlights were turned off it was incredibly black, and even though they never turned off the motor I could hear that steady roar that insects make in the country in summer at night. I was wondering how long I'd have to walk to get a ride back to Atlanta. We were still in Georgia, I thought.

That's all I can tell you, from my own personal experience, about where I am. The physical senses stop, as you may have

Copyright © 1981 by The Antioch Review, Inc. First appeared in *The Antioch Review*, Vol. 39, No. 3 (Summer 1981). Reprinted by permission.

guessed. I was never much on nature anyhow, so it seems ironic that I should be becoming part of it in this literal way. It would probably be better if I am never found, or found much later. The weather has stayed very hot.

I know that in the same way that you know it's hot when you see a desert movie. The physical senses stop, but feeling and knowing, witnessing, all the internal mechanics, go on. But they are heightened. Yes, that's exactly it. It's as if you are high above life. Lying here, I see scenes of how things are going on, anything that has to do with me. I can also look inside people and know what they know, know what they feel, think, know what they are. It's interesting. I've noticed that the things I see this way, things that should scare or hurt me, don't. It isn't that I don't care or have any feelings anymore. It's as if the things I see and my seeing them make some kind of a whole. I feel a completeness. I understand.

I don't know if it goes on like this forever. I read those stories about people who almost died, or did die, and came back. They said it was beautiful. There was warmth and light and some kind of voice or presence that came and told them what to do and made them feel happy and safe. I've been waiting for something to happen to me. I've thought that maybe it hasn't because now I'm just missing. No one, not even my murderers, knows for sure I am dead.

I am only twenty-three. I thought of that when I heard the angry sound that I knew was the beginning of my murder. I haven't done anything, I thought. And that was all.

I think I meant I hadn't done anything to be killed for. But maybe I meant more. Is there something definite you should have done with your life by the time you're twenty-three? I never thought so, but I knew a lot of people who did. My father, my mother, older brother, all my bosses, my teachers, a lot of my friends. They seemed to think that there was something you ought to do with your life, some certain place you ought to be by twenty-three, or any age. The certain places were all different, of course. But I never thought that there was anything definite that could be made of anyone's life, at any age. Making something of a life was too much like arithmetic, and I hate

arithmetic. Lives are much more mysterious and interesting than
sum totals. I still think so, but now I know that a line is drawn.

The two guys who did this to me didn't have to do it. I can
think of at least six things they could have done instead. They're
passing through a little farming town in north Texas right now,
still driving my car, heading west. In Alabama, near the Mississippi line, they stole a license plate and replaced mine.

Neither of them has ever killed anyone before. My judgment
of them was right that far. I wasn't a stranger to them either. I
was a friend, or thought I was. That bothers both of them, and
they think of me constantly so that I can follow them with this
new interior vision I have. I can pick them up any time I want.

Their thoughts so far have been sick and stupid. Stupider than
usual, I should say. They're driven in circles and mazes on back
roads at night, gaining maybe fifty miles westward a day. They
are terrified of human contact and stop only at country stores to
buy food. They park my car down the road out of sight and one
of them walks to the store to buy, making them all the more noticeable and suspicious. They don't know this but I do. I grew
up in a small town, before we moved to Atlanta. If they had
kept me alive and with them, I could have helped.

They don't know what to do next except keep driving on
deserted roads. They are not sure I'm dead, and yet they know I
am. They won't even turn on the car radio for fear of what
they'll hear, and they don't talk to each other unless they have
to. Each of them, to himself, has found the idea of being a murderer so huge and unmanageable that each is convinced he will
soon have to murder again. Committing the huge, inconceivable
act again seems to each the only possible way to wipe out the
first act.

The younger murderer, Rosk, is twenty-five and is a little
brighter than the other. He has made a mental connection about
all of this, and his feelings about it, in a way.

He keeps remembering a time when he was little that he
spilled chocolate ice cream on his best white pants. It was just a
small drop. He was about four or five, he thinks. He knew that
his mother or father would look his way any time and see the

spot. They were at some kind of big family picnic, and his parents had been showing him off to all the relatives, who said how cute he was in his little white suit. His mother and father both worked in a mill. They had told him over and over how cute he looked in his spotless white suit and how much the suit had cost.

So all Rosk could think of when he saw the blob of chocolate ice cream hit right beside his fly was the desperate need to wash the spot away. So he just reached out and tilted his whole bowl of half-melted chocolate ice cream into his lap. Now he keeps remembering what a perfect solution it seemed in the moment before he did it, and what a huge, unchangeable mess it looked like in the instant it was done.

Rosk's full name is Roscoe Amos Bethey. His folks still live in Birmingham, but they haven't heard of or from him in ten years.

The other one is Wayland Furth. Wayland is forty-five, though he doesn't look it. The only thing that is truly real to Wayland is his own body. Feeding it, exercising it, gratifying any need it may have, keeping it in top condition. These tasks, and the minute observation of their success or failure, consume Wayland's entire life. I thought he was just another health nut, but now I see that it is a wonder Wayland hadn't killed somebody long before now.

I was the first dead body Wayland had ever seen, and it made him sick. He cannot get the deadness of the flesh out of his mind. He is also troubled that for nearly two weeks he has not had the right food, cleaning, or exercise. He does not know when he can have them again. He feels that he is deteriorating, withering, melting. Melting, that's how it feels inside his mind.

Rosk, with whom he is trapped in the hot, smelly car, seems like a filthy infection to Wayland. Wayland doesn't realize it yet, but a part of his mind is sure that he will soon kill Rosk. In Wayland's mind, that is the only way to clean himself and restore his body's health.

Rosk and Wayland have been together for five years. They met in a neighborhood tavern in Atlanta and discovered that they both worked for the same big printing company. Rosk drove a delivery truck and Wayland operated a binding machine. They were both alone. They didn't drift literally. They stayed in the same place and held pretty good jobs. But they were both of the drifting mentality. Neither had had any family contact in years. Wayland, from somewhere in Florida, said he didn't have any family. Neither had any close friends.

They got in the habit of having a few beers together after work. They were easygoing and sociable at heart. People, acquaintances, liked them. Wayland was rugged and muscular and impeccably groomed. Rosk was tall and thin and showed in the way he moved and handled objects that he had been a pretty fair high school basketball player.

One evening they went into the men's room at the tavern together, both still laughing at some joke that had been told at their table. Wayland, without knowing he was going to do it, suddenly threw his arms around Rosk in an exuberant bear hug from the rear and ended up fucking him. Rosk let it happen and said nothing. By then he felt scared at the idea of not having Wayland's companionship.

In a few weeks they moved into a boarding house together. The sexual relationship was infrequent, unacknowledged, and always violent. I see that now, but I would never have guessed that they did those things to each other when I was alive. In a way, they never guessed it either but they stayed together. They aren't gay. They're caged up together. There's a difference.

My father, coming awake abruptly at six-thirty, feeling the morning already unbearably hot: How the hell does Cal get mixed up with the weirdos he gets mixed up with?

Then: Surely goodness and mercy shall follow me all the days of my life.

The words keep popping into my father's head. They surprise him. He is a very moral but not a religious man. I, Cal, have been missing for two weeks today, a Wednesday. My father, my family, cannot get anyone interested in looking for me. The police feel that a white male, age twenty-three, with his own car and some money from a decent job, is apt to go missing now and then. They see it all the time. And unfortunately my father, a moral man, has felt it his duty to tell them that I did it once before: disappeared for four days with no word to anyone. That was when Jennifer left.

But there was a *reason* then, my father keeps saying. He is furious, outraged, that no one will look for me. He has spent a lot of his life in movements protesting injustices built into established systems. But he is genuinely astonished and outraged at the indifference of a system that should, but will not, search for his son. He is an innocent, as I always told him. This is the first time that he has felt injustice personally. He vents his anger in thoughts of me. That neither surprises nor hurts me, and wouldn't even if I were alive.

My father gets up quietly, not waking my mother who always sleeps later than he can. He walks down the hall toward the bathroom. This morning, as every morning since I disappeared, he hopes in the five or six steps before he reaches my bedroom door that he will look in and see me sleeping safely there. My father aches to feel the huge shocks of relief and fury he felt on the fifth morning the other time I disappeared, when he looked in and saw me sleeping peacefully where I was supposed to be. He visualizes himself hurrying back up the hall to his and Mother's room, gripping Mother's shoulder until she wakes, and whispering, "He's back."

Cal and his goddamn weirdos. So my father thinks.

My father is a bookkeeper in an architect's office. He's been a lot of other things in his life too, never much of a success and never much of a failure. He has always thought it was more important to do good with your life than to be a success, but he has always thought that you could do more good if you stayed respectable. He's always joining moral causes. Good is always obvious to him.

I never thought you could do much good in big movements. I thought the only way to do good was individually, one on one. I never thought good was all that obvious.

In the kitchen starting coffee, sweating in this hot, heavy morning, my father feels his head pounding with rage as he remembers one of our regular arguments, once when I said,

"You know twice as many weirdos as I do, you and your knee-jerk protester friends. Nothing's all that black and white, Daddy. It'd be nice if it was, but it just isn't."

Three months ago my father had a bad heart attack and almost died. He is still recuperating and now this: Cal disappears. My father suddenly remembers my ten-year-old face grinning at him from a straggly line of spectators at a civil rights march in the little south Georgia town where we lived when I was a kid. My father had an insurance agency there. He was one of only two whites in that march. The other was the Presbyterian minister, who was quietly transferred away a few months later. In my father's case, his customers and his income just slowly dried up and we moved to Atlanta.

Behind my grinning face that day my father remembers the face of my best school buddy, a hulking farm boy named Cliff Burkhalter. Cliff annoyed my father by getting me excited about things like bird hunting and hog slaughtering. Behind my back that day, Cliff was giving the marchers the finger. My father remembers my narrow face and my grin at him. He knew that it was a greeting to him, but he felt irrationally furious with me for not being where I should have been. With him. Marching.

This hot morning watching the coffee perk my father slowly sees what made him so furious that day: his fear for me, his fear of evil.

Surely goodness and mercy shall follow me all the days of my life.

My father doesn't remember any peace or light from almost dying of a heart attack. I was the only one home the day it happened, and I drove him to the hospital. He doesn't remember that I stood by the stretcher in the emergency room and held his limp hand and said the Twenty-Third Psalm aloud over and over. It was all I could remember from my Sunday school days. I thought it was pretty then, the idea of the lamb and the green pastures. I always saw them in bright, bright colors. I stood beside my father in the emergency room and said the Twenty-Third Psalm until they made me go out.

Because of his illness my father hasn't been able to do much

himself about my disappearance. He has had to leave it to my
brother Barry. My father decides that Barry must get the police
moving today. He will call Barry at his office promptly at nine.
My father's mind wanders again to my weirdo friends and, naturally, to Jennifer.

She was a slut, my father thought, which was the worst thing
he could think of a woman. He thought that because she lived
with me for a year and a half, about, and wouldn't marry me.
Then she left me and I walked out on my job and school—I was
clerking in a sporting goods store and taking courses at night—
and moved back home. Then I disappeared for four unexplained
days. That was two years ago.

Cal is such a goddamn flake. That's what makes it so hard to
get anyone to look for him. So my father thinks.

He remembers when I moved back home after Jennifer
walked out. He was glad she was gone, but sorry that I didn't
have anywhere else to go but to him and Mother. He didn't like
having me in the house after I was sixteen or seventeen. I never
knew that. He wanted me gone, on my own. Then if I was
unhappy or flaked out he didn't have to know about it.

He remembers trying to talk to me sitting in front of the TV
and drinking beer the first night I was home after Jennifer. He
told me a story about a girl he loved. The kind of love you know
you'll never get over, he called it. She worked where he worked.
He was just starting out selling insurance then. He courted her,
he treated her like a saint, he wanted to marry her. He thought
she was a saint, she was so beautiful and delicate. Then he
walked into the file storage room one afternoon and found his
boss screwing her up against a file cabinet and saw and heard
enough to know she was liking it. And his boss was married. He
never let her know what he'd seen, my father said, and they sure
didn't notice him. In a way, he told me that night after Jennifer,
you never get over it and you do.

I didn't pay much attention. I knew what he thought of Jennifer and didn't care enough to tell him how wrong he was. I
knew he was trying to comfort me. He exasperated me and I
loved him, as always.

Now, from this new height I have, I see the girl he told me

about was my mother. I understand. He didn't get over it, and he did.

Now my mother is coming awake, her first thought that I haven't come back or my father would have roused her by now.

For years one mental picture has always come to my mother whenever I have been unhappy or in trouble. She sees me in the grocery store where I worked when I was fifteen. I am wearing the meek, resigned grin of nice teenaged boys who have learned that they are always going to look silly no matter how nice or even noble their intentions. In my long white grocery-store apron I am gently and awkwardly approaching a huge mongrel dog that has wandered into the store. The dog has floppy ears and a sad face and is backed into a corner of the produce department holding up one paw and growling uncertainly.

Mother just happened to be shopping in the store that afternoon, and she has never forgotten how everyone laughed, including her, as I clumsily stalked the dog all over the store, missing chance after chance to grab him by the scruff of the neck because I was trying so hard to convince him of my kindness and friendliness. I remember that too. I wanted the dog to understand and not be frightened any more than he already was. My mother sees my dark hair as I keep stooping down to reassure the dog, and my grin when everyone keeps laughing at me, as if I agree that I am a clown. My mother sees the big bony hand that I hold out persistently to the dog, despite the fact that he only runs like hell every time I do it.

My mother lies in bed and puzzles over why she has kept this picture of me, and why she only remembers it when she knows that I am in trouble. She thinks perhaps it is because she feels guilty about joining strangers in laughing at me. But from where I am now I can see that it is because she saw me then, for the first time, not as her son. For just an instant that afternoon I was to her simply another person ineptly and stubbornly trying to do what I thought was right in a matter so trivial that I earned the justified contempt of my fellows. My mother can never escape the terrifying detachment and love she felt in that instant, and the certainty of my defeat, and the dread of the burdens that my trying would bring her.

Her thoughts leap now to my father, shutting the picture of me off. I am amazed how absolutely she loves him and me. Her love shows me the likeness between me and my father that I have never seen before. I see that she has completely forgotten the incident in the filing room at the insurance office. She only let it happen to satisfy her physical curiosity. The experience, the sensations, are now an unremembered part of her being. They have the same importance as her forgotten sensations the first time she tasted sea water.

She wonders, as she swings her legs over the edge of the bed, what my brother Barry is going to do about my disappearance today.

Rosk and Wayland are making their first move towards getting caught. Rosk is driving, almost comatose from bewilderment and the long incarceration in my car with Wayland. He knows from experience that Wayland is about to explode, but he can't tell what form the explosion will take. He has never been able to tell that.

They are on a freeway that will take them into Dallas. They— Rosk, really—have decided that it will be easier to ditch my car and get lost in a big city. A pickup truck with a rifle in a rack in the rear window passes them, then cuts sharply into their lane to reach an exit ramp just ahead.

Rosk's numbed brain cannot work fast enough. The pickup clips the front fender of my car. Rosk and the driver of the pickup slam on their brakes and jerk their steering wheels simultaneously, the wrong ways. There is a screaming collision. Both vehicles crash to a stop, hopelessly entangled, against the guard rail of the exit ramp. The pickup driver emerges shakily, carrying his rifle.

My brother Barry has done something about my disappearance every day since my family realized I was missing. It has been a lot of work.

Barry is seven years older than I. He is a rising executive in an insurance company, in his second marriage. No one cares much about that because no one liked his first wife much anyhow. Barry has always done what my father wanted him to do, but that is part of Barry's unremembered being. Barry thinks that he has followed only his own ambitions. He makes a lot of money and knows some influential people he can ask for favors.

It is Barry who has pressured my bank manager into telling him that there has been no activity in my bank account since the last day I was seen in Atlanta. It is Barry who has found out that no charges for gasoline have been made on my credit card. It is Barry who has gone into what he still calls the hippie sections of the city to ask my friends about me. Barry is very worried.

He first began to worry a couple of days after I disappeared, when he went to the health clinic in the black neighborhood where I worked and talked to my boss. My boss, Clayton Worsham, is a minor black politician with a genius for bureaucracy. He is systematically ripping off the federal, state, and city programs that fund the clinic, but he always sees that the people are taken care of. There's enough for everyone, Clayton has told me, laughing. I like Clayton.

He told Barry that day, no, there was absolutely no reason for Cal to run off. Just the opposite. In the ten months I'd been working at the clinic, I'd been very happy. Excited about the work. Everyone liked me. What's more, I'd known that in a couple of months Clayton was going to appoint me his assistant director. He told Barry that I'd found my calling and was very happy.

That's true. The loose way Clayton ran the clinic, I could help people one on one. Not just their health problems. They came to the clinic with all their problems.

Like Mrs. Simmons. Mrs. Simmons was an old country woman who landed in Atlanta because years ago she brought her husband to be treated in a city hospital. He died and she just stayed on. She was seventy-something and lived in the dilapidated white neighborhood that joined the black neighborhood where the clinic was. Mrs. Simmons's problem was that she took in kids. She had a sort of free, unofficial day nursery at her house. She liked to have kids around, and the ones who didn't have anybody to watch them got to know that they could go to Mrs. Simmons's house for company. Black, white, Mrs. Simmons didn't care. But some of her neighbors said it was a nuisance, then it got racial, then threats were made. Then Mrs. Simmons came to the clinic.

Clayton and I took care of the people. Clayton got together some black folks he could rely on, and I got together some white folks I could rely on. Rosk and Wayland were in that group. I recruited my people from the tavern where they, and I, went in the evenings. It was in the clinic neighborhood. Anyhow, one night Clayton and I took our troops over to Mrs. Simmons's area and did some door knocking and some mild head knocking, white on white, black on black. Mrs. Simmons and her kids didn't have any more trouble. The people knew she had protection.

Clayton didn't tell Barry anything like that. But Barry began to worry after Clayton told him about the promotion I had coming. That Barry could understand.

At seven-thirty on the morning of the two-week anniversary of my disappearance Barry is already in his office. Today he intends to get the police cracking on this. He is assembling his notes, his evidence, making a list of influential people he may have to call. It is a lot of work.

Barry thinks about the work only. I do not see him thinking about whether he loves me or cares what has happened to me. Cal and his goddamn flaky friends, Barry thinks. Always a sucker for strays.

Barry considers all my friends strays. They don't have jobs, or they have strange jobs, and they seem to like to live in slums. He remembers one of them, a black musician, a drug addict who was high as a kite when Barry found him and kept chanting Cal-all-*right*-man-Cal-all-*right*-man-Cal-all-*right*-man.

Looking through his notes, Barry suddenly feels bewildered, almost as bewildered as Rosk and Wayland felt after they killed me. This black guy is just one person Barry never knew I knew. Never knew I went places where I'd meet that kind of person. Barry feels bewildered at how little he knows about me, his brother. He remembers spending all the allowance he'd saved on a baseball glove he knew I wanted when I had my tonsils out when I was seven. He remembers what a sharp, good-looking kid he thought I was, socking my fist into the glove in the hospital bed.

Barry is tired this morning. He finds tears running down his face. He is glad no one else has arrived at the office yet. For just an instant he loves me. Then he thinks of Jennifer.

All this day Barry and his secretary are on the phone trying to find Jennifer. At last they find her parents, in the small town just north of Atlanta where Jennifer was born.

I have not wondered why I cannot see into Jennifer's mind from where I am. I know why. Jennifer does not think of me. There is no mystery, and the greatest mystery, about Jennifer. A couple of days after she walked out on me, she killed herself. I heard, and, knowing how my family felt about her, I had to disappear for a few days until I could be sure I wouldn't blurt it out to them. They would have said they were sorry to me and good riddance in their minds. It was never in the papers. She went home to do it, and her family has some influence in their town.

She didn't do it over me. She wasn't a slut. She wasn't on drugs. She was a nice girl, a small-town girl. When she walked out on me, she told me that she just didn't fit. She had beautiful eyes, the color of a deep lake reflecting the sky, but when she had one of these funny spells her eyes would look empty blue-white like the light in a neon tube. She wanted to be something special, to be taken notice of in life. But she had no special talents except for loving. Everyone loved her, but that wasn't enough for her. That's what made my family dislike her.

I felt that my love should have held her, I loved her so much. I felt that I could have kept her alive, but she wouldn't let me. I never understood. I still don't.

Late in the afternoon Barry finds out on the phone that Jennifer has been dead for almost two years. He calls my father first, then starts on the police.

The Atlanta police have already heard from the Dallas police. Wayland and Rosk had stupidly left the legitimate tag to my car in the trunk. Wayland tried to attack the driver of the pickup truck at the scene of the accident and got a rifle bullet through the chest. He is in critical condition but will probably live. Rosk has been confessing for three hours. A call has gone to a county sheriff in a town near where I am.

My father, waiting irritably all day to hear from Barry, has felt a darkening in his mind and all around him. The world seems remote. He keeps remembering, he doesn't know why, a book he has of pictures, photographs, from the Civil War. About four-thirty, just before Barry calls to tell him about Jennifer, my father actually goes to the bookcase and picks up the book. He turns to a particular picture in it that has always haunted him.

It is a photograph of a dead Confederate soldier stretched out face up in a trench. He looks about fourteen or fifteen. He has no shoes on, and no cap. He wears baggy, civilian, farm-boy pants and a uniform jacket. Both are ragged. His wrists and ankles are dirty and skinny, but his fine fair hair looks as if it has just been combed for church, with just two little sprigs sticking out over his forehead.

"Poor boy," my father says to the picture. "Poor boy."

The telephone rings.

Why, why, why, why? My mother is screaming, my father and Barry, both very pale, both trying to hold her, to embrace her at once. She can't stop the rawboned, dark-haired boy from chasing the dog in her mind.

I see that there is no why, only how.

The tavern where Wayland and Rosk drank every evening is near the clinic, on my way home. I like it. It is a good, warm, working people's kind of place. I used to talk to Wayland and Rosk there. Sometimes we'd go on and eat together and go to a movie, or go on drinking around town. I thought that Wayland and Rosk were plain, lonesome, good old boys, a couple of those boys who ought to be back on the family farm, irreparably uprooted by time and events and set drifting. You see a lot of them in Southern cities. I liked them, and I felt sorry for them.

That evening they were both obviously scared to death. That

was such a switch from their usual easy joking that I asked them what was wrong.

They lied to me. They said they'd had a few too many the night before and got a little rough and had been kicked out of their boarding house. They were worried because they hadn't had time to find another place to stay.

What had really happened was that about an hour before I saw them, when they thought everyone had gone home from the printing plant where they worked, Wayland's boss and another man had caught them in an act of fellatio in the men's room. The boss was a good Christian and he had a witness. There were laws. He fired them and stormed off, he said, to call the police.

It all fell on Wayland and Rosk; all the unacknowledged, unspoken weight of sin was suddenly discovered. Neither of them had ever been in jail before. The idea terrified them.

They didn't know that the man at the plant kept a wad of hard porn locked in a strongbox in his garage and that he mentioned calling the police only because he was frightened of Wayland's popping biceps. The other man was merely delighted to have seen something he had only read about, and to have the story to tell.

I didn't see that Wayland's and Rosk's terror that evening was far more than the kind of worry you'd have over not having a place to stay for the night. I just felt sorry for them and superior to them. I told them I'd take them to a clean, cheap hotel I knew, then we'd check the paper for rooms to rent and I'd drive them around to look.

They didn't have a car. It was the car they wanted.

Rosk got in front with me, Wayland in back. Almost as soon as the car doors closed, a blinding band closed around my throat. Wayland's hands. Once he did that, neither he nor Rosk could think of anything to do but kill me.

When we got to that place by the road in that pocket of wilderness two hours later, they had tied my hands behind me with my belt. Neither of them had said a word to me the whole time, and they didn't speak to each other. I thought it was a joke.

As I stood in the headlights and smelled the pine needles and looked at the thick vines on the bank, Wayland searched the ground behind me silently and found a big, jagged rock. Then the headlights went out. The angry sound I heard was Wayland's huge, muscular arm driving the rock into my skull.

Now a young temporary deputy, not much older than I, is approaching this place where I am. He stumbles on the vines and listens to the nearby voices of the other searchers. He did not really want to be in the party but felt it his duty. He is praying that he will not be the one to find me. The smell, they have all said, seems to cover a country mile. But now he spots a patch of my plaid shirt about three yards below him down the bank. Slowly and carefully he edges closer and identifies the grotesque configuration of my bound hands.

He shouts, and the others shout back, coming to him.

He stands where he is, still about two yards above on the tangled bank. Oh God, he thinks. Poor boy, poor boy.

We are all waiting for discovery. Only I do not fear it. Now something is going to happen.

# THE SECRET LIVES OF DIETERS

## PERRI KLASS

Perri Klass was born in Trinidad and grew up in New York
City and Leonia, New Jersey. She attended Radcliffe College,
did graduate work in zoology, and spent a year in Rome
writing a novel. She has won several writing awards, including
the Elizabeth Mills Crothers Prize at the University of California. Currently living in Cambridge, Massachusetts, Ms.
Klass teaches expository writing at Harvard and is a student
at the Harvard Medical School.

Donald loves to cook, even now, when he and Louisa are diet-
ing. He has bought red snapper, leeks, mushrooms and strawberries for dessert. "How will you make the fish?" asks Polly, who is
in love with Donald.

"I'll broil it," he tells her, "with the vegetables and a little
white wine and some spices."

"Herbs," Polly suggests.

"And lots of pepper. Dry mustard, coriander." Polly sees that
in his mind he is picking jar after jar off a kitchen shelf, shaking
each judiciously over the fish, arranged ready for broiling,
garlanded with leeks and mushrooms.

Donald has also brought groceries for Polly, who has been
home sick with mononucleosis for six weeks. For a while she was
very sick, she had her sister taking care of her and there was talk
of the hospital, but now she is just weak, recovering, and her
sister has gone back to Pasadena. For Polly, Donald has brought
canned broth, cottage cheese, fresh bread for her to toast, all in-
valid foods and incidentally dietetic as well, which is not true of
the Sara Lee cheesecake. Donald keeps telling her how much he

Copyright © 1982 by The Condé Nast Publications, Inc. First appeared
in *Mademoiselle*. Reprinted by permission.

envies her the cheesecake. Polly is small and wiry or, now, after
the illness, small and a little wasted. She wants to offer Donald a
piece of the cheesecake, but she is afraid to rupture what she
thinks of as his Louisa-Diet; suppose he hated her for it later?

Donald puts his briefcase on the table next to the bag of groceries. He takes out a folder of papers, work for Polly to do at
home over the next few days. Donald and Polly both work for
Ground Zero Graphics, and Donald and his girlfriend, Louisa,
live in the building across the street from Polly's, on the western
slope of Nob Hill in San Francisco. It is during these weeks of
her recuperation, with Donald bringing her food and work, that
Polly has fallen in love with Donald. After he leaves she goes to
the window and pushes the bamboo shade to one side, watching
him cross the street with his bag of groceries.

Donald is always willing to talk, to stay awhile; he can probably sense Polly's need for company and conversation, though he
doesn't realize how specifically it is his company and conversation she desires. He tells her what he is going to make for dinner, what went on at GZG, how he and Louisa are doing on
their diet. Before Polly got sick, she and Donald were not particularly close, but these half-therapeutic talks have given them
such extensive (if superficial) knowledge of each other that
when things turn bad between Donald and Louisa, he does not
hesitate to tell Polly all the details. Perhaps he has come to see
Polly as a remote spectator, safe in her apartment from any contact with other lives, able to listen and judge and advise. And
Polly works the details of Donald's trouble with Louisa into her
evening stories: For weeks now, Polly has told herself each evening the story of Donald and Louisa: What they are having for
dinner. What they are talking about. Whether they go running,
and if so, how far (she sees them set out sometimes, matching
their paces, Donald in navy blue sweatpants and a red T-shirt,
Louisa in a green warm-up suit). What they watch on television.
Whether they make love.

It is the night of the red snapper broiled with leeks, mushrooms and spices. Louisa is eating with concentration; all she
has had all day is a blueberry yogurt and a bagel. Louisa is
fifteen pounds overweight by her own reckoning, and she does

not look bad, just a little soft around the hips and thighs. Donald is only ten pounds overweight, by his reckoning as well as by the height-and-weight table in the calorie-counting handbook; Louisa wants to be five pounds lighter than the table says she should be.

Donald divides the last little piece of fish between the two of them. He thinks wistfully about sugar and cream for the strawberries, decides not to mention it, just to serve the berries plain.

"There's something I think we should talk about," Louisa says. It is not a casual statement.

"Yes?"

"I think . . . " She pauses, picks up her knife, puts it down neatly across her plate. "Donald, I think we're getting to be too much of a couple."

He tries to get her to explain. They are eating strawberries, without cream and sugar. They spend all their time together, she says, they never do anything with other people, they take for granted that they will eat dinner with each other, go to the movies with each other, sleep with each other.

"You want to go to the movies with someone else," Donald says.

"Well, after all," Louisa says, "it isn't like we're married. Even like we want to be married. I don't want to be married."

"You want to have an affair with someone else," Donald says. He is staring at the last strawberry, noticing a small mushy place on one shoulder under the collar of little green leaves. "Do you want to have an affair with someone else in particular," he asks, "or just with the next guy who follows you home from the bus stop?"

Louisa takes the last strawberry, mushy place and all, into her mouth, her fingers neatly extracting the stem and leaves as her teeth close on the fruit.

"Someone in particular, huh?" Donald says.

"Yes," Louisa says, "but even if there wasn't someone, I'd still think we were getting to be too much of a couple. I'd still think it would be a good idea for us to see other people."

"Well, but just tell me, who is this other person who just happens to be around, who you just happen to want to sleep with?"

"Someone at work," Louisa says.

Louisa teaches English at a small private high school.

"Michael, the math teacher? I thought he was gay."

"He *is* gay. It isn't Michael." Louisa's tone is patient.

"Well, who is it then?"

"A French teacher," she says.

"Named?"

"Philippe." Louisa leaves the table, goes into the bedroom, closes the door. If she went to the window, she could look across the street and see Polly's bamboo blinds. Behind the blinds, Polly is eating the cheesecake Donald brought her, small square piece after small square piece.

Louisa examines herself in the mirror. The diet is working, she believes it is working, but it doesn't really show yet. She takes out the bobby pins that hold her pale brown hair in a bun, shakes the hair loose over her shoulders. (Is Louisa a cruel and heartless woman? Polly is sure of it, after Donald tells her about this conversation.)

Louisa leaves the bedroom, wrapped in a long quilted bathrobe. She sits on the couch, and Donald comes and sits beside her. Finally he says, "Louisa?"

"What?" Her response is too quick; she was unnerved by the sitting in silence.

"Will you promise not to have an affair if I promise to submit my application and my portfolio?"

She has been telling him and telling him to apply for a Master of Fine Arts program; he can study at night and become an illustrator, what he has always wanted to be, and leave Ground Zero Graphics, where he designs restaurant logos and business stationery. Donald has been unwilling to fill out the application, even more unwilling to assemble the portfolio.

"Will you?" he asks again. "Will you promise?"

"Okay, then," Louisa says. "I'll promise if you promise."

Donald takes a deep breath, lets it out. "What do you say I go out and get us some sweets," he says, "just to celebrate?"

"We shouldn't," says Louisa, but she is giggling. Donald is putting on his jacket. "What are you going to have?" she asks.

"Cheesecake," says Donald.

"I'll have the same," says Louisa.

Donald leaves the building, but Polly is no longer sitting

behind her blinds watching the street. She is working on the assignments he brought her and already feeling tired; she is not nearly recovered yet.

Polly thinks of herself as a small dark animal, though since she's been sick, her skin has turned cheesecake white; her hair, though, is very dark and bushy. She braids it into twenty-three tiny braids one day, waiting for Donald. She is no longer a small furry animal, she is a spider. Her apartment is her lair, or her web, it is always dark, and there are mysterious things piled in the corners and complicated woven rope sculptures on the walls. She imagines that her furniture is part of the web; she imagines that if Donald touches the furniture, he will stick to it.

How can she be in love with someone who can be in love with Louisa? Polly's last (and only other) great love was a tall, impossibly thin man with soft blond hair, who programmed computers in very esoteric, very advanced computer languages and ate frozen food while it was still frozen. His favorite food was frozen burritos. He printed out long poems about Polly on his computers and she drew strange spiky sketches of him, one he especially liked on the inside of a frozen burrito box, and finally he accepted a job in Boston and moved East; he still calls her in the middle of the night to tell her he hates his job, he hates Boston, he should never have left San Francisco, he has become a Red Sox fan, he is drinking too much. But that relationship did not surprise Polly; it made sense to her. Since he left, she has been waiting to fall for another sick personality, and instead here she is in love with Donald of Donald-and-Louisa.

"So did you put the portfolio together?" Polly asks.

"Yes. I even hand-carried the whole thing over to the school. I guess I'll have Louisa to thank if I get into this program."

"And her French teacher," Polly says.

Donald has brought canned salmon for Polly, cucumber and tomatoes, heavenly hash ice cream. For himself and Louisa, chicken breasts, string beans, bing cherries.

"You don't think she pulled all that just to get me to send in my portfolio, do you?" Donald asks, transparently, hopefully.

"No." Polly wonders why he doesn't make some remark about all her little braids. She is a spider, she would like to suck him

dry, all the good cooking and gentle self-doubt about his drawing and late-night expeditions for dessert.

Donald replaces the light bulb in Polly's bathroom; earlier,
when she got on a chair to fix it herself she felt suddenly ver-
tiginous, the grimy inside of the bathtub tilted up at her, and
she grabbed at the medicine chest, carefully stepping down to
the floor. It must be the aftereffects of the mono, since she has
never had trouble with heights before. She is ashamed of the
bathtub, she realizes after Donald has gone to change the bulb.
She should have scrubbed out the bathtub. After he leaves she
thinks again about scouring powder and sponges, but the
thought of bending over the tub makes her nauseous, and it is
some time before she feels well enough to eat her salmon salad.

Polly has begun to illustrate the stories she tells herself about
Donald and Louisa. In a fresh clean sketchbook, saved in a
dresser drawer for some day when she would want it, she has
made a series of drawings. Donald cooking. Louisa and Donald
eating. Louisa telling Donald about the French teacher. Louisa
examining her body in the bedroom mirror (perhaps a little
heavier in the picture than she is in life). Louisa and Donald
running. The drawings are meticulously detailed, carefully
shaded. Polly considers a new illustration: Donald and Louisa
making love. Instead she draws Louisa and Philippe, the French
teacher, wrapped in a hasty stolen kiss in a supply closet.

The diet is working. Two weeks after Louisa agreed not to
have an affair with Philippe, she stands in front of the bedroom
mirror again and knows the diet is working. She is only four
pounds over the weight given on the chart, nine pounds over
what she wants to be.

Donald comes into the bedroom and stands behind her.

"Still too fat," she says.

"Yes, I am," he agrees.

"I meant me."

He pulls a piece of paper out of his back pocket and hands it
to Louisa. It is a letter telling him that though official notifica-
tion will not be for another month, he has definitely been
approved for his Master of Fine Arts program.

Louisa hugs him.

"And I owe it all to you," he says. "You and your French teacher." It is the first time either of them has referred to her promise. Donald draws Louisa back onto the bed. They kiss.

Donald stops kissing Louisa. "You're doing it anyway, aren't you?" he asks. When she doesn't answer, he says, "You're having an affair with him anyway, aren't you?"

"Yes," Louisa says, and gets off the bed. She puts on her bathrobe.

"But I sent in the application and the portfolio." He knows he sounds silly.

"Was it such a bad thing to make you do that?" Louisa asks angrily. She leaves the room and he can hear the water running in the kitchen; she is doing the dishes. Donald lies on the bed, wondering what Philippe looks like, whether Philippe says things in French when he is making love to Louisa. Polly would bet that he does. In her illustrations, Philippe is tall and dark, his legs are good but his shoulders are too narrow. Donald has nice broad shoulders. But of course he doesn't know about Polly's drawings.

What can he do? What does it mean, getting to be too much of a couple? Is it just an excuse to sleep with Philippe? Donald could write to the M.F.A. program and withdraw his application, but he knows he won't. He could sneak calories into the dinners he cooks so Louisa will get fat again, so Philippe won't want her. Polly draws a fat Louisa, a Louisa crouched over an enormous pile of French fries. But Donald doesn't know about Polly's drawings, and he goes on cooking dietetic dinners and he and Louisa both lose more weight. And Louisa goes on washing the dishes, doing the laundry, buying toilet paper and soap. And they do not discuss Philippe. What is there to say? Donald does not get home from Ground Zero Graphics until well after six, even later if he stays at Polly's to talk, and Louisa finishes teaching school at three every day. She can do whatever she likes all afternoon; she is always home when Donald gets there. Donald is hoping, perhaps, that Louisa will begin to feel that she wants them to be more of a couple. They are not at all a couple now, Donald thinks; they do not make love, they do not discuss how she spends her afternoons; they eat the dinners he cooks and watch television. At least he will eventually start that M.F.A.

program so he will be busy in the evenings. He is willing to wait
Louisa out.

A small steak. Salad. Green peas. For Polly, hot Italian sau-
sages, macaroni salad from the delicatessen, three eclairs. Polly
will be coming back to work in two days. It has been a long convalescence, and her muscles are still weak.

"You really have lost weight," she tells Donald.

"Yeah," he says. "The diet's just about over. Louisa is where
she wants to be too."

They both hear a double meaning in that sentence (where,
after all, is Louisa; or at least, where has she been all afternoon?), and they do not look at each other. Polly is wondering
whether she will still be in love with Donald after she has gone
back to work. Is loving him some kind of artificial healthiness to
balance out her illness? Why doesn't she have the nerve to tell
him that if he wants to get even with Louisa, she, Polly, is ready
for an affair? She is afraid he would be ready too, but only because he would be eager to get even with Louisa. Not that he
doesn't like Polly, look how kind he has been during her mononucleosis, and look how he confides in her, but Polly knows that
he does not think of her as a sexual being. Perhaps she should
not have let him come into her apartment; he will associate her
forever with sickness and cluttered smells.

The sketchbook of illustrations is almost full. Louisa and
Philippe, Louisa and Donald, Donald alone. Louisa alone. But
not Polly. She does not belong in those careful drawings.

"What kinds of things will you illustrate when you have the
M.F.A?" Polly asks.

"Children's books, I hope," says Donald, and Polly is pleased
and yet annoyed by the ordinariness of his desires and the sin-
cerity with which he expresses them. She has never wanted to illustrate children's books, she would rather make obscene animated films, not that she ever has.

Donald spends a long time in Polly's apartment; she knows he
does not want to go home and begin another evening of not
being too much of a couple. But finally he leaves, after checking
to see that Polly's eclairs were not crushed during his journey
from the bakery. She wants to offer him one, but she doesn't; she

is angry with him because he is going home to Louisa, because in two days he will no longer be bringing Polly food.

Polly fills the sketchbook. She has a complete set of drawings now: the dissolution of a promising relationship (Donald and Louisa). She does the last few drawings even before Donald tells her the last installment, which in fact takes place that steak-and-salad night. But Polly is as sure of the ending as she was of Donald's ambition. He would want to illustrate children's books. And Louisa will move out. Polly draws Louisa packing. Louisa in the drawing is thin, but graceless.

"I want to move out," Louisa says.

"You're moving in with Philippe."

"Yes. But things weren't working out anyway. I think you really know that."

"Sure. We were getting to be too much of a couple, right?"

"A lot of things," Louisa says. "Listen, if you don't want to understand, then you don't want to understand."

Ridiculously, after dinner she does the dishes. She doesn't begin to throw things into a suitcase like a departing wife in the movies, she doesn't look around the apartment and begin to cry, she doesn't even telephone Philippe and ask him to come get her. She does the dishes.

Donald considers himself in the mirror. He is thin. He will be starting a Master of Fine Arts program. It is as if Louisa has whipped him into shape before leaving him. He is left much the better for her presence in his life, better looking, with new career prospects. He wants to go into the kitchen and smash the dishes and push her head under the faucet. Or maybe make love to her one last time, one unbelievably fabulous and passionate last time, on the kitchen floor perhaps.

He goes to the bedroom window and looks out: Polly's bamboo blinds, though that is not really what he is looking at. She is behind them, drawing the scene he has not yet described to her, but of course he doesn't know that. All he knows is that the unillustrated story is ending, leaving him thin, leaving him about to enter an M.F.A. program, leaving him alone.

# THE DOGS IN RENOIR'S GARDEN

## GLORIA WHELAN

Gloria Whelan moved from Detroit ten years ago to the woods of northern Michigan, and she's been writing ever since. She has published four novels for young adults, and her stories have appeared in various literary magazines. Her latest novella was published by *Redbook* in December 1982.

"There's an extra charge each month if you don't use their furniture." May Elger put down the tortoise shell shoehorn and looked around her small room. She thought of her little collection of furniture as choices she might have made from a burning house. Not the most valuable things, but the first to come to mind. They had allowed her her little satinwood writing table with ormolu mounts and a graceful gilded cane chair. The chest that held her clothes—the few she needed—was Empire. On the chest was a Lowestoft armorial plate which her doctor insisted on using for an ashtray. Snuffing out his cigarettes was eroding the honey gold on the crest, but she never corrected him. He was the one who pronounced her sentences.

Only the bed belonged to the nursing home. They insisted on its remaining. Who could blame them for believing that she would need it as she grew older. The evidence was all around them. With its bulky mechanical contrivances that could manipulate your body into infinite angles, the bed looked like a small factory set down in the midst of the delicate furniture.

Her little Renoir painting which she missed most was not allowed her. The insurance company had pronounced the security at the nursing home inadequate. May considered that ironic. She had found the security so effective that in the year and ten

Copyright © 1982 by The Virginia Quarterly Review. First appeared in *The Virginia Quarterly Review*. Reprinted by permission.

months of her stay, and in spite of the unlocked doors, she had never ventured out of the home by herself. But then her daughter had placed her there, and May was always ready to accept the appraisal of others.

"Why wouldn't it be *less* when you use your own furniture?" Ethyl grasped the slight conversational thread and held on. She saw that May had lost weight. The red-and-white silk dress hung on her waning frame like a large flag draped over a small casket. May's daughter, Susan, obviously hadn't bothered to buy anything new for her mother. But then she never bought clothes for herself. Or if she did, they all looked the same. Susan was a large bony creature, who carried a purse like a suitcase and had a habit of sitting with her legs apart and her feet planted firmly on the ground. She took after her father, who had died of a heart attack in one of the worst November storms on record after refusing to leave a duck blind until he had bagged his limit.

"They charge you because they have to store their own furniture." May was standing in front of the mirror loosening her pearl earrings. She wasn't used to wearing them and had forgotten the aggressive way they nipped into her ear lobes. Averting her eyes from the ghost in the mirror with the pale, blanched look of a weed working its way up through layers of mulch, she tried to recall her last outing from the nursing home. What a hateful word "outing" was, she thought, conjuring up images of helpless babies in prams and little old ladies being aired like musty sheets.

It must have been four or five months since Susan and Richard had taken her out for Easter dinner. An evening of disasters, all of them of her own making, as Susan had been quick to point out. She was surprised Susan had given Ethyl permission for this luncheon.

"The Mengles finally had that old privet hedge yanked out," Ethyl said. It was pleasant to pretend they still had their suburban street in common. The two women had been next door neighbors for thirty years. Luckily May never asked about her own home. Susan and Richard had moved in, telling Ethyl over the brick wall that separated the two gardens, "We're here to keep an eye on things until mother comes back."

If that were true, why were so many of May's things being

carried out her front door? Ethyl had seen a well-known auc-
tioneer leave with two large cartons, and one Saturday morning
a half dozen antique dealers in full cry filled up their vans and
drove triumphantly away. Worst of all had been picking up the
New York *Times* and seeing in an auction notice on the art page
a picture of the little Renoir painting of a garden that had hung
in May's living room. Over the years May had lovingly planted
in her own garden all the flowers that appeared in the painting.
Walking outdoors, you walked right into the Renoir. It seemed a
sacrilege that someone else should own it.

Then there were the dogs. Susan raised German shepherds.
You could see them through the windows careening around the
rooms, skidding on May's parquet floors. May's priceless oriental
rugs dangling from their muzzles. When Ethyl was in her yard,
the dogs peered over the wall smiling their clown's smile at her,
their tongues lolling out between long pointed white teeth. The
stench from their feces, which no one bothered to bury from one
week to the next, was so strong it was impossible to open your
windows.

The dogs had ravaged May's garden, uprooting the lilies and
irises. They jousted at one another with long stalks of May's
delphinium held between their teeth. They snapped off peony
and poppy blossoms and gobbled them down whole.

Ethyl hadn't signed the petition that had gone up and down
the street asking for the dogs' removal. For May's sake she tried
to remain friends with Susan. But Ethyl knew Susan would certainly be angry with her if she knew she was taking her mother
out to lunch. Ethyl had implied to May that Susan knew all
about the luncheon, but of course she didn't.

Ethyl had broached the subject to Susan, trying not to show
her impatience at having to ask permission from someone half
her age, "It's been such a lovely summer, what would you think
of my running your mother over to the club for the afternoon?"

Susan had immediately quashed the idea. "Isn't that thoughtful of you. But you'd never be able to manage mother. Richard
and I between the two of us could hardly handle her last
Easter."

That had not been reassuring. Ethyl had often looked out of
her bedroom window into May's yard while Susan yanked the

big black-and-tan dogs about in their choke collars, nearly throt-
tling them. What was it about her frail ninety-five-pound mother
that made her so unmanageable? When Ethyl visited May in the
nursing home each Thursday afternoon, she seemed perfectly
clear-headed and sensible. Ethyl knew May had problems with
drinking. But surely that could be handled? It was unconsciona-
ble that Susan should allow those great beasts of dogs in the
house but not her own mother.

Ethyl looked at May standing doubtfully in front of the mirror
and felt a surge of affection. What confidences had gone back
and forth over the brick wall. The grieving over the bits and
pieces the doctors had pruned from their aging bodies; Ethyl's
mastectomy and later May's hysterectomy. Susan's marriage to
Richard, who had been the dog warden in their suburb. Ethyl's
son leaving his wife and four children to marry his tennis pro.
And the deaths.

"You look very posh," she said, envying May's trim figure beneath the too large dress. "Yesterday a snotty saleslady at Saks
tried to tell me I needed a size 16." Ethyl looked at her watch.
The nursing home made her claustrophobic. "I suppose we'd
better go. Size 16 or not, I've been thinking about an avocado-
and-crabmeat salad all morning. After one o'clock the ripe
avocados are all gone and you get those stringy ones that are
hard as a rock."

On the way to the club May sat looking greedily out the car
window. It was like watching an old movie. Just as you recon-
ciled yourself to having forgotten it, something familiar would
flash on the screen and you would set to work all over again trying to remember how the story went. They were only a few
blocks from her home, but May saw that Ethyl was not going
out of her way to pass it. Probably a kindness on her part, a
desire not to rub salt in the wound. May contented herself with
looking at other peoples' homes. Even that was painful, suggesting as they did the exotic process of a daily life.

When they reached the Country Club, Eddie, the doorman,
seemed genuinely glad to see May. "Mrs. Elger, you picked
yourself a beautiful day. They're serving on the terrace. You'd
enjoy that." May was grateful for his discretion in not mentioning how long it had been since he had last seen her there. He

helped her out of the car and guided her attentively through the door. Servants had always tended to baby her, and she had encouraged the little game of appearing to be dependent on those who were dependent on her.

Ethyl would have preferred an obscure table in the grill to eating on the terrace, where they would be on display. Not that she expected to run into Susan. Susan despised the Country Club. She had not set foot there since her high school years when she captained the swim team. Only kennel clubs for her.

But once seated at one of the pink wrought iron tables, Ethyl put her misgivings aside. Perhaps it was atavistic, but she believed strongly that nothing unpleasant could happen when you were under the beneficence of the sun. And then eating outdoors, no matter how formal the service, was still a picnic. Still a childhood treat.

May looked past the red geraniums and neatly clipped boxwood to the large blue saucer of the swimming pool and the smaller blue circle of the children's wading pool. In the days when their youngsters were growing up, nursemaids in crisp white uniforms watched over them. Now the mothers seemed to keep track of their own toddlers. She thought of how often she had left Susan in a nursemaid's care, and now Susan was reciprocating. But it was foolish to feel guilty about nursemaids. Look at how the British nannies had produced Winston Churchill and Sir Kenneth Clark.

May sighed and turned her glance to the golf course with its alternating stretches of open lawn and thickets of trees. In the distance she could make out green clouds of willows lowering over a tiny creek. She and Ethyl had sat on the terrace in the summer twilight sipping long cool drinks and waiting for their husbands to stride across the course to their table. She remembered the sharp cries of the nighthawks as they plummeted from the sky, recovering themselves at the very moment you lost hope.

Ethyl glanced at the tables around them, relieved to find no one she knew. No one to come over and ask clumsily of May, "Where have you been keeping yourself?" It was a young crowd. "The girls all look naked," she said to May. Their shirts were sleeveless and unbuttoned halfway down their chests. They were braless, and their nipples showed through the flimsy summer fabric. Even their skirts were slit up to their thighs.

"Nothing to cover them but their long hair," May said, "like a bunch of Lady Godivas."

Ethyl was beginning to think the afternoon would be possible after all when a waitress, neat in a green uniform with a pink apron, stood at their table, smiling pleasantly. "May I bring you a cocktail?"

It was a moment Ethyl had rehearsed. She couldn't refuse May a drink. That would be too obvious. What she had decided to do was to order a glass of wine for herself. It was rude to order before her guest, but she hoped May would take the hint and have something light.

May smiled innocently up at the waitress and said brightly, "I'll have a double martini, straight up." Probably there would be only the one drink. Perhaps her only drink for several more months. Even if Ethyl gave her the opportunity, she resolved not to order a second one. If all went well today, Ethyl might take her to luncheon another time. There might be many afternoons like this one. Ethyl might tell Susan how well she behaved. Or she might say something to someone in the trust department of the bank or to her lawyer who no longer answered her letters, even though he had been a lifelong friend and had gone trout fishing with her husband every spring.

"They've turned one of the private dining rooms into a backgammon room," Ethyl told her.

"Which one?" She was concentrating on the waitress coming slowly across the terrace with two glasses balanced on a silver tray, a tall goblet and a shorter one. The drinks were certainly theirs. She turned her attention to Ethyl.

"The room that had the blue toile wallpaper with the cross-eyed cupids all over it. Conway Studios did it. Remember? And the fake Limoges ashtrays with the gold bees that looked like seagulls."

The waitress put the frosty glasses down on pink paper coasters with the club emblem imprinted in green. May curled her fingers around the stem of her glass like a baby grasping her mother's finger.

Ethyl studied her menu. When she looked up, May had emptied her drink. "What are you going to have?" she asked hastily. "They have those stuffed mushrooms you always liked."

May was appalled at her empty glass. For a moment she thought someone else had emptied it. But, no, she felt the door opening. With it came the feeling things were possible, all kinds of things, one day different from another. Other rooms. Other streets. Other cities and countries.

She had begun drinking too much after her husband's death. Unable to eat dinner alone in the large empty house where forty years of conversations lay about unextinguished like hundreds of small ruinous fires, she took to eating out. Alone, night after night in restaurants and clubs, she felt peripheral. It required so much effort to keep your glance from intruding on that of another diner's. Then there were the salad bars. Even some of the very good restaurants had them. She hated the coarse chunks of iceberg lettuce, the fake bacon bits that tasted like minced shoe leather, the slimy semen-like bean sprouts and the messy ladles you dredged up from the dressing pits. She hated the way they pretended to give you choices.

After three or four drinks, waiters and waitresses seemed kindly. Other diners returned her friendly nods. The food, when she remembered to eat it, was appetizing. Possibilities suggested themselves to her: friends she might call, an exhibition at the museum she wanted to see.

But after her dinner, there was the difficulty of getting herself home. When her driver's license had been suspended, Susan had insisted she see her doctor. The doctor had patiently explained that as one grew older liquor was not as easy to tolerate. She had replied that the same could be said for life and what else did he have to offer. Then she had driven without her license and had had the accident and the parents of the boy on the bicycle had sued her. Susan had consulted with the doctor and her attorney. When they had advised the nursing home "as a temporary measure," she had agreed.

When the waitress arrived with their food, May looked toward her glass, giving it a subtle nudge with one finger. The waitress checked Ethyl's still nearly full wine goblet and left the table before Ethyl could telegraph a warning look to her. Ethyl began eating with little noises of pleasure as one eats in front of a small child to encourage him to eat his own food.

May felt Ethyl's anxiety and tried to nibble at the food but the salad Niçoise she had ordered turned out to be nothing more than tuna with a scattering of black beetle-looking olives. She saw that she must make an attempt to enter the world in which Ethyl still lived and look around a little, remark on something. "Do you remember the time the house committee at the museum spent an hour arguing over how the Lukes sculpture ought to be cleaned?" The sculpture was an enormous piece of commercial felt, a sort of giant fly swatter whose fringes trailed onto the gallery floor and tended to get stepped on.

Ethyl grinned. "And they wrote to Lukes and he said he had planned on the dust and the footprints as part of the effect."

"So they couldn't touch it."

"Ethyl"—May put her hand across the table, upsetting a water glass but not noticing—"do you think we could go to the art institute some afternoon? Just to see my little Renoir. Susan said she lent it to the museum because she was afraid to have the responsibility of it at the house."

"Yes, of course," Ethyl assured her, thinking of the ad in the New York *Times*.

The waitress was at the table again to clear Ethyl's luncheon plate. She had another drink for May. Ethyl had no idea when it was ordered. Then she saw with a sinking heart that May was pressing money into the waitress's hand. "I guess I'll have one more," May said, "the sun is making me thirsty."

Ethyl fixed an icy eye on the waitress. The club had a strict rule against tipping. "May we have our check," she ordered. The check appeared with a fourth martini. Ethyl hastily signed her name and rose. Too late. May had emptied her glass and seemed unable to get up from her chair. The women at the other tables looked pointedly away. Ethyl tried to lift May, but for someone so slight, she was surprisingly unwieldy, like a poorly packed grocery bag.

May tried to help, using the edge of the table as a lever to raise herself but the table began to tilt toward her, the dishes sliding and clattering. May sank helplessly down in her chair. She saw that Ethyl had disappeared. Perhaps they would let her remain there. It would be very pleasant in the evening when everyone had left the club and the empty tables and chairs stood under the black sky and the moon shone on the dark water of the pool. Ever since she had entered the nursing home, May had longed to be alone at night. Although it was considered one of the best homes in the city, the construction was poor, and various snores came vibrating through the walls to destroy her sleep.

Ethyl returned with Eddie. "Mrs. Elger, you just lean on me now. I should never have suggested eatin' out here. Sun's unmercifully hot." They hoisted her awkwardly from the chair and half dragged her across the terrace. Ethyl looked straight ahead.

Eddie gently closed the car door and raised his hand in a smart salute. May was crying, the tears making pale rivulets in her foundation. Her nose needed wiping. Ethyl reached for a Kleenex from the box on the dashboard and handed it to her.

May pushed it aside. "I hate Kleenex." She fumbled in her purse and brought out a linen handkerchief with a wide band of lace. "I wash out seven handkerchiefs each week in my washbasin," she said. "I iron them with my travel iron. They won't do them for me at the nursing home." The rhythm of the car soothed her. Her head began to nod. As a child driving through strange and dark countryside, she had loved falling asleep in the car, knowing her parents were no farther away than the front seat.

Ethyl drove cautiously, husbanding May's sleep. She would continue to see May, but she wouldn't allow herself to become involved again. Their lives were different. She, herself, still had some time left.

When they arrived at the nursing home, Ethyl hurried into the lobby and pushed out one of the wheelchairs that always stood ready. It took a minute or two to awaken May and extract her from the car. An elderly gentleman resident watched but made no effort to help. Evidently he was hoarding his strength.

Ethyl wheeled May hastily down the corridor. May giggled. "You're pushing me too fast. Like a tea wagon."

When they reached May's room, Ethyl quickly shut the door behind then and, leaving May in the wheelchair, she kicked off her shoes and sank down exhausted on the bed, trying not to look up at the blank white ceiling.

"You won't tell Susan?" May asked.

"I won't tell her, but she may hear about it from someone at the club."

"Does she keep up my garden?"

"Yes, it looks lovely. Your delphiniums were gorgeous this June."

"I was worried. She mentioned having dogs."

"Just one. It's very well behaved."

"I'm sorry about the lunch. I don't suppose you'll want to take me out again?"

Ethyl was silent, her small store of lies depleted.

"But you'll come to see me?"

"Every week. Just like I always have." When the time came, would someone come and visit *her?* Ethyl swung her legs over the edge of the bed and rocked her swollen feet into her shoes.

"I do it to open the door," May risked.

Ethyl gave her a strange look.

May decided after all it was best to keep these things to yourself. She saw with a sinking heart that Ethyl believed in will power.

In the late August afternoon the suburban roads were tunnels of light. Sun lay trapped under arching branches that met in the middle of the streets. Ethyl felt she was swimming through gold. Water from sprinklers arched over the spacious lawns looking like Atget's photograph of the fountains at Versailles. She was buoyant, almost euphoric, and then guilty like someone who has ceased mourning much too soon and knows it.

As she pulled into her driveway, she looked into May's garden and saw the dogs stretched out on a bed of crushed daisies warming themselves in the sun. Right out of Rousseau's Peaceable Kingdom, Ethyl thought. It was a painting Ethyl considered full of artful deceit. Rousseau had composed a handful of tame animals to distract you, while the wild ones waited invisible and menacing just behind the trees.

# WORK

## DAVID PLANTE

David Plante was born in Providence, Rhode Island, attended Boston College, and also studied at Université Catholique de Louvain in Belgium. He has lived almost half his life in Europe, and has published eight novels. His new book, *Difficult Women*, published in January 1983, consists of portraits of Jean Rhys, Sonia Orwell, and Germaine Greer.

Robert came out of the old stone house with a sickle. Swifts swooped out over the valley and back into their nests under the eaves. As he sickled the grass and nettles, he thought that there were layers below him of sand and water and rock, and layers above of air and thin cloud, and, above, the layers of the sky, and all the layers rose and fell. From time to time he stopped his work to look at the birds, and as he watched them one hit the stone wall and dropped. He went to it and picked it up, in one hand he held the sickle, in the other the bird, its eyes staring. Across the field below he saw a boy on a black horse trotting toward the house.

Giuseppe jumped off the horse and said in Italian, "What is it?"

"A swift," Robert said.

After the boy tied the horse to a post, he held out his callused hands. Robert laid the bird in his hands, and the boy twisted its neck and threw it down.

Giuseppe, barefoot, in a singlet and shorts, watched Robert sickle.

"He hasn't arrived?" Giuseppe asked.

"No, not yet."

Copyright © 1981 by David Plante. First appeared in *The New Yorker*. Reprinted by permission.

"Maybe something happened."

"No, I don't think anything happened."

Giuseppe shrugged his shoulders. "Things happen."

Robert went on sickling. He said to Giuseppe, "Don't you have any news for me since yesterday?"

The boy stood still, watching Robert strike at the weeds with the dark wet blade, then he said, "The old man in the house by the church is dying."

"I didn't know."

"He goes from his bed to the fire, from the fire to his bed. They don't know what to do with him. He wants to shoot himself."

"What is he dying of?"

Giuseppe stuck out his lower lip. "What my father died of."

Robert stood. He said, "He was a good man, your father—everyone says so. He worked hard."

"I know." Giuseppe pulled his hair over one ear.

Robert imagined he rose tall as he looked down at Giuseppe. "I'm sure your father still loves you as he loved you."

"I know."

Robert bent to sickle.

"Don't you have a father?" Giuseppe asked.

"Yes."

"Is he in America?"

"Yes."

"Why don't you live with him?"

"Because I've grown up."

"How old is he?"

"He's eighty."

"He'll die soon."

"I hope not."

"How old are you?"

"I'm twenty-five."

"My father was twenty-five when he died."

Robert again stood to look at the boy, and, for a moment unbalanced, he felt that he wanted to pull the boy to him and hold him.

Giuseppe turned the dead bird over onto its back with his toe, and the thin black wings opened. He said, "I wish he'd come."

"Beppo, Beppo," sounded from the sky.

Giuseppe tilted his head a little, and, without turning toward his house up the valley, he shouted, "Aou." He listened to the response sung out into the sky in short phrases that rose, in lifts, and fell. Without moving, Giuseppe shouted his answer back.

Robert did not understand any of it. "That was your mother," he said.

"She wants me to go get the bread."

"Then go."

The boy untied his horse and led it, surrounded by flies, to a big stone; he jumped onto the stone and from it onto the horse. "I'll come back," he said. The lilac bushes on either side of the path closed over the flanks of the horse.

From this place, halfway up the side of the mountain, Robert imagined, again, layers of earth and cloud rising and falling over the valley. He picked up the dead bird and went to the patch of earth he had cleared for planting flowers in front of the house; with the handle of the sickle he dug out a hole, dropped the bird in, covered it, and pressed it down with his palm, thinking, Protect us.

In the kitchen he took the broom from a corner, pulling webs away from the walls, to sweep the red tile floor. After he swept half, he leaned the broom against a table and, restless, went into the other downstairs rooms, where the floors were covered with straw, mouse droppings, insects' legs and wings; webs sagged from the ceiling beams. He went upstairs, where he had swept, had wire-brushed wasps' nests from the rafters, and had white-washed the walls of a bedroom. He wandered from room to room. The beds were made, the cushions put out on the wicker chairs, the rag rugs placed on the clean floors. The fireplace was still heaped with ash. Downstairs again, he picked up the broom, but then crouched to look at a basket of kindling, under the table, spun over with webs. He drew it out, and under it found a scorpion. Bending near, he touched the scorpion with a stick; it raised its claws and tail and moved to the side, then stopped. Robert replaced the basket over the scorpion and, smiling, continued to sweep.

He heard, from outside, "Roberto, Roberto," and he went to the door. Giuseppe, his elbows pumping, was racing his horse along the edge of the fields toward the house, and Robert went out to meet him. Giuseppe shouted, "There's a telephone call for you. There's a telephone call at the *posto pubblico*." He pulled up the horse, sideways, in front of Robert. "Get on," he said. Robert tried to throw a leg over the barebacked horse, but he slipped. Giuseppe was shouting as if he were far away, "Stand on the stone," and he swerved the large horse, rearing, toward the stone. On it, Robert again tried to throw his leg over the horse, but the horse moved forward in jerks, and Giuseppe had to run him in. "Come on, come on," Giuseppe shouted. "There's a telephone call." Just as Robert was mounted behind the boy, Giuseppe kicked his bare heels into the horse's ribs, and Robert, thrown against him, clung to him for a moment, then took his hands away to press them to his own sides; he slipped on the horsehair. "Hold me," Giuseppe said. "We're going to gallop." Robert put his arms around the boy, and as the horse galloped he pressed the boy's back and shoulders against his chest. Robert felt the small bones of the boy's body move. He leaned his face close to the boy's neck. The horse galloped along the edges of the tobacco fields, out to a dirt road, across the stream. One of Robert's espadrilles dropped off; he thought that he, too, could easily drop off, and he held tighter to Giuseppe, the boy's small, taut body held in his body, and both of them were carried by the big black horse racing now up a mountain path through elder bushes. The faster the horse raced, the more the flies raged about it. On the white road, Giuseppe kicked the horse and shouted, "Ai, ai," to make it go faster. Round a bend, on a ridge overlooking the valley, was the peasant's house with the public telephone: a yellow-and-blue disc, with the outline of a telephone on it, hung over the doorway, outside of which Robert, half falling, dismounted.

One foot bare, he ran up the stairs to the house above the stables and into the kitchen. The shutters were closed, and he couldn't at first make out who was sitting on a chair by the fireplace—a young man, who got up as soon as Robert entered. The young man said, "Alessandro telephoned; he said he'd telephone again in twenty minutes."

"Thanks," Robert said.

The young man, Gianfranco, rubbed his arms. "Sit down," he said.

Robert sat with him by the fireplace.

"He said he just arrived in Rome. The flight was late leaving America. Don't meet him at the train station; he'll come by taxi."

"What else did he say?"

"He said *Saluti*."

Gianfranco clapped his hands together softly between his knees. He asked, "In America, do you have a house together, as you have a house here?"

"Yes," Robert said.

The telephone, on the wall just inside the door, rang. Gianfranco got up quickly to answer, said, "Yes. Yes. Yes," and handed the receiver to Robert, smiling. "It's Alessandro. He just arrived in Rome. The flight was late leaving America. Don't meet him at the train station; he'll come by taxi."

Robert took the receiver. He said, in Italian, "You're in Rome. The flight was delayed in Boston. I shouldn't go to meet you at the station; you'll come by taxi."

Alex laughed. He said, in English, "And what else?"

"You send *saluti*," Robert continued in Italian.

Giuseppe, among chickens, held his espadrille up to him when he went out.

"Is he coming?"

"Yes."

On the horse, Robert embraced the body of the boy tightly. As they went down into the valley and up past the house, all its doors and windows wide open, toward Giuseppe's house, higher up the side of the mountain, a sense came to Robert of space upon space opening to him. He pressed his chin to the side of the boy's head.

Outside Giuseppe's house Robert slid off the horse. He was covered with short, coarse hairs. Giuseppe got off, and Robert followed him as he led the horse up behind the house, where his mother, in a black dress and a black kerchief, was throwing down corn for the chickens.

"He's arriving," Giuseppe, excited, said to her.

"You must be happy," the widow said to Robert.

"I am," he said.

"Come into the house."

Giuseppe said, "The airplane might have fallen and all the passengers killed."

In the kitchen, the widow washed a glass at the low stone sink, gave it to Robert, and as he held it she poured into it red wine from a large green bottle.

Robert asked, "Where are your other sons?"

"Working in the fields. Beppo doesn't work. He's with you all day."

"I like having him with me."

The widow hit Giuseppe on the head. "He talks a lot," she said. "All he does is talk, he doesn't work, his father would be angry with him."

"I'm sure his father would be pleased with him."

She looked for a long while at her thin son. "He's a good boy," she said.

Robert said to him, "Come on, let's go back to my house."

Giuseppe's mother said to Robert, "Don't you want a son?"

While Robert shovelled the ashes from the large fireplace in the house and put them into a bucket, Giuseppe hefted another bucket and, in a thin gray cloud, carried it in both hands out to dump it near the shed. When he brought the bucket back empty the third time, he clanked it on the hearth. "I think I'll go to my house," he said.

"Was your mother right?" Robert asked. "You don't like to work?"

Giuseppe said nothing.

"It doesn't matter. Stay with me and watch."

"I'll come back later."

"You don't want to stay with me?"

"I'll come back later."

The different levels of earth and air appeared to separate as the daylight lengthened, and the dim upper and lower levels began to disappear. When Giuseppe returned, on foot, a fine livid layer, halfway between the earth and the sky, remained; it was the level at which the swifts flew out and back, out and back.

Giuseppe said, "He hasn't arrived yet?"

"Not yet."

"Let's hope nothing has happened."

"What could happen?"

"The train could have crashed, or the taxi in the mountains—"

Outside, Robert and Giuseppe watched the layer of light fade. The valley went dark. House lights were lit. A woman on the other side of the valley called, "Anna, Anna," and when Anna answered, "Aou," from the near side, they shouted to one another, with pauses between, in high and low voices.

"Let's go in and light a fire," Robert said.

While the fire burned, he and the boy stood at the window. Fireflies were flashing among the elder bushes about the house. Robert pressed his palms to the stone windowsill and leaned out; he felt a pulse in his palms, as if not he but the whole house were pulsing a little.

"There are the lights of a car," Giuseppe said.

"Where?"

The boy pointed. It took a while before Robert could see the moving lights high up on the side of the mountain. They vanished, but a while later they beamed out from behind a bend and from their distance seemed to shine on the house before they swerved away again and descended the road. Giuseppe ran downstairs and outside. Robert came after. He heard, now, the car engine. The lights, rocking as the taxi rocked in the ruts of the dirt road, beamed up to the house. In the light, Giuseppe held out his arms; the taxi stopped before him, and the boy ran to the taxi door across from the driver and opened it. Robert stood back. Alex, saying, *"Ecco, ecco,"* got out. He grabbed Giuseppe, hugged him to him, and asked, "Have you been a good boy or a bad boy?" and released him. Giuseppe simply looked up at his face. Alex turned to Robert and said, "I'm home," and Robert, too, simply looked at him.

His hand on Giuseppe's head, Alex asked the boy, "How is your mother?"

Giuseppe's eyes were large. "She had a bad cold, very bad, but now she's all right."

The taxi-driver got out, opened the trunk, and put two large bags on the ground.

Robert said to him, "Come in for coffee."

"No, no," the driver said.

"Yes," Alex said, "come in for coffee."

Giuseppe dragged the biggest bag into the house, followed by Alex and the fat taxi-driver, and Robert with the second bag.

Alex said, "I'll make the coffee."

"I'll make it," Robert said.

He made it quickly in the kitchen, from where he looked at Alex, the taxi-driver, and Giuseppe at the dining room table, talking loudly. He brought in the little cups, with a bottle of brandy, on a tin tray.

"Bring something for Giuseppe," Alex said.

Robert went back into the kitchen for a plate of sweet biscuits and a glass of vinsanto, which he placed before the boy. Giuseppe's hands, resting on the table, appeared large and rough for his thin wrists. He said, staring at the biscuits, "No, no."

"Take them," Alex said.

Giuseppe said, "No."

"Come on, take them," Alex repeated.

Giuseppe picked up a biscuit and stared at it before he took a bite from the edge.

"Whose son is he?" the taxi-driver asked.

"Mazzini, Enrico," Alex said.

"The one who died?"

"Yes."

"I used to see him often at the market." The fat taxi-driver leaned toward Giuseppe. "He was a good man, your father."

Giuseppe silently ate his biscuit.

The taxi-driver said to Alex, "Now what man does he have to take after?"

"Have another biscuit," Alex said to the boy.

"No," he said.

"Anyway," the driver said, "he is well mannered."

Alex and Robert, Giuseppe between them, went out to see the taxi-driver off. Then Alex said to the boy, "Now it's time for you to go home." Without speaking, stumbling a little, Giuseppe walked out into the dark.

As Alex looked at the rooms, Robert looked at him. Alex touched a damp spot on the wall of a downstairs bedroom and

said, "We've got to get to work on this." They went into the
downstairs bathroom, where the toilet leaked. Alex said, "Didn't
the workmen repair it? I left instructions. Didn't you ask them to
repair it?"

"I forgot," Robert said.

"I'll have to get a lot done while I'm here," Alex said.

In the dining room, he said, "The walls are damp here, too; all
the whitewash is flaking off," and Robert again looked at Alex,
not at the walls. Off the dining room was the storeroom, filled
with bags of cement, buckets, hoes, rakes, scythes, and piles of
floor tiles. It did not have a light, and they stood in the dim light
from the dining room. Alex's head, his black curly hair and his
nose, cheeks, chin, was edged by the dim light. He was big, with
big hands and powerful arms.

Alex turned to Robert and smiled. He said, "You've done a lot
of work getting the house ready for me."

Robert said, "Work?"

The doors to the outside were open to fireflies in the elder
bushes.

Giuseppe appeared at the doorway. He was carrying a
weighted, knotted bandanna. He stopped at the threshold.

Alex said, "What is it?"

Giuseppe held up the bandanna. "My mother sends you some
eggs."

"Come in," Alex said.

The boy came in, put the bandanna on the table, and untied
it; he drew the corners back to reveal, on the blue-and-white
cloth, ten white eggs. He stood away from the table and, his
hands by his sides, stared, as at attention, at Alex.

Alex said, "Sit with us."

Giuseppe sat. He wouldn't take anything to eat or drink. He
stared, listening to Alex talk. In the pale light of the shaded bulb
hanging from a rafter over the table, Robert, too, listened.

He heard, "Roberto, Roberto," from outside the bedroom window, and got out of the high iron bed, crossed the red brick
floor to the shutters, and opened them to Giuseppe, below,
standing in dawn mist.

"What is it?"

Giuseppe said, "My mother wants to speak to you."

"Is it grave?"

Giuseppe hunched his shoulders and raised his arms. "Grave it isn't—no."

Alex, from the bedroom doorway, asked, "What is it?"

"The widow wants to speak to me."

"About what?" He was frowning.

"I don't know."

"They think that because they get up at dawn we should, too."

Robert said to the boy, "I'm coming down."

As Robert dressed, Alex said, "You're letting her take advantage of you again. You always let them take advantage of you. I know what they're like. And they know what you're like."

"I want to find out what she has to say."

"Listen, don't get involved in doing something you don't want to do."

The valley was filled with mist, which drifted up, and the white sun appeared to drift with it. Robert followed Giuseppe through the terraced fields, along a path; on either side of the path, in the broom, webs drooped with heavy white dew. Robert's espadrilles got wet.

Giuseppe asked, "Do you have cows down there in America?"

"Yes."

"And pigs—do you have pigs down there?"

"Yes."

"And sheep?"

"Yes."

"Then it must be just like here."

The path narrowed through the high broom and heather; it gave way to a patch of bare earth around the stone house littered with bottles. The mist was thin, and the sunlight diffused thinly through it; there were no shadows. Chickens were scratching the bare earth before the stables on the ground floor of the house. Giuseppe stood by the outside flight of stairs to let Robert go up first to the floor above.

A fire of twigs was burning in the large kitchen fireplace, and beside the hearth, on a small chair, sat the widow's mother, a large, old woman in black, a black kerchief tied under her chin. She tried to stand as Robert came in, but sat back. A dirty handkerchief, with weeds stuffed under it, was knotted around the swollen calf of her left leg. She leaned over and held her leg and moaned.

As she could not speak Italian but only the Umbrian dialect, Robert hardly understood her, but he knew she was apologizing for not being able to stand to greet him.

He said, loud, "What's wrong with your leg?"

Giuseppe said, "It's infected."

The widow came in from the back room. She was thin, gaunt, also in black; her black kerchief was tied under her hair at the nape of her neck. She hit Giuseppe on the head and said, "Why didn't you offer Robert a chair?" Giuseppe pulled a chair from the table and put it by the fire for Robert.

The widow prepared coffee in a little pot over the coals. The kitchen was very hot. Flies flew about and settled, flew about and settled on the tabletop, the yellow-brown walls, the black hams hanging from a rafter. Robert said to the widow, "La Nonna's leg looks bad."

"Yes," she said. "She can't work."

"Shouldn't she see a doctor?"

"We never go to the doctor."

She stood, barefoot and arms folded, before him as he drank the thick coffee from a small white cup. She asked, "Did you eat?"

"I just got up from bed."

"I'll give you something to eat."

"No, I can't eat at this hour."

"I'll give you something little."

She lifted the lid of a chest in the kitchen and took out a cloth, spread it over an end of the table; she put on it a glass, a knife, a loaf of bread, a round sheep's cheese, and a cured ham from which meat had been cut to the bone, and she cut slices from it. "Bring your chair to the table," she said.

Robert did.

"Beppo, go get a bottle of wine."

She sliced bread, and on the slice placed the ham and a wedge of cheese. Giuseppe came out from a warped door under the stairs with a large dripping bottle of wine, and he poured

Robert a glassful. While he ate, the widow sat on a bench; her elbows were on the table and she held her jaw in her hands. She said, "We've got a lot of work to do today."

"Yes?"

"I don't know how we're going to do it. We've got to pick the tobacco to take it to the cooperative tobacco-drying plant by tonight, and if we don't we'll lose the whole picking. I have my four sons, myself, my brother-in-law. My mother can't work. I don't know how we'll do it."

Robert chewed a dry piece of bread and cheese and swallowed it with wine. "I'll help," he said.

"No, no," she said. "I didn't ask you here to help."

"I'll help," he said. "And I'll go and ask Alessandro to help, too."

"No, no."

"Yes, of course."

"I'll pay you," she said.

"No, I don't want any money."

"How can you work and get nothing for it?"

He smiled. "I'll get something."

She laughed. "Grace?" she asked.

Robert found Alex at a stone table outside the house, drinking coffee. The valley was dun-green in the morning light. Robert said, "I promised her we'd help her pick tobacco."

Alex said, "I've come all the way from America here for a rest."

"What could I do?"

They joined the widow, her young sons, and the old brother-in-law, who had one tooth and wore a black fedora, by a field at the river. In a row, they went down the lines between the tall tobacco plants and, crouching low, snapped off the bottom leaves until each one of them had a thick sheaf, and the sheaves were taken to the widow's youngest son, Candido, a pale six-year-old, who placed them in a metal form supported by a wooden stand by the riverbank. The sunlight flashed through the lines of tobacco plants; picking, they shouted at one another from line to line.

The widow shouted at Alex, "If they don't have room at the cooperative for your tobacco, they throw it out. Do you think that's fair?"

"Why don't you do something about it?" he asked.

She stood, and with the back of her hand wiped her sweating forehead. "What can I do?" she shouted from deep in her throat.

"If it were a Communist cooperative—" he began to shout.

"It is a Communist cooperative," she yelled.

Her eldest son, Ulderico, who wore old trousers torn off at the thighs, shouted, "I'm going to become a Fascist." His large brown body shone in the bursts of sunlight as he worked his way down a line between the tall pink-blossoming plants.

The old brother-in-law laughed.

The widow said, "If you work for anybody but yourself it's always the same. But no one can work for himself today."

Robert's shirt and trousers were sticking to him not only with sweat but with the sticky resin of the tobacco leaves; when he made a fist, his fingers adhered to one another.

"Do you work for yourself?" the widow shouted at him.

Robert didn't answer.

The widow shouted, "Is your father rich?"

"No. My father worked hard."

"Doesn't he work any longer?"

"He doesn't."

"Who works for him? Don't you work for him if he can't any longer?"

Again Robert didn't answer. He looked for Alex, who, lifting a full form of tobacco leaves from the wooden stand, looked toward him and smiled.

Another son, Matteo, came through the lines of plants with a clean glass, a bottle of red wine, and a bottle of well water. He handed each in turn the glass, then poured in a little water, which was used to rinse the glass, and then filled it halfway with water and the rest with wine. The glass was sticky with resin by the time it came to Robert.

His back, arms, and legs ached when the widow yelled, "È ora de magnà."

They went to the river. The bar of soap was not passed around but placed on a stone after each one had used it. They tried to wash the black gum from their hands and arms. There were horseflies, and as they washed they swatted the flies.

Ulderico jumped into the water with the soap, sank in up to his neck, rose, lathered himself, sank in again splashing; he emerged dripping, and crouched on the bank, where the three brothers rubbed his body with thin towels, and he laughed. He had a front tooth missing. He began, still laughing, to hit his brothers' heads, and they hit his legs, chest, back.

The widow shouted, *"Basta."*

From plastic bags, she placed food out on a cloth under poplar trees by the river. They ate with forks the salad from a large white bowl.

The widow said, "Isn't it true that a person who works hard should be paid for his work? We work, we work, and what are we paid? What do we work for? To die? No. We work to live, and the more we work the better we should live." She tapped her narrow chest. "I believe that."

"So would any good Communist," Alex said.

"Are you a Communist?" she asked him.

"Yes," he said.

"So am I," she said. "My husband was a Communist, too." She clasped her hands and shook them. "But does being a Communist mean your work has any more value? They say yes, yes. As a Communist, what is the value of my work?"

Alex lowered his head to eat a piece of cheese.

Ulderico said to him, "When did you become a Communist?"

"When I was a young man in Milan."

"You're not old," the brother-in-law said, "but you're not young. Those must have been the hard days."

"At my school, I used to lock myself in an office late at night and on a machine make copies of propaganda, and I took the sheets to cinemas under my shirt and threw them from the top balconies, then ran."

"Why did you do it?" The brother-in-law's face was covered with small, dirty wrinkles; his eyes were round and sharp black.

"I did it because I believed in the Communist Party."

"Why?"

"It gives our work, however small, meaning in the world."

The old man pointed at Alex. "What are the answers it has for

practical issues? I tell you, Communism is just another idea.
What does it do for me? Last year I got two hundred thousand
lire for my pigs. Two hundred thousand lire for a year's work.
Can a man live on that?"

"Yes, I know," Alex said.

"Do you?" The old man rolled his shirtsleeves up from the
sleeves of his thick, long underwear.

"No," Alex said, "I don't know. You're right. I don't know, because I am well paid for my work in a foreign country. I have
money to buy a *casa di villeggiatura* in my own country and
come back for my holidays."

The old man lowered his head. He said nothing.

A cicada thrilled in the still heat.

Alex said, "But I believe the fundamental of Communism, as I
see it, is right—is right for everyone: it makes us think not just
of ourselves but of others, because we're together in the world."

"The world is big," the old man said.

The widow rolled a pear to Alex. She said to him, "I knew you
were good. I knew it." She said to her sons, "He's like your father." She laughed and slapped her hands together before her
nose. "He had ideas, he had ideas."

Alex threw his pear to Giuseppe, who caught it in dirty hands.

Barefoot, they went back into the blazing field, in which the
tobacco plants shimmered in rising waves. They picked silently,
line after line. Robert dripped sweat. Ulderico left, came back
with a tractor, and he, Alex, and Robert had to lift the metal
frames of leaves onto the trailer. They were heavy. When they
had stacked them, Robert turned to the widow, who was collecting leaves that had dropped from the forms, and said, "We've
finished in lots of time to get the tobacco to the cooperative."

She said, pointing with a big leaf, "There's the field above."

They worked, snapping the big sticky pale-green leaves from
the stalks as the sun moved across the valley. No one spoke, not
even when, as the sun set, they piled the frames onto the trailer;
and when Ulderico put on a shirt and drove the tractor off to the
cooperative, at the bottom of the valley, no one said anything to
him. They stood at the edge of the field. Motionless, Robert
thought he would not be able to move his stiff body ever again,

and when he raised his hand to scratch his cheek his back hurt, down to his buttocks.

The brother-in-law went into the field again to disconnect and heft onto his shoulder a long irrigation pipe. He carried it to another part of the field, dropped it, and came for another. The widow joined him, and as she raised a pipe onto her shoulder Robert went to her to take it from her, but she walked off with it. He reached down for one; it was heavy, and he dropped it. The boys, standing before Alex, were watching Robert. Their faces were streaked with resin. He reached down again, hefted the pipe up to his waist, and almost lost his balance as he hefted it, twisting his body, to his shoulder; he had not got it in the middle, and its weight again threw him off balance, so he staggered backward. The boys laughed. He found the fulcrum and walked across the field, passing the old man and the widow going back for more pipes; and when he slowly walked back for another, he met Alex carrying a long pipe. They had, too, to change the pipes in the field below.

The widow said, "You'll come to our house for supper."

"No, no," Robert said.

Alex said to him in English, his voice strained, "We can't not go. She has to feed us for the work we've done."

Giuseppe took Alex's hand as they plodded up the long path, through moonlit bushes, toward the house.

La Nonna was sitting in the dark by the fireplace, where the fire was out, and she was moaning. The widow put on the small electric light hanging from the rafter among the hams. She said to her mother, "How is your leg?"

"Bad," La Nonna said.

"You let the fire go out," the widow said. She washed her hands at the low shallow stone sink in the kitchen. Then, while the men and the boys washed, she started the fire with a heap of broom, and while the men and the boys sat on chairs and benches and watched her, she got the water to boil in the pot hanging over the fire. When it was boiling, she shoved the spaghetti into it.

She prepared spaghetti with oil and garlic, and as the men

and boys ate this she fried, over the fire, pigs' livers, which she took with a fork with a big oil-filled jar. She did not sit with the others to eat but put bits of liver on bread and ate standing.

Before Alex and Robert left, she asked if they wanted to see her cows. The two men followed her slowly step by step, down the stairs outside the house to the stables below. She opened a large door into darkness and a hot sweet smell, and went in. A dim electric light went on, and three great white cows appeared, tethered by chains to a stone wall; they turned their heads round and stared with wet, black eyes. The widow picked up a broom made of twigs to begin cleaning the dung from the stable floor.

Alex and Robert walked along the riverbank. The tall poplars were still. Robert was drunk. He said, "I keep thinking about my father, who worked and worked, and I think I would like to work for him to repay him for the work he did for me. I've got to get work when I return to Boston, good, hard work—"

"Watch out," Alex said, "we're coming to the ditch with the plank over it."

Robert took his arm.

They went down the path round to the front of the house, which shone among the elder bushes.

# MAGAZINES CONSULTED

*Antaeus*
Ecco Press, 1 West 30th Street, New York, N.Y. 10001
*The Antioch Review*
P. O. Box 148, Yellow Springs, Ohio 45387
*Apalachee Quarterly*
P. O. Box 20106, Tallahassee, Fla. 32304
*Ararat*
Armenian General Benevolent Union of America, 628 Second Avenue, New York, N.Y. 10016
*Arizona Quarterly*
University of Arizona, Tucson, Ariz. 85721
*The Ark River Review*
Box 14, W.S.U., Wichita, Kan. 67208
*Ascent*
English Dept., University of Illinois, Urbana, Ill. 61801
*Asimov Science Fiction Magazine*
380 Lexington Avenue, New York, N.Y. 10017
*The Atlantic Monthly*
8 Arlington Street, Boston, Mass. 02116
*The Black Warrior Review*
P. O. Box 2936, University, Ala. 35486
*California Quarterly*
100 Sproul Hall, University of California, Davis, Calif. 95616
*Canadian Fiction Magazine*
P. O. Box 46422, Station G, Vancouver, B.C., Canada V6R 4G7
*Canto*
11 Bartlett Street, Andover, Mass. 01810 (ceased publication.)
*Carolina Quarterly*
Greenlaw Hall 066-A, University of North Carolina, Chapel Hill, N.C. 27514
*Chicago Review*
970 E. 58th Street, Box C, University of Chicago, Chicago, Ill. 60637

*Christopher Street*

> Suite 417, 250 W. 57th Street, New York, N.Y. 10019

*Colorado Quarterly*

> Hellums 134, University of Colorado, Boulder, Col. 80309

*Commentary*

> 165 East 56th Street, New York, N.Y. 10022

*Confrontation*

> English Dept., Brooklyn Center of Long Island University, Brooklyn, N.Y. 11201

*Cosmopolitan*

> 224 West 57th Street, New York, N.Y. 10019

*Crucible*

> Atlantic Christian College, Wilson, N.C. 27893

*Cumberlands*

> Pikeville College, Pikeville, Ky. 41501

*Dark Horse*

> Box 9, Somerville, Mass. 02143

*December*

> P. O. Box 274, Western Springs, Ill. 60558

*The Denver Quarterly*

> Dept. of English, University of Denver, Denver, Col. 80210

*Epoch*

> 254 Goldwyn Smith Hall, Cornell University, Ithaca, N.Y. 14853

*Esquire*

> 488 Madison Avenue, New York, N.Y. 10022

*Fantasy and Science Fiction*

> Box 56, Cornwall, Conn. 06753

*Fiction*

> c/o Dept. of English, The City College of New York, New York, N.Y. 10031

*Fiction International*

> Dept. of English, St. Lawrence University, Canton, N.Y. 13617

*The Fiddlehead*

> The Observatory, University of New Brunswick, P. O. Box 4400, Fredericton, N.B., Canada E3B 5A3

*Forms*
P. O. Box 3379, San Francisco, Calif. 94119
*Forum*
Ball State University, Muncie, Ind. 47306
*Four Quarters*
La Salle College, Philadelphia, Pa. 19141
*Frisco*
1740 Union Street, San Francisco, Calif. 94123
*Georgia Review*
University of Georgia, Athens, Ga. 30602
*GPU News*
c/o The Farwell Center, 1568 N. Farwell, Milwaukee, Wis. 53202
*Grand Street*
50 Riverside Drive, New York, N.Y. 10024
*The Great Lakes Review*
Northeastern Illinois University, Chicago, Ill. 60625
*Great River Review*
59 Seymour Avenue, S.E., Minneapolis, Minn. 55414
*Green River Review*
Box 56, University Center, Mich. 48710
*The Greensboro Review*
University of North Carolina, Greensboro, N.C. 27412
*Harper's Magazine*
2 Park Avenue, New York, N.Y. 10016
*Hawaii Review*
Hemenway Hall, University of Hawaii 96822
*The Hudson Review*
65 East 55th Street, New York, N.Y. 10022
*Iowa Review*
EPB 453, University of Iowa, Iowa City, Iowa 52240
*Jewish Dialog*
1498 Yonge Street, Suite 7, Toronto, Ontario, Canada M4T 1Z6
*Kansas Quarterly*
Dept. of English, Kansas State University, Manhattan, Kan. 66506
*The Kenyon Review*
Kenyon College, Gambier, Ohio 43022

*Ladies' Home Journal*
   641 Lexington Avenue, New York, N.Y. 10022
*Lilith*
   250 West 57th Street, New York, N.Y. 10019
*The Literary Review*
   Fairleigh Dickinson University, Teaneck, N.J. 07666
*The Little Magazine*
   P. O. Box 207, Cathedral Station, New York, N.Y. 10025
*The Louisville Review*
   University of Louisville, Louisville, Ky. 40208
*Mademoiselle*
   350 Madison Avenue, New York, N.Y. 10017
*Malahat Review*
   University of Victoria, Victoria, B.C., Canada
*Manhattan Plaza News*
   400 West 43rd Street, New York, N.Y. 10036
*The Massachusetts Review*
   Memorial Hall, University of Massachusetts, Amherst,
   Mass. 01002
*McCall's*
   230 Park Avenue, New York, N.Y. 10017
*MD*
   30 E. 60th Street, New York, N.Y. 10022
*Michigan Quarterly Review*
   3032 Rackham Bldg., University of Michigan, Ann Arbor,
   Mich. 48109
*Mid-American Review*
   106 Hanna Hall, Bowling Green State University, Bowl-
   ing Green, Ohio 43403
*Midstream*
   515 Park Avenue, New York, N.Y. 10022
*Mother Jones*
   607 Market Street, San Francisco, Calif. 94105
*The National Jewish Monthly*
   1640 Rhode Island Avenue, N.W., Washington, D.C.
   20036
*New Boston Review*
   Boston Critic, Inc., 77 Sacramento Street, Somerville,
   Mass. 02143

*New Directions*
> 333 Sixth Avenue, New York, N.Y. 10014

*New England Review*
> Box 170, Hanover, N.H. 03755

*New Letters*
> University of Missouri–Kansas City, Kansas City, Mo. 64110

*New Mexico Humanities Review*
> The Editors, Box A, New Mexico Tech, Socorro, N.M. 57801

*The New Renaissance*
> 9 Heath Road, Arlington, Mass. 02174

*The New Republic*
> 1220 19th Street, N.W., Washington, D.C. 20036

*The New Yorker*
> 25 West 43rd Street, New York, N.Y. 10036

*The North American Review*
> University of Northern Iowa, 1222 West 27th Street, Cedar Falls, Iowa 50613

*Northwest Review*
> 129 French Hall, University of Oregon, Eugene, Ore. 97403

*Ohio Review*
> Ellis Hall, Ohio University, Athens, Ohio 45701

*Omni*
> 909 Third Avenue, New York, N.Y. 10022

*The Ontario Review*
> 9 Honey Brook Drive, Princeton, N.J. 08540

*The Paris Review*
> 45-39-171st Place, Flushing, N.Y. 11358

*Partisan Review*
> 128 Bay State Road, Boston, Mass. 02215 / 552 Fifth Avenue, New York, N.Y. 10036

*Perspective*
> Washington University, St. Louis, Mo. 63130

*Phylon*
> 223 Chestnut Street, S.W., Atlanta, Ga. 30314

*Playboy*
> 919 North Michigan Avenue, Chicago, Ill. 60611

*Playgirl*
>  3420 Ocean Park Boulevard, Suite 3000, Santa Monica, Calif. 90405-3397

*Ploughshares*
>  Box 529, Cambridge, Mass. 02139

*Prairie Schooner*
>  Andrews Hall, University of Nebraska, Lincoln, Neb. 68588

*Prism International*
>  Dept. of Creative Writing, University of British Columbia, Vancouver, B.C., Canada V6T 1WR

*Pulpsmith*
>  5 Beekman Street, New York, N.Y. 10038

*Quarterly West*
>  312 Olpin Union, University of Utah, Salt Lake City, Utah 84112

*Quartet*
>  1119 Neal Pickett Drive, College Station, Tex. 77840

*Redbook*
>  230 Park Avenue, New York, N.Y. 10017

*San Francisco Stories*
>  625 Post Street, Box 752, San Francisco, Calif. 94109

*The Saturday Evening Post*
>  110 Waterway Boulevard, Indianapolis, Ind. 46202

*The Seneca Review*
>  P. O. Box 115, Hobart and William Smith College, Geneva, N.Y. 14456

*Sequoia*
>  Storke Student Publications Bldg., Stanford, Calif. 94305

*Sewanee Review*
>  University of the South, Sewanee, Tenn. 37375

*Shankpainter*
>  24 Pearl Street, Provincetown, Mass. 02657

*Shenandoah: The Washington and Lee University Review*
>  Box 722, Lexington, Va. 24450

*The South Carolina Review*
>  Dept. of English, Clemson University, Clemson, S.C. 29631

*The South Dakota Review*
>Box 111, University Exchange, Vermillion, S.D. 57069

*Southern Humanities Review*
>Auburn University, Auburn, Ala. 36830

*Southern Review*
>Drawer D, University Station, Baton Rouge, La. 70803

*Southwest Review*
>Southern Methodist University Press, Dallas, Tex. 75275

*Story Quarterly*
>820 Ridge Road, Highland Park, Ill. 60035

*The Texas Review*
>English Dept., Sam Houston University, Huntsville, Tex. 77341

*The Threepenny Review*
>P. O. Box 335, Berkeley, Calif. 94701

*TriQuarterly*
>1735 Benson Avenue, Evanston, Ill. 60201

*Twigs*
>Pikeville College, Pikeville, Ky. 41501

*Twilight Zone*
>800 Second Avenue, New York, N.Y. 10017

*University of Windsor Review*
>Dept. of English, University of Windsor, Windsor, Ont., Canada N9B 3P4

*U.S. Catholic*
>221 West Madison Street, Chicago, Ill. 60606

*The Virginia Quarterly Review*
>University of Virginia, 1 West Range, Charlottesville, Va. 22903

*Vogue*
>350 Madison Avenue, New York, N.Y. 10017

*Washington Review*
>Box 50132, Washington, D.C. 20004

*The Washingtonian*
>1828 "L" Street, N.W., Suite 200, Washington, D.C. 20036

*Waves*
>Room 357, Strong College, York University, 4700 Keele Street, Downsview, Ont., Canada M3J 1P3

*Webster Review*
      Webster College, Webster Groves, Mo. 63119
*West Coast Review*
      Simon Fraser University, Vancouver, B.C., Canada
*Western Humanities Review*
      Bldg. 41, University of Utah, Salt Lake City, Utah 84112
*Wind*
      RFD Route 1, Box 809, Pikeville, Ky. 41501
*Wittenberg Review of Literature and Art*
      Box 1, Recitation Hall, Wittenberg University, Spring-
      field, Ohio 45501
*Woman's Day*
      1515 Broadway, New York, N.Y. 10036
*Writers Forum*
      University of Colorado, Colorado Springs, Col. 80907
*Yale Review*
      250 Church Street, 1902A Yale Station, New Haven,
      Conn. 06520
*Yankee*
      Dublin, N.H. 03444